HUNTING THE STRANGE

A MYSTERY ROYALE NOVEL

HUNTING THE STRANGE

A MYSTERY ROYALE NOVEL

KAITLYN CAVALANCIA

HYPERION
Los Angeles New York

First Edition, March 2026
10 9 8 7 6 5 4 3 2 1
FAC-004510-25352
Printed in the United States of America

This book is set in Garamond/Monotype
Designed by Marci Senders

Library of Congress Control Number: 2025934661
ISBN 978-1-368-10479-1
Reinforced binding

The authorized representative in the EU for product safety and compliance is Disney Trading B.V., Asterweg 15S, 1031 HL, Amsterdam, The Netherlands
email: DCP.DL-EU.bookscontact@disney.com

Visit www.HyperionTeens.com

Logo Applies to Text Stock Only

To Cameron and Callum,

I could spend the rest of my life thinking up stories,

and I'd never come close to writing one as great as yours.

I.

My fingers fumble with the letters, frozen stiff with fear and frost. The clock in my head ticks in tandem with my heart, two bombs set to explode. The timing must be precise, exact—a second's difference and the entire plan implodes. Time is fickle like that. Nothing given freely, every minute demands blood.

I strategically place the letters, one on the bed, another in the stove, tucked away until she's meant to find them on this hunt for the strange. The rest is in her hands. One misstep and an entire life's work will crumble, washed away like a castle of sand in the tide.

2.

MULLORY

I never thought the seam between the living and the dead would remind me so much of a ham sandwich. A poorly wrapped wad of cellophane flattened beneath the weight of an apple. But that's exactly what it's like—a wall of clingy plastic wrap that separates me from Lyric.

The shadow is warm in my palm, keeping me tethered to the other side. I squeeze it fiercely, terrified of what happens if I let go. Finding Lyric was easy—I only needed to think of him and follow the bats. But each time I return, the light grows more dim, the wall more opaque, and Lyric himself has begun to fade. And with him so have I—wretched from the inside out with guilt. It gnaws at my heart bit by bit. Not for claiming Xavier's inheritance, but for Lyric's death, which was supposed to be my own.

I was hopeful at first, because we finally had the shadow, a necklace with an amber stone—a gift from my mom, hidden in her broken watch along with a cryptic message. But true to her nature, she failed to leave directions in mastering a death-defying magical object.

"Mullory?" Lyric's voice is a hopeful whisper.

"I'm here."

A sigh of relief escapes his lips.

I can't imagine the isolation and utter loneliness between my visits. "I'm here," I say again, because I need him to hear me as I reach through the gelatinous wall of cosmic-crafted cellophane. I graze his forearm, and the contact causes my heart to skip a beat. First with a thrill that's quickly ebbed away by concern. "You're so cold."

"I'm fine," he assures me. His dark hair is windswept across his brow, exactly the same as when he died. In fact, everything about him is the same, right down to the muddy boots he was wearing.

But he's right, I can still reach him, and I know for certain if I tugged, I could pull him through. But Lyric is adamant. Stubborn even in death's rigid grip.

"Let me get you out," I plead, letting my fingers trace a light circle on his skin. "Let me at least try."

His face hardens. "No. Not until it's fixed."

I shake my head, curls falling free. "But I've tried. . . ."

"Mullory." Lyric pulls my gaze to his and I'm certain he can hear my heart thundering in my chest. "If you pull me out now, he'll just kill me again."

We have this argument every day. We haven't been able to split the last magical thread between Lord Thorn and Lyric. The further Lyric slips into death, the more he can feel the magic loosen its hold, but with it so does our connection. The shadow hums in my hand, vibrating to an awful crescendo the farther out he goes. We tested the limits trying to break the bond, but the shadow groaned until splinters of ice began to crystallize on the stone. It's as if there's something blocking it, a type of stopper that restricts its reach and power.

"I know," I finally say aloud.

Lyric nods, inching up as close as he can to the wall, and I do the same, mirroring him. It feels like we're on opposing sides of a glacial block of ice.

"Any progress?" asks Lyric.

My mom's message had directed us to find her where the moon glows black, and it hadn't taken us long to figure out she was referencing a new moon. But once again, her riddles have led to dead ends.

"Not much. The next new moon is in two weeks. I've read all the astrology texts I could find and searched every website that references a lunar cycle, but I still don't know what it means . . ." I say softly, not wanting to state the obvious. We don't have much time. If only I could find my mom, she might know how to work the shadow and save Lyric.

"And my uncle Xavier?"

It guts me not to have any good news to share, because I feel like I'm failing Lyric as he withers away in this prison. We were desperate enough to try to ask Xavier Stoutmire for help. Surely, he would have answers to unlocking the shadow. But winning his inheritance didn't mean I won him over. Not in the slightest. Edwin handled the funds and the paperwork to buy Gran and me a house. Every call I make to Xavier ends abruptly, and any mail I send is returned covered in sugar-dusted stamps, my letters replaced with paper-thin desserts. Cab drivers get lost or stalled on the way to the estate.

Xavier Stoutmire doesn't want to be found.

"No," I finally answer, ashamed. "I can't reach your uncle."

"And the watch?"

Again, I shake my head, crestfallen. I've tried to use it to find Mateo, optimistic he might be able to help. He offered at the party, telling me to use the watch to find him. But it's just another magical object that came without instructions.

"I'll keep trying. I placed a note inside last night, but I have no idea to whom and where it was sent. I've tried to turn the hands to every time combination throughout the day." I cast my eyes at the floor. "I even tried to sing to it." Fire blooms across my cheeks. At this point, I'd try anything. I can practically feel Lyric smiling.

"Maybe try to give it a big kiss, too."

I swat at the wall, and it jiggles like a Jell-O cup. "Not funny!"

Lyric presses his palms against the sticky barrier, his eyes earnest. "Don't worry, Mullory, we'll figure it out."

But that's just the thing: I *am* worried, absolutely terrified of losing him again.

"Tell me about the science fair," says Lyric while crouching down and settling back, a lazy smile creeping up his face.

This has become our routine. First, we get the unfortunate business of Lyric's impending death out of the way, confirming that I've made zero progress in finding my mom or his uncle or figuring out how to work the watch or the shadow. And then we talk. About anything and everything. I used to be petrified of a scenario like this, certain my brain would suddenly forget how to form words, trapping us in uncomfortable silence.

But that's not the case. And even in the quiet moments it's never uncomfortable. If anything, I feel brave. Brave enough to push my hand through the barrier and hold his.

"Mullory, let's go!" Gran's voice is muffled, but somehow, it's still forceful enough to pierce through the barrier of the dead and startle me. A pile of rainbow-speckled rubber ducks tumbles out by my feet, and I feel my cheeks smolder. Xavier's magic has been leaking out of me in nonsensical ways. Filling the kitchen drawers with chocolate eggs tucked in cotton-candy nests, replacing Gran's chair with a lamb, causing the shower to leak cinnamon-swirled espresso. Try as I may, I can't control it. Maybe because it's bound through a magical will, and it senses I don't have Stoutmire blood. That somehow Xavier's magic knows that Lyric was the rightful heir.

I shuffle and kick the ducks aside with my sneakers. Even more embarrassing is when they begin to bark instead of squeak. "I'll be back tomorrow," I call out.

Lyric ignores the barking ducks. "Tomorrow," he says shakily. Because what if there is *no* tomorrow?

Cecilia's mysterious warning from the game rings between my ears. *"Don't wait too long to use it, Mullory Prudence."* I hadn't known what she'd meant at the time; I was too shell-shocked from Lyric's murder. But I know now.

Don't wait too long to pull him back from death.

3. ELLISON

Chicago is still the same historical city, and our brownstone is still an architectural masterpiece, but I've wilted into something less, laid bare like the trees outside the window.

Hollow and leafless.

Empty without Lyric. A shell of my former self, if that's even possible.

And I can't forget the other change—my mother's dream magic is like lead in my veins and mud beneath my Christian Dior boots.

What a great way to start my eighteenth birthday. Hooray.

The minute the clock struck midnight Whitaker lit our birthday candles with a flick of his wrist. His magic snapped into place like a well-oiled machine, and he woke the next morning positively glowing. He melted the snow on our walkway, and then the entire block to the delight and puzzlement of the city borough.

Naturally, my parents were elated, clapping and smiling as he snapped his fingers and defrosted the windows.

They weren't the only ones to notice. It took less than a week for the council to send a representative, who was equally impressed and offered Whitaker an intern position in New York City.

I fought the overwhelming urge to cry and instead forced the muscles in my face to smile. I knew Whitaker would only go if I encouraged him.

So, I did. Even though it broke the minuscule fragment of my heart that remained.

The days since have blurred together. Passing without distinction. It's as if there's a weight pressing on my shoulders, forcing me down, further and further until I split in two.

I can feel my mother's magic worming its way through my brain, pinching and prying at me to channel it. I simply don't have the energy; I'm too busy mourning Lyric while actively avoiding my mother. She's tried to encourage me, leaving subtle clues—teas, tapestries, crystals, and cards, anything to get me to accept her dream magic. But instead, I let it rot, a festering open wound that's slowly turning my insides necrotic.

I hate my mother for what she let happen and I can't stand that a part of her is now hitched to me like a bloodsucking leech. I blame her for Lyric's death, a nightmare she may not have brewed, but one she's still guilty of orchestrating. Blame is the only mechanism I have to soothe my own guilt away.

Because Lyric's death consumes me, morphing from a memory into an obsession—blood pooling beneath him, a knife buried in his chest. I've ripped my throat raw, shredding my vocal cords with screams. It's in this vulnerable state that my mother's magic pounces, seeking a way in.

So, I've given up on sleeping. I fight it with coffee and pure stubbornness, only allowing myself a few hours here and there.

Even now I can feel my body wavering and I dig my nails into the windowsill until the pads of my fingers throb.

"Ellison." My mother's voice slices into my skin like a saw-toothed blade.

I keep my eyes fixed on the window, but I can feel the weight shift on the couch as she eases down beside me.

"Ellison, look at me."

"No."

"I've given you time to adjust—"

I whip my head around, throwing my ponytail over my shoulder. "Adjust? I'm just supposed to adjust to having a dead brother?"

My mother's face hardens, but she refuses to acknowledge Lyric's death. "You can't fight my magic much longer. It's not only unbecoming and preposterous, it's making you sick."

"So?" I settle onto my heels like an irrational child. Being near my mother I can feel the connection building. I squeeze my hands and bite down on my tongue, fighting it.

"You need to accept my magic, or it'll kill you from the inside out."

"Maybe that's what I deserve." Why should I get to live when Lyric is dead?

"Ellison." She says my name like a plea and extends an arm, resting her fingers lightly on my wrist. For some reason I don't pull away and tears pry at my eyes.

My mother stands, keeping her fingers on my wrist. "Come, I want to show you something."

I don't move, slouching deeper into the couch, wishing it would swallow me whole.

"Now," my mother orders.

I rise on unsteady legs, only because I know she won't leave me alone until I do.

My mother's heels clack against the herringbone floors and I follow her to my parents' wing of the brownstone. I haven't been in their room since I was a child, but it still smells the same, like jasmine and smoke. Fire and flowers, a toxic mix of my parents' magic.

"Sit." My mother points to a chaise longue, tufted with burgundy velvet. I oblige, dropping into a heap with a scowl on my face.

My mother throws open the double doors to her closet, disappearing into the depths of her silks and luxurious cashmere sweaters. I hear the rumble of drawers and several grunts before she appears balancing a small wooden tray with three glass bell jars resting on top. Colorful smoke swirls beneath each of them.

I stiffen, terrified of teas and dreams. "I'm not ready."

My mother merely shakes her head. "Not that."

"Then what is it?"

My mother carefully balances the tray beside me. Thick orange smoke billows beneath the first jar, while pale pink swirls beneath the second. But the third is a mere wisp, a single coil of black smoke.

My mother clears her throat. "I extracted a piece of each of your dreams when you were little."

I wince at the word *extracted*. Not entirely sure how she did that, but I'm certain it was a metaphorical bloody mess.

My mother nudges the tray closer.

I can't help but eye the dream magic with repulsion, and yet I extend a hand, tapping my fingers against the middle jar. It feels familiar in some peculiar way, an odd sensation of recognition. I curl my fingers around the glass globe and cautiously lift it from the tray. Laughter spills out from beneath the jar, light and childlike and free. *My* laughter.

My fingers slip and the jar wobbles back into place, the laughter gone. Perhaps one of the few happy dreams I'd ever had, surgically excised from my brain forever.

I can feel my mother watching me, waiting for me to react.

I tap the first jar that's full of orange smoke. "Whitaker's?"

My mother nods.

I walk my fingers across the tray, pausing before the last jar. *Lyric*. The pain in my heart throbs in an awful burst.

"Why would you do this?" I ask, certain some nefarious motivation exists.

"To watch," she whispers. My mother clutches the ink-black pearls nestled on her collarbone. "I'm going to tell you something."

This should be good. "I'm all ears."

"Years ago, before Lyric was born, a woman visited me." My mother pauses, seeming to be choosing her words with care.

I hang on the moment of silence, waiting for the grand reveal. "And?"

My mother rocks nervously on the stiletto heel of her Jimmy Choos (last season, hideous). "She visited me in a dream," she admits, while raising a hand to her lips to hide her shame.

Aha! There it is, my mother's pride. "Someone infiltrated *your* dreams? The great Saffron Stoutmire." I savor my declaration, licking my lips like a delicious dessert.

"Yes," my mother says through gritted teeth. "But that's not important—"

"I'd say that's pretty important. Monumental, even."

"Ellison," my mother warns. "The woman was the strongest dream wielder I've yet to encounter, strong enough to break down my defenses."

"So? You're not the best at dream magic. Who cares?"

My mother's eyes narrow. "It's her message that struck me."

"What did she say?"

"Try to understand, no one knew I was pregnant yet." Shame burns along her cheeks as she turns to stare out the window, unable to face me when she says the next part. "But this woman, she told me to save the child I was carrying."

I gasp at the implication . . . that Lyric might never have been born. "Who was she?"

My mother gathers herself, twisting her pearls into a knot as she turns to face me again. "To this day, I still don't know," she says bitterly.

I glance at the three jars, understanding washing over me. "She told you to do that." I point at the smoky glass.

She nods as something that looks like a tear slips from her eyelashes. But that can't be right, my mother doesn't cry. She's missing tear ducts and a heart. "If the dreams remain intact, so do my children." Her voice is a raspy exhale.

I've never heard my mother refer to us as her children, and I'm momentarily thrown off-kilter. Staring at the third jar, I'm afraid to breathe. "But Lyric..."

"I couldn't look at first. I didn't want to see the jar empty," my mother admits.

"But..." I can't finish the sentence, my eyes are pinned on the faint curl of smoke floating in the center of the jar. "Is he...?" Adrenaline surges through my body as I grapple to understand what my mother is insinuating. "Is Lyric alive?" I blurt out, holding my mother's gaze.

Neither of us acknowledge the tears slipping down our cheeks.

My mother wipes the corners of her eyes and smooths her skirt. "I believe so. Barely."

I gingerly lift the corner of the bell jar, and a voice slips out. So faint and weak. But I hear him. I hear Lyric loud and clear.

4.

MULLORY

Gran insisted on shepherd's pie from Punxy Phil's Café. "You're all bones, you need to eat something," she declared on the car ride over.

I couldn't remember the last thing I ate that wasn't packaged in plastic, and so I agreed. But now, standing in the entrance, it feels wasteful. I should be home researching lunar occurrences or working on cracking the shadow.

"Mullory." Gran pulls my fingers from the windowsill that I've been mindlessly tapping for minutes. She eyes me suspiciously, the twinkling lights from the nearby tinsel-trimmed tree illuminating her face. She's responded well to treatment, her vigor and strength returning, to the excitement of the doctors. But with her improving health comes her growing suspicions of me.

Three bats flutter past the café window behind her, swooping arcs in the night sky. Gran hasn't taken kindly to them or their droppings, but she never says a word.

They follow me, seeming to multiply when I use the shadow, and oddly enough they're a comfort, a reminder of my mom.

"Don't keep it all in, Mullory," Gran warns, shaking her head. "Not like your mother did, because then it has no choice but to force its way out. And you may not like it when it does."

I hold Gran's stare, tempted to spill everything. How I have Xavier's magic, and his money, and it's still somehow not enough. But I'm interrupted before I even get the chance.

"You're here!" The normally grumpy waitress bustles over, giving us a suspiciously cheerful greeting. Usually she just hollers, "Table's ready, move it or lose it." But today she's practically beaming as she peels two sticky menus from the stack. "Mullory, come here. You have a special delivery!"

At this point, I'm overly cautious of special deliveries, and for some reason this causes a row of velvety soft mushrooms to sprout along my jean pockets. "What delivery?" I ask while tugging my coat closed to hide Xavier's unruly magic.

"You'll see, sweetie! The lady who sent them called and already paid your bill." The waitress grins. "And wouldn't you know it, but she told me where Tom-Tom, my cat, has been hiding. He's been gone for weeks! Can you believe it?"

I glance at the table she's stopped in front of. It's piled high with a stack of musty books and a blackened piece of parchment folded atop.

I look at the signature, sucking in air. "Actually, I can."

Gran nestles in, waving the menu aside and ignoring the books. "Shepherd's pie."

"Same," I answer robotically, fingers trembling as I read the letter.

Mullory,

I must admit, most of your existence I've plotted your death. You've died dozens of times, but now I have a vested interest in keeping you alive. It's quite funny how the future changes. I should know, I've seen it. These books may prove useful, or they may make an excellent addition to your bedside table. There's always the unpredictability of your choices that may cause the future to change. Perhaps your gruesome death isn't entirely implausible. I'll be intrigued to see what path you finally choose. And because I'm feeling generous, and quite certain that my mind is unraveling (the armoire just spoke to me, but then again, perhaps it did), I'll give you a hint. The first will help you now, and the second will prove to be important too death.

Cycle your worries away on Cromwell Street.

Don't judge a book by its cover. You'll know when it's time.

Regards,

Cecilia P. Humes

P.S. I'd move closer to the window if I were you.

I barely have time to scoot over just before a nearby waitress trips and spills a strawberry milkshake down the cracked leather side of our booth. I can't forget that Cecilia plotted to kill me, but at this point I'm desperate for a lead.

I ignore the puddle of pink splattered beside me and the plate of steaming shepherd's pie that arrives afterward, focusing solely on the first clue that promises to help. The word *cycle* initially catches my eye. A bike? Some sort of wheel, or . . . maybe it means an orbit of the celestial variety.

The moon technically cycles the earth.

Come find me when the time is right. I'll be where the moon glows black.

My heart beats a mile a minute.

I'm coming to find you, Mom.

5. LYRIC

I'm a paper cut away from truly dying, from being sucked out of whatever hellish crack I've fallen into, and all I can think about is how ridiculous my hair looks. I never cared before—it always just swooped and fell across my eyebrows. Why would I ever care about my hair when I was being tortured by Uncle X?

But now that I'm hopelessly stuck and inches from death, my biggest concern is the cowlick sprouting up on the back of my head. Because of *her*.

Trying for some unimaginable reason to impress the girl who stole my life and left me to die. It's pathetic if I think about it too hard, and I can't help but cringe. I should loathe Mullory Prudence. But I don't. And that irritates me. It's a soul-sucking cycle of wanting to hate her and just hating myself in return.

Something warm and light as sunshine fills me up when Mullory calls my name, and I'm too weak to resist. I cling to it, crave it. Sickening, I know.

I'm more peaceful here, only a seed of hate remains—a splinter of Lord

Thorn's magic that refuses to release. When I veer away from the wall, the magic in me rebels. As if a tiny parasite is clawing its way around my body, grappling for possession of me. It wants what Mullory wants—to pull me out and survive. But that's the dilemma: If I go too far, the magic relents but Mullory can't reach me with the shadow. And so, the magic in me survives.

I'm pacing in circles as I wait for Mullory, dodging the dead as they stumble in. Today, the antechamber to death is as busy as New York's Penn Station. For some reason, it's a popular day to die. Most people just graze through, heading straight to the flickering light, following a stream of enchanting hums. The noise builds like static, calling to me and intensifying each day I remain.

A man with a chainsaw lodged in his skull staggers by. "Where am I?"

I wince. "Keep moving, that way."

"Are you sure?"

Closer, I can spot the exposed parts of his skull, the bloody bits of scalp. "Yeah, positive. You've got something right here." I tap my head and shoot him a devilish smile.

But he just grunts and keeps trudging along.

An elderly woman hobbles in next, taking care to fix her dress as she sits down beside me. "Waiting for someone?" She smells like butterscotch candies and a pile of teddy bears.

"Yeah. You?"

She smiles. "Chester will be here soon. We don't go anywhere without each other."

Something loosens my insides at the thought that Mullory might be the only person who would ever wait for me. I wipe my eyes, playing it off as if some dust got in, even if we both know there's no dust in the seam of the living and the dead.

It doesn't take long. Chester is hunched over, but somehow still proud in his suspenders. His face lights up when he spots us. He doesn't say a word, just takes her hand in his.

And then it's just me for a while, pacing, until someone behind me stirs. I turn to face them, but I'm surprised to find a figure that's less than solid, more like mist that's been shaped into the idea of a person.

"Kill again," the hazy figure mumbles.

My eyes roll and I turn my back on it, not wanting to engage.

But the voice crackles on. "He'll find you again. Find you and kill you if you go back."

I let out a snort of laughter. "Tell me something I don't know. I've got a murderous father, so I guess that makes two of us."

There's a faint buzz as the mist stirs. "She'll let him do it."

I'm content to ignore these mad ramblings.

Something between a groan and hiss before another sharp whisper. "She has the shadow."

I whip around, breathless. "What did you just say?"

The mist wavers, splitting into particles of vapor before reorganizing back into a humanoid form. "She has it. And he'll kill you again."

My pulse pounds. "Who?" I swat a hand forward, trying to grab purchase, but there's nothing solid to latch on to.

A face emerges in the mist with a smirk. "Tick. Tock. Almost out of time."

I glance at my boots, which are starting to disintegrate to dust.

Shit.

6.

XAVIER STOUTMIRE

It's been some time since I've felt this; I believe others call it *desperation*. Call it whatever you like, nasty business.

I'd much prefer to be at my estate enjoying a glass of premium whiskey, playing rummy with Cecilia while periodically bewitching certain cards into mice. Instead, I'm traipsing about, searching in the dark. Desperation is exhausting.

But I need it.

I don't have any other choice but to find it before she does.

7.

MULLORY

I wake with a kink in my neck, peeling my chin from the drool-soaked page of one of Cecilia's books. Groggy, my bleary eyes roam over the text I fell asleep reading last night, *A Comprehensive List of Common and Uncommon Magical Phenotypes*. I'd been reading a section on time travelers, completely engrossed because biologically and scientifically it's a marvel. Apparently, time travel alters light-wave exposure and changes the melanin in the eyes, imbuing them with odd pigments. How was this relevant to the shadow? Or to Lyric? I have absolutely no idea.

In fact, I was starting to suspect Cecilia was messing with me. Certainly, the Bible-size tome entitled *Birds* was some sort of joke. I pictured her by a fire, cackling at the thought of me on page five hundred, reading about the long-wattled umbrella bird.

Pulling the rogue strands of hair from my face, I then tidy up the stack of books. I'd tabbed something disturbing, yet potentially relevant, in *The Genetics of Magical Transfer* that I'll ask Lyric about later.

My Calculus II textbook eyes me angrily from the side, but how can I worry about derivatives when Lyric is a breath away from dying? Cecilia's letter is much more pressing, and her first clue garnered an address; all I had to do was search *Cromwell Street* with *new moon* and voilà.

Sure, Cecilia spent years trying to plot my death, but I have nothing else to go on and I don't think Lyric has much time. That's what forces me to do the absolute unthinkable as I hurry out and hop on my bike, intent on skipping school for the first time in my life. It's the last day before winter break so I doubt I'll be missed, but the thought of ruining my perfect attendance is still painful.

I pedal quickly, barely able to contain my nerves. I'm huffing gulps of frosty air when a strip of storefronts pops into view and I spot a faded red marquee with a large, rust-riddled moon and an inscription: *New Moon Dry Cleaner—We Clean Faster Than a Shooting Star.* A smile tugs at my lips. Murderous intentions aside, Cecilia is clever with her wording, "cycle your worries away."

I toss my bike down an adjacent desolate alley and hurry over to the dry cleaner. Thick dust and grime coat the window, and the top half of the door is a spiderweb of glass. Clearly the dry cleaner is abandoned. The door groans open and a stained rug squishes beneath my shoes.

I whirl around, taking in the broken racks and conveyors piled with trash and discarded plastic wrappings. The air is pungent with mold.

"Mom," I call weakly. My shoulders slump with the realization that she's not here. I weave behind the counter, mindlessly kicking through the trash. What does she want me to find? A memory of her takes hold of me.

"What makes a good clue?"

I glanced up at my mom, who was covered in bits of papier-mâché. "One that makes you think. It's only obvious after you crack it."

My mom nodded, adding pieces to our handcrafted solar system. "And what makes a great one?"

The wet strips squelched between my fingers as I covered Neptune. "A great clue makes the most sense to the person it's meant for."

Her green eyes sparkled. "Exactly. That's what keeps it secret."

"Do you have any secrets?" I'd dared to ask, fully aware even at eight that my mom was the greatest secret keeper I knew. The strange had called to us for years.

"We all do." She paused, plucking the small lopsided blob that was the moon between her fingers. "One day you'll know every secret that I do." Her lip caught beneath her teeth as her eyebrows furrowed together. "Not all secrets are nice, Mullory."

I opened my mouth to answer but my mom shifted moods suddenly, zooming the moon around our patch-riddled Earth.

"How long does it take the moon to orbit Earth?"

"Twenty-seven point three days," I answered.

This earned me the biggest smile yet, and my heart welled.

"You won't ever forget, will you, Mullory?" my mom pleaded, her words heavy with a deeper meaning.

The memory has me sifting through what remains on the racks, searching for the number 27.3. Mostly I find scribbled names and receipts from years ago. Regrouping, I study the entire room, when my eyes land on an oversize old-school cash register. Hopping between a few soda cans I rush over and quickly press the numerical keys in order.

There's a *click* as the large drawer pops open. A solitary wrapped package is squished tightly inside. There's a card with my name scribbled across and a message.

Time for the truth.
Not all secrets are nice, but I want you to understand why.
When you do, you'll be ready.
Start your hunt with this.

The note makes my stomach drop. It's the second letter in two days warning me of something I'll have to do when it's time.

I claw through the wrappings, tearing open a vacuum-sealed bag to reveal a coat that puffs up once released. It's bloodred with golden tassels and buttons and an ornate pattern that swirls to the back of the coattails. It reminds me of some sort of circus performer costume, garish and over-the-top.

I check every pocket, tag, and stitching for some hidden clue, but it's just a coat. Slightly disappointed, I shimmy it over my sweatshirt. It's baggy and I have to squish the sides to fit my parka over it before I hop on my bike and rush home.

I barely feel the snow or the wind that whips my hair into a frozen knot as I pedal. I can't stop thinking of the note. *Time for the truth.* What truth? What are you hiding, Mom? As soon as I reach my street, I ditch my bike on the lawn and race up the stairs. Gran should be out hustling her coffee shop friends at bridge, so I don't even wait until I get to my room to grip the shadow.

I call for Lyric, racing toward the barrier that so cruelly keeps us apart. "Lyric, I have another clue! Lyric?"

But there's no response. My heart plummets to the ground, echoing in the silence.

8.

MULLORY

I nearly drop the shadow when I spot Lyric lying on the ground, disintegrating into bits of light, as if each little piece of him is being siphoned away.

I plunge my hand through the gelatinous wall and grab on to him. At first my fingers slip, like he's made of smoke, but I bury my nails so deeply the muscles in my forearm spasm in pain and my wrist cracks.

The shadow burns in my other palm like a chunk of fiery sun, singeing my skin as if it's reached some limit, a battery depleted. But I don't care. I'm not letting go.

It feels like I'm being ripped in two, cleaved right down the center and split between the world of the living and the dead. My body aches and my bones feel pulverized, but I only pull harder. Squeezing my eyes shut, focusing on the living. On home and Gran, the smell of burnt coffee in the morning. I think of my mom making waffles and tucking me in at night.

I think mostly of Lyric and me during the game. How he soothed me during the night of poison nightmares, helping me only when he thought I wouldn't know. When he offered to help me find my mom even though it cost him his pride.

Lastly, I think of the kiss. It's easiest to remember because it's seared onto my heart, burning a hole straight to my soul.

And then nothing.

My body feels suddenly unburdened and off-kilter and I'm disoriented as I peel open my eyes. Relief floods my system when I recognize the living room carpet and a steadying presence holding tight around me. Lyric is close, so close and real and alive.

He smells like spring, like something grown straight out of the ground, all fresh and dewy, and I can't help but bury my head into the crook of his neck. He holds on to me just as tightly, breathing in tandem.

My heart flutters behind my ribs, and I'm petrified to ask the question that matters most. "Is his magic gone? Do you still feel it?"

"No, I don't think so. You did it, Mullory." Lyric's lips skim the shell of my ear.

I nod into his chest, tears pressing the corners of my eyes.

"You saved me," he says even more lightly. And I can read between the lines and pick up the greater meaning. No one ever cared to save him before. Lyric twists a lock of my hair between his fingers as he pulls me even closer.

My cheeks flush as I remember the kiss and I can't help but wonder if he's thinking of it, too. Lyric loosens the embrace, putting space between us, and he stares at me so intently I feel charged with pure electricity. I'm half convinced he's going to kiss me again, but he only smiles.

"Nice jacket," he says with a smirk.

I cringe, realizing I'm still wearing the ridiculous red circus jacket. The sleeves hang past my wrists and the coattails skim the back of my knees. A shard of ice sits tangled in my hair. I've been waiting for weeks to finally see Lyric, anticipating, daydreaming, and plotting every minute. This isn't how I intended for it to happen.

Lyric takes a step back and looks around. My stomach sinks to my feet. He studies the shelf of porcelain figurines that Gran and I collect, and then smiles at the painting of a tightrope-walking cat framed above the TV. *Oh dear God.* It's like seeing a teacher at the grocery store, only worse. Lyric's at my house. Not in the mansion or trapped in some death bubble—no, he's standing smack in the middle of my living room.

He tips his head toward the couch, and I realize—to my absolute horror—that Gran is fast asleep on it. Was I really going to kiss him in front of Gran?

My tongue sticks to the roof of my mouth and heat burns beneath my cheeks. Lyric smirks, a face full of smug, waiting for me to do something. Anything. We spent months separated by the literal barrier between the living and the dead and it was effortless. Talking and wishing and wanting. And now that he's here—in my living room, no less—my feelings crash somewhere between excitement and panic.

Lyric runs a hand through his hair, shrugging. The tops of his cheekbones are stained pink. . . . Is he just as nervous? The distance between us lessens. Some magnetic pull, lassoing us together.

I don't dare blink.

And I try my best not to cry.

His fingertips graze my shoulder, featherlight and timid. He looks at me, his eyelashes moist, his eyes searing. My body leans closer, a reflex I can't control; his arm slips around my back, tugging me closer. He runs a thumb across my bottom lip, a gesture that speaks the words we can't seem to find. But we find each other.

My lips part, and thoughts of Gran sleeping nearby vanish.

"Mullory." Lyric whispers my name into my hair. I curl onto the tips of my toes as he kisses the space beneath my ear, gliding down my jawbone. A current spreads out from my belly, stretching to the tips of my fingers. Lyric's lips catch the corner of mine—

"Mullory?" Gran's voice shuts off the current and I startle, smacking my head against Lyric's. I'm too frozen with embarrassment to care about the throbbing bump on my forehead. Gran gives me a thin smile and raised eyebrows as she stands from the couch.

What do I say? Do I even know how to talk?

"Aren't you going to introduce me?" Gran says, matter-of-fact.

I will my heart to stay in my chest. "Uh, Gran. This is Lyric Stoutmire."

She purses her lips, giving him a once-over. "You're scrawnier than the last."

The last? I've never had a boy over, much less one that might be more than a friend. "Gran!"

Gran throws her arms in the air, defensively. "All I'm saying is that the last boy to appear out of thin air had a little more meat on his bones."

My brain pauses and restarts. But still, no words come out.

LYRIC

I pinch my arm. Hard. Squeezing the skin near my elbow until it hurts, to keep the laugh in. I can't help the giddy feeling welling up inside me. I might be glowing. Jesus.

And Mullory. Her face is so contorted with shock she looks like a cartoon. I want to laugh and pull her tighter, but instinct tells me that with her gran in the room, right now probably isn't the best time.

Mullory doesn't move and her mouth hangs open. I mean, I'm surprised, too—turns out I'm not the first guy to suddenly appear in the living room. And here I was thinking I was special.

"What does . . . Gran . . ." Mullory tries to get words out. Mostly she just fumbles incoherent sounds and lets out little adorable gasps.

Me? I'm just happy not to be stuck in some antechamber of death. Who cares if I'm not the first? But I will admit—it is strange.

Mullory's gran waves us to the dining table as she passes through to the kitchen, clattering the cupboards. She plunks down a plate of cookies and a few glasses, the plastic kind with faded sunflowers, and a glistening pitcher of iced tea. Lemon wedges bob enticingly on the surface. Suddenly, I remember that I haven't eaten in months.

"Eat," she orders. Her face is weathered, but stern; her tone means business. So, I eat. Happily.

Gran takes her time and sips her iced tea before smacking her lips together, then faces Mullory. "I suppose it's time I explain, seeing as you're pulling your own boys out of thin air."

That causes a mouthful of iced tea to spew from Mullory's lips. Theatrically, like a low-budget sitcom. All we need is for the goofy family dog to come and lick it off the table.

"Oh, Mullory," Gran says sympathetically while grabbing a rag to sop up the mess. "You startle too easily."

I can't help but remember how Mullory spoke of her gran. *"For the first six years of my life, I was convinced trolls would eat my toes if I didn't finish my broccoli. And I'm still not sure if my pet goldfish dived into the toilet bowl to save his family or not."*

"Years ago, before you were born," Gran begins with stoic precision, "your mother made a boy appear here, too."

"Who?" whispers Mullory.

Gran shrugs. "I don't know. Your mother was full of secrets. She was a secret, folded up inside another secret. Ever since the day she was born, they just kept piling up. She'd disappear and then return with more secrets. Some she couldn't hide, like when she showed back up with you in her arms."

I can't help but notice that Mullory's face softens every time her mom is mentioned. "I don't know how to find her," Mullory finally concedes. "Do you?"

Gran shakes her head. Her gray eyes mirror Mullory's. "I don't, but I have something that might help. I suppose it's time I brought it out." She disappears from the living room, shuffling down the hall.

Mullory does an awkward hand roll thing before throwing her arms in the air and looking to me for answers.

All I can do is shrug and throw my arms back at her.

Mullory paces around a sofa, one where I imagine coins continuously hide in the cushions. "What's going on?" she mutters. "Gran has a secret. *Gran.* Another boy. Thin air." Her thoughts are incoherent snippets, and I catch her as she rounds the couch before we both end up dizzy.

"Breathe," I tell her.

Mullory looks up at me, her eyes large. "What is she going to get?"

I catch sight of Gran over Mullory's shoulder, and I spin her around. "Looks like we're going to find out." I run my arms down the length of her sleeves, then lace my hands in hers. "We'll look together," I say. What a sap I've become.

Mullory sinks her teeth into her lower lip and eases forward. I haven't the slightest idea what lies in the small cardboard box clutched in Gran's hands. Truthfully, after almost dying, nothing could surprise me.

Mullory peeks over the edge. "What's all that stuff?"

Gran thrusts the box into Mullory's hand and falls onto the sofa. "I have no idea."

Mullory fails to hide her disappointment. "But you said it would help find my mom."

"I did," Gran agrees, and takes a long sip of iced tea.

Mullory places the box onto the coffee table and stares at her gran. "Why would this stuff help?"

Gran considers the question and lazily swirls a finger around the edge of her glass. "The day your mother was born, every clock in the hospital stood still. Time itself froze. That was my first clue," she says thoughtfully.

"First clue for what?"

"That my daughter, Esther Merrybright, was special." Gran's eyes are wistful and glistening. "They placed her in my arms, and she didn't cry. That was when everything stopped. But then Esther blinked at me and turned her tiny head just as a woman appeared. I saw her in the hall and then she was beside my bed in a flash. Her eyes were odd. Gave me goose bumps just looking at her."

Mullory hangs on every word. "Who was she?"

Gran smacks her knees with both hands. "I have no idea. Can't really remember what she looked like. Every time I try, my brain goes all woozy. But I remember what she said, can't ever forget it."

"What?" I ask before Mullory can.

"The woman leaned over my bedside table and stroked your mother's fuzzy head. Barely any hair on her," Mullory's gran says, reminiscing. "Anyway, I was frozen in my body, stuck in time, like the rest of the hospital. My fear didn't freeze though, thought for sure she was gonna take her. But all she did was leave that box of stuff and instructions."

Mullory's eyes light up.

"The woman, she told me, 'It's not for her,' and she nodded to my Esther. She said, 'It's for the next.'"

"For me?" Mullory questions.

"That's right. She told me I'd know when to give it to you. That time can repeat itself."

"That's it?" Mullory whines.

Her gran nods. "That's it."

"And you thought now was that time?"

"Like I told you, I knew it was time when you yanked that boy out from nothing. Just like Esther. Only her boy had a scar slashed across his perfect face. Yours seems to be in better shape. But time repeats itself and all that, whatever it means." Gran huffs.

Mullory nods pensively. "And you have no idea who the woman was?"

"Not a clue."

"Right," Mullory answers, and kneels beside the coffee table. "Then there must be something useful in here."

I, being ever the pessimist, am less hopeful. Especially when Mullory pulls out an old ivory comb with crudely shaped teeth.

"Could have used that when I died," I try to joke. But Mullory is set on her box of junk and ignores me.

Things don't get much better when Mullory fishes out the next item, a torn receipt for a cup of coffee. She smooths the crumpled fragment.

"Gum?" Mullory declares when she pulls out the foil stick next. Even her optimism starts to fizzle with this latest clue.

"One thing left."

I brace myself for a squished mint or a ball of lint. Turns out, I'm not that far off.

"A yo-yo." Mullory squints at the cheap plastic toy. "Maybe the pictures are important," she says with a shrug. The front has a faded image of two old keys, one white, one black. She flips it over to reveal images of two more items, a baseball bat and hand saw.

"Maybe," I offer, not at all hopeful.

Mullory releases the string, letting the yo-yo spiral down and then back up again. Unsurprisingly nothing happens.

Frustrated, she tosses the yo-yo to the side and runs her fingers along the bottom of the box, searching for other clues, before inspecting the box itself. I blame myself for her disappointment. A week in my uncle's game made her believe everyone weaves elaborate puzzles and hidden messages everywhere. Sometimes an old box of junk is just a regular old box of junk.

I can't stifle the yawn that creeps up. "Maybe we try again later," I suggest while suppressing a shiver. "It's freezing in here."

Mullory shakes her head, now mildly aware that the room is frigid. "Gran," she chastises. "The windows again."

I trace the source of the cold to an open window, drawing in bouts of icy air.

Gran is unaffected. "It's good for my lungs. Cancer is winter shy."

Mullory rubs her temples while placing the junk back into the box. "That doesn't make any sense."

Gran snorts. "Since when does this family know anything about sense." She points a finger my way. "Go shut the window."

I hop to my feet and reach for the window latch. Wintry air prickles my skin before it rushes in, overpowering me. It's a scent and feeling I'd spent months trying to rid myself of. A cataclysmic wave of white-hot pain descends upon me, a thousand needles plunged simultaneously into every inch of my skin, conduits for the torment that suddenly lights up my entire body. Torturous. As if my spine is being twisted and snapped, every bone splintered into shards.

I fall to my knees in agony.

Dying was nothing compared to this.

10. MULLORY

I smell it before Lyric even screams.

Some things you can't ever forget; some things are burned into you so deeply you can't ever get them out.

A festering, curdled smell. It stuck to the charred remains of our family home. It pooled along the surface of the water Lyric nearly drowned in. And now it gags me as every muscle in my body tightens with a sickening realization. I don't want to turn around, because I don't want to face it head-on. But I can feel it, like a lightning strike that decimates the bridge connecting me to Lyric. Leaving a chasm in its place, an impossibly treacherous divide.

"Mullory!" Gran's voice is urgent enough to make me look. My stomach drops to my feet as I spot Lyric collapsed beneath the window.

At first, I can't move. Something in my chest feels ripped right open, and I'm half-convinced if I look down, I'll see a knife protruding from my ribs. Instead, a tangle of plump worms wriggle by my ankles, another useless spurt of Xavier's magic I can't control.

"Mullory!" Gran bellows again, and this time she physically pushes me forward, jump-starting my panic. A tremor skips through Lyric's body as he lets out another bloodcurdling scream. The sound pierces straight through me, vibrating my teeth.

Tears slip down my cheeks as I grab on to him; another convulsion rattles his body. His skin is pure heat, clammy and fever stricken.

"Hoist him up," Gran orders, taking charge. I slide my hands beneath his shoulders as Gran grabs him by the ankles and we awkwardly drag his limp body onto the couch.

"Ice pack and a cool rag," Gran yells. "Hop to it!"

I follow her orders. I'm robotic in the kitchen, grabbing supplies as I listen to Gran grumble about boys from thin air being no good and how women in our family enjoy being tortured.

Part of me wants to tell her what's happening, what Lyric stands to lose. But when I rush back into the living room, her face is softened; the harsh lines creasing her eyes are blurred with the truth. Maybe she can't fully understand what's going on, but that doesn't mean she hasn't seen it before. Because I may have lost a mom to the strange, but Gran lost a daughter. She might not know the specifics, but she knows enough. Loss is loss even if there's magic involved.

Lyric's eyes are closed, and his dark lashes flutter as I put the cool rag on his forehead and squeeze his hand that's hanging off the couch. There's a surge of energy the moment I touch him. It feels like when Xavier's magic latched on to me, but this isn't a steady trickle—it's an avalanche.

"Stay with me," I order between my sobs. My tears splatter across his cheeks. I don't know much about magic, but I know this is too much for one person. There are rules and precautions that are normally set in place.

Lyric's body becomes limp. "Don't you dare," I whisper, leaning in so that my lips are a breath away from his. Lyric's eyes startle open.

"Mullory." His tone isn't kind or gentle.

I startle back, searching desperately for the boy I just saved.

A pain deeper than the physical torture burns in Lyric's eyes.

My insides blaze with guilt. "I can fix this," I say quietly while grasping for anything at my disposal. Xavier's magic, the coat. I grab the box of junk. "This," I say more resolutely. "This will lead us to my mom, and she'll know what to do and—"

Lyric cuts me off. "He knows."

I cower back, letting the truth wash over me. Lord Thorn knows Lyric has his magic again.

II.
ELLISON

"Are you sure about this, Miss Ellison?" the driver asks while cruising the sleek Audi A8 L down the unevenly paved, crumbling road.

The freaking question of the day. Was I sure about this when I boarded a plane and landed in the backwoods airport with a single runway and a café that smelled like the underside of a boot? Was I sure that dropping everything to flee to Punxsutawney, Pennsylvania, was the right decision? Absolutely not. I'm not built to survive in a place like this; my skin has already erupted with angry red patches.

But I won't tell him that. "Keep driving," I order while twisting my fingers in my lap. Of course I'm not sure what the hell I'm doing. But the traitorous rats were all too happy to reveal this address after I gave them one of Lyric's shirts.

And now we're on some bumpy country road, rolling through a town covered in horrific Frosty inflatables and twinkling lights. As if the decor wasn't already sinful enough, each corner boasts a larger-than-life groundhog painted in ridiculous getups, and a mural welcomes me into the Weather Capital of the World. Thanks, but I'd rather not.

And yet, I can't ignore the pinch in my gut, the possibility—no matter how improbable or ridiculous—that Lyric might be alive. Even my own mother clung to the idea. That's a twisting mystery I'm not sure I'm ready to unravel. All this time—behind all those years of stone-cold torture—she was watching out for the three of us. I dismiss the thought. Forgiveness isn't something I pass out easily or often.

I can't stop thinking about the woman who invaded her dreams and warned her. Who is she? And more importantly, why did she want to keep us safe? More secrets. Another mystery. Wasn't Uncle's fake death enough?

"What are you hoping to find, miss?" the driver asks, snapping me back to the present. *What am I hoping to find? Nothing big, just my dead brother brought back to life.* It sounds too ridiculous to even say aloud.

"Something important," I answer, when really, I'm letting hope's poison dare me to think that *someone* important is waiting for me. That Lyric could possibly be close. I gasp at the thought and slice my teeth into my cheek to prevent the tears from slipping out. For the past two months I've wallowed in a listless state of unending guilt. Because even though I'd lashed out at Mullory and would like to think it's all her and my mother's fault, deep down I harbored a darker truth. Lyric was my little brother, and I'd failed him in so many ways. I blamed myself.

"This is it, Miss Ellison," the driver announces, and slows the car. An unremarkable home the shade of wilted weeds stares back at me. I don't miss the plastic Santa poised beside the chimney or the reindeer spotting the front yard.

I pull my caramel-colored peacoat tight, smoothing the pockets, while following the cracked sidewalk and avoiding patches of ice and snow. The heel of my boot slips, and for a horrible second, I'm afraid I might face-plant right in front of Mullory's tacky home.

"Are you all right, miss?" the driver calls.

I gather my pride. "I'm fine," I scream, and stomp toward the door, dragging my bruised ego behind me. I kick the undersides of my boots across a heart-shaped doormat that reads *Home Is Where the Heart Is*, and raise my fist, prepared to knock, when voices catch my attention.

Suddenly, I'm banging the door with both arms, and when it's finally flung open, I rush forward, crashing into an older lady.

She huffs and moves to the side, gesturing me forward. "I suppose you better come in and join them."

I squeeze past her; my heart is beating so fast I'm certain it will burst from my chest. I don't stop moving until I spot him.

Lyric.

Alive.

Sitting on a truly hideous sofa in Punxsutawney, Pennsylvania.

The dam bursts open, and everything crashes over me at once. A tsunami of guilt and relief, disbelief, and unfiltered happiness, but I quickly reel it all in and lock it deep down in my vault of secrets.

"Lyric," I manage to say, composing myself. My hands are twisted so tightly together, I've lost all feeling in my fingers. I don't move closer—we're not the type of family to hug. Even after coming back from the dead.

Lyric gives me a weak smile. "Hi, Ellison," he says. Just like that.

I inch closer, reeled in. "I thought you were dead."

His face is strained, and his eyes darken. "I was. Almost."

"What are you doing here?" Mullory asks, doe-eyed, taking a half-protective stance in front of Lyric. As if I would ever hurt him. In case she forgot, I was the one who saved him. She was the one who had to go and get him killed.

"I'm taking him back," I say, all grit. Time to remind Mullory how Stoutmires handle family business.

12.
MULLORY

I'd thought pulling Lyric back from some pocket between life and death and then wrangling him into my house in front of Gran would be the strangest thing to happen all day. But seeing Ellison Stoutmire, in her posh outfit, standing in my living room—for some reason that feels even stranger.

I can practically *feel* the anger rolling off her. She glares at me, teeth bared, ready to do I don't know what. But I won't back down.

"Come on, Lyric," Ellison orders while flicking her wrist toward the door. "I'm taking you back to Chicago."

"No, you're not." I lunge in front of him.

"Oh, I see. You think he wants to stay *here*?" Ellison turns her nose up, and my blood boils.

"Maybe he does." I hate that I can feel my cheeks flush, especially with Gran watching the whole thing.

"He's coming with me," Ellison snaps.

"Stop. Both of you." Lyric wheezes, his skin is still a putrid gray, and I can tell he's using all his energy. Taking a deep breath, he shimmies to face Ellison. "Lord Thorn's magic is back with me," he says, spitting the last few words like a foul taste.

Ellison's face pales as she nervously tucks a strand of blond hair behind her ear. "We'll figure that part out later."

Lyric slams his arm onto a pillow. "There won't be a later. He already knows."

Shame and fury cloud Lyric's face, and I can practically hear his heartbeat with his rage. I brush the tips of my fingers against his hand, but he pulls away.

Ellison fidgets with her bracelet and picks at an angry cuticle. "We go back to Chicago," she says again, this time less sure.

"To your mother's house?" I question apprehensively.

"Yes. Our parents can protect him."

Lyric plants his face into his hands before running them through his hair, ruffling up the dark strands. "I can't trust Mother."

"But maybe Father—"

"Not *my* father," Lyric interjects.

My mind spins with moves and possibilities. "We need to get him somewhere safe before we can try and find my mom."

Ellison huffs. "And how exactly is your mother going to help?"

I ignore her and lock eyes with Lyric. "Where?" I ask softly.

He looks drained. Like he might shatter into pieces and fall to the floor any second. "It has to be Uncle X's estate."

I know it, too. Even though that's the last place Lyric would ever want to go. Xavier Stoutmire's estate is the most guarded and maybe, just maybe, he might be able to help. There's only one problem.

"I haven't been able to get back there or talk to Xavier," I remind Lyric.

Lyric pushes himself upright and staggers to stand. "He won't turn me away."

"Or me," Ellison snarls.

"You're going to come?" I ask her, surprised.

She lets out a shrill laugh as if her staying behind was never even an option. "Wouldn't miss it for the world."

"Okay," I say with resolve, letting the new plan take shape. There's just one last thing to do—something I've never been good at. Something my mom did to me all the time.

Until now, Gran has been silent, watching this madness unfurl in her living room. She's poised by the tree; the multicolored lights make her white hair glow. Tough as nails, but I can tell by the slump of her shoulders and her faltering smile—deep down she's sad. And I can't help but feel like my mom, caught between worlds, always on the run.

"Don't worry about me," Gran warns, catching sight of me about to break down. "You've got stuff to attend to. Just be back before school starts again." I grab hold of her as tight as I can. "Go," she whispers in my ear.

I'm quick as a flash, darting into my room and stuffing my backpack with only the essentials, and I hurriedly throw Cecilia's books into a shopping bag before grabbing the cardboard box full of clues.

"Some old books and a box of junk," Ellison remarks. "How prepared you are."

"We need them," I answer without further explanation.

Gran brushes Ellison aside. "I've been waiting to give you that box for years. It's time, Mullory." There's a depth to Gran's words, meanings hidden between the lines. She nods at Lyric with approval. "Watch over her," she warns, and squeezes my hand.

"Always," Lyric musters.

"And you." Gran faces me. "Watch over him."

"I will," I promise.

"Mullory," Gran calls as we turn to leave, "that woman also told me you'd be safest here with me until time repeated itself."

Unease rolls across my shoulder blades, but I shrug it away. "I'll be okay."

"Don't..." Gran's voice quivers, and she steadies herself. "Don't make the same mistakes she did."

But at this point, it's perfectly clear that I'm hurtling down the same path as my mom.

13.
LYRIC

I feel like absolute garbage.

At what point does my body simply give up? It doesn't help that all my demons have returned, hissing hostile thoughts between my ears. Lord Thorn's magic draws out my temper and my anger in a burst that makes my head throb.

I hobble out the door, desperate for a reprieve. The air is bitter, biting at my skin and burning my lungs when I inhale, but both are reminders that I'm still alive. At least for now. I can't help but think of the creepy figure from death and the warning he gave. *"He'll find you again and kill you. She'll let him."*

"You're lucky I came when I did." My sister breaks my trance. "And lucky I brought us a car and a driver."

In her own way, I know this is my sister trying to help. This is how she shows she cares. I'm too tired to even ask how she found me.

Mullory is the first to climb inside the car.

Ellison teeters by the door, hesitating. "I'm glad . . ." she starts to say before her eyes shift to her shoes and her voice cracks. "I'm glad you, well, you seem all right." She whips around too quickly for me to answer, bounding off to the front seat.

I collapse beside Mullory, my mind a puddle of soup as she rummages through her bag of books.

"Maybe when you're done reading," Ellison sneers back at Mullory, "maybe then you can do something actually useful and glamour us, so we're concealed during the trip."

Mullory pales, staring down at her hands. "I . . . can't."

"You can't or you won't?"

Mullory's ears turn red as she fidgets uncomfortably. "The magic won't work for me."

A sharp laugh from my sister.

"But that's what I was going to show you, Lyric." Mullory fishes out a book bestowed to her by my eccentric cousin Cecilia. She flips past the cover, entitled *The Genetics of Magical Transfer*. "'There are two rare instances where transferred magic may not manifest. The first is if the recipient is infected with a parasite of magical origin prior to the transfer. The second is death.'" Mullory gulps when she finishes reading.

My eyelids begin to shut as I answer. "You don't have a magical parasite."

"And it appears, against all odds, that you're not dead," says Ellison.

"But then why won't it work?" Mullory pleads, and a trio of blue birds with catlike tails flutter by her face. Ellison lets out a haughty laugh at the misconstrued magic.

But all I can think of is sleep as the last words barely leave my lips. "We'll figure it out."

And then nothing.

I'm occasionally jostled awake, and I have some foggy realization that time is passing as we move. At some point Mullory makes me take sips of water and force down a crumbly granola bar.

Minutes melt into hours before I can finally sit up. Darkness bleeds along the edges of the afternoon, steadily engulfing the tree-lined streets until they're blotted out completely as nighttime descends upon the Hamptons. It feels like a lifetime has passed, but it's only six p.m.—to think that just yesterday I was dead. What a day.

Mullory glances at me, twisting her hair around her fingers; worry ripples off her. "Are you okay?" she finally whispers.

"Why wouldn't I be okay?"

Mullory flinches at my snarky response, shaking her head. "Do you think he'll be there?"

I shrug, trying to ease the stiffness from my shoulders. I haven't seen Uncle Xavier since he trapped me in a game to kill Mullory. Not since he paraded around, pretending to be Edwin, his senior head of staff, like some half-mad puppeteer. Not since he failed to leave me the one thing I was promised—the very thing that now resides in Mullory. His magic.

I sit on my hands to stop myself from punching my fist through the window.

"Are you sure about this?" Mullory's fingertips tentatively brush my knee.

"What other choice do we have?"

Mullory forcefully stuffs her hands back onto her lap. I know she doesn't have the fondest memories of the estate either. Not with Uncle trying to kill her with poison or drop her down a well. But even though Uncle Xavier is the epitome of an asshole, he's still powerful, and he's still capable of providing us with time to sort this mess out. If that's even possible. Maybe I'll be dead again tomorrow.

"Back too soon," Ellison grunts, as the driveway to Stoutmire Estate peels into view. Enormous evergreens, enchanted to look like they've been growing up the lane for years, are strung with soft, glistening lights. Gossamer, shimmering snowflakes fall and catch on the branches in meticulously perfect piles. A large skating rink of picture-perfect glassy ice is situated on the front lawn. Skaters carved from blocks of ice are dotted around, spinning and leaping across the mirrored rink.

Mullory squeezes my hand. She's as taut as a finely tuned violin. "I could never get this far when I tried."

I'm not sure why Uncle wanted to keep her away. I never know why he does anything, but I do know the house won't turn me away. It wouldn't dare.

The driver lets us out at the base of the massive porch. The columns are strung with thick garlands speckled with giant candy canes and silky red ribbons twirled from moonlit threads.

The estate appears to be sleeping, tucked tightly beneath a layer of fluffy snow, but I know better—it's more like a predator poised to lure us in.

Ellison and Mullory are huddled behind me as I give the heavy golden knocker a rap, and then we wait. But it isn't Uncle X or even Edwin who greets us.

"Uncle Zolan?"

"Ah, yes," he says, shifting in velvet slippers that I know for certain belong to Uncle X. A glass bottle full of Macallan 1926 whiskey sloshes in one hand; a fat red cigar is perched in the other. Some of the whiskey sprays his tweed vest that's stretched beyond its limits across his midsection. Uncle Zolan raises an eyebrow. "I thought you were dead," he says before downing the rest of the glass. "Perhaps you still are."

"I was," I answer smoothly, still waiting on the porch threshold.

Uncle Zolan takes a drag. "Well, dead or not, I'm glad someone came. Come in, or do you prefer to dawdle on the porch all day?"

I step past him. "Have you been here the entire time?"

Uncle Zolan lets out a gruff laugh. "I was asked to stay. Official business with the dead, so on and so forth."

Beneath the caramel notes of whiskey, I can sniff out his bullshit.

"Where's Xavier?" Mullory demands, patience wearing thin.

"I haven't the slightest idea." Uncle Zolan brushes her aside. "But as I was saying, I'm glad someone came, because there's been a vermin problem." Uncle Zolan waves his cigar through the air, twirling ringlets of garnet smoke. "Normally animal deaths don't disturb me, especially small ones. I usually just ignore them, but these keep popping up in the middle of the night. Tiny little chipmunk bodies floating in the pond. You know, the ones Xavier kept on the estate to collect trash at parties and string acorns during the Thanksgiving holiday."

"Why do we care about this?" Ellison asks with agitation.

"Because it's a nuisance. Xavier kept everything in magical harmony, but it hasn't been quite right since he left. And more importantly, the cigars are running dangerously low. Merely stating a fact."

"And the dead just insisted that you stay here and indulge in Uncle's cigars and whiskey?" I ask, eyeing him up and down. His ankles are swollen, like his belly, like someone who hasn't moved in weeks.

"I've done no such thing!" Uncle Zolan bellows. "But see for yourselves, the magic here is unwell."

Mullory blushes at the hidden accusation, that the magic is unwell because of *her*.

"Ah, you're finally here." Edwin pops into view, sporting his signature black blazer, and gives us a cordial bow. "Cecilia called this morning and said you three would arrive today."

Of course, clairvoyant relatives tend to do that. If Edwin is shocked to see me back from the dead, he doesn't show it.

"Did Cecilia say anything else?"

"No sir," Edwin answers. "Just that you might attract unwanted attention."

That's one way to put my father's attempt to kill me.

14.

CECILIA HUMES

The armoire has started talking again.

"Cecilia," it says impatiently. "Cecilia, please."

I balance my cup of tea between the furless ears of Sphinxy cat and tentatively crawl toward the armoire.

"What do you want?" I poke a finger at the grainy wood.

"Finally. There you are."

"Edwin?" I ask, opening the door to reveal my phone, clutched between the paws of the ferret I misplaced. I scoop up the furry trickster and pry away the phone Xavier forces me to keep.

Edwin continues. "Yes. I wanted to let you know that they've arrived just as you said."

I glance at the seven clocks sitting atop the fireplace mantel. "An hour late."

My mind whirls with alternate possibilities; an hour might as well be an eternity. I throw a book at the third clock, letting it smash to pieces on the floor.

"I'll keep a firm eye on them," Edwin assures me before hanging up.

I roll across the carpet and settle before the fire. I pluck four feathers from a basket and begin to hum.

On a hunt four little birds go.
Time is precious, fast and slow.
One for a mom to help heal,
Another in dreams for a reveal.
The third wishes to be set free,
But there is a price, honey to the bee.
The fourth, quite old, wants what he lost.
But do the four little birds know the cost?

I weave the feathers between my fingers as the remaining clocks tick away in awful bursts. *Tick. Tock. Tick. Tock.*

"So it begins," I murmur to the now silent armoire while scattering the feathers into the flames. One little bird won't make it to the end of the hunt—of this, I'm sure. Glancing at the clocks, I can't help but wonder: Which will it be?

15.
MULLORY

As it turns out, the real Edwin is much more agreeable than the Xavier imposter. He entices Uncle Zolan away with another expensive whiskey and offers us hot chocolates topped with peppermint-dusted marshmallows. And as a much-appreciated bonus, he doesn't try to kill me.

"I trust that your trip was satisfactory?" he asks cordially.

I nod, taking a swig of rich, velvety chocolate. "Where's Xavier?"

Edwin's green eyes lock onto mine. "He's been gone for several weeks."

"Why?" Lyric demands.

Edwin straightens his posture and flicks a bit of lint from his blazer. "He's been off on business." The way he says it makes the whole thing sound suspicious.

"Business?" Lyric counters.

"Precisely."

The sheer exhaustion from the day presses down on me. "And when will he be back?"

"He didn't say, Miss Mullory. All I know is that Xavier had something important to attend to."

"It's always important, isn't it?" Lyric huffs.

We shuffle deeper into the foyer. The entire estate smells like pinecones and crushed candy canes, festive and sugary. Tiny golden ornaments hang from the bones of the family tree. Striated red ribbons that look suspiciously and horrifically like muscle fibers are draped across the skeletal spine sprouting up from the plot of soil scattered across the marble floor. The winding staircase is wrapped with fresh evergreen boughs, and ruby-red berries pop like blood-stained jewels between the greenery. A light snow falls from the ceiling but never collects on the surfaces. I can't help but stick my tongue out and catch a flake—it melts like sugar frosting.

"You packed light," Edwin remarks.

"I never intended to come all the way here." Ellison stares me down like it's a challenge. "But I won't be leaving anytime soon."

"Well, then I'll take your bags, Miss Mullory."

I hand over my overstuffed bag of books but keep my backpack clutched to my chest.

Edwin studies me with a puzzled frown. "Your belongings appear to be glowing."

I glance down and realize he's right. Something inside my backpack is radiating a warm red light. Pillaging through my clothes, I quickly find the source of the glow. Splotches of shining red dot the perimeter of the yo-yo. I turn it over, ignoring my first thought, which is that it looks like blood.

Lyric examines it next. "They kind of look like fingerprints," he says slowly while rubbing the yo-yo between his own hands, before looking up at me. "I think you must have activated it when you first touched it, Mullory."

Grasping the yo-yo again, I run my fingers along the edge. Lyric's right; my touch reveals the paint, until the entire circumference is alight with fluorescent red. A ring of numbers appears next, like the face of a padlock.

Instinct has me gently twisting the one half, realizing that it spins. "I think I need the correct combination." But what is it? My birthday? My mom's birthday? Both are too obvious for a hunt of this grandeur. My mom would've left a clue intended for only me, one connected to the lock. I study the cartoonish pictures on the yo-yo. "I think the baseball bat and the saw blade mean something."

"Maybe we need to cut the string?" Lyric guesses.

"Or smash it to pieces with a baseball bat," Ellison offers sarcastically.

But I know the clue is something specific to me; that's how the best clues work. A series of numbers I would find significant. "What if the pictures are homonyms?" My fingers run along the collar of my sweater, trailing the shadow tucked tightly beneath. "What if the baseball bat is an actual bat and . . ." My voice trails off as my fingers spin the face of the yo-yo excitedly. "The date I first *saw* the bats." After my mom burned our house down, initiating my journey into the strange.

When I rotate the face to the final number, something grinds, then pops, separating the two halves of the yo-yo, and a brass button, exactly like the ones on my jacket, falls out. I rip off the circus coat, searching for a frayed space where a button used to be sewn.

"Edwin, we need thread!" I practically scream.

"Certainly, let me fetch Greta. I've never seen such enthusiasm for the prospect of garment alterations, but I'm happy to oblige." Edwin moves from the foyer with Lyric and me close behind. "Let me just ring her," he says while pushing a fancy intercom system paneled to the kitchen wall. "Perhaps some light fare while we wait." He sweeps a hand toward the island, which is covered in platters and towers of tantalizing food.

I'm anxious with anticipation, but my stomach growls at the sight of ham-and-cheese sliders glistening in buttered sesame rolls. "Just a quick bite," I agree. Lyric has already barreled toward a pile of meatballs. He picks the meat off with his teeth, discarding the toothpicks into a pile, quickly working through half the tray. Eating like, well, like a boy who hasn't eaten in months. Ellison meanders into the kitchen and opts for a single bacon-wrapped date.

"Greta," Edwin bellows into the speaker.

"Ja."

"You're needed in the kitchen. We require thread to sew a button."

"What color thread?"

Lyric answers with a mouthful of meatball. "Doesn't matter!"

"Tell her it's important!" I add while wiping a smear of mustard from my lip.

Edwin shushes us with a wave of his hand. "It appears this is some sort of button emergency and that the color thread is inconsequential."

If Greta has any question as to what constitutes a button emergency, she doesn't ask. "Very well, I'll be right down."

Three bites later, Greta hustles into the kitchen, sewing basket in hand. She's dressed in a similar black blazer over a crisp white dress. I wipe my hands on my pants and spring up from the island.

"Here," I say excitedly while thrusting the jacket into Greta's hands. "And the button. Right there." I smack the jacket and point at the empty space.

"I see." Greta removes a pair of small reading glasses from her pocket. Lyric and I can't help but hover over her shoulder. She grabs a spool of red thread and laces it through a needle, knotting it with her teeth and spearing it through the jacket.

"A bit of space, Herr," she says. Lyric is practically sitting on her lap, but he eases back. I bounce from foot to foot like a toddler waiting in line for the bathroom.

Greta pulls the thread through the button's hole, securing it in place, but before she can even cut the stray threads, I'm reaching for the jacket. "Good enough, perfect, thank you!" I run my hand over the newly sewn-on button.

"Anything?" Lyric asks.

I run my eyes over the jacket, checking the pockets and tags. "Maybe if I put it on again?" I slip the jacket back on. "Do you see anything?"

"Still hideous," Ellison declares from the island.

"I don't think so," says Lyric, dejected.

My shoulders drop as I glance back down at the jacket, just as a thunderous knock sounds from the foyer. Instinctively, I freeze in place. Has Lord Thorn found us already?

"Are you expecting anyone else, Edwin?" Lyric asks, equally alarmed.

A curt shake of his head. "No, sir."

Another knock, this one even more forceful.

"Someone's here," Uncle Zolan roars.

"Could it be Lord Thorn?"

"No, I don't believe so. He would have triggered the alarm."

"Okay." I swallow. "Then who is it?"

Edwin pales. "Someone we weren't expecting."

16.
ELLISON

I creep behind Mullory as we huddle beneath the staircase, hiding like a bunch of children. Edwin explicitly told us to stay put, but Lyric and Mullory are far too noisy, and I won't dare let my brother out of my sights again.

A gust of air sweeps into the foyer as Edwin undoes the locks and opens the front door. From our vantage point, I can't yet tell who the ominous visitor is.

A young, but confident, voice carries across the foyer. "Evening. I'm here to see the master of the house."

Edwin doesn't budge, holding firm. "I'm afraid the master of the estate is out on business. Indefinitely."

The visitor lets out a cocky laugh. "Not that master. The new one. I'm here to see the girl."

Edwin blusters for a moment as Mullory slips out from beneath the staircase and pops into view. Lyric and I follow, spilling out like a barrel of monkeys set free. Edwin's eyes widen before he purses his lips and reluctantly ushers in the new guests.

A boy who appears to be around my age marches inside: He sports a rich brown leather bomber with a shearling collar. The sides of his dark hair are buzzed to the skin of his neck, while the longer bit on top is flopped back. His jawline is squarely sculpted, and his full lips pull into a devilish grin, a perfectly pinched dimple creasing, when he spots Mullory. There's something frustratingly familiar about him.

Behind him a girl lurks in his shadow. Her eyes are a deep plum color, and her hair is a lilac-shaded bob that grazes her heart-shaped face. She's a full foot shorter than the boy, but her tasteless outfit makes up for it—a light-pink furry vest that fluffs around her frame and lime-green leggings. She smiles at me, all teeth, and I stagger back.

"Mullory Prudence." The boy squares his shoulders and thrusts his chest out, taking command of the foyer. "Thanks for inviting us."

"I d-didn't," she stammers.

I can't help but roll my eyes, because here I was thinking Mullory had finally come into her own. But fidgeting in that absurd coat, she doesn't look like the master of the house at all. She looks ridiculous.

The boy stalks closer, which elicits a protective growl from Lyric. I still can't put my finger on what's so familiar about him, but it's right there, buzzing on the tip of my tongue. The horribly dressed girl stays rooted by the front door, her eyes flitting from us to the windows between glances at her wrist, which has three oddly shaped watches stacked in a row.

"And who are you?" Lyric barks.

The boy snaps his fingers and beams a smile. "Ah, right. Introductions are in order. I believe you've all had the unfortunate pleasure of meeting my younger, less charming brother, Mateo."

I knew he looked familiar.

"My name is Cruz Lagunes and this . . ." he says, waving a hand at the peculiar girl stationed at the front door. "This is my cousin, Reina Lagunes." Reina offers no smiles now and taps her foot, unamused. She keeps her eyes peeled on the windows, and her other hand firmly fixed on her strange stack of watches.

Disgust wells inside of me, because I know all about Cruz Lagunes. After Uncle's wretched Mystery Royale, I pored over every minute, relived every detail. All I had was time to obsess over the game that took Lyric's life, a self-inflicted punishment. I did some investigating into the entire Lagunes family. Powerful. Ancient. Secretive. But Cruz, he's a whole different type of monster, the very worst kind.

The Lagunes family is considered neutral and thus immune to the council and its bylaws. They prefer, instead, something more archaic when it comes to passing magic to their children. Years ago, families with magic would purposefully have multiple children—survival of the fittest with duels and tournaments, all very theatrical and unnecessary.

The Lagunes family believes in honoring that tradition. Five children born into a family with just two possible heirs—it's no wonder only three of them are still living. Cruz murdered his two older siblings to reroute his father's magic and claim it for himself. From what I could find, it was a total bloodbath. After, he was raised up on a pedestal like some gladiator victor of the Colosseum. They actually threw him a party.

"You're despicable," I yell. I can't help the anger swelling my veins; betraying a sibling is a line I wouldn't dare cross.

"I take it you've heard of me?" Cruz winks.

"Get out!" I howl.

Cruz raises a condescending finger in my face. "This isn't your home, Ellison," he says, scolding me like a schoolchild. "And you're not who I came to bargain with."

"Why would we ever make a deal with you?"

Cruz raises a manicured eyebrow. "Well, you haven't heard what I'm offering yet."

Maybe it's his oily suave demeanor, or his casual shrugs, but I can't take him a moment longer. "How could you? You murdered your siblings!" I scream. My hands are shaking, and my mind is a raging fire.

I can feel Mullory stiffen beside me at the mention of murder. "Is that true?" she whispers. Finally, the master of the house speaks.

Cruz taps his forehead thoughtfully. "Technically, yes. But *murder* is such a nasty word."

"You *murdered* them," I say again.

Cruz snaps his attention back to me. "Not such a hard thing to do if you put your mind to it. From what I've heard, you did a good job helping to murder your own brother." Cruz gives Lyric a lazy once-over. "But as it appears, not quite good enough."

I lunge forward, tears and anger smearing my vision. "Get out!"

Cruz doesn't flinch as I approach and instead, he yawns in my face. "I told you I'm not here for you, Ellison. Stop being such an attention seeker. I'm here for *her*." He turns, unbothered, and flashes a perfectly straight smile at Mullory Prudence. Figures. The most boring girl in the world has the largest freaking fan club.

17.
MULLORY

My mind is spinning, causing clusters of tangerine-colored flowers to sprout from the walls. Their silky centers burst and dribble marmalade jam down the artwork hanging in the foyer. Everyone ignores the nonsensical magic spewing out from me.

Maybe I'm in shock from being back at Stoutmire Estate. Or from the darkness I can feel smothering Lyric bit by bit. Or from my mom's insistent need for riddles when all I desperately need is her help. Or the seedling of fear that rooted right in my chest when Lyric returned. Or maybe, just maybe, it's from the murderous older brother of Mateo Lagunes, grinning directly at me like a wicked prince, waiting for an invitation onto the estate I'm supposedly the master of.

"Mullory." Cruz says my name softly, like we're old friends. "I'm here to offer our services." He gestures at himself and his peculiar cousin, who hasn't moved an inch. "Before you say no," Cruz warns, "you should know that you have approximately..." He pauses and glances at Reina.

"Twenty minutes," she says coolly, eyes pinned on her eccentric stack of watches.

Cruz nods. "You have twenty minutes until several members of the council, including the Magnus, arrive."

My pulse thunders beneath my skin; panic propels my heart into a frenzied beat. Can I even trust what he says? "Why is the council coming here?" I fight to keep my squeaky voice level.

"Don't listen to him," cautions Lyric.

The very last thing we need is another complication and Cruz Lagunes has the very distinct air of a terrible complication, but an even worse one would be if the council finds us first.

"Explain," I say. "Quickly."

Cruz waltzes across the marble foyer; his stride is purposeful, his gaze direct, and the very air around him is sharp with his scent. A mixture of mint and a frost-riddled winter's night. There's a deceptive calmness to his demeanor that has me on edge, the unsettling feeling of something dangerous lurking just beneath the surface.

"So much to explain. The question is, where do I begin?" Cruz gets uncomfortably close and dips his head, whispering gently in my ear. "Not exactly how I remember," he purrs, but before I can even question him, I feel a small pinch and then the bud of Xavier's magic that has been rebelling inside of me slips from my grasp.

Cruz smirks. "Don't worry, I'll give it back." He snaps his fingers, and something sparks. The line between his eyes deepens to a crease. "A bit strange," he remarks. There's that word again. The one that started it all.

Cruz makes a complicated pattern with his hands and finally gets the spark to catch. It ricochets into a blaze of embers that stick to my pants. Red-and-orange flecks of flame that feel hot but don't burn. They feather out into a skirt, clothing me in some sort of fiery red dress. Embarrassment creeps up my neck at his effortless use of Xavier's magic. I've tried for weeks but have been unsuccessful at wrangling it.

Cruz leans closer in one smooth arc. His lips skim my hair as he says, "You're different than I thought you'd be." His voice drops to a murmur. "But different intrigues me."

Just as quickly, he snaps back and continues his theatrical demonstration. He taps his chin while examining his work. "Close, but still not quite right." He releases his hands with defeat. The dress disintegrates to ashes and Xavier's magic rebounds back inside me.

"What did you just do?"

Lyric marches up to Cruz, chin to chin like he might punch him square in the face. "He's a siphon. A bloodsucker of magic."

Cruz gives Lyric a light shove. "I prefer *borrower* of magic. I gave it back to her. You're so hostile, Lyric Stoutmire." Cruz clicks his tongue with disapproval. "Perhaps you prefer your true name. Lyric Thorn." Cruz smiles again. "Yes, I know every dirty secret wafting around this place." He pauses behind Lyric and claps his hands together. Lyric stiffens, and I know that Cruz has commandeered Lord Thorn's magic from him.

"I think," Cruz says excitedly, "I think what you need is . . ." He slowly circles Lyric. "Yes, I think I've got it. I just need to lift this side here." Lyric groans as the left side of his cheek rises like a marionette. "And the other," Cruz commands. "That's it! You *can* smile."

But his smile is all wrong and sweat slips down Lyric's forehead as he fights and shatters whatever hold Cruz has on him.

"Enough!" Ellison orders.

Cruz turns his attention toward her, inhaling deeply. "Yikes. Your magic is a tangled knot. I'd get a better handle on that if I were you," he says, dusting off his hands.

It's Reina who finally breaks the hostility brewing in the foyer. "Ten minutes, Cruz."

"What does any of this have to do with the council?" I finally ask.

"But we're just getting to know one another," Cruz answers wryly. "Fine. Now that you know what I can do, I suppose it's time to tell you about Reina." He tips his head toward his cousin. "You've heard of Lagunes gifts, I'm certain. My brother Mateo demonstrated that handy little party trick where he could bind magic to himself. My parents just love to use him like a legal pad—"

"We don't have time to prattle on about the family, Cruz," Reina says sternly, her purplish eyes fixed intently on her watches. Honestly, she has me even more uneasy—lurking in the doorway, silently observing.

"Of course, time is of the essence," Cruz says curtly. "Anyway, Reina can hide things. More specifically she can conceal all magical traces. Smother them so that the trail you three are blazing can go away. She can keep you hidden."

"What trail?" I question.

"What trail? Mullory!" Cruz laughs. "That's how they've found you. You're lucky I saved that message you sent to me years ago. It was Reina who figured out that it was meant for today."

Lyric's brow furrows. "What message?" he asks me.

"I was trying to reach Mateo. I told him we were coming here. But I sent it today."

Cruz gives another haughty laugh. "Ah, that was your mistake, improper use of a time-defying object. You needed to set the hands to a place in time where *Mateo* had the watch, not me. But what a happy accident!"

Ellison groans. "And just how is this happy?"

"Because you got an upgrade, the more charming and, dare I say, skilled Lagunes brother."

I ignore his ego and draw us back to the dilemma at hand. "And what about the council? I didn't send them a message."

"No, you sent them something much bigger. Did you think the little stunt you pulled would go unnoticed? Yank someone back from the dead, using a highly coveted and extremely powerful magical artifact, and you thought no one would notice? It's like you shot up a beacon and put a billboard right above your heads."

I open my mouth to respond but promptly shut it. There's still so much to magic that I have no idea what's possible. I glance at Lyric, and his face confirms my fear. Cruz is telling the truth.

"We can shield you," Cruz offers like it's no big deal.

"Why would you do that?" I know how bargains work, and I suspect ones involving magic are even trickier.

"Let's just say I have my reasons. Good reasons, I might add." Cruz gives a casual shrug. "You'll owe me a favor."

"Mullory," Lyric warns. "Don't."

Cruz clutches the collar of his bomber, momentarily fearful. Whatever he wants from me, he must need it badly. He seems honest in that sense at least. As honest as any murderous sibling can be.

"I thought you'd trust me," Cruz finally says, disheartened. "But fine, consider this a trial run. Test us out and if you want us to leave after the council does, we will."

Every hair on my arms stands straight up in warning, and yet, some deranged part of me knows I have to try. Better to make a deal with this devil than pick a fight with the council.

"Fine," I hastily agree. "Show us what you can do."

18. LYRIC

It takes every ounce of my withering self-control not to pummel Cruz Lagunes in his smug face. I don't trust him at all, but I'll stand by Mullory's decision. What choice do we have? Trust this asshole, who I'm certain has a terrible ulterior motive we haven't yet uncovered, or take our chances with my charming father.

Reina braces herself, eyeing the door. "Two minutes," she warns.

An ear-screeching alarm echoes throughout the foyer, vibrating the walls and clacking the bones of the family tree together. The door groans, and a central fissure splits the wood open, releasing a complicated pattern of locks that snakes across and snaps into place like the barricade to a castle fortress.

"That would be the alarm," Edwin yells. "Certain persons get it excited."

"And that means Lo—" I can't finish the sentence because I don't want to say his name, so I rephrase. "The council's here."

Edwin gives a tight nod. "Precisely."

"Can we hold them off?" I dare to ask.

"Not indefinitely, sir. With Xavier gone, and . . ." Edwin's voice trails off as he eyes Mullory. "And with a different master in place, I'm sure they'll find their way onto the estate rather speedily." He steadies himself. "Best to face them head-on."

I grumble and step aside so Cruz can regain the spotlight.

He claps both hands together excitedly. "Showtime!" He motions to Reina, who smiles wide, baring her canines.

"Get together," she orders. We assemble into a cluster by the base of the stairs with Reina at the helm. Something invisible yet palpable slips over my mental awareness, insulating the group. Reina holds her fingers up and puts them down one by one. Mouthing a countdown. *"Three . . . Two . . . One."*

Someone bangs at the door and my throat tightens. Mullory grabs hold of my hand, the only flicker of movement, as the rest of us remain still as statues, grouped beneath whatever cover Reina conjured up. Either we're protected or sitting ducks, only time will tell. Ellison's breathing becomes labored; she's a moment away from a panic attack. Only Cruz seems at ease, eyeing the door with confident anticipation. Like this is all a grand spectacle he can't wait to watch unfold.

Another knock. This one more urgent.

It's Edwin's turn now. He straightens his blazer and calmly crosses the foyer, slipping past us like we're not even there, remaining at ease even when the knocking turns thunderous. He's all manners when he undoes the complicated locks and slowly opens the door.

"Good evening." A silky light voice drifts across the foyer. A woman who doesn't look much older than us, but who carries herself as someone wiser and more important, materializes. She's dressed in a sky-blue pantsuit. Her dark hair is done in tiny braids and twisted into a bun; her eyes are a warm amber and there's something mesmerizing about them.

"That would be the Magnus, Lucy Martini," Cruz remarks, like he's commentating on a horse race. Mullory gives him a silencing glance.

"Oh, do lighten up. You guys are so tense it's making me cramp."

I glare back at him, but Cruz only sharpens his smile.

"They can't hear or see us, I assure you. We're not amateurs. Reina is quite good at what she does."

"She better be," I mumble. I don't have a single chip to bargain with, but I'm still going to try my best to get beneath Cruz's skin.

He merely brushes me aside and stares back at our unwelcome guests. Something in my stomach coils as more footsteps and shuffling follow the Magnus, who's now poised in the center of the foyer. Several members of the council and associate cronies appear next, including Lawrence Stoutmire, my previously presumed father, who neither raised me nor gave me his magic.

Lord Thorn is the last to enter, clad in a dark suit and with an even darker presence. The sight of him causes my entire body to seize while the magic flooding my veins practically sings. I know he knows. How could he not? *"He'll kill you again."* The mysterious figure's warning won't get out of my head. I can't help but wonder what else it knows.

Mullory squeezes my hand so tightly it's painful, but I don't dare let go. *"He'll kill you again. She'll let him."* I will the memories from death's door away.

Edwin gives the guests a polite bow. Cool as ice, that's what years working for my uncle will do to a person. "I'm deeply apologetic, but Xavier Stoutmire is indisposed at this time," he says. "Perhaps some refreshments."

"We're not here for Xavier, or for refreshments," Lucy says curtly, teasing off her dainty leather gloves. "We're here with a warrant. We have reason to believe an artifact of significant magical value is being hidden here and was recently used illicitly."

"How interesting," Edwin remarks with a level of excitement equivalent to watching the weather.

"Search!" Lucy commands.

A beady-eyed man with a terrible comb-over takes the lead, crouching so that his fingertips skim the ground as he sniffs the air. His spine curves upward, and foul droplets of saliva drip from his lips, rendering him like a rabid wolf.

"They call him the Bloodhound," Cruz says excitedly. "He can sniff out magic. They say each type tastes differently to him, that he's developed an appetite for certain flavors. He's probably the one who led this merry bunch straight to us."

"The Bloodhound," Mullory repeats, trepidation causing her voice to waver.

"Nothing to worry about, Reina's got us." Cruz gives Mullory a reassuring nudge. I make sure my elbow quickly finds his stomach. Cruz groans but holds steady as the Bloodhound stalks nearer. His eyes are covered in some sort of milky web; reddish vessels pop beneath the glaze. He gives our group a drawn-out sniff before falling back in resignation.

Reina smiles proudly. Two points to the murderer Cruz and his useful cousin.

The rest of the council disperse throughout the estate. Frantic footsteps, slamming doors, and drawers being thrown about sound from all directions. Some of the staff members are startled and scream in response. But not one of us moves, and I don't miss the sheen of sweat glistening on Reina's forehead. I don't know the battery life she has on this magic, considering how young she is, but I don't want to find out.

Edwin remains in the foyer, waiting for the group to return. He doesn't even glance in our direction. Uncle can't possibly pay him enough.

After what feels like a lifetime, several of the council members stagger back. The Bloodhound appears disappointed, a hunger left unsatisfied. Lord Thorn is as menacing as a thundercloud, threatening to explode. I feel his magic crackle beneath my skin.

"Find what you were looking for?" Edwin asks politely.

The Magnus, Lucy, shoots Edwin a threatening scowl. "Not yet, but rest assured we will."

"Do come back again," he answers cheerily.

Lord Thorn is the last to leave, like he can't let it go, like he knows he's being duped. He pauses on the threshold and directs his fury at Edwin.

"If you happen to see Lyric Stoutmire back from the dead, please do give him a message. Let him know I won't make the same mistake twice."

Something in my chest constricts and a trickling sound fills my ears as cool water grazes my calves. My lungs burn, aching for oxygen, and my mind spirals into the darkness that followed my almost drowning. Piercing my nails into my palms, I have to physically tear myself from the nightmare my father inflicted upon me.

"Noted," Edwin says coldly, as he slams the door behind Lord Thorn.

We hold our position for another few minutes before Reina lets go, collapsing with exhaustion. "They're gone," she wheezes. "All clear."

"Well done, cousin!" Cruz says proudly. "And what do you think now, Mullory Prudence? Have we passed the test?"

Mullory eyes Cruz unsteadily and my stomach lurches because I already know her answer. What else can we do but trust Cruz and his creepy cousin?

"You'll keep us shielded until we don't need you anymore?" questions Mullory.

Cruz crosses his fingers and places them on the cavity where his heart *should* be. "Scout's honor."

"And in return I'll owe you a favor."

"One small favor." Cruz gives a slight shrug. "Barely anything at all. Dare I say, you're getting the better end of the bargain."

"And you won't tell me what that favor is?"

Cruz winks. This guy, of course he's a winker. "Where would the fun be in that?"

I want to scream in protest, but I know it's pointless.

Mullory reluctantly concedes. "Deal."

19.

MULLORY

"N*ever agree to nothing if you don't know the stakes.*" Gran may be miles away, but her raspy voice still finds me. A quick glance at Cruz Lagunes, and I can tell he's pleased with the terms of our deal. He's practically glowing. What will the favor be? Will I even be able to grant it?

"Cheer up. All of you." Cruz is all smiles, his one perfect dimple out for display, like that invasion from the council was nothing at all. "I have another present for everyone, it looks like Christmas may come early this year!"

"Ho-ho-ho," says Ellison, utterly unenthused. For once Ellison Stoutmire and I are on the same page, scowls out, daggers shooting from our eyes at the guests we now can't refuse. My stomach clenches with worry. We only narrowly avoided the council, and Lord Thorn made his intentions perfectly clear—he's out for blood. How long can Reina keep them away? Worse yet, what happens when she can't?

But Cruz Lagunes is annoyingly unfazed as he marches around the foyer. "Now," he says with an enthusiastic clap. "It's time to address that jacket."

It takes me a moment to realize what he's talking about, because during all the chaos, I'd forgotten I still had it on.

"What about it?" I pull the flaps tight around my waist. I may be tied to Cruz in some way I haven't yet unraveled, but that doesn't mean I need to share everything. If I've learned anything since being thrown into this world, it's to keep your secrets close.

"Mullory." Cruz clicks his teeth together. "I thought we agreed to help each other." His eyes are dark around the rim with a soft amber core. I hate that they twinkle mischievously.

"We *are* going to help each other," I assure him.

Cruz runs his hand through the top of his wavy hair that's longer than the sides, which are buzzed to the skin above his ears. It's hard to deny the resemblance to Mateo, the angular cut of his jaw and the slope of his nose. But where Mateo was gentle, Cruz is hardened, a tenseness that percolates just below the surface. I'm certain if we cut him open, something monstrous would crawl out.

"I already showed you what I could do," says Cruz. "I'm able to sense magic so that I can use it."

"So that you can steal it," Ellison corrects him.

"Borrow it," Cruz says with an edge. "I gave it back, don't forget. But to think I wouldn't notice the magic radiating off that jacket." Cruz raises a dramatic hand to his chest. "That wounds me."

"You can feel something?" I ask excitedly, forgetting for a moment that I've struck an open-ended bargain with a known murderer.

"Of course. Aren't you all curious as to why nothing has happened yet?"

I steal a glance at Lyric and Ellison, whose vexed expressions signal that once again Cruz Lagunes has us dangling from a thread. Worse yet, he knows it.

"You all are just so lucky that I arrived when I did," he says proudly. "Practically blessed."

I bite my tongue, letting the pain anchor me as I force a smile. "Very."

"That's the spirit, Mullory. Now, the problem with your jacket is the buttons."

"But we sewed the missing one back on."

Cruz steps closer and runs a finger down the length of my coat. "But the line of magic is disrupted. I believe they're in the wrong order."

"What's the correct order, then?" Lyric snaps.

Cruz tenses, clearly agitated. "I'm not sure yet. I can't be expected to know everything."

Before they erupt into an argument, I shimmy off the coat and yank each button until all five are pried loose. I arrange them in a line on the floor. Only then do I realize that the number of holes is different on each one. "I think they need to be ordered numerically, somehow." I count the holes on each. "Two, one, seven, six, three."

Everyone huddles around me.

"An equation perhaps," says Cruz.

"There must be another clue." I tap my chin, contemplating where the button came from. "It was hidden in the yo-yo, but we only used the pictures on the one side."

Lyric finishes my thought. "One black key and one white key remain."

I nod, looping a lock of hair around my finger, before scooping the buttons up and hurrying out of the foyer.

"Where are you going?" Ellison calls as everyone chases after me.

"To the keys, just not the kind you think," I shout while leading us into the parlor.

The ceilings are vaulted, and shimmering snow crusts the elaborate molding. Mustard-colored drapes flank elegant windows, while a fire crackles in a stately fireplace. Several frost-speckled trees are rooted in the floorboards; a baby deer grazes between them. Plush reading chairs face a piano that's swirled with glitter and rhinestones to look like a peppermint candy.

I rush to the piano and spill the buttons onto the ivory and black keys. "These keys."

"Two, one, seven, six, three, did you say?" Cruz settles on the piano bench that's tufted with gumdrops. "In addition to my magic, my charming personality, and my grand master chess status"—he flexes his fingers before draping them atop the keys—"I'm also classically trained on the piano."

He taps five keys in quick succession. "If we assume that the alphabet is the cipher, then the numbers correlate to the following musical notes: F, G, A, B, C. That's the order they appear on the piano, and that's how they should be arranged on the coat."

"Edwin, we need Greta!" I yell.

Dressed in a powder-blue sleeping gown and her hair in rollers, Greta isn't nearly as enthused this time as she shuffles into the parlor.

"Another button emergency?"

"Something like that." I sip the tea Edwin sets out for us.

As soon as Greta touches the jacket, we all begin to shout at the same time, rendering her flustered and unable to hear a thing.

She raises a stern hand. "One at a time."

"Let the renowned, classically trained pianist handle it," Ellison declares.

Cruz arranges the buttons in the proper order along the length of the coat. "That should do it."

And then we wait in agonizing silence, watching Greta pull the needle and thread like it's an Olympic sport.

"Finished," she announces, then lets out a scream of likely curses in German. She drops the coat as flames catch along the collar and set it ablaze in a brilliant flash. I lunge to stamp it out, but there's no need. Just as quickly as the fire catches, it smolders, leaving behind an image seared into the breast pocket.

Burned crisply into the jacket is a charred image of a crow mid-flight. The crow flaps its broad wings, and it makes an unsettling *swish*. Its feathers fall into a tumble of ashes, leaving a gruesome carcass behind.

"Not creepy at all," Ellison remarks.

Cruz is more focused. "I know what that symbol is."

"We all know what that is." Lyric puffs out his chest.

All but me, of course. All my studying, and I'm still the last to know. "I don't."

Cruz smiles. "It means we're going on a field trip tomorrow."

I can't peel my eyes away from the crow's skeleton, a formidable omen. "To where?"

"Not to where, but to whom."

Lyric sighs. "The Skeleton Singer. That's who."

20.

I don't let myself question the items being left behind. Ordinary, everyday bobbles that could easily be mistaken for trash. But that's the point, because I can't exactly leave directions or a message that could be stolen and misinterpreted. That's not how this was planned, the future simply won't allow it.

The rest is up to her.

I roll the brass button between my fingers, inspecting my handiwork for the tenth time, my small amendment. This clue might be the most important, because it gives her a reason to trust me. Better yet, it provides a cause to fight for.

I place the button with the other clues. The first of many.

But can she make it to the end?

21.
MULLORY

We linger in the parlor, the tension from the night's activities keeping us tethered in place. I haven't let go of the coat; I'm still ashamed I didn't think to order the buttons properly. They were clues left by my mom, and I should know her best. *"Details, Mullory. The smallest detail will sometimes make the biggest difference. It's the details that make the clues sing."*

My thumb skims the golden tassels of the coat; the cloth is still singed around the image of the skeletal crow, the burning smell still pungent.

Edwin clears away the tea mugs. "I'm going to retire for the evening, unless you require anything else?"

It takes me a moment to realize the question is being addressed to me. I'm technically in charge of Stoutmire Estate.

"No," I say, unsure, as everyone swivels toward me, waiting for instructions.

"Do you see that?" Reina grabs my wrist.

I glance back down, eyes searching furiously.

Reina slides her pointer finger along the perimeter of the button that was hidden in the yo-yo. "There's a crack along the edge."

I yank the coat closer, inspecting the button, only to realize she's right. It's like two halves joined back together, meticulously so, but there's still a joint. I run my fingers along the others but they're each solid.

Curious, I grab a knife from the plate of gingerbread cake Edwin set out. Guiding the sharp tip along the edge, I apply pressure, carefully wedging it between the pieces. A little more, before a satisfying *crack* as the halves separate.

A small scrap of paper, like a fortune in a cookie floats out. I unfold it to reveal the message.

SHE	**ATTIC**	**ORE**	**ADD**
X	**XX**		**X**

Ellison reads it aloud. "She attic ore add. Is that supposed to make sense?"

"It will." I wave her out of the way, trying to focus. Running through combinations and links between the words. Is there a common theme? An obvious repetition of letters? Is the number of letters in each word important? Or the number of vowels? But the line of *X*'s listed just below the words stands out most.

"The *X*'s," I say at the exact same time Lyric does, and I flash him a smile. "That's the cipher." I tap my chin, studying. "I'm just not sure how."

Cruz jumps on board. "Which makes the word *ORE* unique."

"Exactly." I grab a pencil and a sheet of paper, copying down the message. "I think we're supposed to eliminate letters in each word according to how many *X*'s are positioned below it. One from the first." I start by trying to remove the *H*. "I can combine the *SE* with the *AT* in the next word to form *SEAT*, or..." My mind toggles the puzzle together faster than I can articulate. "Or I can remove the *S* and form *HEAT*." I know instantly this is correct. A few more quick slashes.

SHE ATTIC ORE ADD

"Heat to read," says Cruz while glancing over my shoulder.

I fly from my seat, clutching the scrap and rush to the fireplace, gently wafting the paper above the flame, careful not to burn it.

Slowly, a message bleeds through.

Henry Prudence's murderer
is closer than you think.

Shock roots me in place and my mind comes up blank.

"Henry Prudence," says Ellison, slowly piecing it together.

"That must be . . ." Reina starts.

Lyric's hand finds mine, letting me know he's here.

I swallow, finally finding my voice. "My father."

I never met him, never knew anything about him. I only know he died when I was little. But murder feels like the cruelest type of death, because it was orchestrated not by chance or illness, but by someone else. My father was ripped away before I ever had the chance to know him.

As the shock ebbs away, questions start piling up. Why would my mom wait until now to tell me? Something about the message bothers me on a deeper level, but I can't get past the bigger mystery. Who killed him?

"A new murderer," Ellison says coolly, eyes darting at Cruz. "Or an old one?"

I shake my head. "He died when I was young."

Ellison doesn't back away from Cruz. "Or maybe that's what you were told. Obviously, you weren't given all the facts."

"I . . ."

"Does that mean the person is here?" asks Reina.

"Or did they just leave with the council?" counters Cruz.

“It means it’s time for bed.” Lyric wraps an arm around my shoulder and tugs me from the parlor.

I’m glad for the escape, because the secrets left behind by my mom keep growing darker. The darkest one of all reverberates through my mind.

Who murdered my father?

22.
LYRIC

I died.

Horrifically and tragically by the edge of a knife meant to kill Mullory Prudence.

Then she brought me back to life, and somehow, I've managed to end up right back in my childhood bedroom. Not a book is out of place, my green bedspread is tucked tightly along the corners, and a set of flannel pajamas have been laid neatly on top. Maybe the house always knew I'd come back, so it kept my room just so. I can't imagine Uncle keeping it for sentimental reasons; I'd thought for sure he'd turn it into something ridiculous. A room flipped upside down or stuffed full of exotic plants with flesh-eating petals.

But unlike my room, I'm not the same.

I'm worse. Because now Lord Thorn's magic has no choice but to surge back like a tidal wave, no easement or transition. That alone should've killed me, but if there's one thing I'm not good at, it's staying dead.

And where do I even go from here? Mullory seems to think her mom will have answers, that the shadow is blocked. And then what? I die again and we try to do it right this time? Try to sever the connection between my father and me. Can we even trust her mom? She just revealed that Mullory's father was murdered by someone close by. A secret bloody past that I'm certain will unfurl at some point.

I slump on the bed, a place riddled with nightmares and sweat-soaked sheets. When I was little, I'd lie still and quiet, counting to one hundred, waiting and hoping for my uncle to come.

"Sir, I think he'd like it if you'd read to him," Edwin implored my uncle. "Perhaps one of the classics."

"Nonsense, he can read to himself. No one ever read to me," my uncle huffed. "A childish fantasy I won't indulge in."

It was always Edwin who would come to tuck me in, never my uncle. Most of me would sigh with relief, because I lived in fear of my uncle. But my fear was a complex thing, something I still sought out.

I stretch my arms and legs, faintly aware of the buzz beneath my skin. Lord Thorn's magic has begun to settle, spreading its barbed tendrils like a poison, rooting itself deeper and deeper. And the worst part—the part I won't dare admit to anyone but myself in the cover of night—is the feeling of relief. A steadiness that accompanies the return of something that was missing. A homecoming.

Sleep is nearly impossible; I can't unsee the misty figure that warned me in the clutches of death. Who were they? And how did they know of the shadow? What else do they know? These thoughts have me catapulting out of bed and dashing down the hall. I nudge open the door to Mullory's room and rush inside to find her sitting up in bed, hunched over a pile of papers, a furrowed expression on her face.

"Hi," I manage to say.

"Lyric." She gives me a nervous smile, and a stream of pink bubbles erupt around her, which she quickly tries to waft away.

"You made bubbles."

Mullory groans, popping one with her finger. "Strawberry-scented, apparently."

I know Mullory has been struggling with Uncle X's magic, and I quickly try to divert her attention. "What are you looking at?"

She nudges over a piece of black parchment. "A letter from your cousin Cecilia. I think the second clue is supposed to help me uncover who murdered my father. That's why she mentions death. What do you think the last line means? 'Don't judge a book by its cover. You'll know when it's time.'"

I opt for the most obvious answer. "It must mean the answer is hidden in one of these books."

Mullory chews her lip. "I thought so, but it seems vague." Her fingers skim the spines of books splayed out on her bed. "There are thousands of pages."

"That's Cecilia for you. Let's not forget she did try to kill you."

"I know."

"Multiple times," I add.

Mullory nudges me and more bubbles erupt around us as I scoot beside her. "Yes, I know. But I think there's something else we're missing...." Her eyes skim the letter. "She says, 'I'll give you a hint. The first will help you now, and the second will prove to be important too death.'"

"It reads funny and I feel like there's something buried in her words. The word *too* is incorrect," I say. "It should be *to*."

"What if that's on purpose so we notice it, and she actually means the number two? What if..." Mullory trails back over the last line. "*First. Second. Too.* What if they're meant to signify a page number?"

I lean across her and yank the first book from the stack, *The Genetics of Magical Transfer*, and flip to page 122. We both skim a dense passage on Y chromosomal–linked magical diseases. "'Although recessive in females and often hidden, any transference from the father to the son is always dominant and on display.'"

"From father to son?" Mullory furrows her brow. "But that doesn't make sense, given that I'm his daughter." Mullory stifles a yawn before slamming the book closed and addressing what's really on her mind. "Why would my mom wait until now to tell me that my father was murdered?"

"No clue," I finally say, keeping a darker thought to myself. Is it because Mullory herself is now in danger?

That thought ignites a fury inside of me, and I edge closer, drawing an arm tightly around her before I overthink it. Mullory sinks into her pillows. A shiver runs down my body, and I turn to find the source of the cold. Her window is drawn wide open, winter spilling in.

"Aren't you cold?" I ask, teeth chattering.

But Mullory is already sleeping. A lone bubble clings to her cheek, and I gently flick it away, letting my hand linger near her neck. The shadow radiates a pulse; like a living being, it calls to the darkness in my magic.

I should leave and go back to my room, let her sleep, but I have a far worse idea. Impulsively, I hook my fingers around the stone, squeezing until I'm oriented back in the place between the living and the dead. For some reason, it orients me on the side closer to death where I lingered for months. Mullory had a harder time accessing it, and I can't help but wonder if it's because I've been here before. As though I've left an impression, a piece of myself behind.

It takes only a minute for the figure made of mist to appear in my periphery. It hovers nearby, beads of dew twisting so that it appears to dip its head to the side.

"How did you know about the shadow?"

The mist flickers.

"Tell me."

But the mist has other ideas. A slick voice slips out. "He's watching you."

23.

ELLISON

The key to avoiding sleep is to drink an ungodly amount of coffee and then place yourself in an uncomfortable position. The downside is, of course, the jitters and the unfortunate experience of waking up slouched beside a bookcase with a kink in your neck and your tongue plastered to the roof of your mouth. But you can't win them all.

I eye the fluffy duvet and mountain of pillows stacked on my bed with complete disdain. I avoided it last night, too afraid that I might sink into the downy plushness and relax enough for my mother's magic to take hold. Instead, I huddled against this rigid bookcase, slipping farther and farther as the night wore on; the spines of the books edging into my shoulder blades roused me every so often. In and out of sleep, evading the depth needed for my mother's dream magic to truly unfurl.

Ignoring her magic only seems to anger it, causing it to stir inside of me, thrashing like a wild storm contained in a delicate glass globe. The magic isn't used to these boundaries and confinement; my mother let it loose like a rabid dog, steeping her teas and brewing our nightmares. I get the horrible feeling that it prefers the nightmares.

Between fighting my mother's magic and my insomnia, not even splashes of ice water seem to help with the puffiness circling my eyes. I've looked better for sure, but why am I even concerned with looks here? Another day on the estate, following the team of idiots on a ridiculous chase that has a high probability of ending with someone's death. As long as it isn't Lyric's or mine, I don't really care. It's unsettling to think that someone nearby murdered Mullory's father, but that's Stoutmire Estate for you.

I choose an outfit I had left behind in my armoire, opting for my warmest coat and a pair of snow boots that still have the tag. I make my way downstairs, meandering and taking the circuitous route to delay the inevitable. Bitter air whishes across my face and I trace the gust to an open window. Mullory Prudence is curled up on the window seat.

I stumble in a failed effort to quietly avoid what I'm certain will be an awkward encounter. And I'm almost successful, but Mullory catches me.

"I know you won't ever forgive me, Ellison. . . ."

Never.

"But I hope you can understand that we're trying to save the same person."

That awful, dreaded word again, the perpetual thorn in my side . . . *hope.*

I square my shoulders and face her head-on. "You have a funny way of showing it. Might sound crazy, but my idea of saving someone doesn't usually end up with them dead."

My jab hits Mullory square in the face, and she slumps against the window frame. "You're right." She gulps. "It should've been me."

She seems remorseful, borderline ruined, but does she truly understand? Can she fully grasp the depth of horrors Lyric has endured? I think not. I need to push, to make her understand.

"He trusted you."

She sinks even deeper, but to her credit she maintains eye contact. "I know."

"But you don't know!" My voice is a coil of barbed wire, and I lace into her. "He doesn't trust anyone." *Not even me.*

Mullory's face softens as she extends an arm, fingers reaching toward me before she pulls them back. "He does more than trust you, Ellison. He loves you."

My chest tightens and my knees quake—my body's response to the idea of something that should otherwise be effortless. But love was always one of those words that tripped me up. Something I liked to think I felt but could never really verbalize.

Mullory drums her fingertips across the sill, casting her glance outside, giving me a private moment to recover. "I won't let him down again."

I want to believe her, and she sounds so sure, so completely committed to the cause.

"Neither will I," I finally say in a tight whisper. A partial admission on my part that maybe it wasn't entirely her fault. I try and fail to smooth my sweater, yanking it close to combat the wind spiraling in from the window. "Lyric's important," I add, feeling like a dutiful older sister. *He's important to me.*

Mullory extends her arm outside, and soft flakes land in her palm. "Lyric's one of the few people I have left." She closes her hand and places it near her heart. "He's everything."

I nod to the girl who came in fighting to find her mom and who now fights for my brother. He deserves that and more. He deserves an army because no one ever fought for him before. I'm about to leave when Mullory calls to me.

"Ellison?"

"Yeah."

Mullory slowly, repeatedly, curls her fingers into her palm, grasping at air. "What does your magic feel like?"

I scoff at her, completely taken back. *It feels like a punishment, like the cruelest form of torture. A life sentence, to carry around the magic that has only ever caused my family harm.* But I won't share any of that. "It feels exactly like it should."

Mullory eyes her empty palm, perplexed. "How do you know how to use it?"

Another idiotic question. "You just do. It wants to be used."

"But what if it doesn't?" Mullory's gray eyes flicker with concern.

I cut to the truth. "Well then, something's wrong." With that I leave Mullory Prudence staring pensively out the window and march toward the kitchen. An elaborate breakfast buffet is laid out, courtesy of Edwin. Platters of flaky pastries, silver trays of scrambled eggs and turkey sausage, a basket of chocolate croissants, and slices of fresh fruit—orange wheels and grapefruit wedges feathered together like roses.

I don't even have to ask; Edwin has already poured me a large cup of steaming coffee. Black and strong enough to restore my jitters. Everyone nibbles away in silence until Cruz Lagunes waltzes in, his dark hair wet from a shower and dripping down his cashmere turtleneck.

"Beautiful morning," he proclaims. "I've already run ten miles."

I snort into my coffee cup. As if I didn't trust him before—after he murdered two of his brothers in cold blood to claim his father's magic—now I really don't trust him. A ten-mile run. And a turtleneck. Evil incarnate.

No one pays him any attention; I can sense that everyone's minds are elsewhere. And it's understandable because we know our destination today will be most unpleasant. Even Mullory, who doesn't have a clue who the Skeleton Singer is, can pick up on our somber moods.

Edwin clears his throat to get our attention. "I've prepared a car, I just need the address. . . ." He pauses, his eyes dart unsteadily between Mullory and Lyric.

I stifle a laugh and settle for a smile. How awkward. Because who's really in charge? The boy groomed to run this estate or the girl who fell into fortune? Technically, it's Mullory, but I get Edwin's sense of loyalty. He raised Lyric, after all. Mullory hasn't a clue where or who the Skeleton Singer is, so Lyric takes the lead.

Reina sips a latte beside me, clad in a ridiculous teal jumpsuit. I don't hate her purple hair, but I don't like it either. It reminds me of a bruised night sky.

Cruz eyes me over his platter of eggs, and I return the glare. I won't back down and I won't forget—he's just one of the murderers lurking on the estate.

24.

XAVIER STOUTMIRE

Desperation has me phoning my cousin Cecilia, which feels simultaneously like cheating and admitting defeat. I'd wanted to find it on my own.

It rings three times before she answers. "Your call is six minutes later than I'd expected."

"Where is it, Cecilia?" I have no time for her games.

"So snappy. Not so fun when you don't get what you want, now is it? Try watching yourself find what you're looking for, only to realize that it's a thread in the future already gone loose."

"You could end my little escapade if you just tell me where it is." I massage my temple, trying to clear my head. "Why was it even moved? After the party I'd been certain of where it was. Why can't I hold on to this wretched thing?"

Cecilia lets out a bored little gasp. "You know it was destined to find the other. A perfect pair."

My frustration builds. "But I already checked there. And nothing!"

"That's because it's not there, Xavier."

I resist the urge to fling my phone. "I don't have much time, I'm certain *she* wants to use it."

"She does. My best advice without meddling and muddying things up is to kill, dear. Or is it dear, kill? I think that's right. This cheese I'm nibbling on may be expired or maybe it's my brain that's gone bad. Perhaps we're not even talking at all, and this is another loose thread in the future, soon to be snipped."

I ignore Cecilia's pleas at insanity; she's been theatrical since we were children. "Have a good morning, Cecilia."

"Or a good night, depends what way you look at it. Don't forget what I said, Xavier, dear, kill."

25. MULLORY

Reaching for a scone, I knock my coffee mug off the table, shattering it into pieces across the kitchen floor. I can't keep still or quell my trembling hands.

Henry Prudence's murderer is closer than you think.

The last time I was at Stoutmire Estate, I was meant to die. And now this time offers a peek at my parents' history, one tainted with murder.

Add that to the worry of finding my mom, Lord Thorn and the entire council hot on our trail, not to mention the confirmed murderer whom I struck a bargain with and who's currently smiling at me across the island.

But unbelievably so, something else is still bothering me. A low-grade unease that settled inside me the moment we arrived on the estate, like a fire alarm going off several houses down the road. A worry buried in the depths of my subconscious, subtly reminding me that there's something else not quite right.

Edwin senses it too, and he steals worried glances when he thinks I'm not looking. And now, after cleaning up my mess, he pulls me to the side while the others shuffle outside to the car.

"Miss Mullory, a word?" The corners of his green eyes crinkle with concern.

"What is it, Edwin?"

"Nothing too serious, miss. Just one of a few minor occurrences."

Minor occurrences sounds like a fancier way to say *problems*. "Like . . . ?"

Edwin gestures a hand at the cabinet of fine china, before opening the door and pulling out a dainty teacup. It's creamy white with delicate golden swirls patterned like lace.

"I don't understand," I say, feeling silly.

Edwin tips the cup toward me, so I can peer inside.

"There's a hole."

Edwin nods. "That's precisely the problem. Most of the china in our collections has been acting hysterical—sprouting holes, cracking into pieces, some have even begun to weep tears of honey."

I ruminate on the words, trying not to let out my initial reaction, which is to laugh at the absurdity of the problem. With everything else going on, this seems foolish. "Can they be fixed?"

"Xavier kept them in order. Everything here is glamoured and enchanted in some way or another. Xavier's magic is, of course, restricted to illusions, but throughout the years he's brought in experts in other fields. There is magic woven into every brick and beam of this estate. Some are purely for recreation, others for protection. And, well, to be frank these magics recognize Xavier as their guardian."

And then it hits me, what Edwin is *really* trying to say—I'm supposed to oversee this estate, which means I'm supposed to keep the magic in check. The problem is, I feel no connection to Xavier's magic. I may have it, but how do I use it?

"I'll look into it?" I answer as more of a question because I don't have the slightest idea of how to fix it. Do I just politely ask the china to be more manageable? Why is it even weeping in the first place? The far bigger problem is finding my mom before the council finds us.

Our next clue has us hurtling down a pebbled road flanked by thick woods that have slowly begun to strangle the path. Snow-laden branches rattle against the side of the car, scraping the windows.

"Who exactly is this Skeleton Singer?" I finally dare to ask, as the car chugs along.

Ellison shifts uncomfortably and fixes her stare out the window. "You'll see soon enough."

"Tell me, please."

Cruz willingly takes the challenge, crossing one leg and settling back. "To understand the Skeleton Singer, first you need to understand the labyrinth."

Worry sinks like a stone to the pit of my stomach.

"Council headquarters is hidden in plain sight, tucked inside the Metropolitan Museum of Art in New York City. And beneath that there's a sort of..." Cruz gives a thoughtful pause. "A sort of prison."

"Worse than a prison," Lyric interjects.

For once Cruz agrees. "Yes, you could say that. Anyway, the first thing you should know about the labyrinth is that it's constructed to mimic a maze, one without any cells to keep you in or to keep others out. Endless tunnels filled with horrors and monstrous beings that feed on fear and nightmares."

I suppress a shudder. "Why have this maze? For what?"

"There needs to be a place to put it."

"Put what?"

"All of the magic that's gone wrong, that's gone dark. And more importantly, a place to put the people who wield it."

I can't help but notice how Reina has gone totally still, her body stiff. She runs her hands quickly across her cheeks and stuffs her ear pods in, turning herself into the nook of the seat.

"Is she okay?" I whisper.

Cruz looks at her thoughtfully, his admission a whisper: "Someone she loves is there."

Something inside of me softens when I glance at Reina again, a bit of camaraderie in having someone we love impossibly out of reach.

"The second thing you should know about the labyrinth is that no one ever escapes it."

"Not ever?"

Cruz gives me a diabolical grin. "Not ever."

"And this has to do with the Skeleton Singer how?"

"Patience, Mullory," Cruz cautions. "I'm just getting to that part. The Skeleton Singer used to be a resident in the labyrinth and—"

"But I thought you said no one ever escaped."

"That's exactly what I said," Cruz agrees. "He didn't escape, he was let go. The only case ever."

"What was left of him," Lyric mumbles. "You don't just get let out."

I fumble with the tag of my parka.

"He went in and came out completely different. The labyrinth took his brain and scrambled it up until he hadn't the foggiest idea who he was. He only speaks in riddles, but he's essentially harmless," Cruz explains.

"'*Essentially.*'" I gulp.

For the next few hours, we ride through what feels like an endless loop of foreboding forest, thick evergreens nestled on a mountainside plush with snow. Deeper and deeper into the woods, following a dirt road that jostles us side to side. The sky is a threatening wash of gray.

When the car finally comes to a halt, the driver lets us out at the base of a mountain. A heap of craggily rock capped in snow. The quiet is deafening. Tipping my head up and staring at the peak of the mountain, I can't help but wonder—

Where exactly have you sent me, Mom?

26.
ELLISON

The top of a mountain.

The freaking top.

Not the inside of a ski chalet, or a cozy cave nestled on a tropical island.

"Don't look so sad." Cruz waves us over to a set of slick steps that have been jaggedly carved into the rock. He taps the pouch slung over his shoulder. "I brought snacks."

Even craning my neck, I still can't spot the top of the stairs that wind upward in a death-defying spiral. Trudging over from the car, the snow is so deep I have to forcefully drag my legs, and after only a few minutes my lungs ache, restricting my breath to short rasps.

"There's a sign." Mullory swipes a mitten across a metal placard, filling her glove with snow.

Do you like riddles? Puzzles that slink beneath your scalp, burrow into your skull, and eat at your brain? One delicate, sensuous, rotting thought at a time.

"Cheery," I say.

"No time like the present." Cruz extends an arm to help Mullory, but Lyric throws a stiff elbow into his ribs and gets to her first.

Really? "This girl," I mumble. "I'll never understand the allure."

Usually, my comments are purely for my own entertainment, so I'm startled when Reina responds. "I don't get it either."

I ignore her, stepping behind Lyric to begin this treacherous climb. One miserable step after another. My calves burn as I try my best not to slip off the edge and plummet to my death.

We climb.

And we climb.

Did I mention the snow? Falling into the hood of my jacket and sliding down my neck. Collecting on the steps that are already glistening with ice. I'm in pure survival mode, numb from the cold and the lack of sleep.

I hate that I can't stop thinking of my mother, because I already thought I had her figured out, written off as a heartless monster. But a mysterious woman visited my mother and instructed her to surgically excise pieces of our dreams to watch over us. And my mother did just that.

But who was this woman?

Who could rival my mother's dream magic enough to invade her mental fortress and save Lyric all those years ago?

"This is it," Lyric announces a few steps ahead.

I drag my leaden legs up and across an alcove. A large wooden door is seamlessly fit into the stone. In the center the decaying remains of a crow are pinned down with a rusty nail. Its needle-point beak is a husk, and grisly bits of spoiled flesh cling like cheesecloth to the bones. Bile rises in my throat; the air is ripe with notes of rancid meat and rotting fruit.

Cruz—and his severe overconfidence—raps the knocker. "Hello. Anyone home?"

Slowly, the bones of the crow crunch as it turns its rotting head. There are no eyes, just sockets full of fat, feasting maggots, but I get the creeping sense that it's *looking* straight at us. Through us.

The door creaks inward. Naturally, the door with the morbid skeleton knocker on an abandoned mountain would creak. How predictable.

Against my better judgment, we duck inside and follow a narrow tunnel carved through the mountainside. The gloom is as heavy as a thick mist, and our boots slap against the stone as we burrow farther in a single file, sheep to the slaughter. Faint light spills across a stony wall, nudging us to take a sharp right. We're funneled into a cavernous room, the ceilings vaulted to dizzying heights. Rusted metal beams arc across the top; fitted between them are panes of beaded glass, fogged and streaked with a grimy film.

Something swoops past Mullory's head and she ducks mid-shriek. Another crow, or rather the remains of a crow, caws past us. It's a skeletal abomination, the bones mashed together at odd joints so that the wings are uneven and its flight choppy. No eyes in this one either, but it tips its head from side to side, a disturbingly watchful gesture.

With a quick sulfur pinch of kerosene, flames catch on a row of lanterns hanging from the rafters, flooding the space with warm light. There's a *snap, snap, snap*, the creaking of sleeping joints being cracked into place. Bone grinding against bone. Tucked in every corner and perched on the beams are thousands of these skeletal crows. Roused by our presence, their misshapen skulls swivel at odd angles, joints backward and lopsided.

None of us say a thing. Not even the grand master, the classically trained pianist himself, makes a peep.

Eyes adjusting to the light, I notice piles of metal, several feet tall and stacked in every corner. Mullory picks off a piece, revealing an old, rusted key. One of the crows nips angrily at her ankles and she tosses it back. There must be thousands of these antique keys, protected by their dead guardians.

"Why so many keys?" asks Lyric.

Mullory approaches the back wall, a slab of stone that easily reaches thirty feet, speckled with holes, like Swiss cheese. She runs her hand from hole to hole. "Because one of them fits, one of them leads to a door."

"Well, we can't try them all." I state the obvious.

"We don't need to." Mullory points to a message painted on the stone. "We just need to solve that."

Keys that bite, keys that lock.
Keys that shut, keys that flock.
More than one, a murder you get.
Find the right key, or take a bet.
What makes a key, is it metal or bone?
Will you call in the dead to bring it home?

27.

MULLORY

The riddle is clumsily written, letters oozing down the stone wall. The half-dead birds caw, harassing me as I read it again. Somehow this needs to reveal the one key in a pile of thousands that will lead us to the Skeleton Singer. It feels like a test, to see if we're worthy.

Ellison huffs. "Why is it always murder and death?"

"It's not . . ." I stop mid-answer, fixating on the word *murder.* But not for the obvious reasons, but rather because of the giant book entitled *Birds* gifted to me by Cecilia. "Page two hundred and six. A flock of crows is called a murder."

"So that means—" Cruz tries to finish my train of thought.

But I beat him to it. "That means we're not looking for a key, I think we're actually looking for a bird."

"Good thing there's only a few thousand as well," snaps Ellison.

Lyric elbows past her. "There's more to the riddle. But what do you think 'call in the dead' means?"

I twirl a loose curl around my finger, thinking, as one of the crows hobbles near me. Its jagged skeletal toes clack against the floor as it pushes something with its splintering beak. I bend down to retrieve a rusted can. Wiping away the muck, I reveal a faded label describing what was once preserved peaches.

The crow flaps a battered wing, scurrying away just as another takes its place dropping a different item by my feet. I scoop this one up, a small plastic key chain in the shape of California.

"That's it?" Reina asks. "An old can and a key chain?"

I stare at the two seemingly unrelated items. "Somehow these should tell us how to call in the dead so we can find the right bird."

"Are we sure that's something we want to do?" asks Ellison.

I ignore her, working through the riddle. "Maybe we need to open the can? Somehow use the key chain to do it." I inspect the edge of the key chain—it's made of smooth blue plastic. "Or maybe there's something hidden on the clues themselves." I inspect the front of the key chain, but there's nothing written or readily apparent, just a small star positioned halfway near the southern tip.

"LA," Lyric notes. "The star marks Los Angeles, but how does that tie in with a rusted tin can of fruit?"

"Maybe there's something on the can itself?" Cruz postulates.

I roll it across my palm, eyeing the ancient label, *Freshly Picked, Preserved Peaches!* I inspect the bottom—there's a series of numbers, likely some sort of date. "Maybe these? But how does this call in the dead?"

Lyric runs a hand through his tousled hair. "It can't be the actual dead we're calling to, which means that's a clue itself. But to call in a dead what?"

Words pop into my head. *Dead body*, *dead end*, *deadline*, and then it hits me. "Dead language. We need to call to the bird in a dead language." I raise up the key chain. "LA." I hold the can up in the other hand. "TIN."

Lyric flashes me a rare smile. "Latin."

Before I can answer, Cruz interjects. "Allow me. Avis voco, qui ianuam aperiat," he says boldly. "For those who didn't study Latin, I called for the bird that opens the door."

The bristling of feathers, the pop of bones, and a crow swoops from the rafters and lands near Cruz's boots. There's a disturbing gurgle noise as the bird coughs up a bone shaped like a key. The bird then hurries to the back wall, pecking its beak at a keyhole near the bottom.

I lift the phlegmy key and follow the crow to the wall. It's a perfect fit. As I turn it, several stones grind together, and a door appears that wasn't visible before.

A gentle push.

Here goes nothing.

28.
LYRIC

The door opens to yet another dark tunnel that's coarse with crumbly stone and narrow enough that we have to squeeze in one at a time. The walls continue to constrict the farther we go, pressing against my shoulder blades as though they might bury us alive. At one point, we're forced to drop to our knees and crawl.

A procession of crows follows behind us, pecking at our calves as we go. The skeletal creatures are crafted with magic that feels unsettled and reckless. My own magic recognizes it, unfurling with excitement. *Something dark*, it hisses. *Something boundless.*

"I can't go any farther," Mullory cries from the front.

"Guests?" a lone voice croaks from the other side.

"Yes," Mullory pipes. "We're guests."

"Solved my riddle. But did you bring a gift?"

"We think we did," Mullory answers shakily.

There's a splintering sound that vibrates through the stone, some internal mechanism that allows the wall to swing outward.

We crawl through quickly and funnel into a dimly lit room. At first all that's visible is a cat perched in the corner like a doorstop. Not a fat cat, but one built from bones. It arches its skeletal spine and hisses. Needlelike teeth stacked in horrifying rows, set in half of a jawbone.

A ratty chair with two broken legs is set before a lopsided fireplace. A long, cluttered table is pushed against the wall. Dozens more of the skeletal cats watch us, swooshing the spines of furless tails. Some have two heads, others multiple legs, as if the creator couldn't quite remember what a cat should look like.

"Gift?" the Skeleton Singer grunts.

Greasy, graying hair falls to his shoulders, and he's wearing a tattered coat—moldy filth makes the color almost indiscernible. But the lone tassel hanging limp from the side is enough for me to realize it's exactly like the coat Mullory's mother left.

"Gift?" he growls again.

"The gift," I mumble out of the side of my mouth, nudging Mullory.

"Right." She snaps into focus and eases off her backpack, pulling out the red coat.

"A gift." She offers it over with a smile. Only she could muster a smile right now.

The Skeleton Singer's upper lip curls into something that tries to mimic Mullory's expression, but he snatches the coat and abruptly tosses it. "Not a gift."

Mullory looks to me, but I'm just as confused. It's exactly like the coat he's wearing, only way less shitty.

"Oh, for hell's sake." Ellison pushes forward. "Open your backpack and take out the raggedy box. Maybe he wants to trade snacks."

Mullory yanks out the box. "Maybe a different gift?"

The Skeleton Singer leans over and his eyes light up as he yanks the comb from the bottom.

"Excellent choice." Cruz's ass-kissing goes nowhere.

The Skeleton Singer twirls the comb, appraising his prize, before sinking his yellowed teeth between the delicate prongs and snapping them off one by one. He tosses the shell of the comb and holds the teeth in his hand.

"Bones," he says excitedly.

29.

MULLORY

The Skeleton Singer is thrilled with the bits of bone he chewed from the comb. Whoever left it to my gran all those years ago must have known he'd like it. A shudder skips down my spine despite the heat swelling from the fire. Bones from what? From whom?

More importantly, why are we here? What did my mom want me to see? *I want you to understand why. When you do, you'll be ready.*

I brave a question. "Did you know Esther Merrybright?"

"Esther Merrybright?" The Skeleton Singer draws out all his rotten teeth on display, scratching the back of his neck. A long pause, before he says "Esther" again, while crinkling his brows together with recognition.

"You know her?" asks Lyric.

The Skeleton Singer beckons us toward a shadowy door covered in locks. "Come."

My heart pounds behind my ribs as I eye the line of padlocks. *Is my mom in there?*

"Want to see?"

"Yes," I whisper.

The Skeleton Singer grabs the tail of a passing cat and the bony bit snaps right off. He uses this to open lock after lock, yanking the chains free and tossing the used tail to the floor, before nudging the door with his boot.

I slip through the open door. "Mom?"

Ellison gasps. "Oh my God."

"Holy shit."

Nausea rises up my throat, and my knees rattle together. I don't even try to stop the tears.

Cruz is the only one brave enough to ask the obvious question. "Who was that?"

A corpse, mostly skeletal but with sparse flesh still clinging, is propped up in a rocking chair. Its jaw hangs to the left, as if whatever remnant of a ligament holding it might snap free at any moment.

The slightest creak as the chair tips forward and back.

"Did you see . . ." Lyric starts to say.

I grip his arm, because I saw it. The femur stuffed in a boot that kicked the ground. The corpse moved.

The Skeleton Singer rushes over, grabbing a comb from a side table and raking it through the few hairs lying wilted on the corpse's head. A clump of scalp falls to the ground, but he picks it up before squishing it back on the skull.

"I fixed him," the Skeleton Singer says proudly. He lifts a cup to the corpse's leathery lips, and the water dribbles down the exposed collarbone. But the Skeleton Singer is pleased. "See, fixed."

A bit of relief rolls over me because it's not my mom, but it's temporary as I get the unsettling sense that *this* is why we're here. "What happened to him?"

"We killed him."

Reina flinches, but I press on, needing to know. "'We?'"

The Skeleton Singer nods, undisturbed. "Yes. Me and Esther Merrybright."

My vision blurs and darkens as my body sways. Lyric scoops a steadying arm beneath my back. I cling to him for purchase, letting him guide me out of the room containing the half-dead body.

"Let's just finish this," Cruz says quietly to the group of us before addressing the Skeleton Singer. "Don't forget about the lovely bones we've brought you."

The Skeleton Singer eyes the dainty bones and like a fish to a shiny bauble he immediately relaxes in the distraction. He raises his hand. The two middle fingers are missing—crude, bare bones are shoved into the sockets, the skin around them blackened. A long talon-like nail protrudes from the longer bone and the Skeleton Singer pierces it into his forearm.

At first nothing happens, not until the Skeleton Singer twists the nail deeper and begins to hum. A haunting melody that slithers between us like an eerie fog.

The humming escalates, turns into a string of words that makes no sense, but the bones laid on the table begin to rise. Turning slowly, before assembling together. They morph into a skeletal mouse that falls to the floor with a thud. A frenzy of cats pounce at once.

Satisfied, the Skeleton Singer turns to us. "Follow," he orders, and beckons us through a different door that leads directly into an expansive atrium. He lifts and discards a few rusted cages, before he finally settles on one that's tarnished and curves upward in elegant scrolls.

"This." He offers it to me, and I get the sense he will not be elaborating. That the filthy cage is just another clue that needs to be cracked.

"I think we're done here." Lyric gives me a gentle tug.

The Skeleton Singer catches my wrist as I turn to go, twisting his nails into my sleeve.

"One last riddle." His breath is hot and rancid. A bulbous tongue sweeps his blackened teeth. "Esther loved riddles."

Mention of my mom spikes my pulse. *My mom killed someone.*

"Most think it's full, few know it's empty. If up is down, then your hands are twelve in time above," he says before releasing me. "Figure it out by the time the new year ages." The Skeleton Singer cocks his head to the side as several crows let out urgent cries.

"More guests?" he whispers, intrigued. "Or enemies?"

"We better go," Reina implores as the crows squawk, chasing us out of the mountain lair before we have the chance to find out who else is here.

30.
ELLISON

All that fuss, not to mention the puddle of snow ruining my boots. The deadly climb up a mountain, and then a run-in with a deranged skeleton puppeteer who probably wanted to eat us and lick our bones clean so he could hobble together our remains into delightful companions. All that for a cage full of bird crap and a drunken nursery rhyme.

Well done, team!

Add that to the fact that Lord Thorn was probably the enemy the Skeleton Singer was referring to, and we only narrowly avoided him.

"All set, miss?" the driver asks Mullory as we barrel into the car.

"Yes," she barely murmurs while gripping the birdcage tightly. She's been as pale as a ghost since learning her mother is a murderer. Yes, well, welcome to the club.

When we finally arrive back, it's pitch-black, the darkness cut only by the twinkling lights strung up and around the estate. Edwin is waiting in the foyer and quickly ushers us inside, gathering our damp coats and boots. There's warm lobster bisque soup and steaming homemade rolls set on the dining table, followed by miniature chicken potpies layered with flaky crust. After Edwin watches the staff clear the remains of our berry cobbler, he offers up a suggestion.

"Perhaps you'd all care to wash up." He eyes the nasty birdcage positioned by Mullory's feet. She won't dare let it out of her sight, stench or not.

That's a polite way of putting it, considering we stink of the death lair. The staff has been trying not to gag throughout dinner.

I'm all too happy to oblige, trudging up the stairs to my suite. I peel off my clothes and toss them right into the fireplace—they simply can't be saved.

I crank the shower as hot as it will go and shut the bathroom door, turning the room into a sauna. It's here, in the solitude, that I finally allow the tears to fall. Slowly at first, until I'm trembling and forced to my knees.

I thought I was past my nightmare of being buried alive. But crawling through that tunnel only focused my hatred for my mother's magic. I rake my nails across my thighs, angry lines coursing reddened flesh. Is that what I'm destined to do? Hurt those closest to me with dream magic?

"Dreams exist in a place that doesn't exist," my mother told me when I was little.

"I don't understand," I whined.

My mother flinched with annoyance. "When the mind dreams it's as if it grabs on to a balloon and floats away temporarily. Into a space only we can access." There was a haughty quality to her voice, the implication that we were a part of some exclusive club.

"But where is it?"

"I already told you. In a place that doesn't exist."

I paused, still unsatisfied. "But where?"

"Ellison! It's a place, call it whatever you like." Frustration rolled off her. I couldn't then grasp what I know now—my mother didn't have a clue where exactly the minds of the dreamers go.

"All you have to know is that we *can go." Her eyes narrowed greedily. "Build or destroy whatever we like there. Sift through others' dreams like putty between our fingers. Bend the minds of whomever we choose."*

I scratched my chin. "Is it hard?"

She squared her shoulders. "Not for me. One day it will be your burden to bear. Your back needs to be strong enough to handle it."

"Can I build myself a castle, one no one else can get in?" It sounded like a terribly exciting idea. Could I block out my mother's nightmares?

She shot me a twisted grin. "You can keep most out. But not me, you can't keep me out, Ellison. No one keeps me out. And no one gets in unless I say."

And then the water goes cold. Not just cold, but arctic-level frigid, snapping me fiercely to the present.

Every bead of moisture clinging to the shower freezes, and ice spreads like a spiderweb of veins, cracking the glass. The water raining down hardens into razor-sharp icicles. Frost thickens on my skin, burning.

Somehow, I manage to grab a towel and slip across the icy floor, running straight through my room and into the hall.

I'm screaming when Lyric finds me.

"Ellison," he says, rounding the corner and halting his run. "Are you okay?"

Tears trace the frozen tracks on my cheeks because the question is so much bigger than just a cold shower. Lyric takes a few timid steps closer. And there's so much I want to say, so much that *needs* to be said. I want to tell him how broken his death left me, how empty I was for the past few months. How I can't possibly fathom losing him again, even though I don't deserve him. But I'm so exhausted, burdened with my own cumbersome magic that I'm fighting to control. And all I can manage to do is shiver and cry.

"The water froze," I finally say. I push everything else deep down where all the trauma of our family is buried. Because even though we might fight for each other, we can never admit why.

Lyric holds my gaze for a moment, studying the icy clumps woven in my hair.

"The magic here," he says unsteadily before looking over his shoulder. "It's acting strangely, something's off."

I nod and gain my composure. "Maybe you should bring that up with your girlfriend."

"What happened?" Cruz rushes toward us with the rest of the motley crew right behind him.

Oh great. I grip the edges of my towel tighter, trying to hold on to whatever pride I have left. "The shower's broken," I snap with annoyance.

Edwin appears next, flustered and embarrassed. "My apologies, Miss Ellison; come with me to a different suite right away."

Everyone lingers. Lyric looks at me like he wants to say more, like he knows I desperately want him to, but eventually he just turns and leaves. I start to follow Edwin when a warm hand grabs my wrist.

"I can help," Reina offers, and then explains: "With your magic."

"Don't touch me," I snarl, ripping my arm away and turning quickly on my heels, ignoring her as I hurry behind Edwin. *How could she possibly help me?*

31.

MULLORY

My heart thunders in my chest, reminding me that lying in bed is pointless because I'm not going to sleep anytime soon. Maybe never again.

"We killed him. Me and Esther Merrybright."

My mom, who braided my hair, and cut my waffles into stars. A murderer. But why? What could have driven her to that point?

I push the tangle of covers aside, turning on the light to reread the note she left me.

Time for the truth. Not all secrets are nice, but I want you to understand why. When you do, you'll be ready. Start your hunt with this.

I run my thumb across the line, *you'll be ready*. It's eerily similar to the last line of Cecilia's letter.

Don't judge a book by its cover. You'll know when it's time.

But time for what? What will I have to do?

I hurry over to the desk, spreading all seven books across in a line. Most are academic and scientific, the covers an unremarkable smear of burgundy and black. Except for the odd book on birds that's a striking blue color. But what secrets are they hiding? What does Cecilia want me to find? Lyric and I had reasoned that a clue might be hidden somewhere on page 122. That maybe it would provide answers about my father's murder.

Is it a coincidence that murder plagues both of my parents' pasts? I try not to think about that as I start searching through the books.

My first grab is *A Comprehensive List of Common and Uncommon Magical Phenotypes*. It's the same passage I already read, one devoted to time travelers, that delves into the science behind eye pigmentation.

It's interesting, but I'm not sure how it's supposed to help me solve the bigger mystery. Who killed my father?

Henry Prudence's murderer is closer than you think.

I circle back to *The Genetics of Magical Transfer* that Lyric and I first looked at. The passage on page 122 mostly talks about a sex-linked gene passed from father to son, but once again, I can't understand how that's supposed to help me uncover my father's murderer. Why am I supposed to care what's passed from father to son? Is Cecilia just trying to confuse or distract me?

But maybe I'm missing something? I read on:

Almost everyone carries the gene that allows magic to transfer. However, the gene alone is not enough for magic to manifest. For centuries scientists have tried to isolate the magic itself. To separate it from the living host. The closest known account was in 2001 in Prague. A single cell imbued with magic was sequestered and captured beneath a microscope for a moment. Disturbingly, it displayed features of a more complex living organism. There have been a few recorded mutations of the gene throughout history that can make magical expression inefficient.

I snap the book closed and several purple-shelled beetles scurry across the cover. Their wings are lined with fur, and they bellow timid roars. Shaking my hands, I try to dissolve the nonsensical bits of magic seeping out. Is that what's wrong with me? Some sort of mutation?

I can't seem to focus and decide to take a break from the books, turning instead to the latest clue, the birdcage gifted by the Skeleton Singer. Eyeing the book entitled *Birds*, I can't help but think Cecilia must have seen this coming.

I spin the birdcage backward and forward. I count the spokes, searching for some sort of pattern or irregularity. I briefly consider trying to find a bird and place it inside. There'd been no instructions, which meant the clue was hidden somewhere in or on the cage.

Desperation and insomnia finally convince me to pull open the bottom drawer of the cage and sift through the dirty bits. It's a congealed mass of papers stuck together with bird droppings that have turned to cement. Desperate times, desperate measures.

The rising sun slashes my hopes, leaving me crestfallen and filthy as I pry the final scrap free from a clump of feathers. The bottom is torn, but I recognize it instantly. I don't bother to clean up, rushing to find the others.

"It's the missing half of the receipt!" I scream across the breakfast buffet.

Lyric rushes over. He turns his nose up at the nasty bit of paper. "Maybe just tell us what it says."

"It has the name of the coffee shop," I announce proudly. "ZapToast. That's where we need to go next."

Reina pulls out her phone. "It looks like there's only two coffee shops registered with that name. The first is in Switzerland."

My heart sinks.

"But that one is new, only opened two years ago. The other isn't too far from here, it's in Brooklyn, and according to the website it's been serving the world's best coffee since 1940."

"It must be that one. My gran received these clues the day my mom was born."

Reina nods. "I've got the address."

"Edwin," I call.

He pops into view. "Already preparing a car, Miss Mullory."

"Twenty minutes!" I scream as I bound up the stairs and take the fastest shower of my life and then change just as quickly. I'm twisting my dripping hair into a bun as Edwin loads everyone with thermoses and bags of pastries.

"A word before you leave?" he asks me discreetly as the others bustle outside.

The fizz in my stomach suddenly sours. I don't expect good news, not after the tea set fiasco. "What is it?"

Edwin keeps his green eyes calm. "You're familiar with the garden sculptures?"

I think back to the party and the elaborately trimmed circus hedges. Lions, elephants, and tigers. "Yes."

"Well, it seems they've been breeding."

My mind can't wrap itself around the logistics of his statement. "Do they normally do that?"

Edwin shakes his head. "Not usually during this season."

"Okay," I say slowly. "So, there's some miniature baby hedges. Is that a bad thing?"

"No, certainly not. The problem is that Xavier would've maintained a heated net on the shrubbery to keep it stable during the winter. The baby hedges are quite cold and vulnerable in the snow and it's distressing some parent hedges, who are shedding their leaves."

"Maybe this is a silly question . . ."

"Certainly not, Miss Mullory."

"How exactly are the hedges mating?"

Edwin gives me a sad smile, like I'm a lost pupil, years and miles apart from my predecessor. Which in all actuality I am. "As I've alluded to before, the estate is embedded with a variety of magic, some precautionary. Others purely recreational, some admittedly of an odd variety, but regardless of intention or purpose, it all recognizes Xavier as a sort of keeper. . . ."

And we're right back to the same predicament—I'm not Xavier Stoutmire. Not even close. I can tell Edwin is looking to me for the next course of action. But what am I supposed to do? Holes in the china and now cold baby shrubs. Edwin must sense my complete lack of a plan, because he offers a solution.

"Might I suggest we move them to the stables, where it's warmer? Unless you feel up to directing the magic?"

I glance down at my hands—I don't have the slightest idea how to use this magic. "No, the stables should be fine," I agree. I can't shake the feeling that I'm failing. The holes in the china had been laughable, but the ice in Ellison's shower was concerning. Guilt blossomed in my chest when she locked eyes with me, and I could practically hear her thoughts. This was *my* fault.

And now everyone is looking to me as the leader. I'd won the Mystery Royale and beaten Xavier Stoutmire, but could I do it again? How much of that had come down to plain dumb luck?

32.

LYRIC

Immediately, I can sense something's bothering Mullory. Normally, my emotional radar is set to zero, but this is so painfully obvious, it's like an uppercut to the chin. The problem is I don't have a clue how to fix it. Some unrefined instinct urges me to pull her aside before she gets in the car.

"Are you okay?" It seems like the right thing to say, but judging by Mullory's reaction, I've been horribly mistaken.

She slumps against the porch stairs and looks up at me, gray eyes misty. "I don't know what's wrong." She swipes her eyes with a mitten, and that small gesture nearly kills me. Seeing her upset feels worse than dying. But I'm in uncharted territory, wading through emotions I was raised to bury. If I ever cried, I was punished.

"Wrong with what? The clues?"

A nervous little laugh escapes her lips. "Well, of course there's that. And the shadow I couldn't get to work properly, and now..." She hesitates, chewing her lower lip. "It's the magic on the estate, it just isn't right." Mullory gazes through me. "Lyric, what if it's me? What if there's something wrong with me?"

At first my only response is to shake my head side to side, because I'm completely tongue-tied, overcome with disbelief that she could think anything was wrong with her. I may not make it to my eighteenth birthday, but if there's one thing I'm absolutely certain of, it's that there's nothing wrong with Mullory Prudence. Not a damn thing.

I want nothing more than to tell her what's burning up my blackened little heart. And I want to unburden the guilt I'm feeling from using the shadow without telling her, but I just can't. Instead, I pull her as tight as I can to my chest so that she doesn't see my face.

"There's nothing wrong with you," I whisper into her damp hair.

"How can you be sure?"

"I'm sure."

"If you two are done cuddling, the rest of us would love to leave. The coffee shop was *your* idea after all," Ellison barks out the window. Sometimes I can't stand my sister.

We climb into the car. Mullory's cheeks are red with embarrassment, but I'm all smiles, especially at Cruz, who looks visibly irritated. The driver takes us out of the Hamptons and heads toward the city.

Reina is the first to strike up conversation. "Have you given any thought to who is responsible for your father's death, Mullory?"

I freeze, locking eyes with Mullory because I'm not sure if we should share the clues from Cecilia. The slight chance that the answer lies in one of several old books.

"No." Mullory shakes her head. "All I know is what we were told, that it's someone close."

Cruz jumps ahead. "One of the Stoutmires most likely."

"My family are not the only ones to frequent the estate," Ellison snaps. "The council was just here."

"But someone in your family would be the obvious choice." Cruz grins.

Mullory intervenes. "I can't help but think that the mysterious woman who left my gran the clues might be involved somehow. Or at least know something more. I just have no idea who she could be."

"A mysterious woman," Ellison says back slowly, looking as if she wants to say more. Her lips open as if she's on the cusp of revealing something, but she promptly goes silent. My sister can be complicated. And full of secrets.

But then again, so can I.

33.

MULLORY

The streets in Brooklyn are crammed with angry drivers, as if everyone has somewhere important to be all at once. It doesn't help my nerves, wondering what my mom wants me to find at a coffee shop. But then again, everything was always a riddle with her, and I was always expected to solve them.

"You're just like me, Mullory." My mom nudged my hip as she licked a spoon clean of chocolate icing. "We're happiest when we're chasing something. The fun's in the anticipation."

I raised a tube of sprinkles, dashing the plate of lopsided cupcakes in rainbow confetti. "But what about when we find it?"

Her face dropped, and the spoon sagged in her hands before she perked back up. "Then we start looking for something new. We never stop, that's the rule."

I didn't dare disagree, fearful that if I did my mom might leave me again. Instead, I pushed the plate of birthday cupcakes to the center of the table. "Gran will love them."

My mom dragged the plate back to the edge, making a tsk-tsk *sound between her teeth. "Anyone could find these, Mullory."*

"But they're for Gran and she'll be home soon."

"Never leave a clue out in the open where it could be stolen or exchanged." A disappointed sigh escaped her lips. "You love to hide things, Mullory. It's how you have fun, isn't it?" Her face searched mine for confirmation. This is how she doled out her love, endlessly, but always with restrictions.

I couldn't bear the thought of upsetting her. "It's fun," I quickly agreed. "Where should we hide them?"

"You're a smart girl, the smartest I know," she said, smiling. "One day you might solve a mystery bigger than you think."

"How do you know?"

Her expression hardened. "Because you'll have to. Now, where do we put these cupcakes? What makes a clue great?"

I knew the answer to this one, I always did. "A great clue makes the most sense for the person it's intended for. We need a place Gran would look!"

My mother winked with pride.

I scampered around the kitchen, before yanking out the coffee pot with my chocolate-covered fingers. "Gran loves coffee!"

My mom laughed. "That's a good start, but I doubt the cupcakes will fit in there."

My shoulders fell.

"But..." My mom's eyes sparkled. "We could put a different clue inside. A clue to lead her to the next one." Her voice thickened with glee. "Let's not forget, we love the hunt, Mullory."

"Earth to Mullory," Ellison yells from the street. "Get out, it's time for the world's best coffee."

I'm the last to stagger out of the car, and I hurriedly join the others, huddled beneath a striped awning. *ZapToast: World's Best Coffee Since 1940* is stenciled beside a snowman on the large picture front window.

The inside is rich with nutty and caramelized notes of espresso that are so thick they feel seeped into the dark wood paneling. A potbellied stove burns in the corner, and the counter is deep, polished wood with a lower glass display of mouthwatering pastries.

"Welcome to ZapToast," a girl in a beanie says with a yawn. "Here, you're always ready for coffee." Her voice is robotic.

I stumble, taken back. "What did you just say?"

Ellison raises a hand. "Please, not again."

"She said, 'Welcome to ZapToast. Here, you're always ready for coffee,'" Cruz repeats over my shoulder.

Not all secrets are nice, but I want you to understand why. When you do, you'll be ready.

A buzz builds in my fingers, a sense that I'm in the right place. But what does my mom want me to find?

"Are you going to order something?" Beanie Girl taps her boot. "You've got to order something or leave."

My eyes dart nervously around the shop: It's full of patrons sipping steaming lattes, typing away at keyboards. A silver Christmas tree is strung with garland made from packets of tea. The old-school marquee displaying the menu snags my attention.

Hunting for the Perfect Cup? Start here!

My gut prompts me to follow the obvious clue. "I'll take the first one."

"One classic cappuccino. That'll be three dollars and fourteen cents."

I pause, waiting for some reveal. It's Lyric who finally pushes a ten-dollar bill across the counter.

Beanie girl hands over a paper cup with a black lid. It's warm in my palm.

"You gonna order something else?"

"I..."

"She's just so enamored with the world's best coffee," Ellison sneers.

"Foam-to-milk ratio looked a tad off to me," Cruz comments.

I have to block out the chatter and ignore Beanie Girl's death stare. *We could put a different clue inside. Let's not forget we love the hunt, Mullory.* That's when I realize my mom's hunt requires an exchange, just how the Skeleton Singer took the bones.

I shimmy the receipt halves from my pocket, sliding them across the counter. "Can you tell me anything about these?"

Beanie Girl rolls her eyes. "Let me get a manager. Scottie!"

It's a minute before an overly eager looking guy strolls in from the back room. "Howdy, name's Scott." He points to the plastic tag on his tightly buttoned polo, grinning wide. Scott's hair is slicked so tightly with gel it glistens like a helmet in the sun. "We aim to please at ZapToast. Here, you're always ready for coffee!"

I dig deep for any remnant of charisma that might be buried inside me and smile back at Scott.

"I know this is a long shot, Scott, but I'm glad we have a manager like you to work with." His smile grows wider, and I know I'm on the right track. "I have a receipt, and I think it's pretty old, but if you could tell me anything about it, I would appreciate it." I fight all my instincts and bat my eyelashes. Or at least I try.

"Something in your eye?" Cruz smirks.

I ignore him and hold fast to my smile. Cruz tries to hand me a tissue, and even though my cheeks are burning, I keep my gaze fixed on Scott.

"Certainly, though if it's older than twenty years, it might not be in the system."

My stomach drops, because I know this receipt is definitely older than that. I motion to swipe the scraps from the counter, disheartened. "Thanks for your help, Scott."

"Not so fast." He smacks his hand down, catching the corner. I cringe at his proximity to a patch of hardened bird poop.

"I always, always try. That's the ZapToast way. We didn't make the world's best coffee by a lack of trying." He smiles, revealing a line of front teeth that overlap at gravity-defying angles.

I want to tell him that it's pointless, but I've just never been good at disagreeing.

Scotts scans his computer screen.

I shift from foot to foot, anxious to get this over with.

"I knew it."

"Thanks for your time, Scott."

"That's why we always try! This cup of coffee was bought on September fourteenth."

Something isn't quite adding up. "September fourteenth of what year?"

"This year." Scott stares at me strangely. "Just a few months ago."

"This year?" I blurt back.

Scott double-checks the screen. "I'm certain that's correct. I sold the cup myself." He scratches his chin. "Is this some sort of prank?" He glances over my shoulder. "Is that your camera crew? Am I on one of those TV shows?" He flashes a smile and strikes a pose.

"What?"

"I knew it," Scott says again with a laugh. "I knew you looked familiar."

"Me?"

"Yes, you! You're the girl who bought the coffee. Those are your receipts!"

I'm at a complete loss for words, my mouth gaping open at Scott. A million questions pop into my head but I don't get the chance to ask any.

Cruz grabs my arm, tugging me back. "Someone's coming." His eyes dart toward the window. "Someone with magic. Reina," he warns.

"Already on it."

As we scurry out of ZapToast I feel something sheer slip over my subconscious as a figure in a dark cloak lingers at the end of the street, silently watching.

34.

I run my fingers across the torn edge of the coffee receipt. A seemingly useless scrap, but one that threatens to reveal secrets embedded in time. Paper is light and easily moved, but the real clue is something more. The receipt is merely a piece of the map to get her there.

35. LYRIC

I can't pull my eyes from the car window, convinced that at any moment Lord Thorn will pop into view. I know we're chasing riddles to find Mullory's mom, but there's a bigger predator on our trail. We may be hunting the strange, but Lord Thorn is hunting me. I'm certain that's who was at the Skeleton Singer's lair and then again at the coffee shop; I'm just not sure how long we can outrun him.

"How could I buy the coffee?" Mullory asks, distraught.

Her voice helps to pull my whiny head out of my ass, and I finally turn back to face her. "There's a good chance this Scott from ZapToast was confused," I say.

Mullory ignores me, clutching her empty cappuccino cup. "I was in Punxsutawney in September, and I've never been to that coffee shop. Besides, Gran got that receipt from a woman the day my mom was born."

"Maybe we're looking at this the wrong way," Cruz says.

"Do enlighten us," Ellison counters. "This should be simple, given your history of chess mastering and murder."

"At least I'm more proficient than you at both."

Reina intervenes before the two of them go at it. "Maybe it's just someone who *looks* like you, Mullory."

It's the first thing that Mullory seems to listen to, twirling a curl with a pensive look on her face. "My mom," she says softly. "It could've been her. But that doesn't explain the timeline."

Reina continues. "Ignoring the timeline, there's a reason she sent us to the coffee shop."

I have to agree. "She's right. But where was the clue?"

All at once the light bulbs seem to turn on, and everyone's eyes narrow in on the empty cappuccino cup resting in Mullory's hands.

Cruz taps the lid. "That's the only thing we have."

"Maybe something hidden in the folds of the cardboard, kind of like the button?" I say.

"Or we need to burn it to reveal a message," says Ellison.

Mullory shakes her head. "No. My mom would've made sure the clue was meant for me, something ordinary that would catch *my* attention." She shrugs. "That's how the best clues work."

Pride wells up in me, watching Mullory figure this out like it's something only she's destined to unravel.

"My mom knows I love numbers," Mullory says, while turning the coffee cup between her hands. The sticker receipt is stuck to the side, and Mullory lingers on it, before laughing.

"Care to tell us what's so hilarious?" Ellison asks.

"I ordered the cappuccino classico because the marquee prompted me to start my hunt for the perfect cup of coffee there. My mom would've known how much it costs if she'd been there recently. Don't you guys see it? Three point one four?" Mullory laughs again.

Ellison answers, "Still not funny."

"It's pi. A circle's circumference to its diameter. One of my favorites. We would celebrate every March fourteenth."

"But what's the significance?" Cruz asks.

"Right," Mullory answers. "There must be something on the cup that tells us what to do with pi. *'ZapToast. World's Best Coffee Since 1940.'*" Mullory reads the tagline again. "Pi is a number although it's irrational and repeats, which means the year 1940 is probably significant because it's another line of numbers. My mom was always a fan of the alphabet cipher, where each letter is assigned a number. The number zero doesn't have a letter, but one, nine, and four would correlate to the letters A, I, and D."

"We need to aid pi? Pi aid?" I offer, while scratching my head.

Mullory spins the cup in her other hand, reexamining it. *"The 12 Days of Coffemas,"* she reads off the back of the cup. "Twelve would give us the letter L." Another smile. "Dial pi."

"The first ten digits of Pi," Cruz says, catching on. "A phone number."

Mullory whips out her phone, her fingers shaking as she types in the first ten digits of pi, which I'm sure she has memorized by heart. "Exactly."

It rings.

Rings again.

"Mullory."

Tears spring to the corners of Mullory's eyes. "Mom?"

No one in the car moves.

"Don't get rattled now. Head to Coney Island," the voice on the other end of the line instructs.

"Mom." Mullory's voice splinters, simultaneously gutting me. "Where are you?"

But the voice is nothing more than a recording that repeats the same line before breaking into static.

The cup crumples between Mullory's fingers as she wipes her face.

"Well, I guess we know where to head next," Cruz says, matter-of-fact.

I lace my fingers between Mullory's and spend the rest of the ride determined to do something useful, racking my brain around the cryptic riddle that remains from the Skeleton Singer. But I can't get past the first line: *"Most think it's full, few know it's empty."* Besides Cruz's head, I can't come up with a sharable answer.

Between grueling Brooklyn traffic and then a pit stop to a gourmet cheese purveyor—deemed necessary by Cruz—we don't arrive back to the estate until the sun begins to set in a band of orange and pink. As always, Edwin is eagerly waiting to escort us to dinner.

"I thought this might cheer you up," Edwin says to a distraught Mullory.

Her eyes light up at the sight of several pizzas set on silver trays arranged across the dining table. Uncle would be mortified, and the thought has me smiling broadly as I pull up a chair. Hot grease dribbles down my chin as I bite into a slice of pear and Gorgonzola, just as Reina screams.

I lurch forward, prepared to run, certain that Lord Thorn has found us, only to realize there's a fork hurdling toward my face. What the hell?

I duck to the side as it whizzes past my ear and lodges into the painting behind me. It's not the only one; all the forks have gone feral, spearing through the air. The knives bounce off the chandelier, blades flying. The spoons begin to laugh, clacking together.

Ellison screams and snaps her head at Mullory. "Make it stop!"

"I don't know how," Mullory answers.

We all drop to the floor, crawling beneath the table.

Edwin joins us, looking pale. "Dangerous cutlery," he says before retrieving a large stainless-steel bowl and placing it on his head. "I need to rescue the pizzas."

It's a noble mission and we wait for a battle-ragged Edwin in the library. I keep close to Mullory, silently willing anyone to ask her about Uncle's magic so that I might get the chance to snap at them. Any outlet for this fury is welcome, but no one says a damn thing.

"My apologies for the utensils." Edwin drags in a tablecloth laden with pizza pies. Some of the cheese has sloughed off and a few of the toppings trail on the floor, but no one seems to mind. Not even my table-etiquette officer of a sister.

"Do you really have no idea where my uncle is?" I ask Edwin while munching on my third slice.

"I'm sorry, sir. He was quite distraught after the game. Some might say he was a mess."

Something inside of me flickers with the news, some delusional thought that Uncle cared for me even in the slightest sense. He should be a mess. I did die.

We devour the pizzas, using some of the books as makeshift plates. Edwin pretends not to notice the slop coating the antique leather covers.

"More adventure-seeking tomorrow!" Cruz announces while standing up and wiping the crumbs from his pants. I don't miss how his eyes flit to Mullory every time he talks, but she ignores him. Clearly not in the adventure-seeking mood. I give him a giant grin and a thumbs-up, earning myself a scowl.

Everyone mumbles something close to a good night, staggering off to their rooms. Mullory lingers the longest, sharing a glance that means a million little things at once. Not like I can articulate any of them back. Instead, I swipe another slice of pizza as Tulia whisks into the library with a garbage bag.

I'm about to leave when I feel it. A tightness in my neck, a budding pressure in my skull, something akin to an urge. My fingers flex, itching to do something. The magic in me sparks, catching fire and taking the lead.

Make her. It whispers in my head. *Make her do whatever you want.* It's like pulling on an invisible rope tethered straight to Tulia. She claws her free hand across her forearm, nails biting into flesh and drawing blood.

A whimper escapes her lips, and I wait for her to confront me, but she never turns around.

Something ugly inside of me unfurls, like a fat cat in a sun patch, almost as if it's sighing with relief.

It was just a scratch, and I won't try it again. I repeat this to myself as I shuffle back to my room. But it doesn't help to calm the side of my brain wrestling with morality. Was it *me* that used the magic, or the magic using me? Can the two even be separated? Either way, it leaves a lingering bad feeling. A feeling that deserves to be punished.

36.

MULLORY

The "dangerous cutlery," as Edwin called it, does little to lessen my self-doubt. I can't help but wonder what I've done to send the estate into such a state of turmoil. My only solution is to stay busy. And since my mom's latest clue can't be cracked until tomorrow at Coney Island, I shift my focus to my father.

Henry Prudence's murderer is closer than you think.

All I have to go on are Cecilia's implied hints buried somewhere in a textbook. But so far, they've only proven to be full of scientific explanations of magical transfer and facts about birds.

But seeing as my father's dead, there's only one person I can turn to. No matter how reluctant I may be.

Zolan Humes is easy to find—his routine is the only thing that runs like clockwork here. Brandy and cigars in the parlor following dinner.

"Uncle Zolan."

He gives me a glazed look that seems to suggest that he's not *my* uncle. "Mallory."

"Could you help me with something?"

He yawns in my face.

"I'll make sure the cigars are fully stocked again."

This at least gets a response. "I'm tremendously busy, Mallory. Tremendously."

"I know." Although I haven't the faintest idea with what. "But maybe you could help me find someone who died?"

This interests him. "Do you have something, a token of theirs perhaps?"

I'd been anticipating this hurdle. "No," I say quickly. "But I'd thought someone of your caliber might be able to try without it."

Zolan settles into his armchair. "I am, undoubtedly, the most advanced in the field, and I suppose I could use the mental stimulation. I'll need a name."

I nod, trying to mask my excitement. "Henry Prudence."

If he recognizes my father's name, Zolan doesn't show it and he closes his eyes. His left eyebrow twitches. "Dead, yes . . ." His fingers rake through the air. "But I can't find him, not without something of his."

"Thanks anyway," I say, deflated, and turn to go.

Zolan's eyes snap open. "Not so fast. I was able to uncover something quite interesting." He strokes his goatee, baiting me.

"I'm very impressed." I play along. "What is it?"

"Curious that it's *you* who asks."

I gulp, certain from the glimmer in Zolan's eyes that I won't like where this is going. "Curious how?"

"Curious that you're entangled in yet another murder. Even more curious that it involves the very same knife."

I don't give Zolan the satisfaction of witnessing my horrified reaction, opting instead to sprint out of the parlor.

I'm shaking when I finally get to Lyric's room and barge inside, but it's empty. "Lyric?"

"In here." His voice is hushed by the sound of running water.

I gather my courage and walk slowly into the adjoining bathroom.

It's dark, eerie almost. Faint moonlight spills in from the window, casting a soft silvery glow across the tiles. Lyric's long arms are draped over the sides of the tub, his head stretched over the edge, neck fully exposed. Most of the soapy bubbles have popped, leaving a flimsy divide between us.

My already staggered breathing stops at the sight of his bare torso, muscles flexed, fingers gripping the ceramic sides. I'm stunned in place, and it takes me a moment to realize my shoes are wet, that the water is overflowing from the spigot that's still running.

I reach to shut it off.

"Leave it," Lyric growls. Then softer, amending, "Please, just let it run."

I take a cautious seat on the side of the slippery tub. Icy water sloshes over the sides.

"It's cold," I manage. Those are the only words that feel safe to utter as I watch Lyric inflict some self-appointed torture, revisiting his first near-death experience when his father tried to drown him.

His neck twists to the side; a bluish vein pulses beneath his skin. "I've been here a while."

Cautiously and with a featherlight touch, I run my fingers down his arm. Lyric trembles as my fingertips slide over his goose bumps, and my very own crop up.

"Do you think it matters, Mullory?" His eyes are closed, his breathing shallow.

"What?" I whisper.

"Do you think what we're doing matters?" The muscles along his jaw tick. "Or do you think no matter how much we try, we can't fight it? That we are who we are."

My thumb skims a bead of water from his forearm. "It matters. What we do, why we do it, it always matters."

Lyric sits up, sloshing water over the rim, but I don't back away. His dark hair is wet, a stray piece curling across his cheek. "I was remembering something from when I was little. Back when my uncle would still take me places. It was rare, but it happened. We went to the movies once."

It's bizarre to think of Xavier Stoutmire taking a young Lyric to the movies.

"There was a little boy sitting behind us, he kicked me the entire time. Stole my Skittles. Halfway through the movie he fell off his chair and sprained his ankle."

"Lyric—"

But he cuts me off, continuing. "I was insistent that I hurt that little boy, but Uncle X had never been firmer. He grabbed my wrist so tightly the skin burned and he said, 'You did no such thing. People get hurt all the time and sometimes they deserve it.' From that moment on, we never left the estate again. I'd always thought it was a punishment, but maybe it was just a precaution."

"But you were just a child."

"Lord Thorn's child."

His response causes me to falter, suddenly remembering why I barged in here, what Zolan had just said.

"What is it?"

I squeeze his wrist. "Nothing."

He leans closer, water trailing down his bare chest; his eyes are darker than the night beyond the windowpane. "Tell me." His hand cups my chin, tips it. "You can."

It's absolutely the wrong time, but whenever will it be right?

"I asked Zolan to look for my father, to try to find something useful. And . . ."

Lyric is a breath away from me, and yet he feels further than I can reach. He taps his forehead to my chin. "And?"

"He mentioned a knife. The same knife that . . ."

"That killed me." Lyric's voice is icier than the water overflowing from the tub. His body leans into mine. I shudder, powerless. My hands graze his back.

He pulls away, his expression hardened, a mix of horror and disgust.

Neither of us can find the words. But the truth burns between us like a flame, because there's one person who would've most likely had that knife. Who could've used it. His father may have killed mine. The passage about parental magic from Cecilia's book suddenly makes more sense. Was it a nod to Lyric's father? Something more literal than just genes that was passed from father to son? Was she trying to hint at the knife?

Lyric's next words break the spell, nearly cleaving me to pieces. "I'm like him," he says quietly. "I'm my father's son."

37.

LYRIC

Mullory leaves me soaking in my misery, as she should. My father, my *true* father, is likely the reason hers is dead. I towel off, change into sweats, all the while wondering if we can ever truly outrun our past. Or do ghosts like ours linger forever?

I know Mullory's better off without me and I know it's the noble decision to let her go. But when the hell have I ever been noble? And what about what I want? What I want more than anything else.

I fling the towel across the sopping floor, frustration taking the lead. A scream catches in my throat—is any of this normal?

And you know what, screw it.

I'm racing out of the bathroom, minutes too late. "Mullory, don't—" My voice echoes in my empty room.

Of course she's already gone.

My door creaks, and the sound of light footsteps follows. "I'm not going anywhere." Mullory's voice is muffled; she's hidden behind a tower of books stacked precariously in her arms.

Relief washes over me. "You brought books."

She wobbles inside, huffing as she sets them on the floor. "I thought if you wanted to be alone, I would just keep reading Cecilia's books."

It's nearly painful, the bout of happiness that jolts my insides.

In this moment I want nothing more than to kiss her; my lips remember the feeling, but I don't dare move. I won't, not until I'm absolutely certain that this is what she wants. Me, and everything that comes with me. Ghosts and all.

Mullory rises on her tiptoes and swipes her thumb across my forehead, smoothing my brow. "Let's not worry tonight, Lyric." She tugs me toward the bed and climbs up. I follow her, nestling my head in the crook of her arm. She runs her fingers lightly through my damp hair. So tenderly my eyelids flutter shut.

"Tell me about a time you were happy."

I snort.

She jostles my shoulder. "I'm serious."

I sift through the few pleasant memories from my childhood, focusing on one. "Fine. But don't laugh."

Naturally, this makes Mullory giggle. "I won't."

I jump up and rummage beneath my bed, fighting an army of dust bunnies before I find the velvet pouch I'd been looking for. I pour the contents onto the duvet.

Mullory smiles. "Rocks?"

"More than that." I roll a smooth and speckled one between my fingers before lining it up beside the others. "I'd always find them on the very worst days. When Uncle was the cruelest, when his punishment became unbearable." I tamp down my hatred and keep going. "Somehow, Edwin always knew, and he'd leave these for me."

Mullory picks one up, squinting at the plain brown rock.

I cover her hand with my own, gently squeezing her fingers around the rock before turning her palm over. The rock trembles before it morphs into a tiny monkey; its tail curls around my thumb.

Mullory's face lights up.

I touch the rest of the rocks—two kittens, a cow, a hippo, an unruly chimpanzee, a lion—and let them roam about my room. They stampede toward the books, knocking them over.

"Oh," Mullory blurts out.

Now I'm laughing at her as she hurries to put them back in order.

"They have delicate spines," she argues.

I scoop beneath her legs and lift her up before she can finish. "Delicate spines?"

Her gray eyes find mine, a little gasp. "Yes. Exactly."

Then a smile between us that lights my insides on fire. But I won't kiss her, not yet. Instead, I tuck her into my bed and slide in beside her.

Mullory's breathing starts to slow, but I can't let this night go.

"Now it's your turn. Tell me a time you were happy."

Mullory stirs, her voice on the edge of groggy. "Not really a special day. I woke at four in the morning because the power went out. AC shut off; it was hot."

"Wow. You know how to have a good time."

"I know, right?" Mullory yawns as she smiles. "It was more about the feeling, just knowing that my mom was home to stay. Knowing that even though it was a million degrees in our tiny apartment, we had the entire day ahead of us. Just me and her. No riddles or clues for once." Mullory pauses, and I almost think she's fallen asleep, but she murmurs into my arm, "I've been searching for answers about my mom since as long as I can remember." Her voice drops to a bare whisper. "I'm just so tired, Lyric."

My hand skims her shoulder. "I understand."

Mullory's breathing steadies as her body stills, and this time, I can tell she's asleep.

But I can't seem to shut my mind off, not knowing for sure if my father killed hers. Is that my destiny? To be like him? To kill?

I can't seem to fight what happens next, a nightmare born from a memory, one that seems to yank me straight from my body and plunk me into the tub of water my father nearly drowned me in. The seconds before are the worst part, the anticipation and knowing what happens next. I can't move and then I can't breathe, not until the very last moment.

I struggle, gasping for air, twisting beside Mullory.

The magic in me takes advantage, urging me to slip my hand across Mullory's shoulder, fingers flexing around the shadow. I know I shouldn't. But I can't stop myself.

"I'm sorry," I whisper in her ear as I brace myself against the power of the stone.

This time when I face the man made of mist, I'm prepared. Because all of this can't be a coincidence. The figure that found me in death means something more. I'm certain of it. Like father, like son.

"Henry Prudence," I say with confidence, testing out a theory that this memory of a man is Mullory's father. That before he fully crossed over into death, he left fragments of himself behind.

The mist shimmers, and beads of dew congeal together into something more solid. "Henry Prudence," it replies, like it's remembering a name it once knew.

"I know who killed you," I say boldly. "Lord Thorn."

Henry flickers, impassive. "He's watching you."

It's the same thing he said the last time I was here, and I get the sense that his responses are limited. That I have to ask the right questions. "Who's watching me?"

But Henry ignores my question, bending closer and lighting up at the sight of the shadow pulsing between my fingers. "Mine," he growls. "Mine." A gurgle disguised as a laugh slips out. Henry appears frenzied. "Must take it. Take it from her. Take it." A pause. "He's watching you. He killed."

"Lord Thorn?" I need him to confirm my father's evil deed.

But Henry doesn't respond, almost as if the answer is incorrect. But if it wasn't my father then who?

I pry my hand from the clutches of the mist, squeezing the shadow until I'm back in my bed beside Mullory. My heart is racing, the magic in me ablaze.

I look at Mullory, the trail of perfect freckles spilling down her lips. How many secrets can I keep from her?

38.
ELLISON

We opt not to have our fingers severed by dangerous dinnerware and decide to get coffees and sandwiches on the road. Edwin is apologetic and Mullory looks absolutely ashamed of the cabinet that's rattling in place, stuffed with thrashing silverware. Some of the staffers cradle their arms, nursing prong-shaped battle wounds after trying and failing to subdue the rowdy forks and knives. It took Mullory the better part of the morning to apologize to each and every one of them.

"Will they calm down?" Mullory asks Edwin.

"Let's hope so."

I would think it's quite embarrassing not to have control over the magic she stole from our family. But what beautiful poetic justice! It helps brighten my mood and there's a bounce in my step out the door to the car.

The same driver waits for us in the car, steam curling from the exhaust to fight the cold. I can only imagine what he thinks of our mad itinerary. *No shopping for us today, we'd like to visit a closed amusement park! Why would we go to a restaurant when we could visit a madman hidden away in a mountain?* But the driver is stoic and silent as he rolls up the privacy window.

Coffee helps to perk us up, not that Cruz needs the boost.

"I think this is going really well," he announces. "We're doing an excellent job with our end of the bargain."

I want to correct him because, in fact, it's Reina who's doing an excellent job shielding us from the council, but my phone pings and I decide I need a break from Cruz's crap. My heart leaps when I realize it's a text from Whitaker. I didn't want to look too needy while he's on his fancy council internship, but I've never been separated from him for this long and it's been slowly killing me. I swipe to read the first text.

Where are you!!!

Not good. He's not an exclamation-type guy, which means something's wrong.

Driving. I decide that's the safest answer as I keep my eyes pinned on the screen. Dots appear and reappear as Whitaker types his response.

Why are you on a list of suspected accomplices?!

I hiss under my breath and Lyric shoots me a concerned look.

"This probably won't come as a surprise," I say aloud to everyone. "But the council isn't happy with us. I doubt the Magnus liked returning empty-handed."

"But we already knew that," answers Mullory.

I shoot her a menacing glare.

They're after something big.

Not that big, I think. Actually, it's small and hideous and wrapped around Mullory's neck.

I know.

How are you avoiding them?

I steel a glance at Reina.

It's a secret.

I can't stand the thought of keeping another secret from Whitaker. I hate it. I hate it. I hate it. Ever since I kept my mother's affair from him, I've vowed to never do it again. That secret almost broke us, but here I am keeping another one from him.

Whatever you're doing it's working. They can't seem to find you.... How are you holding up?

Part of me wants to tell him how incredibly scared I am to lose Lyric again. But I'm even more scared of sharing the truth. Fine.

Right. Whitaker responds, clearly not buying my lie. And your magic?

Feels like it's eating me alive, and it terrifies me. But I can't share that, not even with Whitaker, the person I'm closest with. It's fine.

It's okay to not be fine, Ellison. Mother certainly isn't. I've never seen her this worried.

Tears start to well, but I won't give in. She's only worried about appearances.

Whitaker responds quickly. She won't come out of her room; she's just been hiding in her closet. I don't think she's sleeping much at all.

I can't help but picture my mother, bleary-eyed and staring at the bell jar containing a piece of Lyric's dream. Does she know he's alive? That he's fighting for his life once again, all because of her mistakes.

Whitaker sends another text. Lyric?... There are rumors here.

Even through the text I can sense Whitaker's apprehension, his timid nature for all things concerning our brother. But what's safe to respond via text? I decide to send him something cryptic instead.

Holding tight to the banister.

It's a reference to a childhood game we'd play, like capture the flag, where only the downstairs banister was safe ground. I know he'll get the embedded message—Lyric's safe—and I know this news will release a weight from his chest. After Uncle's wicked game, we both blamed ourselves for Lyric's death. He was just better able to cope with it—throwing himself into harnessing his newly inherited magic. I chose to wallow and wilt and spiral into darkness. It's no wonder why everyone favors him.

Be careful.

You too.

"Ellison?" Reina asks, unsure.

I snap my eyes from my phone, annoyed that they probably appear puffy and red. "What?"

"Nothing," she answers quickly. "You just seem upset." She gives me a slight shrug, a peace offering. I want to toss my coffee in her face.

Everyone goes quiet, turning their attention on me while I remain frozen in place, burning from the spotlight.

"Fine. My brother, my other brother," I explain to Cruz and Reina. "He's been interning at the council headquarters—"

"That's where the labyrinth is," Mullory interjects.

"That's right," Cruz encourages her.

Reina's jaw tenses at the mention of the labyrinth.

"It's not like he's inside the labyrinth," I snap. Stupid, typical Mullory comment. "Anyway, the council's furious and is trying harder to find us."

Cruz tightens his grip on his thermos. "We'll be ready, won't we, Reina?"

"I'm always ready," she answers, whip-smart. I don't miss how she turned the *we* into an *I*. This whole plan hinges on her ability to keep us concealed.

"It's me they're after," Lyric grumbles.

"And this." Mullory lifts the necklace from the depths of her sweater. "If we could just find my mom, she'll know what to do."

"Isn't that what we've been trying to do this entire time?" I don't tiptoe around Mullory, and I don't coddle her like the rest of them. I'm growing tired of our little adventures.

"We're getting closer," she answers, trying to convince me, and more importantly, herself. "One clue has led us to another. The button led us to the Skeleton Singer."

"Creepy dude who gave us an even creepier riddle," Cruz adds.

Mullory nods, and some of her dark curls fall from the slop of a bun on her head. "Right, we got the riddle and learned how he knew my mom."

"They killed someone together." I'm quick to remind her.

Lyric gives me a side glare. "That's what *he* thinks happened."

It's unbelievable how hastily Lyric runs to Mullory's aid. Doesn't he understand that all I'm trying to do, all I've ever tried to do, is protect him? Mullory stole the magic that should've gone to him, but hey, *I'm* the villain.

"He also gave us the receipt that led us to the coffee shop."

I toss my phone back in my bag and cross my arms. "And now we're headed to an amusement park in the offseason. In the snow."

"We keep going," proclaims Cruz, our brilliant, murderous leader. "Follow the clues until they lead to Mullory's mom."

I give him a wide smile, because I want him to know that I've cut through all his bullshit, and I know he's hiding something. A secret agenda that I'll uncover. It takes one to know one. "Let's just try to not get killed by the council."

"That's the spirit, Ellison!"

Yep, that's me. Our group cheerleader.

Woooo.

39.
MULLORY

Maybe if it was summer and there were hundreds of kids running around, maybe then the giant clown face hanging above the gate wouldn't seem so menacing. Snow collects on the points of the iron posts beneath a sludge-gray sky, making the whole mood feel primed for a horror film. *CONEY ISLAND CLOSED FOR THE SEASON* is printed across a sign that hangs from the lock and chains looped through the gate.

"Still think clowns are fun?" Lyric teases me.

"Not right now." I playfully nudge his shoulder.

Cruz marches up to the gate and grabs the padlock in his gloved hand. "Hmm."

"How do we get around this one? Will our genius leader play the piano?" Ellison asks between chattering teeth.

Cruz ignores her. "Bobby pin," he says with an outstretched hand as if he were a surgeon asking for a scalpel.

I pull one from my bun and hand it over, all the while wondering what other favor he'll ask for when the time comes. What do I possibly have to give?

"Is *thief* on your résumé, too?" asks Ellison. Her hatred for Cruz is conspicuous. I'm not a fan either, but he's really struck a nerve with her.

Cruz only grins. "Among other talents." He pulls off a glove with his teeth and uses the bobby pin with expert precision. Picking and twisting it ever so slightly with steady hands.

Anticipation builds as he works. Could my mom be here, in an abandoned amusement park? Is it any more likely than a dry cleaner or a coffee shop?

There's another feeling swelling through me: bitterness. I'm always chasing my mom, always one step behind with half a clue and a threadbare promise. Why? Why not take me with her? Why does being her daughter require such effort?

"Got it." Cruz tosses the lock in the snow and yanks the chain through the gate posts. When the chain falls, he kicks it with his boot and pushes open the gate. Naturally, it creaks—like the two rustiest pieces of metal in the whole world just slid past each other—upping the creepy vibes.

"Ladies first." Cruz waves a hand through the open gate.

It's like the very air has changed on the other side—thick with queasy silence. Amusement parks are one of those places, like a church or hospital, a place where without the people to fill the space, the bones are left bare and charged with a sort of static current. It's almost like you can feel the spirit of the place lingering.

Thick layers of snow are crusted along the roofs of wooden stands and attractions that are asleep for the winter. Metal gates are pulled tight across windows that are usually stuffed with plush prizes.

"What are we even looking for?" Ellison breaks the silence. The tip of her nose is blue, but oddly enough I don't feel the cold at all.

"I think we should split up," Lyric suggests while clinging to my side.

Cruz laughs. The noise echoes through the empty amusement park. "Let me guess, you three will go one way and Reina and I will go another?" He shakes his head. "I don't think so. This is a team effort, Thorn."

Lyric tenses at the mention of his father's name.

"I can't let you three pull a fast one on me. Not when we've been working so well together!" He pats Lyric's back, and I cringe—certain Lyric is going to pummel him in the face. But he surprises me.

"Fine," Lyric acquiesces.

"A deal is a deal. You and Ellison can take my cousin, and I'll escort Mullory."

"Like hell you will," Lyric snaps. I spoke too soon.

Tension mounts and I can't help but feel like there's something terrible here, something we need to uncover quickly, and arguing won't get us any closer. "It's all right," I say. "Let's just do this as fast as possible. Everyone, keep your phones on."

Lyric's face falls before settling back into a hardened mask. My heart sinks, but there's no time to undo it.

Cruz extends a hand, and I brush right past it.

He laughs again. "I like you, Mullory Prudence." His voice drops to a whisper. "Even more than I thought I would."

40. ELLISON

I can't feel my toes.

Or my fingers stuffed in my gloves and buried in my pockets.

I can barely feel my heart limping along, fueled only by pure frustration.

Snow *and* clowns. I've got to hand it to Mullory—this time she's outdone herself.

I trudge through the amusement park with the enthusiasm of a corpse. Lyric lags even farther behind me, grumpy and pouting. I want to say something to him, something even remotely comforting. But there's a glaring mountain between us and I've spent my entire life poised on the ledge, too afraid to climb. Emotions are something us Stoutmires keep inside, rotting until we decompose. Even if I did save him in the Mystery Royale, it doesn't make up for the sister I was all those years before. When I could have made a difference, I didn't. And now I can't seem to find the courage to admit it.

A stray wrapper blows by in a swirl of flurries and snags on my boot. Still no sign of Mullory's mom. Or anyone for that matter. Only desolation and despair. Truly, I don't understand the point of amusement parks. Why huddle together in the summer heat just for some rickety rides and greasy food? I'd rather not catch tetanus or vomit. But that's just me, and I have class.

"What do you guys think?" Reina has been silently leading us along. She's stopped in front of a fun house. Another clown face twisted into a grimace with a juicy red tongue sticking out. Do I think Mullory's mom's inside? Probably not. But I want out of the cold. "Great. Looks great."

Reina marches beneath the oversize teeth hanging from the clown's mouth. "It's open," she calls while pushing past a sticky tarp.

"Lucky us."

It's dreary inside, full of spiderwebs and musty air. We have no choice but to wobble across some sort of unstable bridge that tips and tilts, creaking loudly until we reach the end. I turn left into some sort of maze, while Lyric veers right into a hall of mirrors.

"See you on the other side," he calls in a monotone voice.

I trudge forward as the walls narrow and curve, painted with rainbow colors in a kaleidoscopic nightmare. I turn left and then left again, not entirely convinced I haven't spun myself into a giant circle.

A muffled whine catches my ear.

This is it.

This is when someone with an ax in a cheap Halloween mask pops into view and backs me into a corner to finish me off. Ellison Stoutmire murdered in a fun house. Of all the ways to go—that reads especially pathetic.

I spin and shine my phone light, heart leaping into my throat.

"Reina," I call feebly, even though she's probably already found a way out. I move my light to the corner and find a mass huddled tight. The scream dies in my throat when I realize it's her.

"What are you doing?"

"I don't like mazes," she whispers between choppy breaths.

I roll my eyes, not that she can see with my light blinding her. "Does anyone?" It would be easiest to leave her, to step past a problem that isn't mine. But I can spot the raw fear brimming behind her violet eyes, the type of fear that consumes you and turns you into a prisoner in your own body. I lived for years under the tyrannical wrath of mine. I crouch down beside her, against my better judgment.

"You can't let the fear win."

Reina glances up at me.

"Take it from someone on the other side, it's not worth it."

Reina's sobs soften. "How?"

"You just do it. You get up and you lock it down and bury it so deep that it dies. Kill it, or it kills you."

Reina wipes her face, and chews on the edge of her nail. "I just... detest mazes."

"Why?"

"Because... Because..."

I try not to sigh out loud and release the frustration building inside. We don't have time for breakdowns, *but* we do need her. More importantly, Lyric needs her, which means so do I. "You don't have to tell me. But maybe it'll help."

Reina gazes up at me, eyes large. "I've seen the labyrinth."

"I guess that's a good reason to be fearful of mazes then."

She gives a startled laugh before shaking her head and burying her face in her hands. "You don't understand."

"I might not understand the labyrinth, but I understand being afraid of something," I say with as much empathy as I can muster.

"How?"

"I lived my nightmare," I say softly, surprised at my own words and unable to look her in the eye. "It didn't just haunt my mind at night, it crawled its way out of the darkest recesses of my brain and nearly destroyed me. But then I realized..." I look her in the eye, steeling back my shoulders. "I realized it's *my* nightmare. I own it, not the other way around." I don't share how broken it left me, how in my most vulnerable moments I still succumb to it.

Reina finally stands, but the tears keep falling. "It's not just mine. . . ."

Then I remember Cruz mentioned Reina had someone inside the labyrinth. Realization hits hard, followed swiftly by suspicion.

"Does this have to do with the favor?"

"What?" Reina answers, confusion distorting her features. "No. No, the favor is for Cruz." Her tone is stern as she starts to walk back through the maze. I trail behind, wondering what Cruz could have possibly promised Reina to make her agree to this.

"Why are you even helping him then?"

Reina shrugs. "He's family."

This I understand perfectly, more than Reina will ever know. If there's one thing I won't budge on—it's that.

We continue silently through the maze.

"Ellison."

"Yes."

"Thank you."

I don't dare respond.

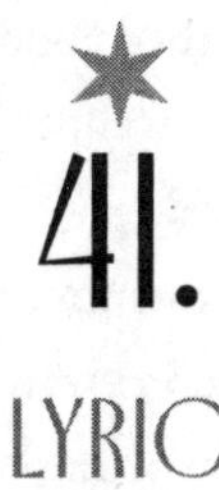

41. LYRIC

Sweat begins to slip down my back as I run my phone light up and down the hall of mirrors. Eyes stare back at me—*his* dark and soulless eyes. And what's worse than just looking like the father who abandoned you and is now intent on murdering you is knowing his innermost thoughts. The tether between us gets shorter and sharper as each day passes. His magic is pure power. Pure rage. Absolute control over whomever I want.

Mullory thinks that it matters what we do, that we choose our own path. But what if I'm destined to choose the wrong one? This magic is corrupt, mutated beyond whatever good or pure intention it may have once had. Generations of being passed down and used solely for manipulation by violent means. A violence it now *craves*. Uncle always said that beasts and monsters were born hungry, that blood extracted by cruel means tasted differently, that it developed a certain appetite. And God... why am I so taken by it? Mesmerized and thrilled. I can't help but hate those parts of me. But hate them or not, they still exist.

I made Tulia claw at her own arm and I can't stop thinking about it, like a sick sort of daydream. The feeling of absolute power cradled in my hands. Maybe some of the lure stems from my disturbed childhood. I'm certain any psychologist would have a field day with me. I don't want to like the magic, but I can't help that I'm itching to do it again. To do more.

And Mullory is caught in the cross fire, because beneath it all I'm a selfish ass. I don't want to let her go. And I don't want to let her in, because I don't think she'll like what she finds. And I know it's impossible to do both, but when has my life ever been remotely easy?

I'd stupidly thought meeting Mullory was destiny. Some fortunate twist of fate. But I'm almost certain my father killed her dad, even if some memory of Henry Prudence has me second-guessing. And I was supposed to kill her. Our meeting wasn't random, it was the collision of two cars set on a direct course for destruction.

42.

MULLORY

For once, Cruz Lagunes is silent. We wander through the amusement park that's perched on a wooden dock. The salty spray ricocheting off the ocean stings my nose. In the summer, I'd bet the air is full of squawking seagulls and squealing children. But in the dead of winter, it's a void. Positioned so that the entire park feels like it's about to collapse and spill into the sea.

I keep my eyes sharp, wondering what my mom wants me to find here.

"Deep in thought?" asks Cruz. His hands are shoved awkwardly in the pockets of his bomber.

I break from my trance.

He shrugs. "You don't have to tell me." Something registers across his face, as if he's been let down. But by what? I've been ignoring his odd reactions, the subtle things he says under his breath, but maybe I need to pay more attention.

I extend an olive branch. "Just wondering why my mom would send me here."

"Ah," he says thoughtfully. "Do you miss her?"

It's an even stranger question, especially coming from him. The boy who murdered his brothers, what could he possibly know about family?

"I always miss her," I answer truthfully. "I'm just not sure how much she misses me." The words tumble out before I have a chance to stop them.

Cruz holds my gaze; his eyes burn dark around the edges, but a caramel softness lingers in the center. "How could she not miss you?" His voice is a whisper that floats across the salty air, stinging me when it lands.

I stumble back.

Cruz must sense it, because he smiles—his one perfect dimple pops as he pushes past me, not the slightest bit flustered. "There it is!" Cruz gazes up at a Ferris wheel. The carts rock in the winter wind, snow sticks to the spokes, and icicles hang from the edges like diamonds.

"Were you looking for the Ferris wheel?"

"I was looking for a way to make this hunt go faster." He points to the tippy top. "So, we can get a bird's-eye view."

"But it's off."

"For now." Cruz flips up the shearling collar of his coat. "One moment, please." He hurdles over the gate in the front of the waiting-line area and hops onto the snowy platform containing the operating apparatus. He places his hands beneath his chin, studying the mechanism. "A key would be helpful . . . or the *idea* of a key," he says excitedly. "Mullory, come here and give me a hand."

I'm not sure how much help I'll be as I try to step over the gate, with much less finesse, snagging my snow pants. I clumsily hoist myself up onto the platform and look to Cruz for more instructions.

"I'll need your actual hand."

I slide off my mitten and let my bare hand hover over his.

Cruz waits for me to make the next move. "I don't bite, Mullory." He leans closer and whispers, "Not usually."

But you do murder. I lower my hand, and he gently laces his fingers through mine. His touch is surprisingly tender.

"Just need a little jump start," he says quietly.

Heat builds in my palm, and I feel the trickle of magic slide between us. Somehow, I can sense the magic settling and transferring over to Cruz's hand, and I can't help being frustrated that he knows how to use my magic better than I do.

"I've had lots of practice," he says, like he can read my mind. "Almost there."

Something clicks, followed by the hiss of lights as the bulbs on the perimeter of the Ferris wheel turn on in a static burst. Twinkling beneath the snow, it's stunning. The Ferris wheel lugs into motion, a slow first turn, gears grinding in protest. Cruz rushes over to a basket and swipes a handful of snow from the handrail. "Time for a ride."

"But how did you do that?" I ask, refusing to budge an inch. "How do you know how to use the magic?" I want to call it *my* magic, but it still feels like a foreign body that's unwilling to cooperate. I can't help but think of the broken china and the irate silverware. The entire estate is pitted against me, and Cruz just casually calls upon the magic and it listens.

He scratches his head. "I grew up with magic and I have a better sense of it. You'll get the hang of it."

"I'm not so sure."

Cruz tips his head and smiles. "I can help you."

"Will it cost me another favor?"

Cruz's smile falters. "No. This I'll do for free. And your first lesson is to relax."

"But I still don't understand how the illusion of a key could work as an actual key."

"It can't." Cruz smiles while dangling a small chain from his palm and gesturing to a metal box near the gears that is now unlocked and swinging open. "But you believed it did. And that's your second lesson, Mullory, you need to believe in yourself."

I climb aboard the snowy seat. The basket rocks from Cruz's weight when he settles across from me.

"I'm relaxed and I believe," I lie. In truth, I'm so tense that I could snap at the slightest provocation.

Cruz laughs. "I don't think the magic agrees."

The ocean is frothy and turbulent as we steadily rise, and I can't help but squirm in place, thinking about the question that's been on my mind since Cruz first arrived.

"You know you can just ask me, Mullory."

I gulp, knowing we're about to go *there*. "You're right." I pause. "It's an easy question."

Cruz shifts closer.

My pulse rises, but I take the dare and press on. "Did you kill your brothers?"

The golden core in his eyes burns, but he doesn't break contact, and his fingers trail across my knee. "Yes." His voice is unwavering. "I killed my brothers."

It's the way he says it, unapologetically. Cruz is a monster, there's no doubt about that. But he doesn't deny it, and there's almost something chivalrous in his honesty. It makes him the type of monster that lures you in, curious to know more. I finally find my voice again. "Why did you do it?"

For once, Cruz doesn't answer with a quick-witted response. Instead, he gazes out across the ocean, deep in thought, but he keeps his hand resting on my leg.

Time seems to stall away in silence as we rise, before Cruz finally responds. "Until you're in the moment, you never really know what you're capable of."

I can't help but think of the magic I took from Lyric. A split-second decision. My body burns with shame.

Cruz raises his hand, ruffling his hair and leaning away. "People think they know themselves. They like to say, 'I'd never do that.' Or 'That's not me,' but it's all just a guess." He exhales with frustration. "You really don't know who you are until you're forced to make a tough decision. Sometimes you won't like what you find."

Regret simmers between us and I can't help but think of my own mom. A murderer. "I don't think I could kill anyone."

"Are you so sure?"

The corpse from the Skeleton Singer's lair pops into my head. "Yes," I answer with more doubt than I'd like to admit.

"What if you didn't have any other choice? What if it was your life or theirs?"

"There's always a choice," I say, raising my voice, unintentionally. "The choice might just seem impossible," I amend, softer this time.

Cruz crosses his arms, stuck in the checkmate I've pinned him down with, but he doesn't stop staring at me. It's the oddest sensation, a look you'd give to someone you really *knew*. I whip to the side, trying to focus as we ascend even higher, almost to the very top.

"Mullory." I can feel that he's still looking at me. It's too uncomfortable to look back, so I keep my eyes moving.

"Yeah," I answer impassively.

Cruz takes a deep breath. "There's something I need to tell you—"

"There!" I exclaim, and point to a tent on the edge of the park, tucked behind some sort of amphitheater. A faint light glows inside, illuminating a large image of a snake. "Don't get rattled," I say, repeating the message left by my mother.

I swivel around and yank out my phone. I need to text Lyric and the others.

Cruz's face is unreadable. "Good spot."

I send the text and will the wheel to turn faster. "What did you want to tell me?"

"Nothing important."

He's lying—that I'm certain of. But I let it be. Something tells me the lie is easier to stomach.

43.
LYRIC

Mullory's text has Reina, Ellison, and me all hurrying toward the Ferris wheel, grateful to have some sort of lead.

I'm enraged when I catch sight of Cruz helping Mullory down, but she's smiling at me so big and eager that I feel my body loosen.

"A rattlesnake," Mullory says in a rush.

I edge past Cruz and step on his boot, harder than I probably need to, but he gets the message.

"It's painted on a tent in the back of the park." Mullory's face flushes. "Do you think she could be there?"

I want nothing more than for Mullory's mom to be waiting with open arms. I want it because she needs it, and because a tiny part of me worries that she won't take another letdown well. After everything we've endured, her heart feels delicate and easily shattered. A breakable, vulnerable thing that I'll protect no matter the cost. Even if that means from myself.

"Let's find out," I say.

Mullory links her arm through mine, and the nearness of her leaves me dizzy—even though she's barely touching me through our winter coats. I can't help but think of when she crawled in my bed, how badly I wanted to kiss her. But I won't, not until I'm certain it's what she wants.

We hastily traverse the amusement park with Mullory leading the way.

Ellison huffs the entire time. "Are we there yet?"

"There." Mullory points to a mismatched tent sewn together from scraps of different patterned canvases. Light flickers from within, illuminating the innards like the belly of a beast. A menacing rattler is painted on the tent, mouth stretched open to reveal daggerlike fangs.

"The Viper?" Cruz reads the bloodred script stenciled beneath the snake. "Who's that?"

Mullory's face hardens with determination. "Guess we're going to find out."

There's no lock or gate keeping us out and Mullory simply lifts the heavy tarp to the side. Inside is warm and surprisingly cozy: Light flickers from the tips of candles, oozing wax down the sides of tables and shelves that clutter the space. I can spot a firepit in the center, burning bright and heating the tent.

"Whoa," Reina whispers as we step farther inside. A large ten-foot acrylic tank blocks our sight line. The tank is multitiered, with several rocky alcoves and large logs scattered about inside. A shriveled, empty snakeskin lies withered on the mulch.

Mullory's eyes widen as she peers inside the tank and whispers, "Where's the snake?"

No one answers as we silently move through the tent. Beyond the tank are two beat-up leather chairs, like the kind you'd find in a dentist's office, poised beneath large halogen lights. There's a cart full of instruments and a tattoo machine. Ink drips from a well, leaking onto a mess of bandages strewn across the floor.

"Another day, another nightmare shop," remarks Ellison.

Behind the macabre tattoo setup are several couches haphazardly strewn about. A variety of exotic animals are stuffed and displayed between the furniture, some frozen mid-leap, paws and claws arching through the air.

Mullory gasps as she stumbles into a stuffed weasel standing on its hind legs. There are baubles and random bits of junk, making it feel like an oddity shop. I spot a fishbowl containing a single eye preserved in some sort of gelatinous mixture.

Mullory stops short in front of a bookshelf, prying out a photo wedged between two books.

Her eyes go wide. "It's my mom."

I rush over to look.

"Hello, Mullory," a voice purrs.

44.

MULLORY

I try my best not to startle at the voice calling my name from the corner of the tent. My fingers remain clutched around the picture of my mom huddled with a group of people I don't recognize.

"You're Mullory Prudence, are you not?" the voice asks lazily. Once I realize it's not my mom calling me, I inch closer. Lyric follows.

I take a bold step to face an alarmingly beautiful woman, who's lounging comfortably in one of the armchairs—she's wrapped in a slinky golden dress that pools by her bare feet. Her bronze arms are exposed, and she's as radiant as the sun. Almost every inch of her skin is covered in a pattern of intricate tattoos that coils all the way up her neck and ends with twin snakes piercing the flesh beneath her chin. Her hair is twisted into tiny braids and swept off her neck into an elaborate bun.

"Who are you?" I blurt out.

"Isn't it obvious?"

Of course it's obvious. "The Viper."

She gives me a coy smile; her teeth are chiseled to fine points, like the fangs of the snakes on her neck.

My pulse quickens. "And you know who I am?"

The woman gives a casual nod. "I should think so, you look just like Esther."

"You know her," I say, grasping the photo clutched to my heart. I feel oddly protective of it, a piece of my mom's history that may belong in this tent, but that I desperately need to understand.

In the photo my mom looks younger, smiling brightly in a group with five others. I recognize the woman calling herself the Viper almost immediately. She wasn't covered in quite as many tattoos, but it's undeniably her.

"I knew Esther. We all did." The way she says *we* makes me think this group of people was something important, something special. "At least we thought we did," she adds softly.

I hold out the photograph and point at a man caught mid-laugh. Long, thick hair tied back into a ponytail, there's something free-spirited about him. He's wearing the same red coat with tassel fringe that my mom left me. "Who's that?"

The Viper holds her smile. "If you're here, it means you've already met him."

Puzzled, I stare back down, searching for some sense of familiarity. He's almost unrecognizable, a wisp of what he was, but when I see it, I tremble. "The Skeleton Singer."

"That's an entirely new title, the unfortunate result of a lost mind. When I knew him, we called him the Crow."

The Crow looks alive and jolly enough to be someone's favorite uncle. A shiver courses my spine at the thought of what he became after he left the labyrinth. Of him and his half-dead creatures holed up in the side of a mountain.

"You wouldn't be able to help us with one of his riddles, would you?"

"Riddles should only be solved by whom they are intended for," the Viper cautions.

I nod, embarrassed by the implication that I'm trying to cheat, and I glance back at the photograph. A slender, elegant arm is draped around the Crow's shoulder. Beside him is a woman dressed in an emerald suit, her shoulders are cloaked by long, lustrous black hair. But her face is obscured by a giant red *X*. "And this woman?"

The smile swiftly falls from the Viper's face. "Dead," she answers coldly, as she gazes around the room, lingering on Reina.

"I'm sorry," I manage to say, because I sense this group of people means a lot to the Viper.

"As am I."

"Who was she?"

"She was timeless." The Viper giggles, like her response is a secret that only she might enjoy. "She was the Dragon."

I mentally log the code names. The Viper. The Crow. The Dragon. "Did my mom go by another name?"

"Naturally. She was the Bat."

I nod, now familiar with the bats that are connected to the shadow. That's when I notice the tear in the photograph, split at the end, where only a solitary arm remains beside the Dragon. There's an electric-blue sleeve that ends at the hand, but the rest is missing.

"Who was at the end?"

The Viper glances down. "Ah, I didn't do a particularly good job of editing that picture, now did I? The Butterfly left before our business was finished."

"Your business? Was this some sort of club?"

The Viper rises from her chair, towering over me. Commanding and exquisite. "I suppose you could call us a club, although I'd considered us friends. We preferred to be called the Continuum."

I wait for her to elaborate because I can sense she has more to say. She's taking her time, but this is her tent. Her rules.

"The council was founded to keep magic in a tight loop. It starts and stops between generations, but we dared to think bigger. Differently. As you know"—the Viper leisurely strolls about the tent like a professor in front of a chalkboard—"magic flows from parent to child." She grabs a water pitcher and pours a few drops into a cup. "It's a slow and steady stream so that there's always a balance, one of the vessels is never completely full and there's never truly an opportunity for either to reach its full potential."

"That's how it's always been," Ellison comments.

The Viper ignores her. "Death was always the tipping point between the two. A bottleneck if you will. *But*"—she strikes a finger into the air and takes a dramatic pause—"if the rules of death didn't apply, well then . . ." The Viper's golden eyes get hazy and far off. "Then there was no limit to what you could do."

I get the unsettling feeling that the shadow hanging from my neck was pivotal to the Continuum's goal.

The Viper takes a sip of the water and shakes her head. "But those were the thoughts of young fools." She smiles at me again and flicks her tongue behind her teeth. "You haven't asked about the last person."

She's right, I haven't. A suspicion took root the moment I saw the photo and I've been holding out hope that I'm right. Standing behind my mother, arms draped intimately around her neck, is a man. Like the Dragon, his face has a red *X* scribbled through it, but unlike the Dragon, someone went to the trouble of trying to scratch the marker off. As a result, his face is half blotched and smeared, but I can just make out a horrid scar running from ear to ear.

I match the Viper's gaze, feeding into the feeling that in this tent it's better if I'm bold. Instead of asking a question, I make a statement.

"That's my father."

The Viper taps her chin. "Henry Prudence."

I try to remain steady and calm, not baring the slightest hint that this is the first photograph of my father I've ever seen. But my voice comes out meek as a timid child. "He's dead."

The Viper's eyes flicker with glee. "Henry Prudence may have died, but that doesn't mean he's dead."

45.

LYRIC

Shit.

Mullory goes eerily silent after the Viper drops the bomb of the century. I'm stunned, but I move closer to her, squeezing her trembling hand.

"But he died," Mullory whispers.

The Viper considers her response, and her eyes dart quickly over me as she flicks a wrist in my direction. "He was dead, too."

I freeze. Mullory spins to face me. "I wasn't the first to pull a boy from thin air," she says quietly. I nod, encouraging her, because we're headed to the same conclusion. "My mom pulled my dad back from the dead."

"I think so," I say.

"I know so," the Viper insists.

Mullory doesn't take the bait the Viper offers and keeps her gaze intently on me. Her gray eyes flicker, uncertainty transitioning to hurt. "Why would she lie to me?"

I don't know how to respond; the moment is too intimate, too heavy, and we're being watched from all angles in a tent of obscure oddities.

"My entire life. She lied to me."

I don't get the chance to respond, because the Viper sweeps in. "She betrayed us, too, if it's any consolation. We were supposed to be her friends."

"She wouldn't—"

The Viper sighs heavily and cuts Mullory off. "She already did. It's her fault the Skeleton Singer ended up in the labyrinth. Her fault the Dragon is dead. Certainly, her fault that I'm reduced to this, a life of solitude." The Viper waves her arms around the tent.

Mullory responds with a single question. "Why?"

"Let's just say it's not suitable for me to be around people for a very long time. When you play with death, death always wins. But that's the price you pay for the things you do when you're young." The Viper flashes a cruel smile.

"Did you kill someone, too?" Mullory's lower lip wobbles.

The Viper's smile broadens, extending to her eyes as she lets out a shrill little laugh. "Do you really want to know?" There's something unsettling about her response, as if she wants Mullory to fall headfirst into a trap so that she might watch her squirm.

Mullory pivots. "Do you know where my father is?"

The Viper shakes a finger in Mullory's face. "That's not why you're here."

"Why are we here then?" Cruz asks boldly.

The Viper takes her time, waltzing past us, barefoot, the excess fabric of her elaborate dress sweeping the floor like a tail. "I believe you brought something for me." She pauses in front of one of the tattoo chairs. "You did bring something?" she asks, irritated. "I was told this would be a bargain of sorts."

Mullory shakes off her backpack and rummages through it. She pulls out the cardboard box, which has taken a beating from all our travels. "This is all we have left." She offers up the stick of gum.

There's no possible way that a measly stick of gum satisfies the Viper, but her eyes glow greedily as she snatches it from Mullory's fingers. At this point I should just accept that I have absolutely no idea what's going to happen.

The Viper holds up the stick of gum; the aluminum packaging gleams as she delicately unfolds it. I catch a faint whiff of something minty with a coppery note. Rusty like pennies and blood.

"Why do you want that?" Ellison braves to ask.

"None of your business." The Viper opens her mouth and gently places the gum on her tongue.

She tips her head toward the ceiling as we wait in anticipation.

For what—I have no idea. Watching a mildly unhinged woman chew a stick of gum was not on today's agenda. Mullory tenses beside me and that's when I notice something bubbling beneath the Viper's skin, as if bugs are trapped and skittering across her bones.

The movement intensifies and the two tattooed snakes peel away from her neck and slither up her face. Their eyes are red as jewels, as are the Viper's. Bloodlust or some magic shit I don't want to understand.

"Pretties," she coos, and the snakes slink back down her arms and onto the floor, their dark oily scales moving in a slippery pattern.

The Viper licks her lips, satisfied.

I have no idea what the hell just happened, and I don't want to. "You got what you want, now it's our turn," I say.

"You're smarter than you look for a boy just back from the dead."

"The bargain," I remind her.

The Viper studies her nails, almost bored, then turns to Mullory. "Fine. For you, Mullory Prudence, the first thing I have is a message."

"Yes?"

"When you get to the party, look for the man with one eye. Tell him you've come for your present."

I can tell Mullory is dissecting every word. "How do you know I'll get to a party?" she asks.

The Viper just rolls her eyes. "Now the second thing I'll offer you is a choice." She extends one empty hand. "You can choose to have all your questions answered. Everything you seek, past or present. Or"—the Viper extends her other hand, palm flipped open—"you can choose an item that will help someone you care about. I'll warn you that it will be something they desperately need."

Mullory considers the offer.

"Take the answers," I urge her.

"How do you know that the person I care about will need it?"

The Viper crosses her arms. "Because that's what my magic does. It lets me see a moment in your future, one of desperation, of grave need."

I know Mullory can't take both and she should choose the answers, end this quest. It might be our only chance, but I also know Mullory. And so does her mother, because she's the one who designed this hunt.

"I'll take the item."

"As you wish." The Viper leads us over to the tattoo chair. She flicks on the light, stretches a pair of black latex gloves over her hands, and pats the seat.

Surely now Mullory will change her mind, but she surprises us all as she plops down on the leather chair.

"Good girl. Now roll up your sleeve." The Viper turns on the tattoo gun and it purrs to life as she dips it in a well of black ink.

Mullory doesn't even flinch as the Viper drags the needle across her forearm.

"And because I'm feeling generous, this tattoo holds a message for more than just you."

More cryptic nonsense. The tattoo doesn't take long, two dainty butterflies with delicate black wings are inked on Mullory's fair skin.

Mullory turns her arm over, inspecting. “What do I do with it?”

“When love is about to fall, use it.” The Viper wraps gauze over the tattoo and yanks Mullory’s sleeve down.

“You’re not going to tell me any more, are you?”

“Not a thing.”

Mullory stands to leave. “Thank you.”

The Viper narrows her eyes. “I wouldn’t thank me just yet.”

46.

This clue is undoubtedly the most deceiving. I can't help but admire the ingenuity of its design as I turn the seemingly simple stick of gum between my fingers. It's what's imbued in the gum that matters. Every member demands a payment, a wicked desire indulged. But that was the price they were willing to pay to cheat death. At the very least that's what they believed.

47.
ELLISON

"I think we're done here, unless anyone else wants a tattoo and hepatitis C?"

No one answers, which I interpret as a resounding yes. "Didn't think so."

I'm resigned to leave this freakish tent behind me when a soft hiss catches my ear. Then another hiss—this one is more drawn out, and I trace it to the vibrating tail of a scorpion tattooed on the Viper's left bicep.

The hissing intensifies and the scorpion peels away, bloating from a flattened tattoo to a physical creature that scuttles down the Viper's forearm, resting on her wrist. Its tail arcs forward, curling over its carapace body before the thornlike stinger pierces the flesh between the tendons of the Viper's hand.

Mullory audibly inhales.

Reina flinches.

I try my best not to scream.

The Viper's eyes roll back, whites exposed, and a sound that's equal parts pleasure and pain gurgles up her throat. Her neck snaps forward, and alarm spikes across her face.

"You have uninvited guests approaching."

Cruz steps forward, insulted. "Impossible."

The Viper only shrugs and traces a finger along the scorpion's segmented shell. "Wait and see for yourselves then."

Reina has panic in her eyes.

Without her saying so, I suddenly realize what has happened. "We need to move."

Mullory matches my stance, ready to bolt.

But Cruz is arrogantly insistent, cornering Reina. "What happened?"

A quick glance in my direction, because I was there in her moment of weakness when all her defenses crumbled. "I may have let my guard down." Reina's voice bubbles up, a plea for forgiveness.

Cruz buries his face in his hands.

Reina clutches her stack of watches. "I can—"

"Don't." His tone is gentler than I'd like to give him credit for.

"But I can fix it," Reina begs.

Cruz shakes his head. "Too risky."

I still feel an irrational need to intervene. "No point discussing it. We need to go."

The Viper glides to the back of her tent, lifting the edge. "This is the most direct route. If I were you, I'd follow the roller coaster. And I'd run." Her eyes glow a murderous red, spiked by whatever poison the scorpion released. "Fast."

Lyric studies her. "Why should we trust you?"

A cruel smile. "No reason to trust me. But then again, no reason not to."

Mullory edges past her and we hurry into the darkness.

48.

MULLORY

Moonlight glimmers on the snow-covered path as a line of gloomy storm clouds rolls in. Squinting in the low light, I note a dilapidated fence that lies on the outskirts of the park, shielding it from the sea. There's a rickety structure of wooden beams that lulls up and down, mimicking the waves, and capped with the metal track of a roller coaster.

I break into a run.

No time to think or bicker about trusting the Viper.

Instead, we dash as fast as the snow permits, hearts thumping in our chests, like hunted prey. Mindless and erratic.

My quads burn, my lungs ache.

Ellison huffs behind me as Cruz eases past both of us.

A sudden burst, and snow explodes around us, descending in a violent surge as a grueling wind howls.

"This way." Lyric's voice strains over the gusts. His hand finds mine, and I follow his tug as the snow pummels our faces.

A blessed break in the storm, an unnatural pause of silence that's quickly followed by a voice that booms across the park.

"I KNOW YOU'RE HERE, LYRIC."

Terror weeds its way down all my limbs.

"I WILL FIND YOU." Lord Thorn relishes his words, almost with a singsong glee.

We race beneath slatted supports; snow crusts my lashes and blurs my sight as we slip beneath the looming coaster. The wood groans and sways as if it's equally terrified of being hunted. Lord Thorn has been trailing us for a while, first at the Skeleton Singer's lair, then the coffee shop; now he's finally caught up to us.

"Reina!" A desperate plea from Cruz. "Can you hide us?"

She's a flickering dot in the snow. "I'm trying, but they still know we're here."

"Don't stop moving." Cruz ignores his own instructions, waving us forward one by one.

Thunder cracks as a bolt of lightning splits the sky. But lightning... in a snowstorm?

"Damn it!" Cruz bellows. "They've brought Eloise."

Eloise must command lightning. Snow bites into my exposed neck, plundering down in an oppressive curtain.

Another crack and a dizzying flash, as if someone turned on all the lights for just a second. Reina's run slows to a jog, and she waves a hand to move me forward. "Don't look back."

But of course, I do.

Another frenzied bolt slices the sky as I spin.

Lord Thorn's shape lurches closer. Others beside him move just as quickly and with the same bravado.

A thunderbolt strikes the merry-go-round, charring the peak and sending one of the horses crashing into the snow.

"Hurry, we're close," someone yells.

A firm tug at my sleeve.

I'm moving again, stumbling. I can almost make out the park entrance when the next burst lights the sky. I can feel and hear them getting closer and my heart rate soars.

We're almost to the end of the roller coaster when another scorching bolt strikes. Something sparks and glittering bits of fire pepper the snow.

"Watch out!"

I'm shoved forcefully to my side by Lyric, who topples down beside me as a metal cart from the coaster plunges through the falling snow. As it slams the ground the metal lurches, twisting and tumbling onto Lyric's leg.

"LYRIC!" screams Lord Thorn, panicked that he won't be the one to execute the kill.

My fear spikes again when I see the gnarled metal pinning Lyric down.

"My boot's caught," Lyric groans. "But I think my leg is okay, if we can just move it." He leans forward, trying to push the cart himself.

Something in my chest tightens and my limbs go limp. Snow slides up my sleeve as I sink deeper, unable to move. The pressure builds, and a quiet voice urges me to run.

Cruz crouches down near Lyric, straining to push the heap of metal away.

Sweat slips down my icy brow.

"Mullory, help," Cruz moans, digging his heels into the snow.

I want to help, I want nothing more than to save Lyric, but it's as if my body is under some sort of spell.

"Mullory." Lyric's voice cuts through the storm and anchors me. "Please."

I surface from whatever fog I was trapped in and spring forward, thrusting my arms against the metal.

"Almost."

I push until the metal sears into my palms, until my calves tremble, and it's just enough for Lyric to shimmy free.

He taps his forehead to my temple and nudges me. “Keep moving.”

We dart forward in a smear of white and wind.

“I’ve got you.” Reina catches us. “This way.”

Her magic feels thicker, some exoskeleton that drapes over us as the front gate finally comes into view.

This time, I don’t dare look back.

49.

MULLORY

No one says a single thing for quite some time.

The only sound is the wind rattling the car windows as we traverse a backdrop of bleak skies. I don't uncurl my fingers from the edge of the seat either; the muscles in my arms have gone numb, anticipating a clap of thunder or a burst of lightning. Even in the silence, my ears still ring from the sounds.

"I think we're in the clear," Reina finally says. "I don't want to hear a word about anything else."

None of us bring up our close run-in with Lord Thorn.

When I finally ease up a bit, my mind races back to the Viper, to whom we gave our very last clue. Now it's gone, and it has the regretful aftertaste of an ending. A finality I'm not willing to accept. In some odd way, the box full of clues was a comfort, a set of possibilities.

And what do we have to show for it?

Life-changing news that I haven't even begun to unpack.

More riddles, a new tattoo that Gran surely won't approve of, and a message. *"When you get to the party, look for the man with one eye. Tell him you've come for your present."* I didn't tell the Viper that my social calendar is wide open, not a planned party in sight.

I can't help but itch the sleeve of my jacket, where my skin is still tender and raw from the needle. Maybe I should have chosen the answers instead, but how could I not help someone I care about?

"Well, that was fun," Ellison declares as she peels off her winter layers, warmed by the heat of the car. "More riddles, more people trying to kill us."

I nod. She does have a point.

"What do we do next?" asks Reina.

Everyone turns toward me, expecting a plan. I shuffle with the contents of my backpack, fidgeting with the zipper. "I did take this." I pull out the photo from the Viper's den. "I had no idea my mom was in this Continuum. Have you guys ever heard of it?" A part of me is embarrassed that I have to ask other people about my mom's past, because I'm the last person who should be kept in the dark.

Cruz shakes his head. Lyric and Ellison mirror him.

Reina shrugs. "Secret society, they seemed to be friends."

The word *friends* shakes a memory loose.

"You don't have any friends." It was the cruelest thing I'd ever said to my mom. But I was fuming, she'd been gone for weeks. She'd missed my first lost tooth.

"That's not true, Mullory," my mom had responded with a whine. "I have friends."

"Then where are they?"

"They're . . ." My mom tried to divert my attention with a cupcake, but I held strong. Her shoulders caved. "They're all over. Sometimes when we try to do the right thing, we can hurt our friends, even if we don't mean it."

"But why would you hurt them?"

My mom pulled at her hair, eyes darting around the room. "Let's go on a hunt instead."

I crossed my arms. "Why would you hurt them?"

"Because they were going to hurt other people. Not on purpose. But because they wanted something."

I tried to understand. "What did they want?"

My mom grabbed both my hands in hers. "One day I'll show you, I promise. Only when you're ready. And one day you'll meet Mina, my very best friend."

I squeezed her hands back, excited by the thought of my mom having a best friend. "Okay."

"Mullory?" Lyric's voice brings me back.

"Yeah." I exhale. "Keeping secrets seems to be one of my mom's favorite hobbies." I don't want to cry. In fact, crying is the very last thing I want to do, but looking down at the photo, I don't know if I can hold back my tears. Is one of them Mina? Why would my mom betray her friends? Why would she want me to know that she did? How is this supposed to get me ready for whatever I'm supposed to do next?

And what about my father? A figure from my past that I never dared to understand or question because I was so preoccupied with chasing after my mom. I'd just always thought of him as gone, so far removed from my life that he was inconsequential.

But he's right here, and although his face is smeared from the scribbled *X*, I can still tell he was smiling. A relaxed, happy smile despite the ragged scar coursing his face. *"Henry Prudence may have died, but that doesn't mean he's dead."*

Another secret kept from me by my mom. Who else knew? Why am I always the last to find out? And why did he never try to find me? Why is it always me doing the chasing?

"Mullory." Lyric nudges me and that's when I realize I *am* crying. "Shoot," I mumble, and wipe my cheeks with my sleeves. "My mom always told me my father was dead, and I just accepted it."

"She must have had a reason not to tell you," Cruz offers softly.

"All she ever had were reasons." But all I ever wanted were answers. I take out my phone and snap a photo of the picture, zooming in, searching for something. Anything.

"His outfit's odd, don't you think?" Reina says.

It *is* odd, some sort of coveralls. I pinch my fingers across the screen and enlarge it. The image gets pixelated and grainy, but I can just make out a patch sewn over his chest. I fiddle with it a bit, but I can make out the inscription.

"Prudence Butchery," I read.

"But is that relevant? Is it even a clue?" Cruz counters. "I mean, the coffee shop led us to the Viper, who gave you that message. The photograph was just extra."

I chew the edge of a nail; I know he's right. Whatever winding maze the search for my father would take us on, it would probably deviate from the course set by my mom. Because for some reason, I don't think she wanted me to find him. I can only hope the two paths intersect, but I have no way of knowing that. A quick glance at Lyric and I know we need to stick to the original plan.

"You're right," I say, and shove the photo back into my backpack. "We work on what the Viper gave us. The only problem is I don't have any idea what party she could be talking about."

"I do." Lyric pulls away from me and collapses in the corner, arms crossed to his chest. "Who do we know who loves to throw a party?"

Oh.

Lyric closes his eyes briefly, accepting the heavy truth. "Uncle's back."

50.

XAVIER STOUTMIRE

Edwin has called several times, trying and failing to hide his rising hysteria. The china has been unruly, and the hedges have been unseasonably active. I fear it will only get worse.

It's time for me to return home.

I may not have found it in time, but I know *she* did.

I may be returning empty-handed, but not without a plan, instructions from my cousin Cecilia. *"Xavier, dear, kill."*

51.
LYRIC

I was tense when we scaled the mountain and ventured into the Skeleton Singer's nightmare of an aviary.

And you could say I was also tense in the Viper's den.

But now I'm *tense* tense. Ready to jump out of my skin tense. I should've known when the word *party* was used. Dead giveaway.

Uncle loves nothing more than a reason to show off. Vain bastard. And I just know—I can feel it in the marrow of my bones—that he must be back. Any lingering connection between us I find unpleasant and unwelcome, and I hate that I know I'm right.

"Oh." Ellison claps her hands together as we wind up the driveway toward the estate. I don't need to look to know that the life-size ice sculptures are once again skating flawlessly across the ice, twirling through the air with precision.

Lately, with Mullory in charge they had begun to wobble and fall, breaking off into chunks. I don't want to look; I liked it better when they cracked.

But the red and green strobe lights swirling around the giant frosted trees are kind of hard to ignore. Blinding me with Uncle's ego. At first, I wanted him to be on the estate—some delusional part of me thought he might be able to help. But he never really helps; he only makes it worse. And every bit of me dreads facing him again.

The air in the entryway is laced with hints of nutmeg and cinnamon. I drag myself inside, not bothering to shake off the snow from my boots. Edwin is much more chipper, beaming in a knit sweater with actual twinkling lights.

"Welcome back!" He grins.

"Your boots," a stiff voice booms from behind. And there it is, my uncle's big welcoming hug—reprimanding me for snowy boots. It takes all my restraint not to lash out.

Uncle X makes his appearance, slow and dramatic, winding around in a red-and-white-striped sequin suit with peppermint-swirled candies sewn onto the sleeves. I don't miss the slight limp in his step. What were you up to, Uncle?

"If you all plan on staying," he says curtly, his voice echoing up the expansive entryway, "then I suppose you'll be invited to my party in two days on Christmas Eve. Dress accordingly."

And that's it. A comment about my boots, and an invite to a stupid party with a dress code.

"Xavier," Mullory boldly calls while attempting to rush after him. She undoubtedly has questions he's been avoiding. But Uncle merely waves his hands without turning around and a stampede of warthogs come barreling toward Mullory.

Their aggressive snorting has her turning quickly on her heels. "Okay, maybe later then," she calls.

The pain in my chest intensifies as I watch Uncle limp away, before he simply disappears.

"A party," Mullory says with determination. "Do you have the guest list, Edwin?"

"Certainly, Miss Mullory, right here." He flips open a binder.

"Any chance one of the guests is missing an eye?"

"I'm not sure, Miss Ellison."

Mullory gazes over the list, turning suddenly pale. "The council's invited?"

"They're always invited," Edwin answers. "Xavier has this party every year."

"Lyric," she says, sinking her teeth into her lower lip. "Lyric, what do we—"

But I can't think about any of that right now, not with my uncle here—my head is spinning. White-hot anger and panic burn up my insides, as well as, dare I admit, some twisted sense of comfort? All three mix in a momentous wave that propels me forward.

I'm moving, practically sprinting, through the estate, trying to find an outlet for my adrenaline. I don't want to talk to Uncle, but I *need* to.

I'm antsy by my sixth go-around, mentally fatigued from playing out different conversations in my head. Pent up with a rage that's slowly being hollowed out by the disappointment of my uncle not looking for me first.

I spot Mullory in the library, a thoughtful expression on her face as she studies the endless shelves of books. The nervous energy coursing my veins makes me impulsive and I don't think as I stride beside her and take her hand in mine. I don't think about Uncle, or the magic I'm steadily becoming obsessed with. I don't dare think about what's best for her, I just think of her touch, how her fingers are interwoven between mine, how her body leans in, guided by some undeniable magnetism.

Mullory runs her free hand across the spines of several books. "I tried to find your uncle again."

"What did he set after you this time?"

"Hyenas. Although they could have been coyotes, I'm not sure."

"Ah, definitely hyenas. One of his favorites."

Mullory twirls the amber stone around her neck. Her voice is tired, yet still inquisitive. "How do you think it works?"

"The shadow?"

"Yeah." She exhales.

I tug her the rest of the way near me. "I think..." Impulsiveness takes the reins again, sharing thoughts that only surfaced in the darkest moments of my death. "I think maybe magic is tied to your soul. When you fully cross over the magic is lost because it can't survive without that part of you still living."

Mullory's brow furrows.

I picture my soul rotting and festering away from Lord Thorn's compulsion magic, a charred, burnt thing. "Maybe."

She tips her chin toward me. A longing in her eyes that nearly undoes me. "I didn't think you'd be one to believe in souls." Her lips twist into a smile.

"Why not?" I slide my arm behind the small of her back and sway ever so slightly. I can almost feel her heart spike. She blushes, and my own pulse skyrockets in response.

But Mullory's arms suddenly go rigid, and a frightened expression spreads across her face.

For a second, I think she can see me. See through me, right down to the parts that I'm desperate to hide. How I've gone behind her back and used the shadow. How I enjoy the feel of Lord Thorn's magic.

"Do you think that's why it won't work?" she finally asks. "Do you think something's wrong with my soul?"

I shake my head. "Never." But then I flash a mischievous grin. "Although maybe it's because your soul is getting too close to mine."

Mullory relaxes and her eyes twinkle as she swings her arms up around my neck and nestles her head, whispering into my shoulder, "You think our souls are close?"

I kiss the crown of her head and start to rock us again, an almost dance. In the quiet of the library, in this improbably perfect moment, I let another truth slip out. "I don't think there's any part of me that wouldn't try to find you." But that truth is tamped down, because in reality I'd tear the entire goddamn world to shreds to find her.

I feel Mullory's breathing hitch, her grip tightens, and she pulls away, forcing me to meet her gaze that nearly cuts me to pieces. "I won't lose you again, Lyric." And then she grabs my neck and kisses me. Fiercely, as if she needs me.

My entire body lights up as snow starts to fall from the ceiling.

"It's snowing."

My voice is husky. "I see that," I say, not giving a damn about the snow. "Sometimes it storms in here." I pull her close again, my body desperate to be near hers.

"Soul to soul," she whispers.

I don't want to let go of her. But my nerves jostle me, reminding me that my uncle is here. I let my fingers trail down her spine, before whispering in her ear as I pull away, "I'll find you later."

And then I dart away before I can think better of it.

I don't need to search for long as I stumble across Uncle shuffling past his study.

"Don't you have anything to say?"

Uncle X pauses but doesn't even have the decency to turn around. "Do you need something, Lyric?"

My blood boils and the magic takes it from there. It's funny how easily it comes to life. It's like there's a set of invisible strings anchored to my uncle and all I have to do is tug at them. His knees give out as his body betrays his mind and he's forced to turn around with the jerky motion of a puppet.

Ahhh, and his face—an expression I've never seen my uncle display. *Surprise.* For once in all the years I've been here, our roles are reversed. I'm the one in power, looming over my uncle.

"I died."

Uncle X's left knee cracks into place as he puts weight on it. "That was never the plan."

I laugh. "Oh right. The plan was for Mullory to die and me to *maybe* win your magic, even though I was the one who lived with you. Who endured all your games. But that was never enough."

Dark circles frame Uncle's eyes, and he looks frailer and more worn down than I remember. "It was always more complicated than that. The plan was to avoid this." Uncle stares at me like a disappointed parent. But he has no right. None at all.

"Your plan was shit," I say boldly. Part of me has already winced, preparing for some illusionary attack. A bear to jump from the walls and claw at me or a fiery lasso to snap around my ankles.

But Uncle only nods, looking dejected. "I've failed you, Lyric, and I'm not sure if I can ever make it right."

I'm too stunned to answer as he hobbles away.

Finally, the closest to an apology I've ever gotten, and him in a weakened state. So why the hell do I feel even worse? Maybe because I wanted Uncle to challenge me, to show some emotion, to fight.

52.

MULLORY

Fleece-lined pajamas in an adorable snowman print are folded neatly on my bed and in just the right size. The floor beneath my bare feet is warm and there's a hot cup of cocoa with reindeer-shaped marshmallows set by the crackling fire. The holly-strung tree in the corner is twirling, and there are a pair of live cardinals nestled in the branches; they hum carols if I get close enough.

No silverware tries to kill us, and the china has all returned to normal. I didn't need to check to know that the newborn hedges are fully warmed and sprouting leaves. Xavier Stoutmire is back. Maybe I should be relieved—one less thing for me to worry about—but it feels more like a failed test. That there's something wrong with me, a reason Xavier's illusionary magic won't work. That maybe my soul is torn or tattered. Or my gene for magic mutated.

I know Xavier has answers; it's his magic, after all. But he's the most stubborn man I've ever met. On my third attempt to find him, I had to bribe and practically beg Zolan to tell me where he'd seen him. I caught a glimpse of Xavier's sequin suit by the library, but when I rushed inside, I was greeted by a large, irate grizzly bear in a top hat.

And I know that right now I should be focused on the clues, on the riddle from the Skeleton Singer and the message from the Viper. *"Look for the man with one eye and tell him you've come for your present."* We already know where and when the party will occur. The only problem is that the council will be there. That's what I need to spend the next two days working on: a way to evade them while still being able to find this man with one eye. That's the rational plan, the responsible one.

But that's my *mom's* plan, her winding hunt and need for riddles. *"Henry Prudence may have died, but that doesn't mean he's dead."* I've spent most of my life chasing after my mom . . . but what about my dad? Where has he been the past sixteen years? Does he even want to be found? Why would he never come looking for me? That's the hardest question to face, because it forces me to consider the possibility that maybe he wants nothing to do with me.

And why is it even a choice I have to make? Why must I pick between them?

"Don't you want to find your presents? You love the hunt, Mullory." My mom's smile was falling, as she stood beneath a bundle of balloons, my birthday clues clutched in her fingers. "This is your favorite part."

I eyed the treasure map, the long-winded riddles I'd have to solve to claim my gifts. But a different question haunted me. "Where's my dad?"

My mom faltered, tripping on the tangle of balloon strings. "You know he's gone."

I shuffled my feet, unsatisfied with the response. "You never talk about him."

Her green eyes welled. "That doesn't mean I don't think about him. One day I'll explain, I promise."

My shoulders sagged, I was growing tired of collecting promises.

"It's hard for me to share." My mom offered this bit of truth: "It's hard to talk about someone we love when they're lost, because they take little pieces of us with them. And we don't ever get those pieces back."

A light knock breaks my memory as Lyric slips into my room. He's freshly showered—his hair sleek and wet—clad in a black sweatshirt and shorts. No snowman pj's for him. My heart does this funny little leap, and every inch of my skin feels fizzy, like my blood is made of soda pop. In the library, I was brave enough to kiss him, unable to wonder any longer what he was waiting for. He was just as desperate, but now his posture is stiff, his expression strained.

"What's wrong?" But of course, I already know the answer. The one he can't seem to say, as his fingers curl into fists and he closes his eyes, dark lashes fluttering toward his cheekbones. "Come here," I say, making room for him to sit.

Lyric crawls onto my bed, nudging my side, so that I can feel him shaking. Vibrating with tension.

"Did you try to talk to him?"

Lyric laughs, curling his knees to his chest. I reach over and brush a strand of hair from his eyes.

"There's no point in talking to my uncle." He turns to me, pressing his fist to his lips, his next words a raspy whisper. "He doesn't even care."

And there it is. Lyric's truth that he's dragged around his entire life. Despite how he pretends to be unshakable and emotionless, deep down what he's always wanted is simple. For Xavier to care. And I have no idea what Xavier Stoutmire thinks or feels, but I know exactly what Lyric does, because I've yearned for the exact same thing. I've spent my life chasing my mom, desperate for her to come looking for me. Wanting her to find me.

I link my hand through his. "I care." My voice doesn't waver, because I believe each word.

Lyric inhales and holds my gaze for what feels like an eternity, before his face breaks into a smile.

I smile back. We don't stop smiling at each other, loopy, stupid smiles, and I have no idea how much time passes. All I know is I want Lyric to kiss me. Why won't he kiss me again?

Instead, he tugs me close so that I crumple into his side. And now feels like as a good time as any: "Lyric, I know we have the party, but—"

"You want to go look for him." He finishes my thought so that I don't have to.

I nod into his side, relief flooding out of me in the form of cotton-candy pink and blue lollipops that rain down onto our laps. Xavier's magic makes absolutely no sense.

"I figured," he says quietly, while smiling at the rainbow-wrapped candies. "We'll go tomorrow."

"But the party."

"We'll figure that out after."

I nestle tighter, letting my breathing match his. Steady and slow. Warmed with the thought that Lyric understands me, he knows exactly what I need, as I drift into sleep.

53.
ELLISON

There are three things I absolutely loathe.

Public transportation of any variety.

Coupons.

And, most notably, asking anyone for help with anything. Except maybe Whitaker, but he doesn't count as just anyone.

That's why I'm currently pacing the solarium, fidgety and flustered. Usually, I'd do things on my own to avoid the inevitable disappointment when the other person fails. Because they *will* fail in some way, at some time. My mother taught me that years ago.

But I'm desperate and out of options and my brother is more concerned with Mullory Prudence than with his own life. A life that, I don't need to remind him, he already lost once because of that girl. And I also don't need to remind him that the council is looking for him and that Lord Thorn has already printed a death certificate with his name on it.

And my plan? Try to find the mysterious woman who infiltrated my mother's dream seventeen years ago. A woman who I suspect might be the same person who gave Mullory's gran that box of clues. It's not exactly foolproof. Or sturdy. It's the do-it-yourself furniture of plans—wobbling particleboard assembled with missing screws.

"Ellison."

I didn't bother to turn the lights on. "You're late."

"Cruz wouldn't stop talking. Sorry," says Reina. "So, what can I do to help?"

I cringe at the suggestion of her help. I barely know her, and I don't like that she's related to a boy who openly murdered his brothers.

"You said you could help with my dream magic." I force the words out.

Reina steps closer, carefully finding her way through the dark. "What are you trying to do with it?"

"That's not your concern."

"Right," she mumbles. "Well, when you're under the dream magic, I can neutralize it, if need be. Make it go away if you get stuck."

"Fine." I settle onto the floor, cross-legged.

Reina does the same. "I'll be here if you need me," she offers. "I've seen people get lost in dreams, and if I see that happening, I can pull you out."

I'm grateful for the cover of darkness that helps mask my panic. Sweat beads across my forehead and my heart hammers in my chest. I'm uncomfortable on every level imaginable.

"You're not alone, Ellison. I'll be right here."

I want to laugh, but I don't. Maybe because there's some comfort in what she says.

"Whenever you're ready," she says softly.

I try my best to take a settling breath, but my body has never taken to meditation, and I end up gasping as I release the inner boundaries keeping my mother's dream magic at bay. It swirls inside me, frantic and excited. My eyelids close and I'm thrown into an absolute darkness that's completely disorienting and detached from my body. To the place that's not a place at all. Spinning, sinking, unhinged. Alice in freaking Wonderland.

The voices come next, followed by flashes and images that don't make sense. Blurred and fused together without purpose as only dreams can be. It's like muddling through someone else's mind. I do my best to focus, to think of a woman who visited my mother, to remember exactly what she said. But I might as well be searching for a diamond in a sandstorm. And that's when I panic and pivot and fall into something horrible.

A nightmare. Someone else's. I can tell right away: The air is pungent with sulfur, and pure panic, setting my teeth on edge. Danger lurks. I'm able to orient myself in some sort of forest and that's when I notice someone lying helpless and wounded. Blood gurgles up from a nasty leg wound and I can sense a predator nearby—this is someone's ending. The type of nightmare that ends with death.

"Hello, brother," a voice hums, as if it's made of the darkness itself. It rattles down my spine. I want to shout at the person collapsed in a pool of blood to run. But I'm just as helpless.

"Don't do this," the boy on the ground begs.

I know this voice.

Cruz Lagunes.

I don't have time to react as his brother lunges forward, and all I can do is scream before the entire scene dissolves into nothing.

"Ellison. Ellison." A voice tugs me back, and a warm hand squeezes my wrist. "You're okay."

Light floods the solarium; Reina must have flicked the switch. I pull my wrist away from her, not wanting to be touched.

"What happened?" she asks.

"Not what I wanted to happen, obviously."

"Are you okay?" Reina's gaze is sincere.

My response is shockingly truthful. "I don't know."

"Most days, I don't know either. But what you're doing is brave."

I scoff. "You have no idea what I'm trying to do."

"Maybe not. But I can guess it has to do with Lyric. Somehow you think you can save him by facing the thing you fear."

I pinch the skin around my wrist. "You're making me sound far better than I am."

Reina shakes her head. "No. I'm stating the truth. Maybe you just need to hear it."

54.

MULLORY

I'm up early. The sun has just cracked the sky open and faint light spills into my room. I'm determined to find out as much as I can about my father today. I have no idea, after all these years of lying, why my mom now wants me to know he was murdered. What am I missing? Can I be certain Lord Thorn murdered my father? And why does it matter so much if my mom used the shadow and brought him back anyway?

Lyric is still here, wound tightly in my blankets. His dark hair has dried in every direction, but he looks peaceful on my pillow. I leave him there and tiptoe out of my room.

I change quickly in the bathroom and steal one last glance at him before I slip into the hall. Most of the estate is still asleep as I meander toward the kitchen.

Hushed voices spilling out of the parlor catch my attention and I press my ear to the door.

Xavier groans. "I'm trying to intervene. That's what I've been doing since I left."

Before I storm in to face Xavier, I have the sense to listen in and gather as much information as I can.

"And you think that's wise, sir?" asks Edwin.

"I'm not entirely certain I've had a wise thought in quite a few years."

A long pause, followed by Edwin, his voice quieter still. "Have you found the other thing you were looking for?"

Finally, a clue. But what has Xavier Stoutmire been looking for?

"I'm afraid in my old age, I've grown slow. Suffice it to say, *she* beat me to it."

I cover my gaping mouth with my hand. Who beat Xavier Stoutmire, and to what? Edwin hurries out, nearly knocking me over with the door. I regain my footing and turn to hurry into the parlor. But of course, it's empty.

"Where did he go?"

Edwin's face remains neutral. "He's busy, I'm afraid."

"Could you at least tell me where he's been?"

"I cannot. Even I don't know the specifics. But perhaps some coffee instead?"

I follow Edwin into the kitchen, still puzzling over what Xavier could be searching for. Over who the *she* was that bested him.

"Breakfast will be ready in an hour. And if I may, Miss Mullory, some advice?"

"Of course."

"I suspect you want answers concerning Xavier's magic."

I try not to seem too eager, but Edwin is far too observant.

"Don't be so hard on yourself. Xavier struggled in the beginning with his magic as well."

"He did?"

"Of course. He turned his slippers into mice, and nearly drowned his aunt while trying to water the flowers," Edwin says with fondness.

"Thanks." I don't have the heart to tell him that this feels like something worse than mouse slippers.

"No, thank you." Edwin gives me a polite bow before leaving the kitchen.

"He's right, you know."

I swivel on the stool to face Cruz. "Were you listening?"

He helps himself to a cup and the carafe of coffee. "Just observing."

"That's the same thing."

Cruz slides up beside me. "It's true what Edwin said. The magic is more settled with Xavier because he's familiar to it."

"You make it sound like it's alive."

Cruz shrugs. "And I know you can use magic, because I've seen you do it already."

I take a sip of coffee—it's bitter and strong on my tongue—as I try to make sense of what Cruz just said. I'd been so preoccupied with the clues that I haven't been paying attention to all his odd little remarks. The fiery red dress he first tried to magic me into, whispering that I was different than he'd thought I would be. Whatever he was going to say on the Ferris wheel. And now this. How could he have possibly seen me use Xavier's magic if I never successfully have?

"What's really going on?" I ask. "No more secrets."

Cruz shakes his head. "Don't spoil the fun just yet, Mullory. Besides, we have a bigger matter to attend to. The council will be at the party. Could be tricky, considering they probably want to arrest you, force you to give up the shadow, and probably kill Lyric."

My panic rises, and I let whatever secret he's harboring go, because he's right, we do have a problem. "Can't Reina keep us hidden at the party?"

"To an extent, but we need to practice and make sure she can do it if we're all moving around. And then there's the problem of you needing to talk to the man with the one eye."

The coffee in my stomach churns as I fidget with my cup.

"Go on already, Mullory."

"Go on, what?" I say in an unusually high-pitched voice.

"If you want to know more about my brothers, all you have to do is ask."

I exhale, happy to change the subject and avoid discussing the council. "How's Mateo?"

Cruz lets out a short laugh. "Mateo despises me, as does Isadora, and I can't blame them. But that's not the brother I was referring to."

I hadn't planned on revisiting this conversation, but a part of me is deeply curious, a part of me needs to know. "Why couldn't you just let your oldest brother have your father's magic?"

Cruz laughs, but this time it's hollow and laced with pain. "I would've, gladly."

"But you didn't."

"No." Cruz shakes his head. "I didn't. I'm sure by now you can appreciate the delicate workings of a dysfunctional family. The unspoken rules and otherwise frowned-upon practices that are buried so deeply in the heart of the family unit you barely notice them at all. Arlo was the firstborn, followed shortly after by Daniel. Two children, quite an ordinary number."

"But your parents didn't stop at two."

Cruz shakes his head. "No, they didn't. When we were little, it was fun. Endless entertainment, we were always getting into something. But we could feel it building like a storm. As soon as Arlo could grasp just the smallest bit of my father's magic, everything shifted. He began to pull away."

"I still don't understand."

Cruz stretches his arms behind his head before swinging them at his sides. "I suppose if you wanted to understand my brothers, you'd have to understand my father first."

I can't help but imagine a childhood similar to Lyric's. "Was he cruel?"

"Not always. He was extremely calculated and often steps ahead of everyone else. But he could be kind in his own way. A kindness he would ration out like crumbs, waiting until we were on the brink of starvation. We'd try to do everything and anything to please him. Studying. Practicing. Listening. Fighting for just a morsel of his affection. If he ever gave it out, it didn't last long. And then you spent every minute after trying to win it back again."

"And your brothers fought for it?"

"We all did. Arlo fought the most fiercely, but he was also the weakest when it came to my father. He was the least resilient, and my father knew how to push him to the edge, only to reel him in with a pat on the back."

"But how does that explain what happened?" *How does that explain why you murdered them?*

Cruz ruffles his hair, clearly thinking, before landing on a moment worth sharing. "Arlo was always obsessed with these miniature kits that let you build skyscrapers. A meticulous, grueling hobby. But he'd spend hours. One day my father gifted him a four-thousand-piece replica of Big Ben. Arlo didn't sleep for days, he barely ate. He just glued those little toothpicks together, one by one, until it was finished." Cruz shrugs. "It was pretty cool I guess, in some insane way."

My stomach tightens anticipating the twist.

"My father told Arlo he was going to display it in his office so everyone in the company could see." Cruz buries his head in his hands. "He gave it to Daniel to carry to the car, insisting that he be the one to do it. Daniel was seven, and a total klutz. I watched him carry it, hidden from the top window. Daniel took three steps before the entire thing fell apart; every toothpick snapped into pieces. Arlo came running out screaming, totally hysteric."

"But it was an accident. . . ."

"I thought so, too, until I looked at my father." Cruz's voice fills with disgust. "He was smiling. Like it went exactly how he planned."

A sharp pain pierces my heart, and I lightly rest my hand on Cruz's arm. "He pitted you against one another."

Cruz refuses to look me in the eye. "He got more creative as we got older, upping the stakes, until Arlo was nearly eighteen and we went to our family's retreat for a grand hunt in the woods. But deep down, we all knew why we were really there."

My grip on Cruz's arm tightens; part of me doesn't want him to say it.

His chin lifts, and the honey centers of his eyes find me. "We were there to hunt one another."

"That's horrible."

Cruz shrugs, a monster who knows exactly what he is. "The truth is I killed them. I killed them both. But just because I did it doesn't mean I wanted to." His voice drifts away and he quickly stands. "Let's not forget we have a mystery to solve."

"We can work on that tomorrow." I leave my half-empty coffee cup and edge away from the island.

"Going somewhere?"

"I . . ." I've never been a good liar.

"Looking for a certain Henry Prudence?"

"It'll only take a day."

Cruz chugs his coffee down. "No problem, we'll come with. What says holiday more than a trip to the butcher?"

55.
LYRIC

I don't have much time before we head out to find Mullory's father. And there's something I need to do in secret before we leave, but for some reason, I can't seem to get out of Mullory's bed. Her pillow smells sweet, like whatever shampoo she washes her hair with, and I can't help but feel like a creepy serial killer as I sniff it.

I'm not thrilled that we're leaving to try and find Mullory's father, not with the council arriving in one day. But the selfish part of me is pumped that it'll be just the two of us, like that moment in the library. No side remarks from my sister and no dealing with Cruz Lagunes. And as a bonus, I get to leave my uncle behind on the estate. I've tried my best not to think about our last interaction.

Hell, today might just be a good day. Someone in my shoes might even smile.

I stop by my room to change into a different pair of black jeans and a sweater, then dash to my uncle's treasury. There's something I need to steal, even though it goes against all my principles. And it's not the stealing part I'm above; I'm just usually not a gift giver. But this year—this year I'm sneaking around trying to find Mullory the perfect gift.

The last time I tried to give someone a gift, I failed miserably.

"Why are you moving so fast?" Cousin Cecilia had grabbed my skinny arm and planted me still in the library.

"I'm thinking," I whined, wanting to break free of her. She had a funny smell about her.

"You're thinking so fast it hurts my head."

"Why does it hurt your head?" Half the stuff she said made no sense. I set one of my stone animals loose on the floor, a lion that marched in proud circles. Edwin always gave the best gifts. And I had thought maybe I could do the same for Uncle. That maybe that *would be enough to win him over.*

Cecilia pinched the skin on my forearm. "Because I know what you're thinking. And I'm willing to help you, so stop moving."

I swatted her away. "You know what gift I can give Uncle Xavier?"

"I know what Xavier will need, yes."

I thumbed through my pockets full of gum wrappers, afraid I had nothing to bargain with. "I don't have any money."

Cecilia reached into her teacup, fingers swimming through steam. She didn't flinch from the heat as she pulled out a golden pin. It was an odd little bird. "All I want is for you to stop moving. Give him this."

I eyed the pin suspiciously. I'd had grander thoughts. A telescope or a sports car. This pin seemed to fall kind of flat, but I had no money and no other ideas. I wrapped my hand around the pin, the metal still hot from the scalding tea.

I held my breath as Uncle opened it on Christmas morning.

"A bird pin," he said flatly.

Cousin Cecilia snorted. "It's a killdeer, Xavier. One of my favorite birds. One day it'll be a favorite of yours too."

"I see," he said, and placed it back in the box.

My heart sank and I resolved never to give him another gift again.

I banish the memory away as I slink out of the treasury, intent on heading to my room. I'm almost there when I hear light humming and catch sight of Greta pushing a cleaning cart. I don't need her spying and reporting my thievery back to Uncle.

Move her, a voice whispers menacingly between my ears, *make her move.* The magic in me flares, sparking alive, and I jump on the opportunity. It's swift and seamless as Greta hurls herself down the hall, a startled cry escaping her lips.

Farther, the voice commands. *Push her farther.*

Greta lurches forward again, wincing as her legs move in a spasm. Her face is completely horror stricken. I can't help but wonder if that's how I looked when Uncle would torment me.

"What's the occasion, Lyric?" Uncle Zolan asks as he rounds the opposite corner.

"Huh?"

"Just now, why, I've never seen you look so happy. You were nearly glowing. I assumed there was a celebration nearby. A supply of cigars, perhaps. Pure speculation."

I push past my uncle and head back to my room, but I'm still lightheaded with the taste of magic. The feeling lingers, the satisfaction of toying with a power that brilliant. I rationalize to myself that I only did it for Mullory, that I want to get back to the feeling in the library with her, not this. But the gift in my hands feels almost inconsequential, an idea a former version of myself thought was important.

"Lyric," Mullory calls from outside my door. "Are you ready?"

I hastily stash the gift beneath my bed. "Coming." I race out my door and almost barrel Mullory over.

"Sorry."

Mullory laughs and crinkles her nose. "Actually, I'm probably the one who needs to say sorry."

"For what?"

"You'll see."

My feeling of a good day drifts further and further away until it slides right off the edge of a cliff when I catch sight of Cruz, Reina, and my sister bundled up and waiting at the door.

"Ready for another adventure, bud?" Cruz gives me a thumbs-up. I debate making him snap his own thumb in half.

"I didn't know *they* were coming."

"Neither did I," Mullory answers.

"Can't risk you going out unprotected," says Cruz. "Reina will make sure we avoid any unwanted attention."

"Did you really think I'd let you go to Prudence Butchery without me?" Ellison asks, aghast. "You know how much I enjoy bloody carcasses hanging from the ceiling. So selfish, Lyric."

I rip my coat from the closet and march straight out the front door. So much for my good day.

56.

ELLISON

I have a harder time than usual ignoring Cruz this car ride. There's something about being in his nightmare last night that has me perturbed. I could practically *taste* his fear—the type of fear that shocks your system and pins every one of your muscles in place like a frog about to be dissected. But the pieces just aren't adding up. *He* was the one who murdered his brothers, not the other way around. Maybe this is some sort of guilt-driven nightmare, not one built from actual memories.

But still.

A quick look at him has me digging at the skin around my cuticles until they bleed. There's more to his story, more to the secrets he's hiding, and I need to find out why.

"What's the matter with you?" Cruz finally asks. "Try to relax a little, Ellison."

"I am relaxed," I hiss through my teeth, and burrow closer to the window.

We've been driving for over two hours all while Mullory and her crew of amateur detectives roll through theories only to stumble upon dead-end possibilities. *Where's her mom? Where's her dad? What's the Skeletal Singer's riddle mean? Who's the man with one eye?* Blah. Blah. Blah. I'm the only one to point out anything of real significance.

"Are we just going to ignore the fact that Mullory got a tattoo in a shady tent by some lady with live snakes on her neck?"

"She'd said someone I care about would need it."

"Yeah, well, good luck using it if your arm falls off from an infection."

Mullory pats the sleeve of her jacket. "It's fine."

"For now." I smile before turning back around, happy to have imploded their conversation. Just here doing my part.

And now we're miles deep into New Jersey, a silly little state full of people who want to pretend they're city dwellers. The street we're currently driving on is shabby, and there's an actual moldy mattress lying in the middle of the road. Sidewalks are overflowing with trash bags and discarded furniture, and most of the buildings are boarded up and covered in graffiti.

The driver slows, turning down a narrow one-way street—the exact type of alley you'd expect to get mugged in. How wonderful.

"I'll wait outside," he says hesitantly.

Mullory's the first to hop out and over a pile of dirty snow heaped on the curb. There's a row of narrow shops and only one with the lights on. I see a metal placard on the crumbling brick facade.

Prudence Butchery. Established 1919.

"I've been here before," Mullory says, awestruck, staring at the ragged storefront. "When I was little, with my mom. I remember because we drove all this way just to get hamburger meat. And she was crying when we left. I remember thinking she was upset the hamburgers weren't cooked, but I think it must have been because of my father." Her eyes are misty and everyone else gives her reassuring looks and the type of camaraderie Mullory Prudence demands.

“How sentimental,” I say while trying to pry open the filthy glass door.

“I’ve got you,” Cruz says over my shoulder, yanking it free.

“I’ve got myself,” I answer while slipping past him.

Inside it’s exactly what I’d expect from a butcher shop on a suspicious alley. The walls are lined with laminate counters, sticky with fingerprints and smudged with who knows what else. Beneath them are shelves displaying thick cuts of meat and bones and other animal parts. Dried salami hangs from the ceiling above my head. I couldn’t be paid enough to touch anything in the entire store.

“Are you the guys who called about the steaks?” A young kid in a bloodied apron leans over the counter; his face is ripe with acne that he clearly picks and scrapes at. To really seal the deal, he wipes his nose with the back of his hand before reaching below to pull out a tray of steaks. White-and-red flesh marbled together.

“It’s fresh,” he adds, like that helps at all.

I don’t have any words. Not enough remarks to let Mullory know that this place feels like more of a dead end than the others by far. I should be home figuring out a way to find the dream woman, and the rest of them should be prepping for the party. But no. Let’s take a trip to New Jersey for salmonella and a pound of fresh snot-smeared steak.

“We’re not here for the steaks,” Mullory answers politely.

“Lamb’s good, too,” the boy says. I’ll give him credit for sticking to a sales pitch.

“We’re not here for lamb either. Actually, I was wondering if anyone from the Prudence family still works here?” Mullory Prudence, ever the optimist.

The boy scratches the side of his face, ripping open a fresh patch of acne and dragging a smear of blood down his cheek. “Almost everyone in the family has died. We only kept the name because it was too expensive to change. Plus, people like the history.”

Mullory’s face falls with such crashing defeat I almost feel bad. Almost. “Okay. Well thanks anyway.”

Before we leave, the boy calls to Mullory. "Pa's still here though. He wouldn't leave the place. Said he was born here, and this is where he'll die."

"Pa?"

The boy shrugs. "That's what we call him. The guy's old. Like old as dirt. He cuts up the entrails for us and helps package the meats."

My stomach churns, but Mullory lights up with the news.

"Could we speak to him?"

"Sure. He's out back in the meat locker."

Perfect. The meat locker, just where I want to go next.

57.

MULLORY

It's a short walk as we squeeze single file through a bricked alley adjacent to the butcher. Discarded sheets of metal, threadbare tires, and rusty car parts are stacked against a wooden fence that butts up against a mobile home. It's the type of place that causes the baby hairs on my neck to stand with a tingly sense of fear.

But I want to find my father any way I can, and that gives me the courage to walk up to the meat locker. At one point, the trailer was probably a shiny aluminum, but now it's smeared with swirls of pink that I try to convince myself aren't blood. I swallow hard. It's definitely blood.

I knock once. Twice. Three times, before giving the handle a turn and a gentle nudge. "Hello."

Cold air rushes in a burst—the temperature inside the locker is even chillier than outside. A single bulb hangs from the center, and sunshine fights through the only dirt-smudged window in the unit. My eyes adjust and my stomach churns.

Whole animal carcasses hang from their hooves and legs, skinned, and cut so that their insides are on full display. A long metal table is covered in chunks and loopy strands that are probably intestines. Perched on a crate with a giant cleaver in hand, an old man is hunched over the carnage. His skin is as thin as tissue paper, hanging like it might slough right off his bones. A pair of giant spectacles, with the thickest lenses I've ever seen, sit on the bridge of his crooked nose. His forehead is covered by a floppy fur hat with flaps that match the plaid jacket bundled beneath his bloodied apron.

He raises the cleaver and hacks down into a slab of meat, unbothered by us. Ellison makes a gagging noise behind me, and I struggle not to do the same.

"Excuse me," I manage to say.

THWACK. Another slice into the meat.

"Are you Pa?"

THWACK. THWACK. For an old man, he wields that large blade with ease. A pause, his eyes finally registering our presence, but he shows no signs of distress.

"Come closer and speak up," he yells. "Only got one good ear."

Even in the freezer, the air is so pungent with the coppery scent of blood, I feel dizzy. "ARE YOU PA?" I scream.

"Do I look like I could be anyone else?" He has a lone tooth hanging from his upper gums.

"I'm looking for Henry Prudence."

Pa studies me; his dark eyes are magnified like he's looking through a fishbowl. He yanks something that looks like a saw from the ceiling, pulling the cord as he brings the spinning blade to a hunk of bone, cutting through it like butter. The air takes on a burning quality that pierces my nose.

"I'm looking for Henry Pru—"

"I heard ya the first time," he yells.

"But you didn't respond."

"'Cause Henry Prudence is dead and buried. Six feet under, and that wasn't deep enough."

"You knew him?" I ask, searching for something, anything.

Pa hobbles off his crate—he's so hunched over he barely reaches my shoulder. "'Course I knew him." He pulls a wallet from his coat pocket. "Henry Prudence was my grandson." He flips through a stack of old photos—his finger joints are swollen—and he points to a sulky-looking boy sitting in the corner by himself.

My father.

"My son and his wife, Lottie, adopted him."

"He was adopted?"

"That's what I said, ain't it."

I give Pa a solemn nod, hiding my surprise, encouraging him to keep going.

"He just showed up one day. Coldest day of the year, all the pipes froze and nearly burst. We didn't find him until morning. That boy spent the entire night in a box on the porch. And do you know the oddest part?"

"No," I whisper.

"He never cried. Can you imagine? What type of baby don't cry on the coldest night of the year? Strange that boy was from the very beginning."

There's that word again. It forever haunts me, following me no matter where I go. Maybe I'm the one who's strange.

"He wasn't right. I told everyone from the start that something wasn't right with Henry. The other kids could sense it, too, they was cruel to him because he was different."

Something inside of me tugs and unspools. A shared feeling of loneliness between my father and me.

"Those kids locked him in this trailer. He spent the night without a jacket. When we finally found him, he just walked out like nothing had happened."

"Jesus," Lyric mumbles.

I'm suddenly embarrassed for no reason, prickly with the feeling of being exposed. Family secrets I didn't know I had, splintering through cracks I feel the need to patch up. "Did you know this woman?" I pull up a photo of my mom on my phone.

Pa wipes his nose with the back of his glove and squints. "Maybe. She looks familiar." The deep creases in Pa's forehead overlap, and he looks at me appraisingly. "You look a little familiar, too."

I don't know why I get choked up or why my body betrays me at the very worst times. But I feel the tears starting to slip. Lyric must sense it, because he intervenes.

"How did Henry Prudence die?"

Pa huffs. "That bit was strange, too. I found him in here on that table."

Lyric raises an eyebrow. "That one?"

"You hard of hearing, too, boy?"

"No, sir."

"He was all cut up like those sides of beef. Coroner said he did it to himself. Sliced from ear to ear and straight open. No sign of anyone else in the room."

My knees buckle and the room narrows, the scent of blood nauseating. "He killed himself?"

Pa hacks up something in his throat and spits into a rusty bucket. "That's what all them smart people were sure happened. All the doctors, cops, and lawyers were happy to think that." Pa kicks the bucket with his boot, shaking his head.

"What do you think?" I ask.

"I don't think he did, never made sense. No one cut meat better or cleaner than Henry. And that there was a hack job on his body."

"Did they find the knife?" asks Lyric.

I know where he's going with this. The knife neither of us can seem to escape.

"Oh, they found it right away. Henry's prints were all over it, but no one else's. Nothing. Then the knife disappeared. How do the cops lose a weapon? They never cared about him." Pa stiffens and picks his blade back up. "But that there wasn't even the strangest part."

"It wasn't?"

"Nope. Strangest part was the other boy found dead in here six months later."

Fear crawls up my spine as Pa spits in the bucket again.

"Cops didn't care to remember. But I did. Nobody cared 'bout that boy either.

Same cuts as Henry, I'm sure of it! I know my blades. But no weapon this time, just a dead boy on the table." Pa slaps the metal top.

"But why?"

Pa waves me off. "I ain't got answers for you. Only one thing I found that I didn't give the cops." Pa pulls out his wallet again, fishing out half a scrap of paper. "Didn't make no sense to me, it's your mystery now."

I take the slip of paper, but before I can say thank you, Pa raises his cleaver and slashes into a hunk of meat.

58.

ELLISON

Mullory insists on clutching the measly scrap of paper to her chest, waiting until we're all huddled in the car to finally open it. It's something that was left with the body of a different boy murdered exactly as her father was. This should be good.

"Well?" I ask. I can't see over Lyric and Cruz, who are practically sitting on Mullory's lap.

"I'm not sure," she finally answers, and turns the paper around for me to read.

Replace

to

Him

Another

Kill

Must

"Replace what to him?"

Mullory shrugs. "I don't know. The bottom is missing."

"Maybe something was taken from him?" Cruz postulates. "Something important."

I tune out the rest of the conversation. All I care about is Lyric. More importantly, how do I keep him safe? Maybe Mullory's mom can help, but maybe she can't. That's why I need my own plan.

Find the woman from my mother's dreams.

Who is she?

Why did she make sure we made it to this point?

What was in it for her to keep Lyric alive?

If I were more trustworthy, I'd confide in the others and confirm my hunch that this woman probably left the clues with Mullory's gran all those years ago. That she's at the center of our massive knot of secrets. But I can't trust a soul.

The estate is in full swing with Christmas cheer when we arrive back. Holly and jolly and whatever. Staff members are set to pre-party mode, bustling by in forest-green blazers embellished with illusionary snow that cascades down their back and arms, landing on a scenic stretch of pine trees dotting the seams.

Perched before the awful family tree is an oversize gingerbread house, with perfectly iced shingles and candy-coated shutters and a red door constructed from cherry-swirled candies. The air is warm and spiced with the scent of butter and cookies. Foot-high gingerbread people, freshly baked with button eyes, totter about on fat feet, stringing spun strawberry taffy. One wobbles atop a ladder built from pretzels, icing the chimney that puffs swirls of cotton candy.

Something tugs at my pant leg. A gingerbread person, with a licorice smile, offering me a handful of gumdrops and a hug.

"No touching," I snap before throwing the gumdrops on the floor.

Tiny reindeer whiz above my head, hauling a sled boasting a laughing Santa who drops a sugar-dusted macaroon into my hands. Mullory couldn't even get the knives to behave. As much as I loathe Uncle, I'm glad he's here. There isn't much time until the party, when the council and Lord Thorn will flock to the estate. And I know my brother won't take my advice and leave—he's too hell-bent on finding the man with one eye. Set on solving Mullory's mystery, even if it ends with him dead. Again.

My only hope lies in the dream world. To stumble in without any direction. That's why my mother prefers her teas, a way to execute her nightmares with precision.

I wait until it's dark and quiet throughout the estate before I text Reina to meet me in the solarium. I have no idea *why* she wants to help me, which sets me even further on edge.

"Ellison?" Her voice pierces the darkness. "Are you there?"

"Over here." I've dug my fingers into my elbow, twisted at the skin until it split open. My eyes adjust as she materializes into view: Her pajamas have fur-lined edges, and her purple hair is wet and tied in a tiny knot.

Reina plops down beside me with a calm I can't possibly match. "Is it difficult to get to the land of the dreaming?" she asks.

"Not for everyone."

"But what about for you?"

I tug at the tender skin beneath my fingers, pinching harder. "It's whatever." I pause before continuing. "If you have dream magic, then you're granted a key or a pass or whatever you'd like to call it. You can get in, but it's easier for some."

"And for you?"

"Not that hard." I spare Reina the details, the agony. I don't tell her what happened the night of my birthday. How the second the clock struck midnight, and a rush of magic transferred, it pulled me under like a riptide. Knocked me from my feet, stole my breath. Like falling into a pit, some weightless terror, limbs freely thrashing and stomach plummeting. Only there was no bottom to this nightmare, just a continuous fall through darkness.

Reina studies me. "What exactly are you looking for?"

"Not a what, but a whom," I answer. Part of me wants to tell her everything, because for some reason I almost feel like I can. Like maybe I don't have to shoulder this entire thing by myself.

Reina doesn't pry for details. "I'll be right here."

I squeeze my knees to my chest and knot my hands together, bracing myself.

"I'll pull you out if you get stuck," she whispers reassuringly.

I nod, secretly relieved that Reina's close by.

My mother's magic simmers before striking once I release my barriers. I leave my body and enter the land of the dreaming. But it's not a land; it's pure chaos. *Stay focused, find the woman*—but I'm pulled and tugged in every direction.

Until I stumble into the very same forest as last time, pine and damp leaves, a smear of fog, watery sunlight breaking through the tree's canopy. This nightmare is ripe with fear and it sends my heart into a frenzy. Fear that demands to be seen, felt, consumed. *His* fear.

Cruz Lagunes lies in a puddle of his own blood. Somehow, in this space, I can discern details I wouldn't usually be able to spot. His heartbeat is something I can almost feel in the palm of my hand; it's slow and sluggish, life seeping out of him and spreading on the grass.

"Hello, brother," the same voice taunts.

"Don't do this." Cruz begs with the reckless fever of someone on the brink of death.

I can't stand to watch this happen again, and I want nothing more than for Reina to pull me out. But the dream soldiers on.

"We don't have to choose this," Cruz sputters. Blood oozes from the nasty gash in his leg.

"But we've already chosen." His brother circles nearer with a predatory gait. "The magic is mine!"

"I don't want it!" Cruz cries out in agony.

"Don't be ridiculous." His brother crouches beside him and places his hand on Cruz's leg. His voice drops to a whisper. "It's the only thing we've ever wanted."

Cruz's eyes bulge as his brother digs his fingers into his gaping wound.

I can't stand to watch or make any sense of Cruz's pleading. *He's* the murderer. Cruz. He killed his brothers.

"Ellison." A distant voice coaxes me back. I can feel Reina's fingers threaded through mine, tugging. My entire body is shaking.

"What is it?" she asks, eyes luminous. "What did you see?"

I close my lips tight and shake my head, but I don't let go of her hand.

"Tell me who you're trying to find. I can help."

Maybe it's because I'm wallowing in a moment of weakness that I soften. Maybe I'm tired of shouldering this secret alone. "A woman," I say quietly.

"Who?"

"I don't know," I admit. "She visited my mother years ago, trying to help us." The plan sounds even crazier when I say it aloud.

But Reina doesn't flinch. "Well, then I think it's obvious what you need to do next."

"Oh, really?"

"Yes," she says quietly. "You need to visit your mother."

She's right. My mother's dreams are where I need to go.

I just don't know if I can.

How do I change something that's already happened? How do I ensure it goes exactly as I planned? That's the problem with time—you can bend it, fold it, tear it, but you can never really control it. Changing one little thing could alter the course of everything. Move a pebble, destroy a city. The rules are in a constant state of flux, scribbled in sand, and washed away just as quickly. But I don't have a choice.

What's important is that she believes this must be done.

60. MULLORY

Another riddle wrapped around another murder.

Replace

to

Him

Another

Kill

Must

The bottom of the message is torn away, leaving it incomplete. This part implies something was taken from the boy who was murdered after my father. A murder that occurred with the very same knife, in the exact same place. But why?

I have all the clues my mom left, but I just can't seem to unravel the bigger mystery. I can't seem to get anything right, including Xavier's magic, which has recently caused a line of trumpets to appear in midair with black flowers spilling from their horns.

I read through all my notes until my vision clouds and don't stop until Lyric appears at my door. I shimmy to the side of my bed, and he crawls on top of the blankets I'm nestled beneath. The only barrier between us, which might as well be a fortress.

Lyric points to the paper. "Something about this whole thing is bugging me."

"What do you mean?"

"Pa said the knife only contained Henry Prudence's fingerprints."

"That's right."

Lyric shakes his head. "But do you remember how the knife works?"

I inhale sharply, thinking back to the Mystery Royale. "Someone in Lord Thorn's bloodline needs to be touching the knife for it to make a cut."

Lyric raises an eyebrow. "I don't think it was him. Why would he plant a knife only he could use? It seems too obvious."

I can't accept us going backward on the little progress we've made. Circling back to the beginning of a murder that was then undone. Even worse, going back to considering that my mom may have been involved in both. "Maybe he wore gloves."

"Maybe." Lyric shrugs. "Or maybe someone just wanted us to believe it was him."

"But what about Cecilia's hint about the father in the book about genetics, doesn't that count?"

Lyric eyes the stack of books. "We don't know for sure which book contains the clue."

Suddenly I'm frantic, pulling them out and flipping through until each is set open to page 122. "Let's look then." My eyes blur as I read. "'An uncommon disease that is often associated with a magical rash that causes lichen to grow on one's extremities.' Or this one." I point to the giant book entitled *Birds* with a laugh. "Maybe a bird killed my father?"

Lyric tries to yank me away, sensing my breakdown, but I'm adamant. "Or something here, in this book, *Death: Beyond Our Plane.* Cecilia does love death. 'The final light is often described as warm and bright, a merry welcoming into the afterlife.'"

My lip trembles, snagging on the two most obvious words. *Merry* and *bright.* Esther Merrybright. It can't be my mom again, not something else that she ruined.

"Mullory, I need to tell you—"

I cut him off, dispelling all thoughts that my mom was somehow involved in my father's murder. "No."

Lyric pushes the books aside. "Let's give these a rest for now."

I don't argue and instead shift to something else heavy on my mind. "Earlier today, I overheard your uncle talking to Edwin. He's angry that someone bested him. Xavier said that *she'd* found what he was looking for. Any ideas who it could be?"

Lyric gives me an earnest look. "I've only ever seen one person beat my uncle at anything."

I'm about to ask who, when I realize why he's staring at me intently.

"Only you, Mullory."

My cheeks heat and I look away, embarrassed by the praise Lyric's offering. I don't deserve it, especially because I can't control Xavier's magic. I shake my head. "I don't think it's me. I don't have . . ." The thought dies in my throat, and I clutch the shadow resting beneath my shirt.

Lyric's eyes track my movement. "He's always wanted that."

"But then why has he been avoiding me? It doesn't make any sense."

"Uncle X has never made any sense." Lyric lifts my notebook and tosses it on the side table. "Mullory, I've been thinking," he says slowly.

My heart threatens to leap out of my chest. Even with so many lives in the balance and a seemingly unsolvable mystery, I can't help that my heart is sixteen years old. I can't help that I'm giddy.

"I've been thinking about the party."

I sink down, disappointed.

"I was thinking that we need to be there, but also not be there at the same time. Maybe between you and Reina, we can pull it off."

"Me?"

"You have my uncle's magic."

His words sting a bit, leaving residual guilt and a feeling of ineptitude. "But I can't use it."

Lyric shimmies closer, and his damp hair grazes my arm. "Try it on me."

I freeze, eyes wide. "Try what?"

"An illusion."

"But it won't work."

Lyric gently pries my fingers from the covers, resting them in my lap and tracing the tender spot on my palm. A sensation that races up my arm as if my entire body were hot-wired. The only light is the soft glow coming from the lamp on my bedside table. His square jaw is relaxed, but his dark eyes are intently fixed on me, like he's never been more certain of anything in his entire life. This feels like one of those moments where the physics of time seem to falter, briefly standing still. The ones that all the movies build up to. Somehow, we've gotten closer, bridged the gap until just our cheeks touch.

"Try, Mullory." His voice is a whisper.

I close my eyes. Slowly, I tease out the magic. It's resistant, like yanking on a weed that's rooted itself in deep, but I don't let go. Thread by thread it feels like something might be working, and I imagine myself spinning the illusion around Lyric.

I open one eye, half afraid to check.

And: Oh. My. God. A little gasp escapes my lips followed by a shriek of laughter.

Lyric jumps back, eyes wide like a gun just went off. "What is it?"

But I can't stop laughing—it's hard to breathe, let alone answer.

"Mullory," Lyric says slowly. "What?"

I raise a hand to my lips. "I'm sorry," I blurt out. "You better look for yourself."

Lyric swipes his phone from his pocket and turns on his camera. It's one of those things that he just needs to see because an explanation couldn't possibly do it justice.

The very wimpiest collection of ragged hairs beneath just one nostril. The saddest excuse for a mustache.

"I'm not even worth the whole thing?" There's a playful tone in Lyric's question.

His face sends me back over the edge into hysterical laughter. Lyric smacks me with a pillow. Beautiful, dark, mysterious Lyric with the saddest excuse for facial hair I've ever seen.

"I'm sorry." My stomach hurts from laughing.

Lyric smiles. "I like when you laugh."

A hiccup escapes my lips, and my belly gets the fizzle-pop feeling as Lyric leans closer.

His thumb traces a circle across my shoulder blades, and heat trickles down my entire body. "Is this what you want?"

"Yes."

But he keeps the distance, hesitating. "Are you sure?"

I try not to second-guess myself, to misinterpret his reluctance, choosing instead to leap. "Yes."

It's the softest kiss at first; his lips barely brush mine, as if he's still not quite certain. His skin is still dewy from the shower, fresh and tinged with something spicy.

Lyric kisses the corner of my lip, pausing, a request to keep going. My arms snake behind his neck and I pull him in tighter. This time the kiss is anything but gentle.

The entire world melts into nothing. Lyric leans in, pressing his weight against me, then kisses my jawline in a trail that leads right back up to my lips.

He breaks away, breathless, and I snuggle into his side, waiting for my heart to stop pounding. But even after this, a little blip of guilt worms its way over me, reminding me that the magic I stole was supposed to be Lyric's. I can't help but think that if he did inherit it, he'd have no problem running the estate.

I clear my throat. "Have you tried to use yours?" I don't specify Lord Thorn's magic, but I know he understands.

Lyric exhales, distraught. "It's not good or kind, his magic."

I note how he ignores my question, so I try a different angle. "But it matters how *you* use it."

Lyric looks me in the eye. "Mullory," he says, and leans closer, lips skimming my hair as he whispers. "I don't think I'm kind either."

61.
ELLISON

Truth be told, I've been putting this off. Deep down, I've known. I've always known that at some point I'd have to face my mother. It took hearing it from Reina to make it real.

But that doesn't mean I want to.

Not even close.

I've been pacing the solarium for an hour, tugging at a thread in my sweater until it unraveled, much like my mind, which has begun to spiral. What will I find in my mother's dreams? What makes me think I could even make it there? What are the chances this mysterious woman returns? What the hell am I even doing?

Reina has been quietly watching me the entire time. "Ellison."

"Let me be."

"Ellison." Reina catches my arm, yanking me back as I try to skirt past her. "What are you so afraid of?" Her grip on me doesn't relent.

I square my shoulders and meet her stare, challenging her to back down. "Isn't it obvious?"

Her purple eyes soften. "No."

I don't owe Reina anything, explanations included. But part of me craves a release. "My mother's mind is the place my nightmare was born. The nightmare where she buried me alive every night since I can remember." I expect this to shut Reina up.

"But it's over. You told me that you've already lived your nightmare."

My mouth hangs open as I search for a retort. Exhaustion and the pressure to save Lyric seep through my vulnerable armor, threatening to break me. I jerk away from her, dabbing my cheeks. "You don't understand." A pathetic response, but it's all I can muster.

"Help me to."

My voice breaks as the tears fall. "I can't face her alone in there."

"But you're not doing this alone, Ellison. I'm here. I've been here the entire time." She gives me a smile. "You know it's not the worst thing in the world, to have a friend."

I force out a nervous laugh. "It's a close second."

"Let's just do the damn thing." Reina claps her hands together and sits cross-legged on the floor.

"I don't know how to reach my mother's dreams," I blurt out, while settling beside her.

Reina gives me a thoughtful glance. "I think your magic should be able to help with that."

I force down the lump in my throat. "I hate it," I say so softly I don't think she can hear me.

"I don't love mine either." She shrugs. "But it's all I have left of my dad. . . ."

I can sense there's more to the story; maybe he's the one in the labyrinth. "Is he . . . ?" I can't find a delicate way to ask.

"He's not with me," she answers bluntly. "I wasn't a fan of how he used his magic in the end, but that's what *he* did. Not me." She grabs my hand. "Not us."

I must be delirious. "Let's do the damn thing."

"I'll be right here."

A deep inhale and I close my eyes, releasing myself once more. But this time, I'm ready for the dream magic, the chaos that exists in the minds of the sleeping. Instead of trying to find someone specific, I hold tightly to the magic itself. A slimy rope that I securely wrap around my arm, winding it up tight.

I know who's waiting on the other side.

I just don't know if she'll let me in.

I imagine this is exactly like opening Pandora's box.

What I don't expect is to be transported right back to the room my body is currently anchored in. Sunshine filters into the solarium, bouncing off champagne glasses held between manicured fingers, beaded dresses swishing between laughter and chatter.

A party.

Not just any party.

I know where and when my mother is dreaming of; I just don't know why she'd willingly do it. Not when she has total control of her dream self.

Beneath the sparkle of balloons bursting with confetti and gold-dusted chocolates, there's an ominous undercurrent to the dream. Something rotting along the edges. And the timeline is warped, flexing at an unnatural speed. I follow my mother outside; her hand is gripped tightly on Lord Thorn's shoulder. Even in the dream world, I hate him.

The sky is a murky black, and monstrous clouds hang just above our heads. The air feels heavy, like it's on the precipice of being split open with a storm. But it's not Mullory who's slumped and bloody over Lyric's body—it's my mother.

Her scream rips through my spine. I've never seen my mother like this—so completely undone, raw with unimaginable pain, her eyes fixed on Lyric's dead body. The clouds open, but the rain is sticky and red. Blood pours from the sky in a way that only a nightmare can produce.

And even my immense contempt for my mother isn't enough to wish this on her. I stagger through the grass, which is slick and syrupy.

"Mother." I drop to my knees across from her. I don't know if she can hear me, I don't know how any of this magic works. My voice is weak and lost in the blood rain.

"Mother!" I scream, but I'm not a match for the noise. I panic, but a distant squeeze to my physical body gives me courage to do the thing I hate. My hand trembles as I place it on my mother's shoulder.

A crack of thunder and then a pause. Her eyes find mine, searching as I hold on to her. Then silence. Her expression changes.

The scene disappears until there's nothing around us, some empty void, and her voice echoes.

"Ellison?" she questions. There's something else there, beneath the surface, something she's just realized.

"How do I find the woman who visited your dream all those years ago?" I ask her.

My mother shakes her head with disbelief, ignoring my question and refusing to accept something she's realized. "Ellison." She says my name again, but her voice is sluggish and distant. I know I'm losing her.

"Tell me how to find her."

My mother sways in place, fighting to hold our connection. "She said she'd be at the party," she whispers fearfully. "She said you'll look right at her."

I'm tense but I need to confirm what she just said. "The woman from your dreams will be at the Christmas party?"

My mother's face contorts. "How are you . . . ?"

And then the dream dissolves before I can ask anything else.

62.

MULLORY

As soon as I wake, I know exactly what I need to do, even if it pains me to leave Lyric. There was a shift last night; some invisible door between us was finally unlocked and I'm afraid that if I go it might shut again. Not just the kissing, but the after. The hour where he held me close. Like I truly mattered to him.

Lyric is curled into a ball with his lips slightly parted, and for some reason it makes me giggle. I lean closer and whisper into his ear, "I'm going to find your uncle. I won't let him disappear or spring a pack of hyenas on me this time."

Lyric's serene face twists into a scowl before he opens his eyes. With his ragged bedhead and half a mustache, it's hard to take him seriously. I smile so big I can feel it in my stomach.

"That's a terrible idea." His voice is hoarse and dry.

"I have a better one. Maybe find a razor."

Lyric grabs his face with his hand. "Oh." He laughs. "You don't like it?"

"I'll see you later." I grab a change of clothes, scurrying to the bathroom to get ready quickly.

I need to corner Xavier Stoutmire and find out what he's been searching for. Call it a hunch, but I suspect it ties into my own mystery.

The estate is already bustling, staff members skirt around me, balancing cages containing snow-white turtledoves and yards of tinsel.

I march past the kitchen, determined to find Xavier, when I run into Edwin.

"Mullory," he says briskly.

"I need to find Xavier." I try to keep pace with him.

Edwin is juggling a bolt of shiny silver fabric, a fishbowl full of tiny swimming snowmen, and a holly branch.

I gingerly take the fishbowl from his hands. "Let me help."

"No worries, Miss Mullory. I'm off to the ballroom, much to prepare for the party."

Greta flits past me and plucks the bowl from my hands in a graceful swoop before darting away.

"Much to do," Edwin exclaims. "Xavier's in his study."

"Great, thank you!" I call out, but Edwin is already five steps ahead, shouting orders and balancing decor.

The intricate wooden door to Xavier's study is shut.

I knock. Timidly at first.

Another knock. Polite, but more assertive.

When that doesn't work, I bang both fists. "I know you're in there!"

The door sweeps inward and I stumble, nearly crashing into Xavier. He looks tired, clad in a bright green suit with a vine of holly berries snaking up his arms.

I don't miss his limp as he hobbles inside and gestures for me to follow. Where has he been? What has he been searching for?

He lazily raises one eyebrow. "You finally found me."

I huff. "I've been trying to find you for weeks! Why have you been avoiding me?"

"Is that what you think I've been doing? It's not my fault you have poor timing and a terrible sense of direction."

I can tell that whatever reason Xavier has for avoiding me, he won't be sharing. Time to get to the point. "Are you purposefully blocking your magic from me?" It's the one scenario I'd been secretly hoping for, an easy explanation for why I'm failing miserably.

Xavier shakes his head as he sinks into his desk chair. "Even if I wanted to," he says sharply, "that's impossible. Once the transfer begins, I have no way to stop it. Sure, I could try and tamper with it, delay it... but that would prove utterly pointless."

"But with Lyric—"

Xavier clenches a paperweight on his desk. "I never began the transfer with Lyric. I never got the chance." His words are dipped in acid. "Not that it's any of your business."

"Well, something's not right." My eyes drop to my shoes, ashamed. "It won't work for me. And I don't think I have a magical parasite, and I'm not dead." I quote the possible reasons cited in the book left to me by Cecilia.

"What astute observations," Xavier says rudely. "I'm certain there's nothing wrong with my magic, but with you..." He pauses. "You're so eager for answers, but I'm not sure if you're ready for them. You may not like what you find."

I stiffen, certain Xavier is trying to scare me. What other horrifying truths could I possibly uncover? "Are you referencing the fact that my mom killed someone?"

I'd blurted it out for the shock factor, but Xavier doesn't flinch. "You're on the right path, but tread lightly. When it's time, I'll call for you."

"Time for what?"

Xavier gives me a sad smile. "You'll see."

His vague response leaves me unsettled, but I know which issues to push. "What have you've been searching for?"

A laugh, the truest sound I've ever heard him make. "You're far too much like Esther. Meddling in things you haven't a clue about."

I can tell Xavier is nearly done with me and that I won't be getting any answers, so I pivot. "We need your help at the party."

Xavier doesn't lift his eyes from his desk. "First you accuse me, then you request my help. A word of advice, Mullory."

"Yes?"

"Don't do that."

I can feel the conversation slipping away from me, but I don't see another way around this. "Please," I croak. "We need an illusion so that we don't look like ourselves. The council—"

"Will not be pleased to see you." Xavier grabs a pen and signs his name dramatically across the bottom line. "Fine."

"Fine?"

"Yes. That's what one says when one agrees."

I turn on my heels before he can change his mind, about to bolt out of this study, when Edwin enters.

"Sir, they've readied the helicopter."

"Helicopter?" I can't help but ask, even though it's not my place. "What about your party?"

Xavier rises slowly. "Not that it's any of your business, but I'll be back in time for the party. I'm few things, but an excellent host is one of them."

I'm curious as I shuffle out of the study, wondering what Xavier is still chasing. If not the shadow, then what?

63.

LYRIC

"We need to practice," Cruz announces. His hands are tucked behind his back, and he's ordered us in a line as though we're on our way to a championship game. I'm surprised he doesn't have a whistle.

We assembled in the library after Mullory announced that my uncle would help disguise us physically. The only thing left to do was to make sure our magic would be hidden as well. I have no idea how she coerced the favor from my uncle, but she's constantly surprising me. The Christmas Eve party is tonight, and we need to be ready. Game time approaches.

My pinkie grazes the side of Mullory's thigh, and she smiles, acknowledging our touch. All I can think about is last night. I have zero room for any other thought, especially about anything that pops out of Cruz's face.

"Right." Cruz claps his hands together. "I took the liberty of scouting out the ballroom." He pauses, like he expects us to praise him; instead, we stare back in silence. "The size of the main floor is roughly equal to this room, plus the added square footage of the mezzanine level that circles the second floor. We want to avoid that level, isn't that right, Reina?"

She salutes him and Ellison snickers. Since when does my sister snicker? I haven't been paying much attention to her, but now that I am, I notice something's different. She looks more . . . relaxed? And there's a sureness in her eyes, almost as if she's up to something.

"Reina needs to shield our magic, but not cover us completely, which will take a tremendous amount of concentration."

"Will it be similar to when the council first arrived?" asks Mullory.

Reina shakes her head and answers before Cruz can. "No. That was more like a blanket that I draped over all of us, hiding us completely. This will take more finesse. I need to conceal certain parts and not others. It's just exponentially more difficult."

"How long can you keep it up?" This wins me an encouraging nod from Mullory.

Reina shrugs. "If you all stay close to me, I can hold it longer, but even then, I don't think more than an hour." This whole plan hinges on her ability to keep our magic hidden. One tiny mistake and Lord Thorn will sense me, like a shark with blood in the water.

"Of course, I'll have full reign of the ballroom seeing as though I don't need to be concealed," Cruz says.

"How lucky."

"Yes, Lyric, it is lucky. We only have one hour to find the one-eyed man."

"Shouldn't take long," Ellison sneers. "The missing eye should be a dead giveaway, don't you think?"

Cruz taps his chin. "I don't think anything. All I know is when we find him, Mullory is the one who must approach him."

Mullory nods excitedly. "That's what the Viper said. I need to tell him I've come for my present."

"Okay, Reina, you take your position near the center," orders Cruz. "According to the staff, the dance floor will be illusioned to look like an ice-crusted pond with a swan fluttering through gold-dusted snowflakes."

Of course there's an ice swan and golden snow at Uncle's party.

"That's where Reina will stay so that she's equidistant from all of us. We just need to figure out her range. Reina." Cruz extends an arm and she shuffles over. "Everyone fan out around her."

We listen to Coach Cruz's order and group round Reina, whose brows are furrowed together in concentration. At first, we stick to a tight circle.

Reina nods and we take a step back.

I have no idea if it's working, but of course the rat, Cruz—with his gift to smell and steal magic—can tell when it is.

"That's good. Let's try another foot."

Reina nods. "You know," she says, while a bead of sweat glazes her temple, "if we cut down the size of the group, I can extend it farther."

I know what she's getting at, and I won't have it. "No chance in hell," I counter back.

Reina huffs and blows a strand of hair away from her cheek. "Just thought I'd mention it."

"When we locate the man with the one eye, we'll need to converge around Reina and get Mullory to him." Cruz gives a complicated series of stupid hand signals.

"You'll stay near me, Mullory." Cruz eagerly rushes to her side and his fingertips brush her shoulder. His touch and tone are different with her, like she's something that deeply intrigues him. There's uncertainty and concern and a . . . tenderness that has me furious with jealousy.

Anger builds—a quick and clean break.

The rest is easy.

Cruz howls and lurches backward, his body slamming to the ground. Mullory yells and falls to her knees. It only takes a minute to figure out what happened. Maybe Cruz is too ashamed, but he doesn't even look at me.

"Lyric?" Mullory's tone is pleading, like she doesn't want to know the truth of what I've done.

But I did do it. And it felt good.

"Way to go," says Ellison.

Reina throws her arms in the air, hurrying over to Cruz. "We don't have time for this."

"Is it broken?" Mullory keeps a gingerly touch on Cruz's wrist.

He leans closer to her. That bastard. I clench my fists as tight as possible to prevent myself from making another move.

"Just a sprain, I think."

Everyone huddles around Cruz, icing me out. Mullory shoots me a look that stills my heart and not in a good way. More of a *Titanic*-sinking-to-the-bottom-of-the-ocean type of way. She helps him up and keeps a steadying hand on his back. The jerk milks his performance, cradling his wrist. Like falling on his ass was somehow heroic.

"This isn't you, Lyric." Mullory's voice is heavy with disappointment, and it burns me worse than anger.

I don't answer her—because what if this is me?

It only took me a day to ruin what I had with Mullory last night. Record-breaking time. But I'd told Mullory the truth. I'm not kind. I just don't think she wanted to hear it.

64.

MULLORY

It's like the most elaborate Halloween costume I've ever worn. Only more. Much more. Staring at the mirror, I feel like my brain's short-circuiting trying to locate myself beneath the disguise. My normally gray eyes are now the palest shade of blue, piercing like shards of ice. Strawberry blond hair, twirled with every shade of gold and garnet, cascades down my back. This must be how Xavier felt during the game, stepping into someone else's skin.

He lined us up an hour ago—Ellison, Lyric, and me. Ellison wasn't pleased with her short dark bob and the curve Xavier added to her nose.

"Seriously?" she whined when Edwin handed her a mirror. "I get this and Mullory gets to look like *that*."

Xavier flicked his wrist and replaced her bob with a bald spot. "Is that better?" His voice was ragged and worn thin.

Ellison pouted and he put her hair back. She didn't dare say another word. Xavier gave Lyric soft blond curls, green eyes, and stretched him out by a half a foot, but I couldn't stomach looking at him, not even in costume, not after what he did. He was so fast to hurt Cruz. And the worst part, the part I still can't wrap my head around, is his lack of remorse. It's almost like he enjoyed it. But I can't think of that now, because I need to focus.

Find the man with one eye.

I run a hand nervously up my arm—fingers tingling where the now-hidden tattoo from the Viper normally lies. My skin is perfectly smooth, but somehow beneath the enchantment, I can still sense it.

"Miss?" Greta calls from the hall.

"Come in."

"Your party dress." She pushes in a rack and then unzips a garment bag.

"Wow."

Greta smiles. "Let's try it on."

The fit is perfection. The long sleeves are lace, detailed in a pattern of red roses that sweep up my collarbone and melt into a bodice that plummets with a deep V cut. It has me blushing the same bloodstained shade of red.

Greta takes my hands and gently pulls them to the side, standing behind me like a proud mother. "Tonight, you can be someone else," she whispers.

Panels of silk drape elegantly from my waist, sweeping the ground, and I can't help but spin in circles. As stunning as it is, there's something oddly familiar about the dress.

"Have fun," Greta calls, and disappears.

It's less than a minute later when there's another knock.

"It's still open," I call, convinced Greta forgot something.

"Beautiful," a deep voice murmurs as Cruz materializes behind me in the mirror.

He's fitted in a black tux that highlights his every muscle. His bow tie is red silk, the same as my dress. The sides of his head are freshly trimmed; the top is longer and swoops across his forehead. There's a glint in his dark eyes that makes me swallow.

"Just like I remembered."

I puzzle over his strange words and think back to the first night we met. *"You're different than I'd thought you'd be,"* he'd said. "What's that supposed to mean?"

"You think this is the only family with a seer in it?"

A seer . . . like Cecilia. My fingers skim down my sides, slipping on the silk. Realization presses against me—this dress feels familiar because it's exactly like the one Cruz tried to magic me into that first night. Some part of me buzzes with the knowledge, another recoils. "What did your seer say?"

I scurry over to the bed and busy myself with my heels, not wanting to face Cruz when he answers.

"I've known we'd meet for a while, and I must admit there's always been something fascinating about you. But now, I finally understand why that is."

I gulp. "Why's that?"

Cruz doesn't falter. "You don't belong here. You have no true claim to magic and yet you find yourself inheriting one of the elite's most sought-after magical lines. You're like me."

"You?"

Cruz closes the distance between us, leaning nearer so that every bit of me is acutely aware of his presence. "We're course correctors. We change the tide, beckon in the storm. If Lyric had inherited Xavier's magic, none of the Stoutmires would be so shaken." He flashes me a smile, his nose inches from mine, his voice dipping low. "And then where would the fun be? I much prefer those who challenge the status quo. Who shake things up." Cruz kneels and his hands find my feet, guiding the strap that's flapping open around my ankle. His touch is featherlight, reverent almost.

"Just like Cinderella," I say, trying to keep it light.

Cruz pulls the strap; his fingers linger near my ankle when he's done. "Don't sell yourself short, Mullory." His voice is stern. "You're so much more." He lifts his head. "And this is far from a fairy tale."

65.
MULLORY

I politely decline a second mug of hot buttered rum offered by a gingerbread person in ice skates gliding across the frozen dance floor. Christmas trees soar to the second level of the mezzanine, an off-limits area, as Cruz reminded us several times. The branches glisten with snow, lights, and edible desserts that replenish themselves after they're plucked. Penguins waddle around the snowbanks and snow sculptures that dot the perimeter of the dance floor. In the center, the ice swan's delicate glass wings flutter through the golden-tinted snow. Sugar plums, candy canes, and twinkling lights are wrapped and stacked on every surface.

If there's one thing Xavier Stoutmire knows how to do, it's throw a party. But what was so important that he needed to leave this morning? What is he after? Lyric thought it was me, possibly the shadow, but then why leave?

Uncovering Xavier's motives will have to wait because focus is critical if I want to find the man with one eye. And it's becoming increasingly complicated as guests arrive wearing elaborate masks crusted with jewels and feathery fringes. This is a masquerade.

Someone brushes my shoulders, followed promptly by a rude shove. I teeter unsteadily on my heels and whirl around to spot the back of a man, balding and squat. His neck cracks as he tips his head side to side, vertebrae snapping into place before he goes eerily still. The hairs on my neck raise from some ominous familiarity as the man inhales and swivels around to a crouch. *The Bloodhound.* I count to ten before daring to glance at Lyric, checking that he's okay.

"See anything?" Cruz whispers from the corner of his mouth. He's stayed close to my side, eyes alert on our every movement, keeping us in a tight carousel around Reina.

"Nothing." I must seem both frustrated and unhinged because Cruz places a reassuring hand on my shoulder.

"We just need to keep looking. The masks are making it more difficult than I anticipated."

"Yes, but he must be here somewhere."

"Fancy party, am I right?" an older gentleman asks, breaking my concentration. He's dressed like some sort of naval captain, in a fitted blue suit with a shiny tag that reads *Corporal Jim* flanked by a series of badges and medals. Disappointingly, he has both eyes.

"Yeah, it is," I answer politely, trying to break away.

"I don't like parties much, just here doing my part."

I don't want to be rude, but I don't have much time for conversation. "Yes, I'm not one for parties, either," I say quickly.

"You looking for something?" he asks, as I turn to scan the party. This poor man won't catch a hint.

"You could say that." The words escape my lips in a staggered breath as the doors fly open.

Lord Thorn storms into the party; he's dressed in a sinister black suit with a horned mask, looking like something that stepped straight out of a bad dream.

Every guest pauses and murmurs fill the ballroom. His presence taints the energy. I steal a panicked look at Lyric even though I'm still upset with him, and then I glance at Reina, making sure she has him concealed.

Lord Thorn raises an arm and my heart races, certain he's going to call out Lyric. But he quickly ushers in the same woman who came to the estate the first night we arrived. The Magnus. He bows cordially at her.

Behind Lord Thorn, other council members and highly positioned people, including Saffron and Lawrence Stoutmire, make their way in, each paying their respects to the Magnus.

Suddenly, my skin feels tingly and my breathing hitches. Even in this lightweight dress, I'm unbearably sweaty. My eyes flicker between Lord Thorn and Lyric. Why did I think this was a good idea?

"Mullory."

The snow beneath my feet crystallizes to ice.

"Mullory." Cruz calls my name again, but his voice is distant. Before I know what's happening, I'm being tugged forward and one arm snakes around the small of my back.

Cruz grabs my hands, raising them to his shoulders.

"No," I cry out when I realize where I am. The very center of hell itself—the dance floor. I'd rather drink the poisonous tea or shimmy down the well again than dance in front of people.

"Just follow my lead."

My hands can barely grip Cruz's; they're too slick with sweat. "I'm a terrible dancer."

"Lucky for you, I'm an excellent teacher. One, two, step. One, two, step," Cruz's voice is even and melodic. "It's like math. You like numbers, don't you?"

I barely dip my head. "I like numbers."

"One, two, step. One, two, step."

Somehow my feet follow the pattern and eventually by some miracle bestowed on me by the dancing gods, I catch my breath and miraculously stay upright.

"Thank you," I whisper. When I finally feel stable enough, I tip my head and look up at Cruz. The centers of his dark eyes are golden like honey, and I can't help but feel like there's a secret hidden behind them. If only I could crack him open.

He murdered his brothers. He's a monster. It should be as simple as that. But he's a monster who doesn't hide from his past. And there's something freeing in that. Could I blame my lack of decisiveness on the past my parents hid from me? I'm struggling to understand where I came from. What wicked things were done before I was even born? I'm wondering why I'm the one forced to pay the price.

66.
LYRIC

Ever since I can remember, I'd begged and pleaded with Uncle X to let me come to this party—the grandest event of the year. His legendary Christmas Eve soiree. But every year I was tucked away in some corner of the estate by myself, alone and miserable. Ever since the accident. Some years, if I was lucky, I was close enough to hear the music and I'd imagine myself in a tuxedo, dancing and laughing with the other guests. Edwin would smuggle me cookies and I'd eat them until my stomach hurt, and then fall asleep in a sticky pile of sugar crumbs.

Well, I've finally made it to Xavier Stoutmire's Christmas Eve party.

I'm even wearing a tuxedo.

But I'm not dancing. Certainly not laughing. I'd rather be hidden away again than have to endure another minute of Cruz twirling Mullory around the dance floor while I simultaneously hope my father doesn't try to murder me.

I can feel the tug. The magic inside me is elated that he's here. And I can't deny the sheer power he commands when he enters the room. There's a sharp brilliance to his manners. He forces the staff to do better. People move out of his way whether they want to or not.

But I'm not here for that.

It takes all my willpower, but I stay focused on the task. At the very least, I owe that to Mullory.

Find the man with one eye.

It's the only way to make up for what I did.

A slip, where I lost control and Mullory caught a glimpse of what I'm capable of. The look she gave me was the most painful part. All I can do now is stay on target. I stick to our plan, not straying too far from Reina, and forcing myself to engage with guest after guest. Once I confirm they have both eyes, I leave them mid-sentence and move on to the next. Some are trickier than others, with masks that curl and obscure their faces—these conversations are especially difficult, waiting for them to adjust their mask or take it off.

"Xavier Stoutmire throws the best parties."

"Good thing his nephew didn't inherit his magic and ruin all of this."

"I hear the girl who won can't even get the silverware to behave."

I have to squeeze my fingers so tightly in my palms that I draw blood.

Finally, after what feels like an eternity in hell, I spot a lanky man leaning over the edge of the second-story balcony. He's sporting an eye patch that glitters black.

Gotcha.

67.

ELLISON

If I'm being honest, I've totally abandoned Mullory's little mission. Why would I search for a man with one eye when the person I really need to find is a mysterious dream-walking woman? Statistically speaking, she will probably have both eyes.

The only problem is I have no idea how to find her. The ballroom is a wintery spectacle bursting with Christmas cheer and guests spinning carelessly as the drinks continue to refill. I've already downed three cranberry foam spritzers and pilfered five macaroon buttons from the coats of unsuspecting gingerbread people.

I'm aimlessly searching when I stumble into my father and mother. Her nearness throws me and I sway, unsteady. Then I spot Whitaker nearby. The one and only person I've ever counted on and he doesn't even recognize me. My mother's shrill laugh slices into me and I feel my panic taking the lead.

Gentle fingers lace around my wrist, and Reina steadies me. Brings me back down.

"You're right," I whisper to her. "My mother is worse."

"Worse than what?"

I can't look her in the eye when I say the next part. "Worse than having a friend."

Reina keeps the contact, smiling.

"I think the woman I'm searching for is at this party."

"How do you know?" Reina whips her head around the crowd.

"My mother told me in her dream."

"I'll be on the lookout," Reina says, letting me go. Then softer still: "I'm here, Ellison."

I nod, accepting the odd sensation, the lightness, when a burden isn't mine alone.

Weaving between guests, I grasp at any remanent of dream magic that might be floating around. Something tugs me toward the ice pond, a lady outfitted in a golden corset and tiger-striped cape. But she's so drunk she's nearly asleep. Groaning with frustration I glance at my reflection. Pitiful.

My phone pings six times in quick succession and I know the messages are from Lyric, who's currently trying to signal to us. His sights are set on a man sporting an eye patch.

Why couldn't my mission be that easy? Seriously. Mullory gets the clue to find a man who is literally missing a body part and all I get is a vague message.

I shrug at Lyric, as if to say, *Figure it out.*

Not my concern.

Let Mullory Prudence handle it—she looks better than she deserves with that glorious garnet hair and that dress—she's already gotten the better end of the deal. Let *her* figure this out. That's when I catch sight of Mullory, eyes wide and her red-stained lips open, primed to scream.

What. The. Hell.

68.

MULLORY

It all happens in a horrifying moment.

Lyric finds the man with the one eye. But his expression isn't triumphant—it's muddled with regret, like he's already searching for my forgiveness. Like he's about to do something stupid.

I don't have time to react as Lyric makes a mad dash for the stairs.

My mouth opens, about to scream, as I lurch forward, but Cruz grabs my arms and keeps me in the safety of Reina's protection. I know he's right, but logic doesn't always sit well when the heart is concerned.

I look to Reina, frantic, as her eyes nearly bulge out of her head. Straining and straining, until she's looking at me with the same sorrowful expression. Lyric scales the first three stairs, and as soon as he finds footing on the fourth, Reina exhales and releases.

There's a loud screech.

The violin strings pull and stop mid-note in an awful lurch beneath the grip of Lord Thorn's magic. He raises a hand in the air and several people are pushed to the side in a heap. His beady eyes glow with rage and recognition. He can feel the magic even if Lyric is hidden behind Xavier's disguise.

I want to scream at Lyric to stop, but I don't want to draw attention.

This is the worst possible time for Lyric to play the hero.

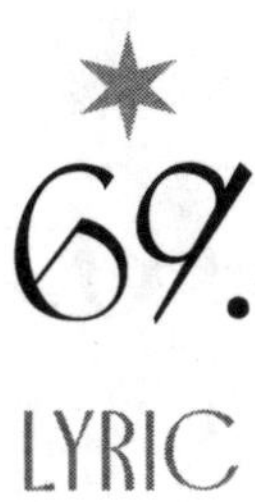

69. LYRIC

Sometimes I do really stupid shit.

This is one of those times.

Usually, the reason behind my stupidity is more selfish or powered by the rage firing up inside me. This time I don't think about myself; I just want Mullory to get what she needs.

Is this a stupid idea that will likely end terribly for me?

Absolutely.

70.

MULLORY

"I know you're here." Lord Thorn's voice is cruel and just a bit excited as it thunders throughout the ballroom. Two of the ice-skating gingerbread people slam into each other and crash into a pile. Even the decorations are terrified.

There's a flicker of amusement in Lord Thorn's face. This is a game. A chase. He just needs to follow his magic through the crowd and collect his prize at the end.

"What's going on, Thorn?" asks the Magnus. Her keen eyes dart around the ballroom.

"He's here," Lord Thorn purrs.

The Magnus steadies her stance. "Who?"

"Lyric Stoutmire." Lord Thorn's lip curls into a devilish smile.

Saffron Stoutmire's cocktail glass shatters into shards by her heels. Her face is drained of all color, pale and sickly.

"But he died," someone in the crowd argues.

"Yes, died, but apparently not dead," someone else responds.

I keep an eye on Lyric, who is stealthily slinking behind guests on the second floor, trying to reach the man with the eye patch.

Lord Thorn raises an arm, his fingers curled into his palms, almost as if he could reach out and yank his magic back. It will take only seconds before he pinpoints exactly where Lyric is.

For a moment, my fury outweighs my terror. Why would Lyric do something so incredibly dangerous? Better yet, how am I going to fix this?

I turn to Cruz, who's just as panicked, and tug him closer to Reina, all while keeping my sights on Lyric. He's closing in on the man with the eye patch, but Lord Thorn has already made it to the top of the mezzanine. The guests parted in a lopsided wave on the stairs; anyone that didn't get the hint was physically pushed out of his way.

Reina holds on to Ellison. If we all get closer together, we can move toward Lyric.

In one swift motion, Lyric rips the patch from the man's face. I can't see much except that his shoulders drop with frustration as the man shoves him aside. The commotion only lures Lord Thorn in faster.

Lyric is distraught as the man (who I can now see has two eyes) hurries off.

"Stay here," says Cruz, before dashing toward the staircase on the opposite side of the room, the one that isn't flooded with people trying to leave.

"Hurry," I call to Ellison and Reina.

Lord Thorn locks eyes on Lyric, smirking at his disguise before he raises a hand. My legs buckle and I brace myself... but nothing happens. Lord Thorn's smirk is quickly stifled with rage as he whips his head around the room, searching for the culprit of his fury. It dawns on me that it must be Cruz interfering with Lord Thorn's magic. But how long can he possibly keep this up?

Lyric recognizes his opportunity and sprints toward Cruz, whose face is flush with concentration. A snarl escapes Lord Thorn's lips as he yanks a candelabra from the wall and hurls it at Lyric's head. Cruz grabs Lyric's arm and yanks him behind a bar cart as the candelabra crashes beside them.

The last few guests on the mezzanine escape, clearing a path for Lord Thorn. He takes his time, striding across the catwalk, savoring his hunt. He raises both arms menacingly above his head, poising himself like some sort of god.

Cruz shouts in agony as his body slams against the wall, and he crumbles to the floor. Lyric rushes in front, thrusting the bar cart at Lord Thorn as he places an arm under Cruz's torso.

"Pathetic," chides Lord Thorn. Both his arms slice through the air again, fully on the offensive. Lyric's back arches in an unnatural snap and he takes a few jerky steps before shakily diving headfirst at the mezzanine railing.

Somehow amid all the chaos, Lyric finds me with blue eyes that aren't his, but I still feel his pain. I'm right there with him as he curls his fingers around the banister in a death grip, fighting. If he falls, we both fall. Lyric moans, battling within himself, before his body finally betrays him and he hoists his torso over the ledge.

His head dangles above the ballroom, hands slipping on the rails.

Lyric's face flickers with remorse, a silent plea for my forgiveness.

"I'm not kind," his voice resonates in my head. But he is kind. He is. I won't let him give up.

Death knocks on his door again.

Time slows like molasses, stills into nothing as Lyric slips inch by inch.

I want to scream and run to him, to catch or be crushed. But it's as if I'm not in control of my own body. The fear in my chest swells into a wave that crashes over me and pins me in place. Every bit of me feels wrong, foreign, ruined. Something deep within me just wants to watch.

I can't lose him again. I simply won't.

I'm at war with myself; my limbs shake as I crumble to my knees.

Another scream, this one in futility, as Cruz pulls at Lord Thorn's magic just enough to keep Lyric teetering on the balcony edge. If Cruz relents even a little, Lyric will fall to a certain death.

And then it hits me.

The Viper's words drift back to me in a flurry. *"When love is about to fall, use it."*

I know the tattoo is still there, just hidden beneath Xavier's illusion. I rush across the dance floor, grabbing a shard of Saffron's glass, piercing the pad of my finger and smearing the blood up and down my arm, hoping I get enough on the tattoo. In this moment of panic I think back to the Viper, who wanted the stick of gum, which likely contained blood.

In a few painfully slow seconds, the tattoo seeps to the surface of my arm before curling away from my skin like a strip of bark. The butterflies lift and come to life, their wings soggy and red, and it takes a second for them to get into the air. All my hope free-falls to the floor. How are a couple of butterflies supposed to help me?

Lyric screams.

I force myself to run. Suffocating the dark thing inside me.

Reina thunders close behind.

Lord Thorn's dark figure is closing in, chipping away at Cruz, who's strewn across the floor, his face mangled with pain. Defeat simmers along the edges as he extends a hopeless arm at Lyric.

I run faster.

A subtle *snap* fizzles in the air. I barely notice it beneath the screams and my racing heart. But another *snap* follows. And another. My head turns toward the sound. Glossy spheres that look like droplets of blood float beside the butterflies.

Every molecule of air in the ballroom vibrates before the dewy red spheres hovering above guests explode.

A deafening bang followed by a smothering darkness that devours the room. I wave my hands through the inky dark, and it pulses in response. Hundreds of thousands of butterflies. Thrashing wings in a wall so thick, I can't see a thing.

Reckless, unhinged chaos. A living shield of butterflies, beating against my skin, making it feel like the darkness itself is fluttering. The crowd panics, a swell of motion that can only be felt, not seen, as the guests topple over one another.

The perfect distraction.

I could almost hug the Viper.

Another loud crack cuts through the madness and immediately all of the butterflies hover in place before falling to the ground. I blink away dots as my eyes adjust to the light and I search for Lyric, but I can't see him or Cruz or even Reina.

Xavier Stoutmire snaps his fingers and strolls rather unfazed through the butterfly carcasses. "Well, it seems as though this party is over."

71.

LYRIC

I try my best to catch my breath along with my swiftly evaporating pride. Judging by the splintering pain in my side, a few of my ribs are definitely bruised.

Huddled with my sister and Cruz beneath a shield cast by Reina, I can't do a thing but wait and try my best to breathe even though it feels like a knife is being twisted around my insides.

"Can they sense us at all?" Cruz winces from the effort—he's just as banged up, but if he expects me to apologize, he should know he'll be waiting for a long time.

Reina is drenched with sweat, barely steady on her feet. "No," she grits out.

"Maybe let her save her energy in case you idiots try something stupid again," Ellison whispers between her teeth.

For once Cruz and I share the same thought and we both back down in silence. The ballroom has begun to empty—apparently a fight followed by a flash mob of butterflies will do that to a party. Uncle X stands in the center, arms crossed, watching everyone leave. He absent-mindedly traces a faint scar on the back of his left hand. I'd always wondered why he never glamoured it away.

"What's that?" I'd asked him when I was six. Brave enough to push my grubby little finger on his hand and touch the half-moon scar.

For once he didn't punish me. "My father believed pain was the loudest way to get a person's attention."

I twitched, certain he'd unleash some unholy illusion on me.

But he simply looked away. "I don't think we can run from our fathers, Lyric. The best we can do is face them head-on."

I hadn't known who my father was at the time. And I certainly didn't think of Uncle X as one to fill the void. "I can outrun anyone," I said proudly.

"I hope so." Uncle X paused, then spoke more quietly, his fingers tracing the scar. "I couldn't outrun mine. He was the worst type of cruel."

"Crueler than you?" I blurted it out, and then immediately cowered behind the table, certain Uncle would punish me.

"Yes, Lyric. He was worse than me." Uncle's voice dropped again. "I'm cruel for a reason."

I peeked my head back out. "And why's that?"

"Because the world will be cruel to you."

I stamped my foot. "No, it won't."

"Hopefully not indefinitely, but I'm afraid it's inevitable."

I'd never forgotten what Uncle had said, and maybe that was the point when my anger was first carved out. But Uncle was right, the world could be unnecessarily cruel. It could give you a father who would try to drown you without any remorse. And a family that almost let it happen. It could give you a mother who spun nightmares and a childhood trapped on an estate with a ruthless uncle. But it could also give you a girl who might just make you forget it all. Make you want to start again.

Noise from the party reels me back, and I watch Uncle X give his final goodbyes.

“Interesting party,” says a lady in a fur-lined fox mask on the way out.

Uncle X nods. “Until next year.”

My mother is next to go, trudging through the dead butterflies, her lips pinched in a tight line. She pauses in front of Xavier, eyes darting wildly around the room. I know she’s looking to see if the council is watching, which of course they are. “Do whatever it takes,” she says cryptically.

“Don’t I always?” Uncle X smiles.

“Don’t fail him again.”

“Let’s not forget why we’re in this predicament in the first place.”

My mother’s mouth hangs open and I can tell she wants to say more. Maybe she wants to believe that I’m still alive. Or maybe she doesn’t care at all.

“Come on, Saffron. I think we’ve had enough excitement for the night.” Lawrence grips her arm, but not before she turns her head, eyes frenzied. Searching.

72.
MULLORY

It's exactly like the end of a middle-school dance, when the fluorescent lights are unceremoniously flicked back on, the DJ shuts down, and everyone blinks through sweaty bangs, wiping smudged mascara across hot cheeks. All the party high that swirled in the dim lighting and pulsing stereo system is sucked out of the room, leaving you on wobbly feet that suddenly hurt, and in a gymnasium turned dance hall that stinks like a locker room.

This is that.

The party is over.

Guests leave in a sluggish swirl, draining out of the ballroom that no longer feels like a Christmas Wonderland, but instead is littered with bug parts. Something about the magic from the Viper's tattoo caused the air to take on a sulfuric tang. Like the inside of a battery. And boy does it really kill the mood.

The ice swan stopped swirling and has begun to melt into a sloppy puddle, leaking into the butterfly carnage. I watch the crowd file out and any hope I had lessens as the numbers dwindle. Thankfully, most of them have taken their masks off, but no man with one eye appears.

Tonight, we were supposed to find the next clue—I even dared to hope it might be the last, because I'm out of ideas and out of items to bargain with. The trail ends here.

The council members are the last to file out, hesitant and keeping keen watch on the party and its passing guests. The Magnus finally claps her hands and signals that it's time to go. She has a way about her, a presence that has me on the edge of my toes.

"I trust I don't need to say this, Xavier, but if you are harboring persons of interest from us, well..." She gives him a dazzling smile, her amber eyes seared with challenge. "Well, then you'd be in contempt, too."

"I'm aware of the rules, but thank you for the reminder."

She leaves it at that, stomping out of the ballroom in her magnificent silver cloak with the rest of the council close behind. Only Lord Thorn lingers. His face is a stone mask, but the rage simmering beneath his beady eyes alludes to the storm currently brewing inside of him.

"I hope you enjoyed yourself," Xavier says coolly.

Lord Thorn looks poised to kill. "Where is he?" A long drawn-out pause, tension rising. "I won't ask again."

"Perhaps if you were more specific with the *he* you were looking for. I don't read minds. Unfortunately."

Lord Thorn smiles. Xavier Stoutmire is catapulted into the air. There's a terrible *clank* as his body slams into the metal nutcrackers, which tumble down like a line of dominoes. Xavier crumbles, momentarily stunned, but he staggers to his knees and throws his hands in the air.

The nutcrackers quickly reassemble, with robotic precision, forming a tight line before charging Lord Thorn, and because they're not technically alive, he has no sway over them. Instead, he's forced to dodge and kick the once-jolly soldiers who have now become combative, punching their arms, and attacking like a pack of knights, swords swishing through the air.

The soldiers are enough of a distraction for Xavier to limp to the side, but Lord Thorn is relentless. A line of blood trickles down his cheek as he ducks beneath the blade of a nutcracker, sprinting toward the stairs and scaling the mezzanine, eyes locked on Xavier.

A stifled groan escapes Xavier's lips as he wavers near the refreshments, arms shaking in protest before he collapses, smacking the table in a nauseating crunch of wood and joints. Victory flashes across Lord Thorn's face, but it's premature, as Xavier extends a shaky hand up from the debris.

This time the counterattack is subtle, a barely perceptible *buzz* near Lord Thorn, but it strikes with lethal precision. A crack in Lord Thorn's face as he sinks to his knees, arms gripping the railings. Tears stream in silent agony.

This is a volley for control, because when it comes down to it, illusions are just tricks of the psyche and Lord Thorn is a master controller. But Xavier has other magic here: Edwin alluded to protective elements that recognize him, not me.

Several of the looming Christmas trees topple toward the mezzanine, cornering Lord Thorn in a prison of evergreens. And it looks like Xavier nearly has him, until the veins in Lord Thorn's neck bulge, and his jaw clenches.

Xavier sinks to his knees and a resounding *crack* rumbles throughout the ballroom. The ice pond splinters and Xavier pries a shard loose. He lifts the jagged fragment above his head in a choppy motion, pausing, before lowering it to the edge of his throat. A bead of blood bubbles beneath the delicate skin of his neck, dangerously close to pulsing arteries.

Fight it. Come on, Xavier. Why should I care if the man who tried to murder me dies? I reason with myself that it's because he knows something, but maybe it's because I care too much.

My heart pounds. I can't watch another person die. I jump out of my hiding spot, and I rush to Xavier's side, trying to pry the sliver of ice away.

Lord Thorn barks out a laugh. "Mullory, so nice of you to join us."

I glance at my once red hair, which has returned to a mass of tangled, dark curls and I don't need a mirror to know the illusion has lifted. It must have come off when Xavier was overpowered.

I swallow and try to breathe while holding Xavier's arm, fighting to keep it steady. My only assurance is that Reina is holding tight to whatever cover she's thrown over Lyric and the rest of them.

Think, Mullory.

No butterfly tattoo left to use. No one to save me.

It feels hopeless, but I try to use the only thing I have left, frantically pulling at Xavier's magic, but it resists me like a stubborn child. What would I even do with it? Give Lord Thorn the other half of Lyric's mustache?

Lord Thorn takes his time getting down the mezzanine stairs, almost as if he knows it will all be over soon. I hear Gran's voice. *"There's fight in you, Mullory. But you got to be willing."* Easier said than done. But I manage to stand up and face Lord Thorn. He doesn't need to know that my knees are wobbling beneath the silk of my dress.

Lord Thorn takes the time to fix his hair, sweeping the singular red streak back before raising his hand.

I try not to cower, but my eyes seal shut as I brace myself.

But nothing happens.

Prying them open slowly, I glance up at Lord Thorn, who has his hand extended, palm side up.

"Hand it over."

I know exactly what he's talking about, but it doesn't make any sense. Since when does he politely ask for anything?

"I don't know what you're talking about."

He flexes his fingers. "Give it to me."

Why isn't he forcing me to hand it over?

"That's enough, Thorn." Xavier has somehow risen from the ice, and if he's in pain, he doesn't show it. "She doesn't have it."

Lord Thorn's eyes narrow to slits.

"You can ask her all day. Or take her with you to the council, it makes no difference to me."

Seriously? After I just tried to save him.

Lord Thorn huffs, clearly mulling it over.

"You know you won't get it that way," Xavier adds. "That's not how this works and you know it."

And whatever that means, Lord Thorn must agree because he relents and stomps toward the door. "This isn't over."

"Trust me, I'm well aware." Xavier sighs.

Only when the door is slammed closed does Xavier finally exhale.

"Are you al—"

"Absolutely reckless!" Xavier's voice booms and I realize he isn't just speaking to me; he must know the others are hidden somewhere. "Complete foolishness and utter stupidity. I want this entire ballroom cleaned up. No staff. No magic," he howls.

I watch him stagger toward the doors, which lock themselves after he leaves, along with the windows. A line of black garbage bags falls from the sky like deflated balloons.

Well, the no magic part shouldn't be a problem for me.

73.
ELLISON

The air inside of the magical bubble Reina constructed is hot and sticky—like we've been vacuum sealed in one of those ridiculous little ziplock baggies. To make matters worse, Cruz and Lyric have spent the last twenty minutes arguing over how to best save Mullory from Lord Thorn.

All those idiots managed to do was throttle each other and elbow me in the side. Lyric was seconds away from exposing our cover and I could've killed him. How many freaking times can he play the savior for Mullory Prudence? It's getting a little old.

Now, for whatever reason (probably fear), Reina has kept us hidden until Uncle Xavier leaves. When she finally releases the bubble, we all spill out in a flurry. Reina slumps against the wall, face flushed as if she just sprinted several miles.

Lyric wastes no time, staggering over to Mullory, clutching his bruised body and ego. Cruz is right behind him, because of course, with this girl it's always an undeservedly dramatic cavalry entrance. Cue the fireworks. Launch the parade.

But among all the chaos, I spotted something in Mullory, something minor that the others probably overlooked. The anxiety in me recognized it straightaway. How she faltered, too frozen in panic to act.

"That went well," I announce while downing a fresh flute of champagne. My heels crunch through the revolting layer of butterfly carcasses and I toss the empty glass on top of them.

"Ellison," Reina scolds.

"What? We have to clean all this up anyway. What better end to a fabulous party than shoveling trash. I, for one, am elated."

Cruz is the first to confirm that, in fact, my deranged uncle has sealed us in this party pit. What a complete waste of a night. Besides the obvious horrors, I accomplished nothing. No mysterious dream woman appeared, and if she did, I had no idea how to identify her. Just perfect.

Mullory is the first to pick up a trash bag, I suspect because she's the most familiar with them. "We better get started," she says.

There's really nothing to do but scoop handfuls of desiccated butterfly parts into the bags. Repulsive. I do my best to make it seem like that's what I'm doing, but really, I just shuffle around and make noise.

"I don't understand," Mullory finally says, clearly on the verge of a breakdown. "The Viper said to find the man with one eye, but we checked every guest."

"Did we?" Reina answers. "Our plan went off the rails pretty quick." She shoots Lyric a death glare.

He raises his hands and flinches from the pain. "Don't tell me that an eye patch wasn't a giveaway."

"Rule number one," Cruz thunders. "Don't go up to the mezzanine level, because Reina can't extend her power that far. Simple instructions—obviously you haven't mastered listening skills yet."

"I had to improvise."

Mullory rushes between them, trash bag clunking behind her. "It doesn't matter. We didn't find him. If there was a man with one eye, he's gone now."

"Maybe we just misinterpreted what the Viper meant," I say. Mullory looks at me, hopeful, like I have some miraculous answer. Really, I'm just winding her gears because I feel the same sense of hopeless desperation. "Maybe . . ." I continue, "it wasn't the man with one eye, maybe it was the man with one leg."

She stoops back down, shoveling crunchy bits into her almost-full bag. That's the only horrifying noise that fills the ballroom for what feels like hours until Mullory gasps, yanking an old leather-bound book from beneath the piles of butterfly bits. "What's this?"

We all hurry over, grateful for a distraction that doesn't stink like rotting bugs.

She quickly flips through a few dusty sheets. "They're notes of some sort, I think. Look at this."

I glance over her shoulder at the inner flap that has several images embossed in the leather. Six animals: snake, bat, lion, dragon, crow, and a butterfly.

"I don't understand," Mullory says, perplexed. "This is my mom's handwriting. And it mentions the shadow. But who could have left this here?"

The pieces snap quickly together. But I'm the only one who knows what my mother told me. I don't want to share secrets, but this could be important. "I think I know who left it."

"Ellison?" Lyric poses my name like a question.

I roll my eyes at him. "What? I think it's the same mysterious woman who left Mullory's gran that box of junk all those years ago. Because I think the same mysterious woman infiltrated our mother's dreams years ago as well. And before you ask, no I don't know who she is. But I did know that she would be at the party tonight."

"But how could she know that we would find it? It doesn't make any sense." Mullory chews her bottom lip.

I don't have time for her pouting. "You wanted a clue, now you've got one. Just read it."

74.
MULLORY

Seeing my mom's handwriting causes my nerves to spike with excitement, but also worry because something about this feels off. *"Never leave a clue out in the open where it could be stolen or exchanged. A great clue makes the most sense for the person it's intended for."* This clue wasn't hidden like the others, but Ellison seems certain that the woman from her mother's dreams left it.

I can't deny that my mom wrote this, and I can't put off reading it any longer as everyone stares, waiting.

"Okay," I say as I clear my throat. "'It has been well established that the shadow possesses the ability to pull someone back from the dead. However, it should be noted that in most instances, the dead often cross over immediately and thus are harder to retrieve. There is a pocket, or a seam, that exists between the folds of the living and the dead. Only the most stubborn and resistant to death can linger there for some time.'"

I glance up and smile at Lyric. Stubborn and resistant for sure.

"You can make googly eyes at each other later," Ellison whines. "Keep reading."

I snap back to the book. "'Retrieval is easiest from the seam, as it serves as a halfway point, like a crevasse in the spine of a book. Not quite in or out.'"

I pause, skimming the next bit, which gets technical. "It goes on about the shadow and it looks like my mom was chronicling it. Almost like a journal."

"What comes after?" asks Lyric.

I'm frantic—my eyes feel like they're moving at warp speed before I stumble upon something else. "I think this is the day she brought my dad back," I whisper before I start to read. "'I had to go past the seam, further and further into the icy grip of death, when the oddest thing happened. I could sense a divide on the side of the living. It was like I could see a physical bond between the magic and the person possessing it. Mina was standing beside me, and I felt the fragile links between her and her magic.... Even scarier, I knew I could break it. But I stayed focused in the land of the dead. I had to find Henry. Whatever was left of him. I pushed the limit that day.'"

Everyone is silent. I can't stop reading.

"'I hadn't told a soul about what I suspect the shadow can do at full potential, not until Henry pulled it out of me. (He always knows when I have a secret. Who knows how much longer I can hide the secret growing inside my belly.) It was his idea to share the shadow's power with the others. Cora had a scientific explanation. She always did. Before joining the carnival, she was a geneticist. Cunning and sharp.'"

"That's the Viper," Ellison says.

I nod and continue reading. "'Cora hypothesized that the shadow's power depended on the instability of certain covalent bonds, but it barely made sense to me. Give a scientist a straightforward problem and they'll give you a five-hundred-word answer, most of which is just a roundabout way to state a simple solution. But I have my own theory. When magic is passed, it's bound to us, but I suspect it goes even further than that. I believe it twists itself around whatever our souls are made of.'"

I pause, sharing a secret glance with Lyric, hoping he's thinking of our souls being close, before I continue reading. "'That's why the further into death you go, the harder it is to pull you back, because the tether is stretched too far. Your soul has departed. And then I got to thinking, if you were on the other side, if you went deep enough, you could visualize a person's soul, view it as a tangible entity. And even though you didn't belong, not your physical self at least, you could start messing with things you have no right to mess with. You could access the tether and, well, you could cut it. A bond that is imperceptible and therefore inaccessible in the land of the living.'"

No one says another word, and I flip through the pages to busy myself. They're heavy with science and theories of magical transfer. Elaborating on how magic has been traditionally inherited, and then posing the question as to why blood should be the sole determinant. The final few pages feel reckless, handwriting messily scrawled in every direction. Dark and secret thoughts spilling out from my mom. One in particular catches my eye.

What have I done?

75.

MULLORY

Maybe it's instinct or embarrassment that causes me to quickly shut the book, sealing my mom's secrets inside. "We can read this later; let's finish up and get out of here."

If anyone is suspicious, they don't show it. Instead, we continue to trudge through the crunching bugs. Some of them are now moist from the ice sculptures that have begun to melt. The smell only seems to be getting worse. Whatever type of magic these butterflies are, it stinks.

I grip tightly to the book, curious and fearful of what lies inside. Xavier's warning floats back to me. *"You may not like what you find."*

Lyric nudges past me and my heart aches from the moments that burned like hours when I watched him nearly die again. My breath turns into shallow little bursts and my feet sway beneath me.

"You need to learn to shut all the other doors." Ellison's voice is a light but acidic whisper, something intended for only me.

I turn my head to face her. "What doors?"

She plucks a slimy wing from her shoulder and flicks it to the ground. "I saw you before. It takes one to know one. That ache in here." She presses her nails to her chest. "That pit that you free-fall into, unwillingly without end. Shut the door. Shut them all. They all lead to nothing, they're all wrong."

I stiffen uncomfortably, almost angered at the accusation that there's something *wrong* with me... even if I know she's right. Even if Xavier's magic can sense it, too.

I continue with the cleanup and after filling three trash bags something stirs from under the table.

At first my mind goes to a dark place, picturing some monster rising from the depths of a bog, covered in leaves and mud. But as the butterfly debris falls away, I realize it's just a guest, the same man in the naval uniform from the start of the party. What's he still doing here? Did he somehow fall asleep?

There's a dazed expression on his face; his light blue eyes focus in on me as he rubs a lump on the top of his head.

"Are you okay?"

He grimaces when his fingers touch the tender egg on his head. "Must've been knocked out. Did I miss anything?"

"Nothing good."

The man scans the empty ballroom and peels a tattered wing from his forehead, inspecting it, before shrugging and tossing it away as he eases himself up. "This wasn't how my night was supposed to go," he says while standing on wobbly legs.

"If it makes you feel any better, that makes two of us."

The man gives me a weak smile as sweat begins to shine across his forehead. "You don't understand. I was here with a very specific purpose."

My thoughts whirl together trying desperately to make the pieces fit. "What did you say your name was?"

"Jim. Corporal Jim Stuart."

My eyes dart to his polished name tag, the very same one I spotted before all hell broke loose at the party. Of course. The answer has been staring me right in the face since the beginning. "Jim, your name is Jim," I repeat back slowly, gathering my thoughts. "A name spelled with one *i*."

He nods. "That's right, that's how I spell it."

An excited little laugh bubbles up my throat. I can't help it. The whole time the man with one eye was really Jim, with one *i*. "Jim, I think we can help each other out."

Jim takes out a pocket hankie and wipes his sweaty face. "How so?"

I drop my garbage bag by my feet, dusting my hands on my dress. "I'm here to collect my present."

Instantly, Jim sighs with relief, a palpable weight lifted from his shoulders. "Thank goodness."

"What do you have for me?" I'm expecting some bauble, or another box of clues stuffed in his pockets.

"I have a message."

At this point, the others have realized someone else is still here and they've circled around us.

"Guys, this is Jim. Spelled with one *i*."

Cruz swears under his breath and Lyric burrows his head in his hands. "Really?"

"Really. It's been him the whole time and now he has a message for me."

Jim clears his throat. "The message is this—to unlock it, check the seam."

I don't know what I was anticipating, but somehow this message falls exceedingly short. I'm exhausted, covered in insect parts, and seconds from a delirious, desperate fit. "Is that all?"

"That's all."

"But did this person say where or what the seam was?"

"Not a thing." Jim brushes off his pants, suddenly in a sprightly mood. "Well, I'm glad that's done." He turns to leave.

"Wait!" I call after him as he crosses the ballroom. "Was it a woman who gave you the message?"

Jim shoots me a puzzled look. "Yes. Of course." His tone suggests that this should be obvious.

My pulse quickens. *My mom.* "Did she look like me, this woman?"

"Did she approach you in a dream?" blurts Ellison.

Jim looks between the two of us and shakes his head, still very much confused. "No, no dreams. And she didn't look like you at all." Jim turns toward the corner of the room where Reina is huddled in the shadows. "It was her," he says.

16. LYRIC

The ballroom doors open, allowing a visibly relieved Jim to exit, before sealing us back inside, which is just fine considering we have an interrogation to conduct. Without saying a word, we've formed a tight circle around Reina, each of us burning with questions. I don't buy Cruz's fake attempt to pretend like he didn't know. Sure, you had no idea your cousin was planting clues.

"Reina, it was *you* who left the message?" Mullory asks, completely stunned.

Reina squirms as we tighten the circle and the pressure.

"Care to explain?" Ellison's voice is ice, even more frigid than normal.

Reina's purple eyes dart around the ballroom, searching for an escape, like she's a wild animal who has only just realized the confines of her cage. But there's no escaping from this.

"Well, did you?" Mullory presses. "Did you leave Jim the message?" I can tell a part of her is hoping it isn't true, that we weren't duped from the beginning, but another part just wants answers.

Reina swallows hard. "Sort of."

Ellison lets out a high-pitched laugh. "Let me explain a few scenarios that can be classified as *sort of*," she says while thrusting up air quotes. "You can *sort of* study for an exam. And you can *sort of* enjoy an oat-milk latte. But you cannot, under any circumstance, *sort of* give someone a weird message. Either you did or you didn't. Which is it?"

Reina throws her hands into the air, as if they might stop my now-rabid sister. Good luck with that. "Okay, okay. I left the message, but—"

"Unbelievable. This whole—"

"But it wasn't my message to leave," Reina cuts Ellison off.

"Let me tell you what we're not going to do—" Ellison begins again.

But it's Mullory who takes a stand and finishes her sentence. "We're not entertaining any more riddles."

"Just get to the point," I say.

Reina fidgets, clearly teetering on the edge of some internal debate, before she turns to Mullory. "Do you still have that picture of your parents?"

Mullory's expression turns suspicious. "Why do you ask?"

"Just trust me."

"That's the thing. We don't." Ellison spits her words.

Mullory pulls the wrinkled photo from a pocket of her dress and guards it tightly against her chest.

"I'm not going to do anything to it," Reina huffs. "I just want to show you something."

Tentatively, Mullory extends the photo and Reina points to the woman whose face is marked with a red *X*.

"The Dragon?"

"Yeah," Reina says softly. "The Dragon. Mina. She was my mom."

The pieces of the puzzle begin to shift and reorganize. It's all at the tip of my fingertips, urging me to solve it.

"Your mom is the Dragon?" Mullory raises one brow.

Reina nods. "*Was* the Dragon."

The past tense stings and we all know what the *X* means.

"I'm sorry," Mullory mutters.

"Sorry or not, it still doesn't explain anything," Ellison snaps. My sister isn't prone to the warm and cuddly.

"Ellison," Mullory scolds.

"No," Reina intercedes. "She's right. My mother died before she could finish it."

"Finish what?"

She looks at Mullory softly. "She couldn't finish what your mother started. I don't know every detail of the plan, I just had bits and pieces of what had to be done and when to set it into motion."

Her use of the word *when* and her strange watches suddenly help something else to click into place. "You don't have any siblings, do you, Reina?"

She looks at me with relief, like I've finally figured it out. "No. I don't."

"And your father's magic allows you to conceal things." I know he's locked up in the labyrinth for something, but that's a mystery I don't give a damn about right now.

"Yes." Reina's eyes glisten like she might cry.

Now I understand. "You got two."

Reina shrugs. "I thought you guys would've figured it out sooner."

"Figured what out sooner?" Mullory asks.

"She inherited both of her parents' magic. Her mother, the Dragon, she was a timewalker," I say.

"I prefer time traveler."

"Which direction?"

Reina gives me a sly smile. "Both. That's why I have these watches." She twists one. *"Forward."* She twists another. *"Backward."* And she twists the last of the stack. "*Now.* I thought it was obvious with my eyes and all."

Ellison smacks her forehead with annoyance. I can tell she's furious that we missed something so blatant. Rare eye colors often accompany time travelers.

"Time travel affects the melanin in your eyes," Mullory says slowly. "Cecilia must've known you'd find us, that's why she gave me that book. She wanted me to figure it out."

Reina shrugs. "Your mother had a list of items and specific messages that needed to be planted in time. I just followed the instructions."

Mullory opens and closes her mouth several times before speaking. "You visited my gran the day my mother was born?"

Reina nods. "Yes."

"If you helped plant some of the clues, that must mean you have some idea where my mom is. Right?"

"I don't know much more than you do."

Ellison steps forward, closing in on Reina. "You expect us to believe that you just randomly took up some mission your mother couldn't finish? Why would you do that?"

"Because . . ." Reina's eyes brim with tears.

It's Mullory who finishes the sentence. "Because it's what her mom would've wanted."

Reina nods and lets the tears spill freely. Something heartfelt passes between the two of them.

"But why didn't you tell us?" Mullory asks softly.

"Because time travel is extremely sensitive. The items had to be discovered like our mothers planned. I couldn't risk messing it up." Reina's wipes a palm across her tearstained cheek. "One small mistake and the whole thing could have been ruined."

"Oh, like it hasn't been already?" Ellison snaps.

"Reina." Mullory calls her name gently. "Do you have any idea where my mom is? Any idea at all?"

Fresh tears spring in the corners of her purple eyes. "I'm sorry."

Mullory sinks her teeth into her lower lip. "Do you have any idea what the message you left to Corporal Jim means?"

Reina shakes her head.

"I believe you," Mullory concedes. Even Uncle must sense a shift because the doors to the ballroom spring open. Cruz, who's been suspiciously quiet the entire time, is the first to exit. Mullory takes my hand, and I follow her.

Only Ellison and her extremely pissy attitude stay behind with Reina.

77.
ELLISON

How could I have been so incredibly naive?

"Don't ever be foolish enough to let down your guard, Ellison." My mother's best advice. When I was six, I lent Margaux Chutney one of my favorite pencils—mechanical with a soft, perfectly intact eraser and a gel grip handle. High quality and extremely functional. She returned it five days later, empty of lead with the eraser chiseled down to a pathetic nub. *"Don't trust people with anything you value,"* my mother told me that day.

Reina is just another Margaux Chutney. This is exactly why I created a list of nonnegotiable rules, and the golden one at the very top of the list is *don't trust anyone*. Trust is as flimsy as the off-brand sneakers Mullory bumbles around in. That's partly why her posture is so abysmal, but that's beside the point.

I'm glaring at Reina in a whole new light—an illuminating, traitorous light.

Part of me is almost jealous of her blatant deception because she was artistic in the execution. Mullory may have bought her story, but I won't be fooled again.

And to think I let my guard down.

I nearly trusted her.

Reina looks up at me, her face is still sticky with tears. I almost tell her to save the dramatics for someone else, when another thought pops into my head.

I work through it in silence. Neither of us has moved an inch since the others left and we're squared off in the trashed ballroom, locked in a staring contest. Only the occasional rusty squeak of a dying nutcracker can be heard. The type of Christmas cheer fit for a nightmare.

When I think she's about to crack, I beat Reina to it. "Are you her?"

Reina tips her head to her shoulder, confused. "Am I who?"

"Don't play dumb. Clearly you're smart enough to mastermind a time-travel version of Clue. I'm sure you can figure this out." I feel like there's steam spouting from my ears; I'm furious with Reina, but also with myself for not spotting this sooner.

"I'm not playing dumb."

"I guess I have to spell it out then. Are you the mysterious woman who visited my mother's dreams?"

Reina scrunches her nose, then opens her mouth before promptly closing it.

"Tell me."

"Oh, Ellison. NO," she shouts. "How could I be?"

I raise my voice to match hers. "How could you be?" I parrot back. "We don't know a thing about you, you could be anyone!"

Reina drops her eyes to the ground. "I don't have any dream magic."

"Oh, you don't?" I fake a shocked gasp.

Reina furrows her brow like she's thinking of something. "Wait a minute. . . ." Her face lights up. "This must be why we're drawn together."

"We're not drawn anywhere near each other."

Reina ignores me. "Think about it, Ellison. This mysterious woman visited your mother years ago and she warned her to save Lyric."

A lump forms in my throat.

Reina mumbles to herself and moves her hands around excitedly. "And your mother said she would be at the party." Reina smiles triumphantly. "Don't you see, Ellison?"

But I don't want to see what's been right in front of my face. I shake my head vehemently. I won't accept this. I can't.

Reina raises her chin to meet me, her violet eyes blazing. "It's you."

The tears start to well. "No."

"You're the mysterious woman. It's your magic, or rather your mother's, that infiltrated her dreams all those years ago. You couldn't believe that someone was strong enough to do it, but it was her magic and you using it all along."

I swallow, refusing to accept the ludicrous truth she's proposing, because to accept it, I'd have to accept the even harder one—there's no one left to turn to for help. Only myself.

"That's impossible," I whisper shakily. "It was years ago, before I even had any magic."

"Impossible by yourself maybe." Reina taps her watches, a cunning smile tugging at her lips. "But not with me."

"Absolutely not."

Reina keeps her distance, but her determination doesn't waver. "Why are you so set against visiting your mom's dreams again? Was she that terrible?"

"She wasn't the motherly type. . . ." For some reason I let the statement breathe.

"But . . ."

"But . . . maybe she knows that. She doesn't have the gene that bestows patience and kindness and whatever." I'm forced to reflect for a moment if that's really her fault. How can you possibly know if you'll be a good mother before you try? You can think it. Hope it. Want it. Even believe it, but maybe the rest is out of your control. What even makes one mother good and another bad?

"So maybe she's not so terrible?"

"Motherhood never suited Saffron Stoutmire, but I think that maybe she tried in her own twisted way." I've never admitted that aloud to anyone. Not a soul. It's always easier to lump my mother and her nightmares in a neat drawer labeled *evil*. Not to give her circumstance a second thought.

"I don't think relationships with our mothers are ever straightforward," Reina says softly. "Mine never was."

I glance up cautiously from beneath my lashes. "What do you mean?"

Reina tucks her lilac hair behind her ear. "I think there's a point when you notice their flaws, things you never saw when you were little, but then you kind of realize that they're just people and they mess up."

I raise an eyebrow at Reina, thinking to myself that I realized that straightaway.

"I grew up in a bubble; my parents always *seemed* happy. That's all I knew. I never imagined it could be any different. But it turns out they weren't happy. It was slow to catch at first. Raised voices, my mother crying, but it got messy. You can only hide unhappiness for so long, before it kind of just spills out, infects everything. It does what those of us who mess with time do." Reina's voice drops off.

"What's that?"

"It changes things. Goes back to all the stupid little memories... dinners, trips, parties, and it ruins them. Because when my parents stopped getting along, it felt like they weren't getting along with me. And pretty soon it felt like I was the problem, and I needed to pick a side. We weren't a unit; we were a divided war front."

"Seems a bit dramatic, and not entirely fair," I admit.

"Who said anything about being fair?"

I nod my head in agreement. I can't help but wonder if it's better to feel as though your family is broken from the beginning to keep expectations low. Or is it better to know happiness only to have it ripped out from under you?

"Those memories aren't tarnished," I finally say.

"No?"

"No." I keep my voice stern. "Because they're yours and only you get a say in how they change."

"Ellison Stoutmire." Reina full on smiles. "Was that something insightful, and dare I say, optimistic?"

"Don't be ridiculous, that was bleak at best."

"So, you'll let me help you use your magic to reach your mom's dreams in the past?"

I snap right back to my senses. Dipping into the anger that was momentarily abated. I almost trusted Reina, but I won't make the same mistake twice. Even more foolish, I almost trusted my magic, and look where that got me. "Not a chance. Let me handle my own business."

78.

MULLORY

After the party, I circled the library clutching my mom's journal, far too nervous to open it. Why, after years of searching for her and searching for answers, am I afraid to finally face them?

"You may not like what you find." Xavier is holding something back, something I know he'll use against me when I least expect it. That's why I need to figure this out first. The shadow. My mom. My father. Xavier's magic. All of it.

Tonight was terrifying and I can't unsee Lyric dangling from the balcony. But by far the strangest part was Lord Thorn's reaction when my cover was finally dropped. Why did he let me keep the shadow? Why not use his magic and force me to hand it over? Was that Xavier's doing? Was it mine? And all of that to gather yet another riddle to add to the list. *"To unlock it, check the seam."* A dark thought presses itself to the forefront, fueled by my frustration. Will I like what I find?

I keep the journal an arm's length away when I open it, as if the distance might guard me from whatever secrets lurk within. Most of the entries are purely documentary, scientific in their exploration of the shadow. It's near the end that the writing is almost unrecognizable, a frantic scribble.

Something's wrong with me.
Does Henry know?
Why?
Why?
Why?
Why?
Kill.

I promptly shut the pages as my mind whirls. *"We killed him. Me and Esther Merrybright."* Maybe Xavier was right, maybe I won't like what I find. Enough for tonight. I slip out of the library, hurrying to change out of the silken dress I'm still wearing.

But when I reach my room, I'm surprised to find that I'm not alone.

"Hi, Mullory." Reina is sitting on my bed, her eyes puffy.

I stow the journal behind my back. "What's wrong?"

"I wanted to tell you guys. Especially *you.*" She wipes her cheeks, crestfallen. "Our moms were friends."

"And one day you'll meet Mina, my very best friend." My mom had wanted me to meet her, she told me as much, but her daughter would have to do. I scoot beside her on my bed, slipping the journal behind my pillow before grabbing her hand. "What happened to her?"

Reina looks away. "I don't know, but it was me who found her."

My heart breaks at her loss, and it feels more personal because Mina—Reina's mother—was also my mom's friend. Another person in the Continuum killed. It can't be a coincidence. But by whom? The same person who killed my father? A darker thought creeps along the edges. . . . Could my mom be responsible?

"At first, I was too mad to do anything. But then I found everything my mom and yours had been working on. Their plan, the clues that needed to be given to your gran, the message to be delivered to Jim. All of it. And it kind of just gave me a purpose, you know?"

I look to Reina, searching for something, some distant connection to my mom. And even through all the deceit, I can appreciate the friendship our moms shared. Knowing that, in some warped way, we share a history. "I understand."

"Ellison doesn't." There's hurt etched in the lines of Reina's face. "It's her. She's the mysterious woman who visited her mother's dreams all those years ago."

"How is that possible?"

Reina wipes her face and stands up. "Because of me. I'm meant to help her travel back."

I nod, now noticing a small gift on my bed, where she'd just been sitting.

"Did you leave that?"

She smiles. "No, not from me."

19. ELLISON

I'm not her.

I can't be.

Because that would mean it's up to me now. That I'd have to trust in the magic I've only ever seen used to inflict pain. To trust in Reina to get me to my mother's dreams seventeen years ago. I'd dared to hope that the mysterious woman would be a mysterious savior. Especially when my mother said that this woman was more powerful than anyone she's ever encountered, someone able to rip down the mental fortress surrounding Saffron Stoutmire. But could I really be her? All-powerful in my mother's eyes? I've never been anything to her.

I'm rushing to the bar in the parlor before I can think better of it, but I'm not the only one. Stoutmire family problems.

Lyric's slumped against the wall. He wipes his mouth with his sleeve. "Here." He hands over a bottle of vodka.

I settle beside him, accepting the bottle and taking extra care to wipe the rim clean.

"My bad luck isn't contagious," he says.

"Are you sure?" I take a sip that ends in a sputter and a full-body tremor.

Lyric rubs his forehead with his fingertips.

"What's wrong with you?"

He slides even farther down the wall, wincing and grabbing his side. "I tried to fix it. I tried to do something brave."

"More like something stupid." The next sip of vodka is easier but still burns my throat.

"You don't understand, Ellison."

"Make me," I challenge him.

"To understand you'd have to care for someone so much..." He stumbles on his words, cracks each knuckle. "So much that you'd do anything for them. Anything at all."

His answer calls for another swig of vodka because it hits way too close to home. Do I care for Lyric more than I fear my magic? More than the fear that I'll mess this up? "Don't be ridiculous. Mullory obviously cares about you," I finally say. "You two spend all your time staring at each other and then moping about when you're not together."

"It's not that I don't think she cares." Lyric slams the bottle to the ground, before his voice drops. "But what if I don't deserve it?"

"Impossible."

"Do you ever wonder if it would've been any different if I'd lived with you instead? If *I'd* be any different?"

My heart races. *Every single day of my life.* "Sometimes."

"Maybe I'd be better."

I give my head a furious shake, trying to dispel the tears, and choose, instead, to deflect. "I'm not sure I turned out any better."

Lyric flashes a genuine smile. "You dress better."

I can't help but to laugh. "That is true." I stand, wobbly legged. "Just go to her already, Lyric. That's what you want. You should have what you want."

A groan as he stands, hesitating before me like he might hug me. But he thinks better of it. "You do too. Whatever had you happy the past few days, don't let it go."

Reina's last words float back to me. *"Impossible by yourself maybe. But not with me."*

80.

MULLORY

The mysterious gift is wrapped in lacquered red paper and tied with a crisp black bow. I turn it over, my fingers sliding on the satiny wrappings, but there's no tag. From Lyric, maybe? It's Christmas Eve, after all. Snow falls in giant flakes outside my window, backlit by all the dazzling lights spun around the trees, painted like a picturesque Christmas card. Brass bells have sprouted from the light bulbs, softly jingling a holiday tune.

Beneath the paper there's a simple wooden box. The top slides open to reveal a beautifully rendered miniature Ferris wheel. I curl a finger through the delicate spokes and place it in my palm: A string of bulbs lights up the wheel and the tiny carts tip and sway as it begins to move. A note slips out.

Don't be afraid to be the storm.
The magic is yours; you just need to take it. –C

Cruz. Something inside me unspools, spreading slowly like warmed honey. It's thoughtful and personal in a way that makes me fidget. I don't have much time to think about it because there's a knock at my door, and I quickly stash the gift beneath my bed.

And just in time. Lyric tumbles into my room. He's still wearing his tuxedo, but it's rumpled and untucked, and his hair is askew.

"Mullory." He hiccups.

I laugh and almost forget that I'm still mad at him.

"Not." *Hiccup.* "Funny." *Hiccup.*

I smell something sweet and sharp on him. "Are you drunk?"

Lyric holds up two fingers a smidge apart and squints at me with one eye open.

"You *are* drunk."

He shrugs and looks up at me from beneath the swoop of his messy black hair. "Drunk and sorry."

"Sorry for what?" I need to hear him say it.

Lyric squeezes his eyes closed, wincing. "For all of it." He sighs. "For what I did to Cruz, for starters."

"You should tell him, not me, that you're sorry." I instantly blush because I feel like Gran when she would scold me.

"Trust me, I did. That's why I had to have a drink after."

"*A* drink?"

Lyric smiles, and slurs, *"Drinkssss."*

"Was Cruz mad?"

Lyric scrunches his face up like he might be sick. "No, it was way worse. He understood completely and he told me it was no big deal. I wish he'd tried to fight me. . . ." Lyric slumps on the edge of my bed. "Then I wouldn't feel like such an asshole."

I scoot closer to him. "I think there was enough fighting already."

Lyric's left cheek is mottled with a fresh bruise and his upper lip is sliced on the corner. Part of me wants to soothe the cuts and scrapes cropping up all over him. "Does it hurt?"

"Doesn't matter if it hurts. I deserve it." Lyric's voice drops to a whisper. "I'm sorry for tonight, too, Mullory." An adorable little hiccup escapes at the end, and I try my best to keep a straight face.

"It was stupid and reckless," I tell him softly.

"Worse than stupid."

"But . . . kind of brave. Maybe even a little badass."

Lyric's head perks up. "Oh?"

I mimic his gesture from before and raise my thumb and pointer finger, leaving just a little space between them. I give him the same one-eyed squint. "Just a little."

Lyric gives me a lopsided smile before snapping his fingers together. "Oh, yeah. I came to bring you this." He twists his hand into his pocket, searching and grunting, a little disoriented. "Too many pockets. Stupid jacket."

"Wait!" I scream.

Lyric jumps to his feet, alarmed. "What?" He turns in a sloppy circle.

"The jacket," I proclaim. "Lyric, you're a genius! That's what Jim's message means. To unlock it, check the seam!"

Lyric gazes back at me, befuddled.

"The seam in the jacket from my mom."

81.

LYRIC

I'm not going to lie, the room is beginning to spin. The vodka sloshing angrily around my stomach seems to be the source of the issue, more so than Mullory's epiphany. But I don't want her to know how shitty I feel, not when she's on a mystery trail. It's adorable. Not that I find things adorable—clearly that's just the alcohol speaking.

After my botched hero attempt and then Cruz's actual heroic interception, not to mention my good old murderous father, I needed a drink. Okay, maybe I didn't need quite as much as I had.

I grip the post of Mullory's bed as she rips through the room, searching for her backpack. She's moving way too fast and it's only making the spinning worse; now the floor has begun to slide up the walls.

Mullory roots and kicks through a pile of clothes, setting aside the box the clues came in and yanking out the rumpled red coat. The same one she wore when she pulled me back from the dead.

She hoists the coat victoriously above her head, like it's the Stanley Cup. "'Check the seam'!"

I want to be excited, but most of my energy is focused on keeping myself upright and not face-planting onto the floor.

"Scissors." Mullory rummages through the desk, tossing a stapler and several sheets of blank paper before finding a pair. She slices them through the air like a mad scientist and looks to me for a quick approval.

I nod as the floor continues to melt into the wall. *"Gooo for itttt,"* I cheer in a slur.

It's forty-five minutes of intense cutting, followed each time by a high and then a low after every stitch is split and no secrets spill out. I do my best to be supportive, but all I really manage to do is sway side to side and sweat profusely; not that Mullory notices, she's too focused. When the last thread is pulled loose, Mullory tosses the scissors into the pile of red scraps littering her room.

"I don't understand. The message was to check the seam." She lifts a curl of fabric and lets it drift back to the floor before slumping onto her bed.

Some part of my brain rumbles alive and reminds me that this is the part where I step in and try to make the situation better. It's a sloppy transition from the floor to the bed as I crawl up beside her. "We'll figure it out," I muster.

I must have done some part of it right, because Mullory slides against my side and nestles her head beneath my chin. For the first time all night, I feel a sense of calm. She yawns into the crook of my neck, and I glance at the clock on the bedside table: 12:03.

"Crap, I'm late." I stagger to my feet.

"Late for what?"

I fish out the box from my pocket, the reason I came here in the first place, and I hand it over. "Merry Christmas, Mullory."

The shy smile she gives me makes it all feel worth it.

"Open it," I say. Jesus, butterflies in my stomach. Fluttering unsteadily above the violent waves of alcohol. By now, I should be sick of butterflies, especially after the party, but somehow, inexplicably, I'm not.

Mullory takes her time with the wrappings; she's one of those people who undoes every corner and meticulously lifts the edges without ripping. She's careful with it, even though I used a dusty magazine that I found beneath my bed as makeshift paper.

Mullory beams. "It's beautiful."

Now I feel embarrassed, heat and alcohol firing up my face. "Your mom found it. Or maybe it found her, I'm not sure how it works."

Mullory bites her lip as she lifts the delicate gold bracelet from the discarded doughnut box I shoved it in. Four charms shaped like tiny treasure boxes hang from the links.

"If you open them," I say as Mullory gently runs her fingers over the charms, "you can store sounds inside."

Mullory looks like she's about to cry, and I don't know why. *What did I do wrong?* Words blubber out of me. "I think your mom must have liked it because she filled them all up. Try it."

She lifts open the lid of one of the boxes. An excited voice skips through the air. "My favorite sound," and then it cuts to a little girl's laughter, and I know that it's a young Mullory, happy and carefree.

Mullory snaps the box close, sending the room into silence. I'm worried I've messed the whole night up even worse, and I don't have the slightest idea how to fix it.

"Stupid again?"

Mullory clasps both my hands and forces me to look at her, tears glistening. "I love it, Lyric. I love it so much."

Damn those butterflies. They flap their cheerful wings, taking advantage of my alcohol-induced fog, and shut down all my defenses, exposing the parts of me normally hidden. I lift my hand, tracing a finger along Mullory's jaw. Equal parts intoxicated and mesmerized.

Mullory stills in anticipation.

"You're just so . . ."

Her voice is velvet soft as it brushes my cheek. "So *what*?"

Enchanting. Brave. Loyal. Kind. Rip-my-soul-straight-from-my-body type of beautiful. But the word my brain finally dredges up and out of my mouth is decidedly safe and plain. "Just so . . . good."

Mullory's nose crinkles. "Good? Are you saying that you're not good, Lyric?"

The magic in me spikes, a not-so-kind reminder that I not only use it, I *enjoy* it. That in my moments of weakness, I relish controlling others. And try as I may, I can't ignore the truth burning a hole straight through me. I didn't inherit just Lord Thorn's magic. Excising him isn't as surgical as just removing one piece. Which begs the age-old question: Can we fight who we truly are? Can I?

"Lyric?"

"How do you know if you're kind? I mean, how do you really know if you're good?" Raw and painfully honest questions that sort of just tumble out.

Mullory inches her hand toward mine, running her fingers up the length of my arm. My entire body quivers from her touch. I'd do anything she says right now, anything at all.

"I don't think anyone is only good or only bad. I don't think it's this or that—"

"But—"

"But you seem to forget about the good in you. You saved me, Lyric."

"But how do you know if you're mostly good?" My voice ruptures, a half scream not just at Mullory, but at the universe. At anyone who will listen. Something in me feels dangerously close to fracturing, to cracking me open and seizing absolute control.

Mullory digs her nails into my arm like an anchor as she leans closer. Her lips brush the shell of my ear. "I know what you are, Lyric. I know." And then she kisses me. Softly. Not at all afraid.

The room finally stops spinning as Mullory drifts off to sleep and I lie awake with my thoughts. It doesn't take much to push me closer, to let my hand grip onto the shadow Mullory never takes off. Another betrayal, another secret. There's something dark about it, something that beckons to me on a deeper level.

"Henry," I call to Mullory's father, a memory that's trapped in the space of death.

He's more defined, almost corporeal, as his eyes swell with bloodlust at the sight of the shadow.

"This is what you want, right?" I bait him.

"Yes."

Swinging the stone closer to his face, I ask another question. "Is this what got you killed?"

The memory of Henry tenses, hisses. "Yes."

I edge closer, taunting him. "Tell me who killed you. Was it Lord Thorn?"

But nothing. Henry's memory doesn't stir. The wrong question then. I try another. "Was it Esther Merrybright?"

Mention of Mullory's mom causes Henry to splinter, wavering into fine particles that buzz like a swarm of flies before reorganizing back into a human form.

"She let him," he says when he finally settles. "She let him. He's watching you."

"Who?" I scream, done with all the riddles. "Who killed you?"

Henry looks me dead in the eye. "A friend."

82.

ELLISON

I wake to the sound of drums.

The beating matches the tempo of my headache, and my tongue is sandpaper in my mouth. The entire horrible party and the aftermath come crashing back in a painful burst.

Lyric nearly dying, then cracking himself open into a million little pieces. And Reina, who won't get out of my head. *"Impossible by yourself maybe. But not with me."*

Time travelers are notoriously full of themselves. Rare and coveted in a world that's already composed of the rare and elite. But who really cares if they can bend the very fabric of time? They're arrogant.

The drums grow louder, interrupting my hungover thoughts, as a troop of toy soldiers in green-and-red uniforms marches into my room, drums tapping to an annoyingly cheerful Christmas song.

"Go away," I yell, burying my head in the pillow.

They only play louder.

"What do you want?"

More gleeful drumming erupts as one of the soldiers tugs my duvet off the bed. Of course. They want me to follow them. Another soldier pulls a small sleigh containing a set of fleecy reindeer pajamas.

"No."

The drumming escalates. I want to kick them into tin parts, but I'm too sluggish to fight, so I go against every fashion instinct in my body and put on the polyester blend abomination. I won't dare admit that they're kind of soft. The toy soldiers turn in their polished boots and head toward the door.

"I'm coming. I'm coming."

I meet a sleepy-eyed Lyric in the hall; he's also wearing a matching reindeer pajama set. I raise an eyebrow—he never wears anything but black.

"What? They're comfortable," he says with a clumsy shrug. "You're in them too."

"I was forced."

"Sure." Lyric smirks.

Our toy soldiers converge into an even larger formation, a symphony that parades us down the hall.

"What is all this?"

Lyric shoots me a confused look. "It's Christmas morning, Ellison."

I'd forgotten about that. "Forgive me if holiday celebrations don't seem important while I've been struggling to keep you alive."

"Merry Christmas to you, too."

A small part of me feels uneasy—we haven't spent a Christmas together in years. *"Do you ever wonder if it would've been any different if I'd lived with you instead?"* Since he was five, Lyric has been alone on the estate for the holidays. Maybe he has an entire drawer full of fleece pajamas with tacky prints. I want to tell him I'm glad we're together, but the words ball up in my throat like a wad of wool.

I follow Lyric and the Christmas entourage to the library. An enormous fir tree commands the room, covered in sparkling snow and gold ribbons that weave and twist beneath glass ornaments encasing Christmas scenes. Tiny spinning trees, flying reindeer, chestnuts roasting, the works.

"Merry Christmas." Mullory beams. She's in the same pajamas as me. The first and last time this will ever happen. Reina, Cruz, and Edwin also have them on. Even Uncle Zolan, who's propped up in an armchair by the fire, is wearing them. Everyone's here in matching Christmas cheer like a dysfunctional family, everyone but my uncle Xavier.

And then I notice the presents beneath the tree, stacked and wrapped with glittering bows and shimmering metallic paper. Edwin sets out cinnamon buns glazed with orange-cranberry sauce and candied bacon.

I don't know why I get choked up. It's stupid. All of this is stupid. I blame my hangover.

It's just that at home, Christmas was a catered dinner and pre-picked gifts I bought for myself. Sometimes Whitaker and I would play games. But my parents were always busy, and I mostly spent the day alone.

"Oh, just sit down already, Ellison. It won't kill you," Lyric tells me. I curl into an oversize reading chair and accept a peppermint latte from Edwin.

"Merry Christmas, Miss Ellison," he says with a soft smile. "Now, it's time for gifts!" It's clear that Edwin is the busy elf behind all this glee, and he's ecstatic to sort the presents, reading the tags and passing them out. I sip my latte and sink even deeper, expecting just to watch.

"From me," Mullory says with pink cheeks as she hands over a lumpy-looking package.

I nearly spit out my drink. "You got me a gift?"

She blushes a deeper red.

"Why?"

"It's Christmas."

I set my cup on the side table and undo her wrappings. Mullory watches me open it, tensing as I remove each layer. Jesus, she actually cares what I think.

"Oh." I pull out a scarf. Chunky, tacky, and made of some strange weed-like yarn. It's the consistency of a matted hair ball you might yank from the drain.

Mullory feels the need to explain. "Because you're always cold and you don't have one?" She says it like a question. "I gave Edwin specific instructions on exactly what to get."

Edwin raises an eyebrow. "Very specific."

I stifle every impulse to tell her that there's a reason I don't have one of these. "It's . . . a scarf," I manage.

Mullory gives me a wide smile.

I keep the scarf on my lap, worried Mullory might burst into tears if I crumple it on the floor. Surprisingly, it's not my only gift. There's one from my uncle Xavier—a salt stone with an inscription that promises to wash away the day's worries. I snort. I'll believe that when I see it; obviously whoever imbued this rock with magic wasn't prepared for the type of worries I might need removed. Lyric gives me a pair of earrings carved from a clear glass that refracts the light into rainbow facets. He claims they're full of stardust and perhaps they are, but I eye him with the suspicion that he pilfered them from Uncle's treasury. It only makes them that much better.

Reina keeps shooting me anxious glances, reacting to my every move, trying to gauge my temperature. I keep all interactions with her on a frigid level of bitchy.

She finally attempts to hand over a gift. "I got you—"

I toss it back beneath the tree without so much as glancing at her. "I'm good, thanks." She needs to know my trust can't be bought. That it's not even for sale.

Next, I unbox a luxurious cashmere sweater from Edwin, the only one in the room with a modicum of taste. Then I settle back and watch the others, and it's almost kind of, well, nice. I can't help but wonder if this is a moment of love. It's a ridiculous thought, almost as ridiculous as the tears that threaten to fall.

I subtly wipe my cheeks, turning my head. That's when I notice Mullory turn over an oval-shaped velvet box with a puzzled expression. She opens it quickly and then promptly shuts it and tucks it into her pocket.

"What's that?" I ask.

Her voice squeaks. "Oh. Just some candy."

She really is a terrible liar.

The rest of the morning is filled with desserts disguised as breakfast foods and fancy Christmas-themed beverages. At one point, Uncle Zolan bumbles off with the excuse that he has *work* to do. A lull hits the room and all of us stare at each other in silence. Edwin must sense it too because he finally relents.

"All right. Get back to whatever it is you've all been doing," he tells us.

Because truth be told, there's still more than one mystery to solve.

83.

MULLORY

I call Gran with a mouth full of toffee crunch and a heart full of guilt.

I've never spent a Christmas apart from her, but she's in high spirits when she answers the phone and informs me she's headed to the casino with Eleanor Pitosky and Lena Markmutt.

"Don't worry about me." She brushes me off, but I can tell she misses me.

My heart nearly splits wide open from just the thought.

"Any word?" she asks, fighting to keep her voice light. I know she's talking about my mom, but she's too afraid to say her name, some superstitious caution.

The very last thing I want to do is to let Gran down. How do I even begin to sum up all the bizarre places and people the clues have led me to? How could I ever tell her what my mom did? "Almost," I croak.

A beat of silence, then static.

"Don't give up, Mullory. You've got more fight in you than you think."

"I love you, Gran. Merry Christmas."

"Love you too."

I waddle back into the library, wiping away my tears with sticky fingers. The wrapping paper has been cleared and Edwin has left, leaving behind some brain food: apple-cinnamon glazed doughnuts and gingerbread French toast. Everyone is gathered by the tree still in their matching pajamas, waiting. Looking at me like I'm meant to march us straight to the next clue.

But I don't really want to be a leader, and I'm tired of parading around like I have any idea what happens next. I clear my throat and fumble around for the right thing to say. My arms swing awkwardly by my sides, skimming my pocket that contains the secret gift. It came in another unmarked package, but it wasn't from anyone in the room. This was meant for me and for me alone to figure out. It's a coin, familiar but different, bronze and stamped with a butterfly pattern, just like the tattoo from the Viper. And almost immediately I knew what I had to do with it.

"Mullory and I checked the coat her mom left," Lyric says encouragingly, trying to jump-start the discussion and fill the silence.

I give him a quick look of thanks and dive right back into the mystery at hand. "I thought maybe the message was meant for the coat because it was the first clue my mom left me."

"Any luck?" Cruz asks.

I shake my head.

"But it wasn't the first," Reina pipes up. "Your mom left you the shadow."

Hearing her say it out loud, I note her eagerness to finish her own mother's work. The feeling resonates with me as I clutch the amulet that I refuse to take off.

"But there's no seam on it. It's a stone."

Lyric dips his head to his shoulder, mulling something over. "But you did say you felt like there was some sort of blocker on the shadow. Maybe it doesn't fit the second part of the clue, but it could fit the first. What if there's some sort of lock on the shadow itself?"

I stare back at him, astounded. "The message is meant as a way to unlock it."

"And if we unlock it, then we can cut my connection with Lord Thorn." Some bare thread of uncertainty, maybe even fear, is buried in Lyric's words.

This information gets Ellison perked right up; she was only just lazily listening and simultaneously scrolling on her phone. "Then we need to unlock it," she declares hastily. "We need to go back over every single clue and find this damn seam. What else do we have?"

I've never seen her so excited.

"We still have the riddle from the Skeleton Singer," Cruz offers. "'Most think it's full, few know it's empty. If up is down, then your hands are twelve in time above.'"

Ellison types it out on her phone and rereads it several times. "But it has nothing to do with a seam."

"We still have to solve it, every other clue has been useful," I say.

Nearly an hour later, we'd done nothing but argue over the origin of the word *time*.

"From the Old English word *tīma*, which translates into 'limited space of time.' Maybe it's referring to a particular space or seam."

"That's a rough translation at best," Cruz counters.

"I didn't know I was with an expert," Ellison sneers.

"Enough," I shout. "Let's just put the riddle away for a little bit. I don't think the seam fits with it anyway. My mom does reference the actual space between the living and dead as a seam, but there's nothing there."

Lyric shifts uncomfortably, looking like he might say something.

"You've already been there, and never found a clue. Besides how would your mom get a clue there anyway?" Reina asks, dismissing my theory.

Cruz paces the coffee table, trying and failing to look serious and astute in his reindeer pajamas. "Let's circle back to the beginning and make sure we're not leaving anything out. There's a seam somewhere."

I rewind us to the day I pulled Lyric back from death. I leave out the almost kiss in front of my not-so-sleeping gran.

Then I go even further back, tunneling through time, searching for the point this mystery started. "The day my mom was born, a woman left my gran a box of random items. Every clock in the hospital stood still the moment the exchange happened."

"That would've been me." Reina clutches her watches.

"Right, you left my gran a box of clues. There were four in total, plus the coat I found at the New Moon Dry Cleaner."

Ellison raises an eyebrow but keeps her sassy comment to herself.

"When we sewed the button on the coat in the correct order, it led us to the Skeleton Singer, who we later found out was a member of the Continuum."

"And he gave us the unsolvable riddle and a cage full of bird crap," Ellison is quick to remind us. "How could we forget."

"And the bird . . . *droppings* contained the receipt that led us to the café," I say, "where Scott thought that I was the one who bought the coffee, even though it was my mom."

"And the other half of the receipt led us to the Viper," Cruz continues.

"Who gave me the tattoo," I finish for him. "And the instructions to find Jim."

"And that brings us right back to when Jim gave us the clue to check the seam, to hopefully unlock the shadow," says Ellison, dejected.

We're all silent, the list of places and clues buzzing through our ears, searching for some scrap we may have missed. In my head I can't help but recount what I've learned along the way. My mom murdered someone. Betrayed her friends. Had her heart broken with my father's death. Was possibly involved in other murders.

"And there was nothing else in the box?" Cruz asks.

"No, nothing." I sigh.

Lyric's eyes light up. "I think I know where to look next," he says triumphantly.

84.

LYRIC

Mullory's face is lit up like the Christmas tree twinkling behind her. I know that look. A part of me might even love that look. Shit, all of me loves that look.

"The box," I say. "I thought it was nothing, some random packing container that was only meant to hold the clues. But what if *it* is a clue?"

"The seams of the box," Mullory says slowly, shaking her head. "But I already inspected the whole thing." Her teeth sink into her lower lip. "Maybe I missed something?" She gives me that look again, and I feel it on a molecular level. Every single part of me is hers for the taking.

"Are you two just going to smile at each other like idiots? Go get the box!" Ellison orders. "Now!"

Seriously, my sister is the worst. But she's right.

Mullory rushes past us, her fuzzy socks glide across the polished floor, and she smacks the edge of the wall.

"I'm okay," she shouts over her shoulder, racing toward the stairs. She returns quickly, breathless, with the dented cardboard box in hand.

Reina has already taken the knife from the hazelnut-cream Yule log and licked it clean. Naturally, the next step is for all of us to instantly declare ourselves experts in the art of box cutting.

"Top to bottom," Cruz instructs.

I try to pry the box away from him. "Absolutely not. This side first."

"Idiots," Ellison proclaims. "That's not how it's done."

While we bicker, Mullory takes the box and begins to delicately slice the knife through the thick corrugated edges. "That's odd, I could have sworn this side was sealed," she says, puzzled. "I thought I checked this, but there's something in here." She flips the box, shakes out a flattened scroll of paper, and quickly unfurls it.

"Well?" Ellison taps her foot.

Mullory eyes the sheet. "I'm not sure."

We all huddle behind her, squinting in unison. There's a cluster of dotted lines traversing the paper, with no discernible pattern. "It just looks kind of random."

Mullory pinches the spot between her eyes before double-checking the seam and pulling out a clear sheet, the same size as the paper with the random dotted lines. She runs her finger along the transparent paper. "There's a series of tiny, raised bumps on this one." She takes a step back, studying both.

"Are we sure nothing else is hidden in the box?" asks Ellison.

"Maybe not inside, but on it?" Cruz ponders and taps the front of the box depicting a treasure chest and map. "*Happy Pirate's Liquor Chest.* That could be important."

"Booty and Booze." Ellison reads the tagline and snorts. "Call it a gut feeling, but I think not."

Cruz dismisses her. "Maybe we're meant to bring this paper to the liquor store?"

"It doesn't feel right. My mom . . ." Mullory shakes her head, her frustration palpable. "There's got to be something that links the two sheets together." She slowly turns the box from side to side before flipping it over. Her gaze lingers on the underside of the box.

"What is it?" I ask.

"'Fold along the dotted line.'" Mullory reads the instructions stamped on the box itself. "I think we need to fold the first paper." She taps her chin. "But which line do we fold first? That's what the clear paper must be for." She holds it up to the light, puzzling at the raised dots. It's not long before a smile tugs at her lips.

I can't help but be in awe of Mullory. Smart as she is, I couldn't appreciate it in the Mystery Royale even when she solved every riddle. Beat my uncle at his own game. Drank poisonous tea and climbed down a deadly well. But now I see her for what she truly is. Brilliant. "Go on," I encourage her.

"It's clear so we can lay it over the first." She pulls a pen from her pocket. "Each cluster of dots signifies a number, the order that the lines on the first paper need to be folded."

Cruz extends an arm. "May I?"

"Another one of your hidden talents?" Ellison sneers. "Origami master, perhaps?"

"Actually, yes."

That shuts up my sister and I'm so eager to solve this thing that I don't care if Cruz is an origami master or not. Or even if that's a real thing. But he is quick and oddly skilled at folding, I'll give him that.

We watch him make crease after crease with expert precision.

Cruz makes the final fold and showcases the creation in his palm. "It appears we have a miniature house."

"Not just any house," I counter. Several of the once broken lines have joined to form two letters: *S.E.* "This house. Stoutmire Estate."

"Any thoughts on where?" I ask, hopeful she's figured that part out, too.

"The estate is enormous," Ellison is quick to point out. "How will we know where to look?"

Mullory's gray eyes get all twinkly again. "Only one way to find out."

"We should split up and cover more ground," I suggest while taking a step closer to Mullory.

"Lyric and I will start inside," Ellison declares in a forceful blurt.

"We will?"

"Yes." She grits her teeth and gives me a look that strongly suggests I don't ask questions. I can't help but notice that she's given Reina the cold shoulder all morning.

"Lyric and I know the inside of this estate best," she says, recovering.

Cruz claps his hands like he's won a prize. "Excellent. Then the three of us will search the grounds."

Yeah. How excellent.

85.
MULLORY

I don't bother changing out of my reindeer pajamas and instead shimmy into a snowsuit (courtesy of Edwin), snapping the overalls right over top, along with a pair of fur-lined boots. Then I shove on my parka and fling my mittens over my shoulder as I rush outside and crunch into the snow. I'm vibrating with the excitement of the mystery; I can't help the thrill pulsing through my body. *"Let's not forget, we love the hunt, Mullory."* Maybe I'm more like my mom than I think.

Something is hidden on the estate, something most likely left to me by my mom when she was last here. But what? Something about this clue isn't sitting right with me; it feels different, but I can't pinpoint why.

I stomp through the snow, hurrying to the back of the estate, building up a sweat in the process. I rip off my parka minutes into my expedition.

"Aren't you cold?" Reina asks with chattering teeth. Only her eyes are visible beneath the hood of her electric-pink snowsuit and the orange scarf wrapped tightly to her chin.

"Not really."

Reina shrugs and burrows her mittens into her coat pockets. "Where to first?"

I look over the sprawling grounds, layered in snow and crusted with ice, like a faerie kingdom fit for a winter queen. Swirls of frost pattern the glass walls of the greenhouse, a place forever drenched with horrific memories. But I'm certain that fear will only hold me back. "There."

"Any idea what we should be looking for?"

"I guess we'll just know it when we see it," I say with a forced smile, and trudge quickly ahead.

Inside, the air ripples with moisture, and I feel as though I've just buried myself in a plot of soil so thick I taste it in the back of my throat. Returning to where Lyric nearly died rouses the darkest parts of my brain, the parts that ooze adrenaline and pump a sweat that glides down my neck. My muscles twitch in response, an involuntary impulse to run.

"Must be strange to be looking for clues from your mom," Reina says, reminding me that I'm not alone. "Even more strange to find out your dad is still alive."

There's something wistful about her voice, not necessarily jealousy but more somber, a projection of her own predicament. I can't help but to compare us and wonder which would be worse: To know exactly where your parents are, even if one of them is dead and the other is in an inescapable prison built from the kindling of nightmares. Or to not know anything at all, swaying between ignorant bliss and imagined horrors.

"I'm sorry about your mother," I say softly.

Reina pauses by the water basin. "Me too." She raises a hand to swipe her cheek, tears catching in her lashes. "Most days I can almost forget that it happened. But somehow that makes it so much worse, because in those few seconds when I do forget, that's when I can finally breathe again. But it always catches up to me, I always remember and"—the words stick in her throat—"it hurts just as much."

I place my hand on Reina's shoulder, a show of solidarity. "It hurts because you care."

"So, I need to stop caring?"

"No." I squeeze her shoulder. "I don't think we ever stop caring, I just think the pain eventually becomes bearable."

Reina shakes her head. "My dad's not dead, but it's still just as painful."

"What happened to him?"

Reina absent-mindedly twists the faucet, letting the water pour out before turning it shut again. "He was betrayed while trying to do what he thought was the right thing. But regardless, he did break the rules. The council doesn't care if your intentions are pure." Reina's voice drops to the barest whisper. "Someone ended up dead... so I get it."

Her admission renders me speechless, parting the way for that tingly feeling that creeps along the base of my neck. *"Someone ended up dead."* What does that even mean? Like her dad killed someone? I swallow past my shock; we have more in common than I thought. "I'm sure you miss him."

Reina sighs. "I miss them both. Losing them sent me to a dark place.... That's why, when I found my mother's things..." She shrugs. "I dunno, it gave me a purpose. Even if I didn't understand exactly why I was doing what I was doing, I knew it was what she would've wanted."

Her words resonate with me because I understand better than anyone the aching need to fill a void. I lean closer and hug her. "I'm glad you're here."

Reina squeezes me back. "Me too."

I break from the embrace and feel the need to lighten the mood. "Even if you did bring Cruz along."

Reina laughs. "Cruz brought himself. If you haven't already guessed, he can be annoyingly persistent until he gets his way."

"And what does Cruz want?"

Reina gives me a mysterious wink. "Our abuela is a seer."

I nod. "He told me that, but what—"

"But did he tell you she is most gifted with matters of el corazón?"

El corazón. The heart. Oh God.

86.
ELLISON

Lyric isn't pleased with me. He has the emotional range of a toddler. Like I care. I haven't been pleased with him since he started down Mullory Martyr Road, but he's my brother and we need to stick together.

This has absolutely nothing to do with the fact that I haven't been able to even look at Reina. It's better if Mullory handles the traitors anyway, although I do feel a little guilty as I shove the scarf she gave me into the deepest corner of my dresser. We're not friends by any means, but her clumsiness does grow on you. Like a fungus.

"Ready?" Lyric asks while lingering in my doorway. Grumpy and in his signature black.

"Don't pout, it's just a few hours apart, I doubt it'll kill you," I say. "Actually"—I push past him and into the hall—"it might be safer to search for clues with me, given Mullory's track record."

"I'm not pouting. I don't pout."

"Please, everyone in our family pouts; it's genetic."

Lyric stiffens at the mention of the word *family*, and I know he's thinking that he isn't really a part of this one.

"You're still my brother," I say, feeling the need to fill the air with something substantial. I want to say more. It's all there, tucked away beneath my ice-clad heart, but baring our emotions makes us Stoutmires sick. Worse than the flu.

"Half brother," Lyric corrects me.

"I don't do halves." It's the most sincere thing I can think to say, and Lyric must recognize the sentiment because he breaks into a smile.

"I never did thank you properly." He gives me a sheepish look.

"Well, your manners are abysmal."

"I'm serious, Ellison." Lyric halts, gripping the stair banister. He looks at me, but it's far too intense, and I fix my sights at the ceiling and study the detailed molding, because now my eyes are getting all itchy and bothered.

"Thank you."

Something in my chest tightens with a terrible pressure, building and budding, and all I can manage to do is nod at him. Maybe in a different life or in a different family, now would be the time for us to hug, but that's not me, I don't hug. And neither did Lyric, not until Mullory Prudence. "Thank me when it's done," I say, and march down the stairs.

"Where do we start? Not really sure what we're looking for. Maybe we try the map room?"

And because I literally have nothing else to go on, I agree. The map room is adjacent to the library, the door to which is hidden in a panel that springs open after you spin a globe counterclockwise forty-three times. Tremendously tedious and unnecessary, thank you very much, Uncle.

The room is squat and terribly cluttered, and the walls are a gridlock of cubbies, each stacked with rolled maps stuffed in cylindrical cases, labeled by year and origin. Historical significance and blah blah blah. But what are we looking for? Where is the clue?

Lyric starts poking around, pulling atlases and unfurling maps, but I can't seem to concentrate. My mind wants to replay the conversation with Reina, the impossible explanation she proposed.

"Lyric?"

"Hmm," he mumbles while nose-deep in a dusty map.

"Do you think it's possible that mother's dream magic isn't entirely evil?"

Lyric looks up, puzzled. "What are you trying to say?"

"Nothing. Keep searching," I order. *Nothing at all,* I think. *Except I might be the mysterious woman, and I may have already saved you twice before.*

87.
LYRIC

"This is pointless," I groan while tossing another map to the ground. "It could take us years to search Uncle's entire estate."

"The clue wasn't exactly illuminating. What else are we supposed to do with a miniature house?" Ellison snaps back at me. "Play dolls?"

"Wait a minute . . . a miniature house," I repeat back slowly. "I think I know where we need to go."

A quick text to the group and everyone hurries to meet in front of the library.

"The clue's in there?" asks Cruz.

"No. Not that door, this one." I point to the wall that abuts the library. The lower half is covered with wood paneling, and the top boasts a red damask wallpaper.

"Funny. I don't see a door."

I give Cruz a firm back pat that's more of a shove. "That's because you're not looking hard enough." I crouch down and tap the one of the panels in the woodwork that conceals a door. "Miniature house. Miniature door." I push the panel, and it pops open.

Ellison huffs. "Ridiculous. We won't fit through that."

"We will. I've done it before." I extend my arms through the small door and shimmy through the tight space. "Watch your heads," I call through the opening.

Mullory pulls herself through next, crawling on her knees to avoid bumping her head. It's a tight squeeze as everyone piles in, yanking themselves through.

"What that hell is this?" Ellison asks, aghast. She picks up a tiny bed from one of the countless replica rooms modeled after the estate. "Is this *my* bed?"

"Yes."

Every room, every candlestick, every cup. Only miniature.

Mullory plucks a doll-size version of herself, dressed in the very same reindeer pajamas.

Cruz sticks his finger in one of the fireplaces, only to retract it quickly. "It's actually burning. Fascinating. But why all this?"

"That's a question you'd have to ask the great Xavier Stoutmire," I answer back.

"Creepy doll room aside, where's the clue?" Ellison scoots around on her knees.

"Look." Reina points to the bathtub that's the size of a lemon. She splashes her fingers in the water and retrieves a Scrabble letter.

We search the dollhouse-size Stoutmire grounds, bumping into one another every few minutes. The next letter is in the kitchen oven, scalding hot, next to a petite loaf of baking bread. The rest are hidden in armoires, beneath rugs, tucked in beds, and floating in the fountains.

"But they're right here in the open," Mullory puzzles aloud when we can't find any more letters. "Why would my mom leave them like that? And when did she do it? How could she have known no one was going to move them?"

Ellison, however, doesn't care to entertain any of those questions. "I doubt anyone was coming into this room. We've got the next clue, let's not waste time."

"It just doesn't feel right," Mullory mumbles.

"Your mom liked board games," I remind Mullory, trying to get her going again.

"I guess so. . . ."

Ellison flips over the pile of tiles. "Great, a bunch of letters."

SGNBROGNLUI

Mullory studies them. "We need to arrange them."

Obviously, we all grab for the tiles at once, inciting an argument in which no one can make any progress as we each hoard pieces to ourselves.

"Slob," Ellison announces proudly. "I've spelled *slob*."

"Highly doubtful that *slob* is the big mystery reveal," Cruz answers.

"Oh, and I'm guessing you have something better?"

"As a matter of fact, I do. I've spelled *gun*."

Ellison's eyes narrow to slits. "You would spell *gun*. Murderer."

"Everyone, be quiet," Mullory orders.

"What about *gun slob*?" Ellison proposes.

But Mullory's not in the mood for games. "It's not that either. We need to use every letter."

I nudge Cruz aside and Ellison drops her tiles so that they scatter across the floor. Mullory ignores her and starts sliding letters up and down, right, and left. It only takes a few minutes.

"There."

"'*Burning logs,*'" I read.

Mullory nods. "Isn't it obvious? It's a fireplace."

"Good thing the estate only has forty-four million fireplaces," Ellison grumbles.

"But how many of them are wood burning? Aren't most of them gas?"

It's satisfying to watch Mullory school my sister, whose lips have suddenly pursed.

"I dunno, maybe two," says Ellison, clearly pulling that number from her ass.

Mullory gives me a private smile, excitement brimming over. "We're getting close."

88.
ELLISON

After checking with Edwin—and enduring an unnecessary lesson on the history of converting most of the fireplaces on the estate to gas—we're finally rewarded with the location of the ten remaining wood-burning fireplaces. Mullory looks elated with her discovery, but I'm slightly less sore knowing it's ten and not two. More work for us, but it's worth it.

The first fireplace, in the library, has a creamy marble hearth lined with jade-green tiles that glisten like mossy jewels.

"Well, are you going to light it or what?" I ask, while everyone stares at the fireplace, dumbfounded. In the end it's our resident survival girl, Mullory, who nearly lights her shirt on fire in the process but does eventually get a sad-looking fire going.

We hover around the flames, waiting for God knows what to happen. Mostly we just breathe in lungfuls of soot.

"Try the next one?" Mullory finally decides.

"Obviously," I answer, because someone needs to keep this group on track.

The next two fireplaces are both duds. All we've managed to do so far is make ourselves smell like a troop of Boy Scouts.

"This is taking too long," Mullory declares, visibly distressed. "Let's split up."

And before these idiots start arguing over who gets to go with Mullory, I beat them to it. "Girls will take the first-floor fireplaces, you two sweep the upper levels. Clock's ticking."

The three of us scramble forward, leaving the two very best of friends behind.

"Happy hunting." I smile, thinking Lyric will thank me the next time he's paired with me. "Don't, like, kill each other," I shout over my shoulder.

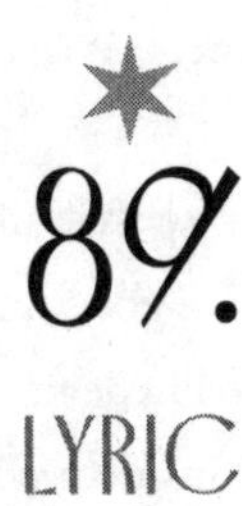

89.

LYRIC

Cruz stops to tie his boots three separate times, clearing his throat dramatically in a pathetic attempt to talk to me. I continually ignore him, focusing instead on lighting the fireplaces and keeping on task.

No clue.

Fine.

On to the next.

I already got my drunken apology out of the way; we don't need to be friends. I'm perfectly fine coexisting in strained silence. Truth be told, I thrive in it.

But apparently, Cruz does not.

He lets out another fake throat-clearing cough, before finally caving. "Lyric, wait."

"No time to wait."

"We need to talk."

"No. We. Don't. We need to keep going." I keep my pace quick, and my eyes on the hall ahead, before marching into the next room.

But Cruz presses on, like an annoying gnat that refuses to die. "Well, I'm going to talk and maybe you'll listen."

"Maybe." He may have saved me, but that doesn't mean I trust him. Or that I like him.

I take a sharp turn into another guest suite, edging my shoulder into his side.

He grunts. "Look, I know you've got something going on with Mullory."

It's the way he says it, like it's no big deal. Like she's not absolutely everything. Like I didn't die for her. The magic inside me hisses, imploring me to make Cruz suffer. Or maybe it's just me. How can I possibly know what parts of me are my father and what parts are me? Every day the line separating the two blurs, and I'm certain at some point I won't be able to pry them apart. "What are you getting at?" The question slips from my lips like venom.

"I'm not getting at anything." He puts his hands up in surrender.

I crack each knuckle in a futile attempt to calm myself. At the next fireplace, I pull a match from my pocket and strike it against the box. The flame catches.

Cruz backpedals. "Maybe we should just let it be." Perhaps he senses me coming undone, leaking rage.

I toss the match onto the logs. He doesn't get to just volley back and forth; if he wants to start this conversation then he'd better be prepared to finish it. "You don't know Mullory."

Cruz adjusts his stance, arms bracing in defense. "And you do?"

How could I even begin to tell Cruz what I feel, when I've barely been able to tell Mullory herself? That she's broken down all my defenses, found a way in when no one ever cared to before. She's my only constant, who for some inexplicable reason fights for me. But why do I have to defend myself to Cruz Lagunes? "Yeah. I think I do."

"Well, I think I do, too." Cruz is more matter-of-fact, borderline defensive.

I start to open my mouth.

Cruz interjects. "Just hear me out."

I cross my arms, threateningly.

"I haven't been entirely honest."

I narrow my gaze. "Got that part. Murdering your brothers doesn't exactly make you the trustworthy type."

A sly smile tugs on Cruz's face. "Understandable. But I was referring to Mullory. I know her— Well..." He pauses and backtracks. "I've known *about* her for a while."

My mind scrambles to find a logical explanation. "After my uncle's will was settled, plenty of people thought they knew her."

"No." Cruz shakes his head. "Before that."

"Bullshit." I don't like his tone or the threat it implies. That he could have something with Mullory that I don't. He must be lying. "She had no idea who you were when you got here."

For some reason this comment triggers Cruz. Not the comment about him being a murderer, but this one.

"I know," he says much quieter. "But I've known who she is for a while."

My stomach drops, an uneasy sense that he's telling the truth. His truth, at the very least. "How?"

Cruz takes the bait. "My abuela, she saw that our paths crossed, she shared several visions, including the one from your uncle's party. One of us dancing..." He holds back, evidently enjoying the moment, savoring the fact that I'm squirming in place. "We were meant to find each other."

I won't entertain the idea that Mullory has some preordained destiny with Cruz Lagunes. To hell with destiny. "Did you tell Mullory?"

Cruz shakes his head. "No."

I toss another used match on the floor, kicking my foot against the fireplace. It's time to go.

"I'll admit, at first I didn't care about the visions. Some random, seemingly ordinary girl...but there's something intriguing about her, don't you think?"

Cruz smirks. "I like people who disrupt. When something doesn't belong, but it forces itself in anyway, changes everything around it. Mullory Prudence rattled the Stoutmire family, she rattled *you.*"

I pause, because deep down—in the only space I can be honest with myself—I'm not sure what or who is best for Mullory. But I know what I want. "Those are just memories that never will happen."

"How can you be so sure?"

My fingers curl into fists. "I won't let them."

Cruz holds his ground. "Maybe you can't stop them."

I want to punch him, but my mind starts to spiral. Thinking of the lengths Uncle went to for Mullory to die in my place. The game, my cousin Cecilia. All that for me to die anyway. But I came back. I damn well came back. I square my chest up with Cruz. "I misspoke. Those aren't memories. They're just possibilities. Chances you won't ever get."

Cruz twists his face into a scowl, the most emotion I've seen him show since he's been here. "She's in my future."

"Then I'm in your future, too."

90.
MULLORY

"It has to be this one," I say, hope running dangerously low, as we trudge over to the last fireplace. But as the flames die down in the billiards room, my soot-speckled smile cracks. "I don't understand. What did we miss?"

"Maybe it's something in the logs themselves and we need to go back over each one," Reina suggests.

"Gun slob," Ellison says with a smile. "Still sticking with it."

"Look." Reina points beneath the mantel.

Burned into a sooty tile is a name. *Pollock.*

"Before either of you idiots tries to overcomplicate this and suggest we dance naked in the moonlight, please follow me," implores Ellison. "Uncle has quite the art collection and most of them are authentic and not magicked with illusion. I know exactly where his Pollock is. Framed and hanging in the second-floor hallway in all its abstract, colorful glory."

Reina hurriedly pulls out her phone. "I'll text the boys to meet us there."

We both scamper behind an overly confident Ellison.

"This is the Pollock?" I ask, tapping the glass casing.

"It's one of his earlier works—the drip style is a dead giveaway." Cruz suddenly appears behind my shoulder.

"Maybe there's something hidden in the image?" puzzles Lyric.

"Or maybe we just do this." Ellison gives the casing a light push and it opens with a satisfactory *click*.

There's a dark and shallow cavity behind the painting, and I reach my arm inside, fingers skimming a loose sheet of paper. It slips from my fingers, fluttering.

Cruz snatches it up and my pulse quickens as his eyes glance over the text.

"It's some sort of contract."

"A contract for what?" Lyric makes a grab for it.

Cruz narrows his gaze, studying the text. "Some sort of lock that's been placed on the shadow. I believe to dampen its power until an agreement could be made on how to best utilize it."

I wasn't crazy after all; there *is* something blocking it.

"Does it say how to undo the lock?" asks Ellison. "I doubt it, because that would actually be useful."

"It can only be broken with the blood of three," Cruz says with a shrug.

Three what?

"Gross," answers Ellison. "Why is it always blood?"

Even more disturbing are the six fingerprints lined up at the bottom of the contract. The animal symbols for the Continuum are stacked neatly underneath. Red and faded, but unmistakably done in blood.

Cruz turns over the contract to reveal a message scrawled on the back.

When it's time, trust it with your friends.

91. MULLORY

Cruz keeps hold of the blood-bound contract as I clutch the shadow tucked beneath my collar, resting atop my frantically beating heart. If we can break the lock on it, Lyric might just stand a chance.

I jump on Ellison's suggestion that we all shower, because according to her, we smell like a group of grubby chimney sweeps. And even though I head to my room like everyone else, I have no intention of showering just yet, because it's time to face a different mystery. I pull the tag-less gift I received this morning from beneath my mattress. A single bronze coin, heavy and marked with an engraving of a butterfly. In this world, there are no coincidences. The butterfly tattoo given to me by the Viper was purposeful. *"This tattoo holds a message for more than just you."*

I hadn't paid much attention to it at the time, but now seeing the butterfly on the inside cover of my mom's journal—I know who was exiled from the Continuum and ripped from the photograph.

The coin fits perfectly into the eye socket of the skull carved on the door, and I twist it clockwise, just like Lyric and I did a few months ago during the game. Xavier Stoutmire is at his desk, ankles crossed with green velvet slippers perched on his resting feet. His silken pajama set is patterned with presents that spin and periodically open to reveal trinkets. The cuffs are lined with vines of holly berries.

"Time to face the truth."

"Merry Christmas to you, too." I lay the coin flat on his desk, butterfly side up.

Beneath the sweep of his hair, which is colored a festive red, Xavier gives me a weak smile.

"You're the Butterfly."

Xavier merely shrugs. "Was. Am. Not sure if I ever truly got out."

"Of the Continuum," I say, making sure to finish his statement and confirm all the facts.

Xavier smiles more broadly, his canines on display. "That's a name I haven't heard in many years. Some things are better left in the past."

I'm not in the mood for vague responses. "What were you and the Continuum after?"

Xavier rolls a clear, spherical paperweight across his desk and it transforms into a serpent that rattles its tail at me.

"What all bright-eyed groups of talented young people want. To change the world. To break the chain and free magic so that it wouldn't be tied to any one bloodline. Why should only the powerful benefit?" His tone hums with sarcasm.

The rattler's tail hisses at me, but I hold my ground. It's all part of the test. "And?"

"And that little endeavor unfolded exactly how all great ideas unfurl."

"Which is?"

"Badly. The problem arises when the young bright-eyed people get a taste for the power they're so valiantly trying to divide. They often find excuses to justify keeping it for themselves."

I swallow past the pit forming in my throat. "That's why the lock was placed."

Xavier snorts. "Every lock can be broken. There's only one way to truly finish this and fix everything."

For a moment I'm hopeful. "How?"

"I brought your mother into the Continuum. You see, she was the missing link, the ultimate tool that eliminated our need to hunt, because the magic came to her. I'm afraid everything that has gone wrong since is my fault." His expression is blank, matter-of-fact. As if this was only a small error on his part—one that ruined countless lives.

My fingers curl into the flesh of my palms. "How do we fix it?"

Xavier plucks a berry from his cuff and pops it into his mouth; another instantly replaces it. "Hand the shadow over to me. Your mother was right, it needs to be destroyed."

I'm shocked. "Destroyed?"

"Yes. You've been traveling around visiting all your mother's old friends. Have you not seen the path of destruction the shadow leaves in its wake? Nothing good comes from meddling with death."

"How do you know where we've been..." I pause, puzzling through his admission. "It was you at the Skeleton Singer's lair, then again at the coffee shop. You've been following us." I clutch the shadow, worried this is what Xavier has been after.

"Keeping an eye on you is more like it. Now hand it over."

I think back to Lord Thorn, who also asked me for the shadow. This would be the second powerful man, clearly in control of illusionary magic, who could easily force me to hand it over, and yet he's asking. In fact, he's almost being polite about it.

The snake on Xavier's desk transforms into a light bulb that glows. "Ah, you've figured it out. Clever like your mother, hopefully not as shortsighted as your father."

I ignore the taunt about my father. I doubt Xavier will share anything about him freely, but I have figured something else out. Feeling bold, I lift the pendant from beneath my pajama top. The amber stone reflects the light, illuminating the fly stuck within. All this trouble and bloodshed for a fly.

"You can't take it," I say.

"That is correct."

I try not to feel smug, but it's hard. "Not unless I give it to you."

"Mullory," Xavier implores, "let me destroy it." He pushes against his desk and hobbles to his feet. "You must trust me, Mullory."

How could I possibly trust the man who plotted a game and then faked his own death all so that his nephew could murder me? I think not. I don't know his exact angle yet, but I suspect he already hinted at it. Power. I tuck the amulet safely beneath my reindeer pajamas. Gran's voice hits me with a burst of advice. *"Don't burn bridges you ain't yet crossed."*

"I'll think about it," I tell him coolly.

"You don't know what you're dealing with."

Anger spikes inside me at his accusation. Just another condescending, careless remark meant to prey on my insecurities. It's not a direct hit to my inability to control his magic, but that's how I take it. Like he sees me as inadequate. "I had no idea how to deal with your game either, but that turned out just fine."

A laugh rattles from Xavier's chest before he answers. "This is no game. Aren't you curious as to why I insisted upon your death?"

"Because you wanted to lure my mom here, to steal this." I run my fingers along the cord containing the shadow, and its power steadies me.

Xavier's blue eyes crinkle at the corners, his smile patronizing. "Is that all?"

The question is unnerving, the implication that I'm missing something. And now I can't help but question everything. The lock on the shadow. My own blockade to Xavier's magic. The worry and the wrongness that sit heavily on my chest. The unspoken whisper in the darkest corner of my mind that *something isn't right.* I start to open my mouth, then promptly shut it.

Xavier pounces on my hesitation. "Ah, so you *do* feel it. The imbalance."

The word *imbalance* is a barbed hook that catches in my chest. "I..."

Xavier tugs at the hook, shredding muscle, rattling my bones. "Did you think you could just bring Lyric back without consequence?"

"What are you talking about?"

"I admit, even we thought it was that simple at first. An object that lets you defy death."

I interpret the *we* to mean the Continuum. "But that's what it does."

"Oh, Mullory." The way Xavier says my name makes me feel as though I'm eight years old. "There's no way to defy death. Deceive it maybe, but not without repercussions. No, I'm afraid all you can do with death is make a deal."

"But I didn't make one."

"I'm afraid you have no idea what you did."

I want to argue the point, but the truth holds me back.

"It's small at first, a suggestion that something is off. But it will grow, push, and pry, and send you into a maddening fit, until you right it. Until you satisfy the deal you made with death."

Several horrifying thoughts weave themselves together in my mind, spiraling tighter and tighter. My hesitation to help Lyric in critical times—when Lord Thorn's magic rushed back, when the cart fell on him at Coney Island, and then again when he almost dropped off the balcony. What I mistook for anxiety was perhaps something darker. Pa's last words creep back over me. *"Strangest part was the other boy found dead in here six months later."* My breathing shallows, my mind slotting the final piece in place. *"We killed him. Me and Esther Merrybright."* My mom and the Skeleton Singer killed the boy to satisfy death. To take Henry Prudence's place.

"Perhaps you're further along than I thought. You'll only fall faster now, Mullory."

I can't accept Xavier's truth, can't let him see how fiercely my legs are shaking. "Merry Christmas," I say, as I turn to leave.

Xavier's face sinks as I pass by. I don't miss how the light bulb shatters on his desktop when I finally leave.

92.

ELLISON

I spent most of the night trying not to think of the blood soaked on the contract or the blood required to unlock the shadow. Honestly, why must it be blood? But now, alone in my room, I can't shake the thought.

Just a little blood. Merely the blood of three, I tell myself, while applying moisturizer to my desiccated skin—all the fires and smoke haven't done my pores any favors. But the blood of three what? I can't help that goats pop into my head. *What the hell is wrong with you, Ellison?* For once, Mullory Prudence pulled through and there may be a way to cut the connection between Lord Thorn and Lyric. All it takes is the blood of three goats. *No, Ellison! Not goats.* But if not goats, then what?

I know the contract and the lock on the shadow are all anyone else can think about, much to the annoyance of Edwin, who orchestrated an elaborate Christmas dinner complete with an actual singing choir of chipmunks. For vermin, they were surprisingly good. And the food was Michelin-star quality, but who felt like eating a perfectly seared steak (oozing blood, I might add) when we're so close. Mullory was especially quiet at dinner, her mind clearly distracted.

And Lyric. My heart aches just thinking of him. Sitting at dinner, covered in bruises, not so subtly staring at Mullory. *"Do you ever wonder if it would've been any different if I'd lived with you instead?"* How could I not think of this every single day? If Lyric had been spared the torturous childhood Uncle Xavier inflicted upon him. If *I* had been there for him, the way an older sister ought to be. And all I have to offer him is the magic that was an equally ruinous part of all our childhoods. How does this not end with more despair?

The pot of moisturizer crashes to the bathroom floor, spewing glass and globs of cream. What if Reina's right? What if I *am* the mysterious woman who saves Lyric? What if she's right and if I don't do it, then there won't even be a Lyric left to save this time. In my mother's dream, she told me I'd look right at the mysterious woman. I'd almost forgotten I'd stared into the mirror and gazed at my own reflection the night of the party.

But what if I'm not enough?

"Impossible by yourself maybe. But not with me." Reina. I'm marching to her room before I can think better of it.

Reina answers, sleepy eyed and in her pajamas. She doesn't say a thing; she just stares at me with her deep-set violet eyes, waiting. And okay, it was me who did the knocking, but she must know why I'm here.

"There's an infinitesimally small chance you were right."

She kicks one eyebrow up. "About what?"

She's really going to make me spell it out. "Right about me being the mysterious woman or whatever."

"I see," Reina says casually, and the door creaks open wider. "You better come in."

My skin is suddenly feverish the moment I cross into her room. "How does this work exactly?"

Reina shrugs. "Never time-traveled in a dream before. But I can't imagine it's that hard."

Seriously? "That's reassuring. How will we even know when to do it? I know my mother was pregnant with Lyric, but that's all I have. A time frame of nine months. Kind of broad, don't you think? And I don't know a thing about time travel, but I would imagine it requires extreme precision and planning and purpose."

Reina doesn't seem worried and spins the hour hand on one of her watches. "So that's what, seventeen years ago? That should do it."

My head spins with the circuitous logic of time travel. "But haven't we already done this?"

"In theory. But we still need to do it now to make it happen then and keep the same timeline."

The dizzy feeling only intensifies. "But how do we know when?"

"The fact that we've recently met and you've sought me out now tells me it's time."

"That's it?"

Reina scoots onto her bed and folds her legs. "Only one way to find out." She pats the spot beside her.

My pulse races. "But I don't know how."

"You know how to enter dreams, and I know how to bend time. We'll do it together."

Together. A word that's so sparse in my vocabulary it feels like a foreign language.

How can I save Lyric from Lord Thorn if he's never even born? It all comes down to this: Can I trust Reina? Enough to place my brother's life in her hands? Half of my entire heart. I've never let anyone in, but this feels different.

It takes all my wobbly-kneed courage to climb onto the bed. I resist every impulse to run when Reina grabs my hands. The sensation of her skin touching mine triggers a fear response in my psyche, eliciting a pain that I know is irrational and nonsensical, but agonizing, nonetheless.

“This may be disorienting, but hold tight to my hands. I’ll be the anchor. And then in your mind, just let go, let your magic find your mother.”

My heart is a fluttering, wild thing, and for a second, I’m convinced I might pass out.

“Just let your magic find your mother,” Reina repeats. “Say it.”

I close my eyes and breathe. “Let my magic find my mother.”

“Do you trust me?”

I dare to take the leap. “Yes.”

Reina whispers, “Hold tight.”

I don’t get to respond because the words get lodged in my throat. Everything goes freakishly still before rocketing forward in a blur that feels as if my entire body is being compressed and squeezed, atom by atom. My brain is mush, all my senses completely useless. I’m upside down and inside out. Only one thing rings clear. Panic. It fills me up and wrings me out.

“Let your magic find your mom.” Reina’s voice is so distant, like we’re miles apart and underwater.

It takes everything I have, but I find the magic and I let it pull me—it wants to find my mother. Now or before, I don’t think it has a preference in time.

She snaps suddenly into focus, all crisp edges. Saffron Stoutmire, years younger. Some of the lines not yet altered by Botox are just faintly showing themselves on her face. We’re in a field but the flowers grow from the sky and clouds brush our feet. Whimsical, not anything like the nightmares she forcefully served.

I concentrate, distorting my appearance so that I’m cloaked in bands of light.

“Who are you?”

It’s a strange feeling, to be in my mother’s dream and for her to have no idea that it’s me. Her eyes search mine. Perhaps she can sense our magic or maybe it’s all muddled by time. I want her to know that it’s me, that I’m the one with the powerful dream magic, but I can’t risk altering the timeline.

“It doesn’t matter who I am.” My voice sounds different, more musical.

“How did you enter my dream? No one has ever done that.”

If only my mother knew the half of it. "That's not important either. I know your secret, Saffron Stoutmire. I know about the baby you're carrying."

Her hand reflexively brushes her stomach. "You don't know anything."

"It's a boy," I say softly. "And you need to protect him." I can feel the tears welling up inside me, the first person to fight for Lyric.

Saffron shuffles back, running a nervous hand through her hair. "But how? His father..." She bites her lip. "It won't be allowed," she whispers.

It's her fear that nearly undoes me, unraveling every rigid bit of me, exposing the soft fleshy parts. I step closer to her, so close that I let my fingertips brush hers. "There's a way to fix this in the future, but you have to get him there first."

My mother's eyes flicker, watery and brimming with tears I didn't know her body could produce. This is Saffron Stoutmire before she had to do the hard work, before the world required her to isolate her youngest son to keep him safe. Maybe this is when the fragile maternal bond inside of her was forced to snap, because she didn't have a choice.

"It won't be easy." My voice wavers. "On any of them."

"I'll do whatever it takes."

For a moment I think she almost recognizes me, her eyes crinkle in the corners, but she shakes her head at the impossibility of it. *It's me*, I want to cry out. I want her to see me. More than that, I want her to tell me that her magic, *our* magic, can fix this.

"Tell me what I need to do."

"There will come a time when it becomes unsafe for him to stay with you." The pressure inside me builds, the tears threatening to pour out, but I push through. "When that happens, you must send him to live with Xavier."

"Xavier? A child... there? All alone?"

I can't believe I'm the one sentencing Lyric to a life of isolation, one riddled with fear, a prisoner to our deranged uncle. But he must be kept out of Lord Thorn's sights for as long as possible. "Yes." My voice cracks into a rasp. "It's the only way. Keep a piece of his dreams. And the dreams of the others, too. Watch over all of them."

My mother nods as tears slip down my own cheeks.

"When it's time, don't hesitate with the nightmares." Fear crawls up my throat like bile, and the bitter taste of guilt coats my tongue.

It's always been *me*. I'm the one who doled out our childhood of suffering, and I'd do it all again if it saves Lyric. But I'm not done, not yet. The future hangs on a precarious edge. "Give Ellison this message. Tell her the woman she wants to find will be at the party. Tell her she'll look right at her."

"How will I know when to tell her?"

I squeeze the tears back. "When she finally lets your magic in."

My mother hesitates, her eyes large. "But won't they hate me for this?"

A sob bubbles up my throat, the truth burns. "Yes. But try not to hate yourself."

Something tugs at me, and I'm compressed and pulled through a vacuum composed of time that's tangled with dreams and threatening to dice me into pieces. Every muscle and bone throbs with pain, and it takes me a moment to reorient myself on Reina's bed.

"Ellison?"

I'm still crying; a sob wrenches my body. Reina doesn't hesitate or ask for my permission as she pulls me into a hug. I hate the contact, the closeness of another person pressed against my skin.

But I don't let go.

I simply can't.

93.
MULLORY

Xavier's warning hangs in my periphery like a storm cloud, grim and threatening. *"Perhaps you're further along than I thought. You'll only fall faster now."*

Is that what I've been doing since I got here? Falling to an end I can't seem to change or control? The same path my mom found herself on.

The idea burrows inside me, nagging. Just like this mystery, how some of the clues have felt misplaced. The journal that was simply dropped at the party. The Scrabble letters supposedly left by my mom, but when? And if Xavier's magic can't seem to trust me, can I trust myself? Am I simply questioning the mystery because I don't know which way to turn?

It's time to face the dark secrets preserved at the end of my mom's journal.

I leaf through the pages, a timid turn of my thumb. The neat, almost meticulous writing spirals to an illegible scrawl the further along I go.

I fear it's inside of me. In my head.
It whispered.
Now it screams. Screams. Screams. Screams.
What is Henry worth?
How much do I love?

The same scribbled note as before. Xavier's laugh echoes in my head. *"You may not like what you find."*

Why?
Why?
Why?
Why?
Kill.

The final entry.

I know what to do.

An ominous end. I turn over the last page, realizing there's a ragged edge tucked in the spine, a final page that was torn out. My fingers glide over the indents that pepper the back cover. I spring up from the floor, grabbing a pencil.

Light strokes colored with lead reveal the entire message Pa gave us.

Replace
to
Him
Another
Kill

Must

Henry

Save

To

The message in its entirety, still the meaning's a scramble. Until I realize the bottom is actually the top. I read up. *To Save Henry Must Kill Another. Him to Replace.*

There it is. The final proof that my mom murdered the second boy found at the butcher. All to save my father.

The journal falls from my shaking hands.

Is this my destiny? A murderer? Eternally plagued by regret, all to satisfy what Xavier called an imbalance. *"Did you think you could just bring Lyric back without consequence?"*

All I can think about is Lyric as I sprint toward his room. The truth is like poison in my chest, spreading down every limb.

Lyric's door is open, and I spot him nestled on his bed, staring pensively out the window. The rocks animated like animals, gifted to him by Edwin, teeter around his bed by his feet. The hippo waddles up his arm.

My hand flies to my mouth, trying to catch my sob. He doesn't hear me, doesn't feel me staring at him. Every bit of him, the bruises everyone can spot, and the ones he's only shared with me. A boy broken by those around him. A boy who died for me.

How much do I love?

Lyric senses me and turns around. A hopeful smile creeping up. "Mullory?" He lowers his chin, resting it on his knee.

The sob finally leaves my lips and turns to a tremor as he rushes over and folds his arms around me. I sink into his chest, pressing myself to him as tightly as I can.

His lips find my ear. "There's no kindness in me. At least not from my father."

He tucks a strand of hair from my cheek. "And my uncle didn't raise me to be kind." He lifts me up, gently wrapping my legs around his waist.

My thumb ripples across the mottled bruise on his cheek.

Lyric holds me to his level.

I can't find the words; I'm numb to everything but the venomous truth. Let Lyric die again or kill someone to save him.

Lyric breaks my trance. "But you're kind, Mullory."

All I can do is shake my head. Can murder ever be kind?

"Too kind for me." He lets me slip down and puts me on my feet. Distances himself.

My arm lurches and claws at his wrist. "Don't," I warn. "Don't act like this is over." I force myself to pick up the pieces, wipe my tears, and get us to the end. Whatever it takes. "I saw your uncle," I say, steering us back.

"Why? Were you in the mood for self-inflicted torture?"

"Because he was part of the Continuum."

If Lyric's surprised, he barely shows it. "He's a part of everything. But not really a part of anything at all, if that makes any sense."

"I get it. . . . It's just . . ."

Lyric's dark eyes bore into mine. "Just what?" The heat of his gaze speaks truer than the phrasing of his question. There's depth there, a gentle probing to find the greater truth we've both been circling around. He slides closer, his arm thrown protectively around my shoulder. "Tell me."

"What I mean is, there's something very wrong"—I let the moment press between us before I finish—"with me." *What if I'm willing to kill someone to save you?*

He doesn't dismiss me or imply that I'm half mad, because Lyric listens to me. Better than that, he *believes* me. "Wrong how?"

"Something about this whole thing feels off to me, and your uncle told me we should destroy the shadow. He practically begged."

"Destroy it?" Lyric pulls away. "Why? Knowing Uncle X, he probably has some complicated plan that ends with him getting it back."

"But what if he knows something we don't?" He knew I'd be left with an impossible choice if I used the shadow to save Lyric. One he was willing to burden, killing me instead. What else does he know?

Lyric studies me silently, a thousand thoughts flickering beneath his lashes, before he speaks. "I'll do whatever you say. You want to destroy it. Or hide it. Or use it."

"How could I destroy it if that means destroying you?" My voice is a whisper that fades to silence.

"But what if I'm already set for destruction?"

My heart silences my erratic mind. "I won't let that happen."

94.

LYRIC

Mullory is tucked beside me, and it's a painstaking, gut-wrenching exercise in self-control. I'm hyperaware of every point of contact between us, the dip of her shoulder, her thigh pressed against my side, her hand that finds mine, fingers threading, heart rate soaring.

This is me *trying* to be kind.

But I'm also weak when it comes to her, and when she tugged me on top of my bed, I simply followed.

And I meant what I said. Mullory can do whatever she wants with the shadow, and I'll follow her without hesitation, my future be damned.

"Lyric," she says with a timid smile. "I've been thinking."

"Mm-hmm." I know where she's going with this, and I know I have to let her say her part first.

"Once we break the lock on the shadow, we can destroy your bond to Lord

Thorn's magic. And..." Her voice gets all pitchy. "And I've given it a lot of thought..."

"I see."

"And I think we should destroy mine, too." Mullory wraps her arms around my neck, changing her position so that she's squarely in my lap. "Because it's never really been my magic. And in some strange way, the magic must know, too, because it won't work for me. Xavier's your uncle and I want you to have it. You deserve it."

I give myself a minute to indulge in this idea, one that I know I could never agree to. Mullory peers up at me from beneath a tangle of her dark curls, waiting for a response. I keep a fierce hold on the moment because I've never met anyone else like her. Not just selfless—but selfless for *me*. I know with absolute certainty that I don't deserve it.

"It won't work," I finally say, crushing the dream I held on to for years.

Mullory slaps my knee. "And why not?"

"Lord Thorn would still find a way to kill me."

"Why would he kill you if he had all of his magic back?"

I understand him on a level no one else ever could. "Lord Thorn isn't one who takes chances, and he'd always be afraid that I might find a way to take it back."

Mullory grumbles. "So that's it? No matter what we do he kills you?"

"No," I say, letting Mullory gather the pieces for herself.

Her eyes grow wide as saucers, and she gives her head a furious shake. "Absolutely not."

"It's the only way," I counter. "We destroy his bond and then I fully take on his magic, and it will...what's the saying, kill two birds with one stone?"

Mullory doesn't find me funny at all.

"I get his magic, all of it, and we dethrone the asshole."

Mullory lets out a heavy sigh. "But you hate his magic."

I shift on the bed uncomfortably, worming away from the truth, from the darkness that is stitched up into every little bit of me. From the ease and the thrill that his power brings me. Maybe this is the nexus in my story, where I fully embrace my villainous future. No going back.

"I can handle it." I give her my best smile.

Mullory looks at me, clearly conflicted. Some battle storming in her head. The furrow between her brows demanding to be kissed.

I want to kiss her.

I want it bad.

But instead, I scoop her up so that I can tug back my comforter and tuck her beneath.

"I'm not tired," she protests mid-yawn.

"I know." I fluff her pillow and ease her back, sliding beside her, one arm propped up.

"Not. Tired." Her eyelids droop and it's only a matter of seconds before she stills, giving in to her exhaustion.

I press my lips to her cheek, a featherlight kiss, but I don't move when I'm done. Instead, I hover by her ear. "I'm sorry."

Mullory doesn't move, and I pray that she hears me somehow.

I finish the admission in a whisper. "I might be too selfish to let you go."

95.
MULLORY

The days after Christmas spiral dangerously close to New Year's, passing by in a rush of salted caramel cinnamon rolls, circuitous attempts to unravel the remaining riddles, and a borderline obsession with the dark truths contained in my mom's journal.

So much needs to go right to save Lyric. Unlock the shadow. Remove Lord Thorn from the equation. Address the *imbalance*. *"You'll only fall faster now, Mullory."* Xavier and his cryptic warning, the certainty that he's holding something else back from me. That he's searching for something, playing his own game.

The longer I sit on it, the more feverish my thoughts become. Can my mom even help me? I dare to hope that she left me the clues because she has a way to fix it. I can't believe that she'd leave me the shadow, knowing the price I'd have to pay if I used it. But am I willing to bet Lyric's life on it?

Thinking of Lyric makes my stomach sink. He's been with me and not with me at all these past few days. He hasn't left my side, but he's kept a guarded distance. And it's torturous.

Tomorrow is New Year's Eve and according to the Skeleton Singer I need to solve the riddle by the time the new year ages.

A knock at my door—my heart is hopeful it's Lyric—but I'm surprised to find Cruz instead. I haven't exactly been avoiding him, but I haven't sought him out either. It's for stupid reasons that barely make sense in my head—why should I feel like I'm betraying Lyric when Cruz is around?

"I come bearing gifts." Cruz balances a tray of hot chocolates.

My fingers curl around a steaming mug and I take a sip. Velvety chocolate swirled with a thick, creamy froth.

Cruz clears his throat. "When I first got here, I made you a promise."

I take another sip, now aware exactly why Cruz is here.

"I told you we'd help you find your mom, and a deal is a deal."

"Is this the part where you finally tell me what you want in return?"

Cruz places his hot chocolate on my nightstand; clearly, he never had any intention of drinking it. "This is that part. The one where I ask for my favor."

My throat clenches. As the days ticked away, I'd given more thought to Cruz's vague favor. And I could draw only one conclusion—he wants the most powerful thing I have to give. If not my magic, then the very thing of power itself. The shadow. To undo what he did to his brothers.

"Cruz." I start to speak, unsure how I'll even finish.

"Hear me out first. I require the use of an item in this house."

I keep my guard up. "Which item?"

"One I'm sure you don't even know exists."

"But how could I—"

"Because this is *your* house, Mullory." He's the first one to be so bold with the declaration. "You can do whatever the hell you want with it."

"Tell me where it is."

"I'll do one better, I'll show you."

Cruz leads us down the stairs and through the halls, my curiosity piqued. "How do you know it's here?"

"Reina told me. She was the one who convinced me to come here in the first place." Cruz brushes my arm, a gentle nudge to turn left. There's something important in his admission, something that bugs at me.

"Ah, here we are." Cruz shuffles us into the billiards room, and my thought is distracted away as he gestures to a glass timekeeper full of golden sand.

I easily lift it from above the chessboard and no cruel illusions attack us. "But you could have just taken it."

Hurt flashes across Cruz's face. "It's not mine to just take."

"I didn't mean . . ." Flustered, I hand it over. "It's yours if you want it."

Cruz wraps his fingers around the bronzed metal base before slowly turning it over. "You see, Mullory, when Arlo died the magic in him temporarily latched itself on to the next heir in line, my brother Daniel."

When you killed him, I can't help but think as I watch some of the grains of sand turn black, and a putrid smoke fogs the glass.

"And then it passed through Daniel, jumping from host to host, before finally passing to me upon his death."

The darkness clouding the timekeeper only thickens. "What is—"

"Arlo loved to play chess, and Daniel was exquisite on the piano," Cruz says quietly. "There's a gene in our DNA that allows the activation of magic, and the rules of inheritance are understood. But there's still some parts they can't predict. There's always something more that comes with it, as if the magic can't let go of its old home, as if it must bring pieces with it. Souvenirs, if you will. Especially if it's rushed, if it doesn't have time to properly detach itself."

I can't help but worry that Lyric got more than just his father's magic. "And you?"

Cruz tightens his grip on the timekeeper; the smoke inside is tumultuous, obscuring everything. "I have both Arlo's and Daniel's final memories." His eyes darken. "You can't imagine the pain and fear that accompanies your last moments, especially at the hands of your own brother. It's one thing to execute the kill, but quite another to be forced to remember it as if you're the one dying." He sighs. "Then again, maybe I deserve it, some sort of penance. That's why I want the timekeeper, so that some part of me is still forced to remember."

Tears threaten to slip down my cheeks. Cruz may be a monster, but he's not heartless.

"Those memories were all I could think about." Cruz pauses and places the timekeeper down. The smoke clears; only golden sand is visible. "Now they're gone, trapped in that."

I eye the timekeeper, tempted to remove the memory of my mom being a murderer. "It's full of discarded memories?"

"Yes. Gone, but they still leave a scar."

Something inside of me softens and I can't help but gaze at Cruz differently, with a gentler lens. "I'd thought for sure you'd want the shadow."

Cruz shakes his head. "I can't just bring the dead back. Not without more death."

His words strike a chord. Does he know the price the shadow demands?

"My brothers would just come back with a more ravenous taste for blood. I did what I did. I'll live with it."

Worry claws up my throat. "What would you do if you'd already used it? What then?"

"Mullory."

My voice trembles. "The shadow demands another. Someone to take Lyric's place. I think that's why Xavier's magic won't work for me. It can't. I'd read that the only reasons a transfer wouldn't occur was either because I was infected with a magical parasite or because of death. The shadow is interfering, forcing me to give it another's death, that's why it won't work." My hand flies to my mouth, trying to cover up the secret that's been eating me alive. One that Cecilia obviously saw coming.

"I see," Cruz says slowly. "What will you do?"

It's a simple question, completely straightforward. And yet, I'm baffled. Will I kill someone else to save Lyric? Follow in my mom's footsteps and end up like her? Wherever she is. Has that been her plan all along? The big secret at the end of this hunt, the one I'm supposed to be ready for. Or will I lose Lyric again, this time for good? I can't face his question head-on; instead I respond with another. "Was it worth it?"

Cruz holds my gaze, the honey centers of his eyes smoldering. "Honestly, I don't know. But I do know I'd make the same choice again."

96.

LYRIC

Most people ring in the New Year with champagne—us, well, we're huddled around a suspicious contract bound with bloody fingerprints. Kind of the same thing, I guess.

Mullory called us all into the library, and she starts right out with a banger. "I think we know how to unlock the shadow."

"How?" Ellison is equally skeptical and eager.

Mullory glances at Cruz, which I force myself to overlook. "We think the blood of three refers to three members of the Continuum. It makes the most sense because that's who placed the lock in the first place."

Ellison crosses her arms. "Great, let's just run back and gather blood from the Viper and then swing by the Skeleton Singer's creepy lair. Then we can pop by your parents' house, Mullory. Oh wait, that's right, we have zero idea where they are. In fact, we've been searching for your mom this entire time and we haven't gotten any closer to finding her."

Mullory doesn't cower or back down, and it's because she's already figured out a loophole. And so have I.

"You have the blood of two," I tell her, and she reveals a brilliant smile.

"And I have the blood of the third," remarks Reina.

Mullory nods her head enthusiastically. "Because we're descendants." She gathers the necklace from beneath her sweater and pulls a knife from her back pocket.

Adrenaline bursts beneath my skin. I can't help but think of Mullory with the knife in the Mystery Royale and how it ended up in my chest. "Careful," I warn her.

Mullory holds out the knife while raising her pointer finger of the opposite hand and presses her flesh to the blade. A moment of hesitation, followed by a slight wince from Mullory before she drops the knife and positions her finger over the shadow so that a few drops of blood ooze out. The stone sizzles as if Mullory's blood is acid burning straight through it.

"Is that supposed to happen?" Alarm registers in my voice.

"Let me think." Ellison taps her chin. "The last time I broke a lock on a death-defying object the same thing happened." She whips her hair over her shoulder and motions to Reina with far less bite. "Your turn."

Reina picks up the knife without hesitation. She punctures her thumb, squeezing the flesh until a bead of ruby blood spills onto the amulet. A terrible *crack* follows. Tendrils of ice slither up the sides of the stone, spreading like a rapid frost across Mullory's hands, but she doesn't let go.

"I think it's working." She trembles. Thick clusters of ice crystals spread beneath Mullory's feet, and her breath escapes in visible puffs before the ice encasing the shadow shatters like glass.

The amulet is now a red so deep, it appears black, pulsing like some preternatural heart pumped full of Mullory's and Reina's blood. There's also a tangible weight to it now, a presence I can feel because the brunt of its magic fills up the room.

"I think it worked," Mullory whispers, eyes brimming with tears as she stares only at me. I want to lift her up and spin her around, because now we have a way to take Lord Thorn's magic completely away from him. Permanently.

"We actually did it," Ellison says, dumbfounded.

"We did it." Mullory's face is slack with disbelief, but also worry. "But tomorrow is New Year's Day, and we still haven't solved the riddle from the Skeleton Singer." Concern creeps along her voice. "We won't find my mom unless we do."

Something's changed in Mullory. Before she'd wanted to find her mom to use the shadow, but now there's something else that's bothering her, and I just won't accept that. I want this girl to have everything she's owed, plus more. "We'll solve the riddle. Right here. Right now."

97.

MULLORY

I try to tamp down my fear; I should be elated, after all. We broke the lock on the shadow, which will enable us to cut off Lord Thorn from his magic. But only Cruz knows the other price that demands to be paid. Someone else must die to take Lyric's place.

My last hope is that my mom has some sort of answer for me.

Actually, I want answers to it all.

I *deserve* them.

We lock ourselves in the library with two pots of dark roast coffee and a mission. Nobody leaves until we crack the riddle from the Skeleton Singer. Easier said than done.

Ellison falls asleep. Twice.

I don't understand how, because I'm so hopped up on caffeine I've taken to sprinting laps beneath the bookcases. Some of the spines have begun to leak espresso beans onto the floor; I think Xavier's magic feels just as caffeinated as me.

And maybe we didn't need my mom to unlock the shadow . . . but *I* still need her. Not like I used to, not for comfort or safety. Now I need her to explain.

"We know we have to solve the riddle by the time the new year ages. But what does it mean? 'Most think it's full, few know it's empty. If up is down, then your hands are twelve in time above.'" Cruz repeats the riddle.

I poke Ellison with my foot. Seriously, how is she sleeping right now?

"I'm awake," she grumbles. "Not like I'm dead, or maybe that would be better. A nice quiet grave where I'm not kicked awake every three seconds."

My entire body hums, every nerve vibrating in jittery harmony. Watery sunlight squeaks through the windows. Happy New Year. My tongue is stuck to the roof of my mouth, dehydrated from my overload of coffee. But something Ellison said is trying to get through my caffeine-soaked brain.

"What did you just say?"

"I said I'm awake."

"No. After that."

Ellison gives me a tired eye roll. "The part where I said I wasn't dead but might prefer to be so that I could sleep."

"Yeah . . ." My voice trails off. "That part." This entire time, my mom has been leaving me clues, whispering secrets, with the greatest being that my father is still alive, but when we visited the butcher, Pa was still certain he was buried and dead.

Oh. My. God.

"My father!" I blurt out. "Most think it's full, few know it's empty. It's the coffin at his grave."

"If up is down," Cruz starts.

"Then your hands are twelve in time above. 'If up is down' means that each word should be replaced with its opposite. Hands should be feet and the number twelve on a clock would be positioned opposite of six."

"Six feet under," Cruz finishes. "Of course. The only problem is we don't know where your father is buried."

But that's just it. I do. There's only one cemetery we would visit, for no reason at all, hours wandering a weedy plot speckled with stones and the dead. My eyes flick to the window as the sun rises. "I know where we have to go."

Everyone hurries to change. Today is a new year. Hopefully that means it's a new start. I can't help but think of the clues that led us here, the hunt for the strange. The button hidden in the yo-yo, the coat, the receipt, the bones, a stick of gum. Each unfurling fresh secrets, unexpected twists. *Henry Prudence's murderer is closer than you think.* This one still feels half-solved, misplaced in the greater mystery.

I squeeze the shadow; somehow it feels heavier. Rushing into the hall, I run into Reina.

She smiles. "You did it."

"We did it."

Reina checks her odd stack of watches. "Plenty of time to make it to the cemetery in New Jersey."

My foot catches and I stumble forward.

"Mullory, are you okay?"

I eye Reina, my mind wheeling. A fine sweat begins to bead across my skin. Suddenly, there's something I need to do. "I'm fine." I turn around and call to her as I hurry away. "I'll meet you outside."

A split-second decision, one where I have to trust my gut. Not Xavier's magic. Not the shadow. Not anyone but myself. There are a few stops I need to make before hurrying to the car Edwin prepared. Choices that could change the course of everything.

I stop by my room first, frantically gathering my things.

The end is near, and I'm still not sure what Cecilia or my mom intends for me to do. *Don't judge a book by its cover.* But how could I not? At first it seemed obvious that the reference to a father meant Lord Thorn had killed mine. But then, as secrets were revealed, I couldn't help but question my mom. Every little thing I thought I knew about her.

And now I know it's time, but I'm still not sure what to do. Or maybe I just don't want to face it.

I wearily eye the stack of books Cecilia sent. One stands out among the rest because of its ridiculousness. The five-hundred-page behemoth on birds.

Could it be that?

The bird on page 122 is adorable, with a tufted white chest, fluffy brown tail feathers, and a series of odd black rings that circle its neck. Like it's wearing a sweater made to look like a zebra. It's the name of the bird that stops me in my tracks though.

Killdeer (Charadrius vociferus)

The killdeer is a fairly docile bird known for its loud and shrill call. Fiercely protective of their young, the killdeer will often pretend to have a broken wing to lead predators from their nests.

My eyes skim all the quaint facts about the bird, but my mind can't seem to get past the first word. *Kill.*

You'll know when it's time.

98.
ELLISON

What better way to end our little tour de nightmares than with a cemetery? Honestly, I couldn't care less about this part. Mostly I'm just keeping Mullory happy so we can track down Lord Thorn, use the shadow, save Lyric, and I can put the last few months behind me. Far, far behind me.

Our ever-faithful driver whips the car down the highway. The ride is a few short hours—it turns out Mullory's dad is fake-buried somewhere in New Jersey. She blubbered on about the details of it, but by that time I'd already tuned her out. This thing is as good as wrapped up. Maybe her mom is there waiting, or maybe she's not. Either way, this all ends today. Thanks for the clues and the good times, Esther Merrybright. May I never have to do it ever again.

Then it's back home to Chicago, this time with Lyric, who will for the first time in his life actually get the chance to live there. Where he belonged from the beginning. A rare calm settles over me, disrupted only when I steal a glance at

Reina. I don't like the prickly feeling on my skin, or the fact that I'm even considering where she'll go when this is all over. But she did help me, possibly in more ways than I'd ever be willing to admit.

"This is it." Mullory is propped up on her knees, nose pressed to the window as the car pulls through a rickety metal gate. Rows of gravestones pepper the snow-draped hills, and a few classier mausoleums peek down from higher plots.

"Left. Right down there," Mullory instructs the driver. She's practically bouncing in her seat—a little shrill of glee flits out of her.

I follow her gaze out the window and spot a woman: The resemblance is so striking I know instantly that it's her mother. Esther Merrybright, the final freaking clue. Tears fall freely down Mullory's cheeks, and she's moving before the car even stops, flinging the door open.

"Mullory, wait." Reina grabs her. "Give us the shadow."

Hesitation creeps beneath the tears on Mullory's face as she turns to Reina.

"'When it's time, trust it with your friends,'" Reina urges her, reciting the last riddle on the back of the contract. "It's time."

"Of course." Mullory unwinds the shadow from her neck, a brief pause before she passes it over. "Keep it safe." Then she darts out of the car in a blur.

Reina grasps the amber stone, stowing it safely around her own neck.

Oddly enough, I'm okay with that. I hate to admit it, but I trust Reina.

Enough to place Lyric's life in her hands.

Enough to call her a friend.

I suppose there are worse things. Few, but I'm sure they exist.

99. MULLORY

I don't feel the cold.

Or my legs pumping up the hilly expanse of snow.

I don't feel a thing but sheer, unfiltered happiness. It blooms in my chest like a rocket.

Mom.

I've dreamt of this moment so many times, so many ways, but nothing compares to the real her. Hair as dark and wild as mine peeps out from a hood, her green eyes find my gray ones and my knees go out as I crash into her side. I'd thought I'd be more reserved, more hardened by her absence that stings like betrayal, but right now I'm nine years old again. Completely unfiltered and unbiased and just so, so happy.

She still smells the same and I latch as tight as I can, clawing my hands into her, rewinding time back to my childhood. To the feeling of being safe.

"Mullory."

I nuzzle into her side, afraid if I let go, she might disappear.

My mom bends her head and whispers into my ear so lightly I have to strain to hear her. "There isn't much time."

I edge back slightly, confusion spreading down my limbs. "But it's over, I found you," I blurt out, unsure, and unwilling to admit I don't know what to do next. My mom tips her head as if she were afraid someone might see her. Panic flourishes across my skin as her fear hits me in a heady burst.

"Do you understand what must be done?" Her green eyes are luminous with fear. "I sent you on the hunt so you would understand. So you would know *why* you must do it."

My toes curl in my shoes, ready to react, but my mom is still holding me, tears pinched in the corners of her eyes, waiting for me to answer. I've missed something. "Do what?"

My mom glances quickly over her shoulder before plunging an arm into her cloak and pulling out a knife.

I'm too stunned to react. It's not just any knife—it's *the* knife. The one that killed Lyric. The sun catches the bone-white handle, reflecting off the snow.

My mom thrusts it into my hands.

I can't find the words as my heart tears through my rib cage. Is this how my mom is going to help me? By passing along a murder weapon?

She grabs both my shoulders, shakes me from my stupor. "He needs to be touching it."

"Who—"

"Don't go all the way," she says, her words feverish. "We'll take care of the rest."

The next question gets lodged in my throat as she pushes me away. Who else is coming?

Footsteps from every direction as I grip the knife.

"I love you, Mullory. You and me. It's always been you and me, don't forget."

100. CHRISTMAS EVE, SEVERAL DAYS AGO

A REMOTE BAR IN NUNAVUT, CANADA

XAVIER STOUTMIRE

"You felt the need to drag me all the way out here?" Esther's tone is anything but playful. She snappily twirls the calling card I'd sent between her fingers.

"No. You insisted we meet; I merely picked the place that has the best fish-and-chips." I shrug. "I had a craving."

"That craving had me on two separate planes."

"The best fish-and-chips in the world are worth at least seven planes."

Esther grunts as I shimmy into the booth seat across from her, wincing as I ease myself to sit.

"What happened to you?" she asks, finally taking in my probably haggard appearance.

"I've been traveling."

"Traveling where?"

“Places.” I snap my fingers and trade my orange peacoat for a periwinkle tuxedo. “Better?”

Esther’s green eyes glance at me quizzically; they’ve hardened to a deep emerald over the years. Not at all curious like when she was a student and I’d first met her. When this entire winding, chaotic spiral was merely a point, a beginning.

Esther takes a sip of an amber ale; the glass is frosted, chilled like the blistering snow beating the pub windows mercilessly. “I’ve been traveling, too,” she says, and reaches into the breast pocket of her raincoat, carefully pulling out a wrapping. Laying it on the table, she unfolds the cloth to reveal a knife.

One of a set.

One of a set used to kill Lyric.

This knife and I have a long and sordid history. I haven’t seen it since my Mystery Royale, because this knife has a peculiar way of disappearing, intent on being reunited with the other in its set.

But here it is. My heart rate soars, the memory a painful wound doused in salt. I’d been searching endlessly for it again. But she beat me to it.

“It appears that you’ve bested me.”

Esther’s face hardens. “Do you think I enjoy this? I’m tired of the games. I’m not you, Xavier. This isn’t the life I want. I’ve been trying to find the knife, to find the perfect time and place to use it. Don’t you think I’d rather be with my daughter? I’ve been running from her, trying to right the wrongs of our past, all to keep her safe.”

I nod, knowing the lengths she went to, the sacrifices she made. She had me help her find someone to employ a protective ward around Mullory, keeping her hidden with her gran. Trying to shield her from this world, just for me to drag her into it. And now, I won’t dare admit it, but I understand, because I’ve tried and failed to keep someone I care about safe.

“Go on,” I encourage her.

“I have a plan,” Esther says more quietly.

My eyes don’t leave the knife. “I figured as much.”

"One that doesn't involve you killing my daughter."

Ah, so she's still bitter about that. Rightfully so, I suppose. "I wouldn't think that would be part of your plan. But of course, I hate to assume."

Esther gives me a cruel smile. "Assume only when you're dead. You taught me that, Xavier."

"So I did."

"I won't give you all the specifics; forgive me if I'm not entirely trusting of you. But I would assume at this point you've deduced that Mullory has the shadow. I gave it to her for safekeeping."

"I had figured as much. Lyric coming back from the dead was a subtle hint." I try to contain the pure joy pulsing my veins. Every time I'm reminded that Lyric's alive, that he gets a second chance, relief floods my system.

"Yes. There was that. Which means you know why I called you here."

My momentary happiness subsides. "Naturally. The shadow demands another."

An uncomfortable pause presses between us. Years of kinship, of studying, searching, then the unfortunate fallout when the shadow proved to take more than it gave. A hard truth not all in our group were willing to accept. One some still won't accept. More death in the name of beating death. Preposterous.

The leather booth creaks as Esther shifts her weight. "I can get all the necessary players in one place, come New Year's Day."

"Players. An interesting choice of words."

"What else do we call those ensnared in the game we started?"

I nod in agreement. Esther is too much like me now. Her whimsy has been dulled to a skeptic's edge.

Esther sets her glass down. "Mullory. Lyric. Lord Thorn. Me. You." She counts the names off on her fingers.

"I see."

Esther reaches across the splintery tabletop; her icy fingers grip my wrist, her dark curls sweep across her face as her eyes steel into me. "Then you understand what must be done?" Her voice cracks. "You understand it must be one of us who finishes it. Their souls are too pure." Tears slip freely down her face.

I gingerly yank my hand away and take a sip of the bourbon sitting before me. "I understand," I answer quietly. Even though my mind is set absolutely against what she's proposing. I know who has to die. I can't forget my cousin Cecilia's sage advice. *"Xavier, dear, kill."* I've known for a while. I simply won't allow it to go any other way.

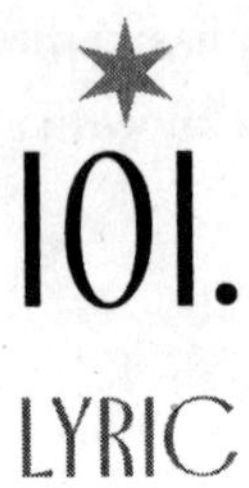

101.
LYRIC

We spill out of the car, rushing after Mullory, who sprinted ahead to her mom. Cruz, Reina, and Ellison are right behind me as we weave between snowcapped gravestones.

But we're not alone.

Several figures emerge from the woods. Members of the council, my own parents.

My heart stills.

Uncle X storms in like some sort of god, fit in a suit of liquid gold, the metal molded to his frame. A cane of twisted glass filled with rainbow bursts is clutched in his palm, and he wields it in a wicked arc. The council lets him draw closer—maybe he's on their side now, maybe he always has been.

A dramatic sigh escapes his lips as he spots me, and he finally speaks. "Lyric." It's the gentlest he's ever said my name. The closest to affection he's ever dared.

"Uncle?" I can't help that my voice betrays me.

He edges closer, marching through the snow, and part of me recoils. My instincts are honed to a razor edge from a childhood of nightmarish cruelty.

Uncle X's eyes are cerulean in the sun. "I'll admit. I got most of it wrong," he says. Shame burns across his face. "Some of us aren't fit to raise children, perhaps because we were never allowed to be children ourselves. But alas, the cards we are dealt."

My insides deflate, the admission I'd always desperately wanted, and it wrings me out. Leaves me empty.

"Try not to judge me for that, Lyric. I've always said the last move is the most important. The final act."

My suspicion escalates. "Final act of what?"

"Judge me for this, Lyric." Uncle's voice splinters. Almost a plea. He extends a palm and on it lies a flat, smooth stone.

I curl my fingers around the stone as it transforms into a butterfly. Like all the others that had been left to me. I'd always thought it was Edwin looking out for me on my most troubled days, but I was wrong. "You."

Xavier nods, keeping his hand extended, clad in a golden glove. "Give me the shadow, Lyric. Judge me for this."

My other hand skims my pocket, the one that contains my salvation. The one thing that can set me free. Mullory frantically sought me out before we left. *"You take it,"* she urged. *"I can't explain now, but I will."* And now the shadow lies with me. And the man who raised me, who shoved me into a box of his own nefarious design, wants it.

"Do you have it yet, Xavier?"

Any thoughts I had burn up instantly. Lord Thorn's voice splinters across my skin and my hand grips the shadow like a weapon. I linger on Uncle X for a moment; his blue eyes are suddenly volatile, but his face is a neutral mask. He keeps his palm outstretched as I spin around to face my father.

I have his blood.

His genes.

His magic.

All the parts I can't control or change. They're etched into my being. Would I be any different if it was him and not Uncle X who raised me? Crueler? If that's even possible. Or set free? Maybe it makes no difference where I lived, who loved or didn't love me. Maybe the parts of him in me were always destined to bleed to the surface and consume everything else.

"Lyric." My name sounds wrong coming from him. Lord Thorn squares his shoulders. "You won't win. You can't."

My fingers curl around the shadow, its edges piercing into my skin. I can feel its power surging. Fury pounds between my ears. This is when I take what's mine. What I deserve. The air trembles. A bat swoops past my shoulder.

"Lyric, don't," Uncle X murmurs as my vision blurs.

This is the only ending that makes sense, the only way to serve justice. This is what I deserve.

I push further, squeezing the shadow and blurring the final lines between the living and the dead. I'm going to take my father's magic and then I'm going to kill him. I don't feel anything close to remorse. If anything, I feel alive.

"Lyric!" My name again, another plea, but this one makes me pause. Mullory's voice finds me. It doesn't matter that I'm inches from the gates of death. She could find me anywhere. "Lyric, don't."

Part of me wants to ignore her, to cut her free from me forever. It would be the most selfless thing I've ever done. The noble way.

But I just can't let go.

Not of her.

"Lyric." Her hand finds mine, a tether that yanks me back. "If you don't trust your uncle, at least trust me."

This is the moment that will define me, my cosmic reckoning. Am I my father? Or am I something more?

How do you know if you're kind?

Mullory whips me around and presses her nose against my chin. "I know you, Lyric. I *know* what you are." Her eyes are earnest. Her belief in me absolute.

How could I not choose her?

I spin toward my uncle and slam the shadow in his palm.

A bloodcurdling scream rips through the cemetery. Have I just doomed us all?

102. ONE WEEK EARLIER

This is the grand finale. Time to tie up the last bits of this mystery and wrap it with a silken bow. I needed to get creative with the last clues since I'm veering from the plan. It's imperative that Mullory believe her mother planted them—I need to nudge, not force, her to the answers or she'll question it. And I needed her to trust me, explicitly and without hesitation. A few shared tears and I knew I had her.

Her mother's journal was supposed to be given to her earlier, but I needed more time to go through it. And for good reason. To make sure nothing was left to chance. That's why I had no choice but to dump it during the masquerade.

This letter was tucked so tightly in the folds that I'd missed it on my first three passes.

Mallory,

You need to see what the shadow is capable of. What it broke, who it ruined, so that you understand what must be done. How it must be done. I've always been afraid to tell you the truth, perhaps this is the cowardly way, showing you instead. I can only hope that in revealing my mistakes, you can learn. Be brave, my Mallory girl. I'm afraid we're both running out of time. I'll meet you at the end.

—Mom

I toss the letter in the fire, watching until it's little more than a pile of ash.

But now, how to get the final cog in motion?

How do I get her to look inside the cardboard box where I planted the next clue? When I snuck in her room and then pretended to cry over our mothers.

What would Esther Merrybright do? The Scrabble set catches my eye—yes, something exactly like that. I scoop up the velvet bag of tile letters. Make it feel like some grand game. I'm quiet, melting in the shadows, taking a circuitous route outside to avoid anyone seeing me.

My fingers fumble with the letters, frozen stiff with fear and frost. The clock in my head ticks in tandem with my heart, two bombs set to explode. The timing must be precise, exact—a second's difference and the entire plan implodes. Time is fickle like that. Nothing given freely, every minute demands blood.

I strategically place the letters, one on the bed, another in the stove, tucked away until she's meant to find them on this hunt for the strange. The rest is in her hands. One misstep and an entire life's work will crumble, washed away like a castle of sand in the tide.

I'm so close; my plan is days away from culminating at the cemetery. Final breadcrumbs. I already took a chance with Jim by changing the original message Esther wanted to leave him. In her version of this game, Jim was the final clue, and his message was this: *"It must be destroyed in the seam."* It was a gamble changing it, but I kept most of the words the same, planting a new clue. . . . It's just not the seam Mullory thinks it is. And of course, there'd be no destroying it. That's simply not part of *my* plan.

How clever am I?

The ghost of my mother's voice haunts me. *"Quite clever, my Reina girl."*

103.
MULLORY

The scream ricochets through the graveyard like a bullet.

Reina falls to her knees, her throat ripped raw. The illusion on the shadow breaks, leaving her with a pile of paper clips in her palm.

The true shadow lies in the hands of Xavier Stoutmire. Lyric clings to me, still shaken, as Reina's red-rimmed eyes find us.

"How?" Her voice catches on a sob, then builds back up to a roar. "HOW DID YOU KNOW?"

It hit me in flashes, in tiny moments that made me question everything. The clues that felt wrong, misplaced. The discarded journal at the masquerade, the Scrabble letters left carelessly in the tiny room. But I ignored them, too preoccupied with the notion that there was something wrong with *me*. Obsessed with understanding why Xavier's magic wasn't working. But I should've known all along. I should have trusted my instincts.

"Never leave a clue that can be easily moved or spotted," I tell Reina while glancing back at my mom and smiling. "I know you tampered with things, I'm just not sure how far the deception goes. But to answer your question, I knew for sure when you told me the cemetery was in New Jersey. I'd never said a thing about where it was."

Reina yells again, clawing her hands in the snow.

"Reina told me, she was the one who convinced me to come here in the first place." What Cruz had said in the billiards room suddenly makes more sense. "You planned this all along."

Ellison blows past me. Her voice is barbed wire and arsenic. "What have you done?"

"I did what my mother would've wanted. What my weak-minded father couldn't understand." Reina howls the last words. "He's the reason my mother's dead."

Ellison shuts down, twisting her arms tightly to her chest, her lower lip trembling.

My heart splinters into a million little pieces that tumble out into the snow. "Your father's in the labyrinth . . ." I don't finish the sentence out loud. Her father's in the labyrinth because he killed her mother.

Reina cracks, folds forward. Completely extinguished. "And I'm the reason he's there."

"Enough of this," Lord Thorn bellows. He's broken away from the other council members, his eyes locked firmly on Lyric.

My mom sways behind me, giving me a firm nudge. "Mullory, you know what to do."

My mom sent me on a hunt, chasing clues to illuminate her past. One bloodied by murder, ripe with the betrayal of her friends, and studded with heartache. But maybe I was missing the bigger picture, the reason she wanted me to see everything. Because there's one object that's been constant throughout her history.

My mom's voice grows more intense. "It's time."

You'll know when it's time. Cecilia's final advice from her letter. The knife hidden in my hand feels hot on my skin. My eyes flash to Lyric, the boy who carved out a piece of my heart. Lord Thorn looms near him. Xavier Stoutmire is eerily still, the true shadow clutched in his palm.

Was it wrong to give it to him? Our one chance at Lyric's freedom? A power that I grew used to wearing, almost like a shield. My eyes catch on Xavier's golden suit, on a seemingly unrelated detail. A small bird pinned to his chest with an oddly striped pattern up its neck, the same as the one from Cecilia's book of birds.

Killdeer are fiercely protective of their young.

My eyes dart to my mom. Then between Lyric and Xavier Stoutmire, finally understanding. It was never about the kill. But rather about relinquishing the power we had, releasing the shadow to Xavier, who was meant to protect Lyric from the beginning. My mom wanted me to know why the shadow had to be destroyed. Cecilia wanted me to know how.

You'll know when it's time.

104.

LYRIC

Uncle X hasn't taken his eyes off me, almost as if he has more to say. But the confines of time or pure stubbornness keep whatever's in his head firmly stuck there. That's when I notice the bird pin secured to his chest, the one I gave him all those years ago. The killdeer. A seemingly stupid gift, one Cousin Cecilia assured me he would need one day. Somehow that feels like the message, a declaration meant for only me. A gift he kept until this very moment.

Lord Thorn has the entire council poised behind him.

And me utterly defenseless before him.

Is this truly the end?

"For this," Uncle X whispers.

And then I'm whipped around as Mullory's hand yanks mine, but this time she's gripping something else as well.

The bone-white handle of the knife that led to my death protrudes from her palm. She hastily wraps my fingers around it while keeping her grip steady.

"To satisfy death, but just barely," she whispers before jerking us around and lunging. Momentum carries us forward before I even realize what's happening.

Lord Thorn tries to react, but it's too late as we collide. More specifically we lodge the knife into his stomach.

A scream from my father with whom I share magic and blood but nothing more.

A final nod from Uncle X, the man who raised me but failed to define me, as he squeezes the shadow.

And then they both disappear.

105. SEVERAL WEEKS AGO

REINA

The front door is ajar.

Instantly, my pulse soars, and sweat crests my brow. Anyone else might think this was just a careless mistake, but I know my mother.

Something's wrong. A wrongness that curls inside me, leaking dread. My fingers tremble as I push the oak door open, stepping over the green mat littered with snow boots. For a moment I stare at the shelves, pictures, and ceramic treasures—mundane and familiar enough to stifle my worry.

But the stillness is too eerie to ignore.

The pressure inside me builds to a roar as I round the corner. My mother's eyes find mine, matching sets of lilac. *"My lilac loves,"* my dad had called us. But my mother's eyes don't move; *she* doesn't move. Syrupy blood has dribbled down her forehead and congealed like tarry soup beneath her head. Her cream rugs ruined. It's my first thought—the stain she won't be able to get out.

After that my mind goes blank.

My vision a smear of red.

I turn explosive, ripping the town house to shreds for reasons my fractured mind can't make sense of. My body needs to move, to break everything else around me.

Minutes or hours later—time is inconsequential—I find it.

My mother's secret.

One she was plotting with a woman named Esther Merrybright. An elaborate, time-jumping scheme, all in the hopes that Esther's daughter might destroy some shadow. The tears slipping across my cheeks slow to a drip as I read. About Stoutmire Estate, Mullory, the clues to get her to the cemetery on New Year's Day. And of course, the shadow. An item with the ability to bring back the dead.

One my mother was out to destroy.

A settling breath precedes my sudden calm.

I'll do you one better, Mom, I think as a plan starts to form.

But how much would I need to change? Things like this require planning; otherwise, I could just go back in time and try and save my mom. But that's not how this works, there's too much unpredictability, and I've barely just scraped the surface of altering moments in time. No, my best bet is to augment the plan my mother already took the time to conceive.

I read journal after journal, all the bloody history containing the shadow, the devastation it brought. The detailed plan, containing maps of Stoutmire Estate, names, places, times—everything I need to execute it.

But if I want to change the rules of Esther's game, I need her daughter to trust me. And what could be more fortuitous than bringing my cousin Cruz along? His fate is already entwined with the girl, his history a shiny distraction that will surely place all the focus on him. Let them think it was his idea to come, that he dragged me along.

And to win over Mullory Prudence, the answer lies with her father. It's all here, who killed him, and why. I just need to plant the doubt, water the seed with the shared loss of our parents, and then get her to give me the shadow.

I'll get my mom back, no matter the cost.

106. SEVERAL HOURS AGO

MULLORY

I never told anyone, including Reina, that my father's grave was in New Jersey. This tiny bit of doubt spreads, hooks its roots in me.

How could she know, unless she knew all along?

And if she knew this is where the final clue would take us, then she lied. What else is she not telling us?

In a split second, my mind has already forged an alternate plan as a precaution. My fingers strum the shadow resting on my collar. I need to keep this safe so I can keep Lyric safe. Which means I need to put my trust in two others. *When it's time, trust it with your friends.*

I don't have long before the others, waiting to leave for the cemetery, grow suspicious. I sprint to Lyric's room, intercepting him before he shuts the door.

"Mullory." He takes a tiny step back, a small space that feels like an abyss.

My fingertips curl at my sides as I resist the urge to reach out and touch him.

"Don't," I warn, afraid of what he might say. "We don't have long, and I need you to take this." I slide the shadow's chain off my neck, removing it for the first time in months. It's harder than I thought it would be, removing something that's been a steady reassurance of power. I can only hope I'm making the right decision.

But Lyric keeps his distance.

"I need you to hold on to it." Extending a palm, I offer it over. "Please. I can't explain now, but I will."

Lyric's dark eyes glimmer, momentarily transfixed by the stone pulsing in my hand. "You trust me, Mullory?"

My throat tightens as I look him straight in the eye. I need him to hear me. "You're the only one I trust."

"Maybe you shouldn't," he says, ashamed. "I've used the shadow without you knowing. It called to me, showed me some memory of your father."

I'm momentarily shocked. "What did he say?"

Lyric casts his glance downward. "It wasn't my father who killed him. Or your mother."

I swallow. "Then who?"

Lyric shrugs. "He said it was a friend. But Mullory, I don't know if I can be trusted with it. I've seen what it did to your father. It turned him completely obsessive. And I . . ."

"No matter what, I trust you." I slam the shadow in his palm. I don't care that he used it without telling me, because he's telling me now. And I need him to trust himself. To know that despite everything stacked against him, he's still kind. I give him a fierce hug and dart away. There's one other person I still need to see.

I turn the butterfly-imprinted coin in the eye socket of the skull adorning Xavier's study door. I'm breathless as I barrel in, but Xavier barely flinches from my intrusion. His garnet pajamas have flames that flicker around the edges, much like the roaring fire on the far wall.

Eyeing his desktop for something suitable, I grab a chain of paper clips and get right to the point. "I need you to make this look like the shadow."

"And can I ask why?" He seems satisfied, likely because I need to ask for help with his magic.

But I'm past feeling sorry for myself. "Because I need someone to believe it's real."

"I see. And where, might I ask, is the real shadow?"

A test. I square my shoulders when I answer. "Lyric has it."

Xavier waves a hand, and the chain of paper clips transforms into a convincing replica of the shadow.

I pick it up, expecting the feel to be subtly different, but it vibrates at the exact tempo as the original. "How do you do that?"

"You play a larger role than you think, Mullory."

I look up at Xavier, searching for a hidden meaning, but his expression is solemn.

"It's easy for people to see and feel what they think should be there. I merely offer a suggestion, and your mind fills in the gaps. People believe what they want more often than they believe the truth."

"I've only ever been after the truth." The admission falls from my lips.

Xavier studies me. "That, I believe."

"Then maybe you can share the truth as well. What were you looking for?"

"I would be remiss if I didn't say that your mother found it first. Waved it right in front of my face. The mentee outshines the mentor, I suppose that means it's time for me to retire."

My mouth hangs open, my brain short-circuits. "You saw my mom?"

"I believe that is the correct term to use when one meets someone else."

A ridiculous little laugh bubbles up my throat. Everywhere we've gone, all that we've done, and Xavier knew where she was all along. "It would've been useful if you shared this."

Xavier shrugs. "Not as useful as you think."

"And what exactly did my mom find first?"

"Ah, that. Something you're quite familiar with, actually. Something that appears in both our histories at particularly terrible times. Yours more recently than mine."

My mind racks through every horrible thing that's happened. My mom leaving. Her burning the house down. Lyric dying. I snap my head up, certain. "The knife."

Xavier curls his lip. "I detest that knife. It will not leave me alone, and yet when I need it, it's never around."

"But what do you mean both our histories? It was just with Lyric at the party. . . ." I struggle to finish the sentence as something else suddenly becomes clear. A different reason for the knife to be in Xavier's past. I remember what Lyric just shared, that a friend had killed my father. *Henry Prudence's murderer is closer than you think.* "It was you."

"I'm afraid so."

"You killed my father. Planted the knife, because you couldn't use it yourself."

"Yes. But utterly pointless, because Henry Prudence lives."

"Why?" It's the only word I can manage to get out.

"Henry was out of control. Reckless in his endeavors. There's a reason your mother wanted you to stay with your grandmother, away from all this. Away from *him*."

The answer unnerves me, and I want to press him more, but I don't have the time right now. Grabbing the illusionary shadow, I secure it around my neck. "We're not done."

Xavier forces a weak smile. "Certain things will draw to an end shortly. And perhaps now I owe you another answer. You remind me of my greatest failure."

"Excuse me?"

"You asked me before why I've been avoiding you. Truth be told, I'm a bit of a sore loser. You were supposed to die and instead you won the very thing that defines me. The only thing I ever had to give."

"Well, that was childish. We could've used your help," I say with one foot out of his study.

"Don't hold my sins against him." A sigh as Xavier calls to me, and then a whisper I almost don't hear. "Lyric deserves better."

107.
ELLISON

A gust of wind howls, sweeping snow against the gravestones and across the spot where my uncle and Lord Thorn just stood. All it took was a single moment and Lyric's horrid history is simply erased.

His father who wanted to kill him.

And our deranged uncle who wanted to save him all along.

Gone.

Reina's betrayal burns deeply, but mostly at a simmer, tamped down by the fact that my brother is still alive. My knees are weak, my joy so intense it nearly knocks me over. Maybe this is love. Not something gentle or easy, but a storm that steals your breath and forces you to fight with everything you have.

My mother scurries around the council, barking orders, trying to pick up the pieces. It takes a moment for her to even acknowledge me. "Ellison."

I could scream a million hateful things in her face. I could brag that it was me, the mysterious woman behind it all. That I saved Lyric using her magic. That I'm stronger than she ever was.

But what I do next shocks even me. Marching straight up to her, toe to toe, I grab my mother, digging my nails into her back, yanking her fiercely close.

And then I hug her.

Because we may share dream magic, but that doesn't mean I have to let it ruin me. I don't have to see this as a burden, letting it drag me several martinis under like it did for her. It can be a tool, a gift to break through. To set us free.

And because this day is a hair away from the apocalypse, my mother hugs me back. A whisper grazes my ear. "This was my best. But I'm certain you'll do better." Then she straightens like an arrow, right back to barking orders. Pointing a firm finger at a despondent Reina. "She'll need to be dealt with."

"Leave her," I say commandingly.

An almost-hidden smile tugs at my mother's lips as she backs away. "You heard my daughter."

Reina doesn't stir from the ground; instead she slumps deeper into the snow, a complete surrender. "You were right," she finally croaks. "You shouldn't have trusted me." Then quieter, "No one should."

"Don't give yourself so much credit. You lied. Multiple times. In multiple points in time," I say, simple as that.

The winter sun catches the tiny purple flecks in Reina's glassy eyes. "I did."

"But you had a good reason." My eyes dart first to my mother; our relationship is as raw as a freshly turned bruise, but at the same time it feels like there's an understanding between us that never existed before. Then I look to Lyric, someone I know I would lie for, as many times as it took, in as many timelines as I could if it meant I could save him.

Reina gulps. "I thought I could bring my mom back."

"I don't forgive you," I answer honestly. I'm not the forgiving type.

A final blow that causes her to deflate further.

"But I respect you." I offer a hand to help her up, and her fingers slide between mine.

I don't let go even when she's standing.

108.

MULLORY

The stone butterfly flutters across Lyric's hand as he watches it, transfixed. It defies logic; the stone should sink, but it soars, beautiful magic bestowed—previously unbeknownst to Lyric—by Xavier. I want to rush over to Lyric, but my mom grabs me first and yanks me away.

"I owe you a conversation," she says, wiping her flow of tears. "I owe you a year's worth of conversations." She embraces me tightly.

I nod my head against her shoulder, caught in this surreal moment. Of all the questions lighting up inside me, one surfaces. "Why did you lie?" The others are background noise in my head. Why put me through all of this? Why didn't you find me yourself? What happened to my father?

My mom tucks a dark curl behind my ear. "Because I'd do anything to protect you. Even if it was the hardest thing I've ever done in my life." She squeezes me harder, a hug that almost hurts. "We have time now, me and you. No more hunting for either of us." There's something different about her, a steadiness that didn't exist before. No need for her to deflect. She eases away and tips her head. "Now go to that boy."

There's so much buried in those words and in her teary green eyes. A history almost repeated, but somehow saved. Because in the end the hunt wasn't about the clues, or the places we visited. It was about picking up the pieces of my mom, no matter how sharp or broken, so that I could understand her. So that I could get rid of the shadow, and in doing so help to mend her past and secure my future. *"We have time now."* Time, above magic and money, is what we've always wanted most.

Before I can reach Lyric, someone else intercepts me.

"I'll admit, this didn't go like I thought it would," Cruz says slowly, his one dimple out.

"I didn't see this coming either."

Cruz looks to Reina with a pained expression on his face. "We do anything for the ones we care about." His sentiment resonates, because I may not condone what Reina did, but I can understand it. In the end, she wanted to save someone she loves. Just like the rest of us.

I extend a hand for Cruz to shake. "I guess this is goodbye."

A smile as he gently brushes my hand aside. "I wouldn't be so sure, Mullory. We'll see each other again soon."

I let Cruz leave with his mysterious parting, as I make my way across the graveyard.

Lyric is still and serene, standing in the snow.

My stomach clenches as I approach him, fearful of what he might say, because all that remains is us. There's no longer a riddle to hide behind or a father to run from.

His voice is quiet and calm. "One of these days, let's do something that doesn't involve a knife, or a death-defying fly." He rubs his chin, a smile creeping up. "One of these days, let's not almost die."

A laugh breaks through my tears. "Well, there go my plans for our first date." I step closer.

Lyric closes the distance slowly but purposefully. His hands cradle my face; his expression is soft, bordering awestruck.

"What happens next?" I dare to ask.

At first, he doesn't answer. His hands slide quickly down my sides as he picks me up. "Whatever the hell we want." He presses his lips to my ear, whispering, "I just know I'm not letting go."

109.
CECILIA HUMES

Finally.

My eyes snap open as all six of the clocks on my fireplace ring out in alarm.

It's over.

I can't help but hum.

Four little birds, their hunt has an end.
A mother found with love to mend,
A father lost, but a life gained,
Magic embraced without strain,
And the fourth little bird, peace at last,
Setting right his failure from the past.

I pluck a snail that's been gliding up my arm and storm over to the hearth, snagging a pair of candlesticks along the way. Presents from Saffron that I'll finally put to use.

Taking my best aim, I wind my arm up and smash the first clock to pieces. Springs and cogs litter the carpet. Satisfied, I move on to the next four.

The sixth one continues to ring. And ring. A celebratory sound. I toss the candlesticks to the ground and cradle the clock in my arms, carefully removing the back and retrieving the bird from within. Its soft brown feathers are warm between my fingers, and I stroke its oddly patterned neck. A killdeer. My favorite bird, and now one of Xavier's favorites, too, I'm sure.

I can't help but laugh.

Mullory Prudence, against all odds. All twists of fate.

It's a good thing I never got around to killing her.

110.
THE SEAM BETWEEN THE LIVING AND THE DEAD
XAVIER STOUTMIRE

I take a settling breath. My lungs quiver from the effort, releasing the stresses that have clung to me my entire life.

Peace at last.

Never mind the dark void I've willingly catapulted myself into. Trapped in an unknown abyss, and I can't help but smile.

"Xavier," growls my unwilling traveling companion.

My smile relents, but just slightly; not even he can ruin this moment for me. I'm slow to turn around, escalating his fury I'm sure. "Ah, Lord Thorn. I'd almost forgotten you'd joined me on this rather indefinite sojourn. One neither of us will be returning from, I'm afraid."

Lord Thorn flexes his wrists, fingers curling as his frustration builds.

I'm all too happy to point out the obvious. "Unfortunately Thorn, we're both powerless here. Just two regular men. Although, I suppose I'm an old man now."

I don't have to look to know my glamours have faded; I'm probably hideous. Even better. My smile perks right up again.

"What do you want, Xavier? Name your price." Lord Thorn's normal pretense is waning, panic scraping at the edges.

Again, another smile that makes my face ache. "No one's ever asked me that. What do *I* want?" I pose the question to the stillness of death's antechamber. I've had riches, a taste for unregulated power, hosted parties that should only exist in the beguiling minds of dreamers. I've chased magic and it's chased me. But what do I want? The answer is simple—to repair the one thing I've botched horribly. To fix my greatest failure. To save the boy who needed me most. "I've already got what I want," I say, while slowly raising a hand and uncurling my fingers to reveal the shadow.

Lord Thorn inhales, fixing his murderous gaze on the necklace I'd spent half my life lusting over and the other half loathing.

Lord Thorn takes an aggressive step forward and pauses.

I extend my free arm, waving a hand at him. "Please, be my guest and try to take it from me. You're certainly strong enough, despite that." I wince at the knife lodged in his stomach. "Nasty luck."

"We both know that's not how it works."

"Do we?" I chuckle. "Silly, I guess I'd forgotten how the shadow works. That's right." I smack my forehead. "I have to willingly give it to you." I place the shadow gingerly by my feet, positioned between the two of us. "Just to be clear, I'm *not* giving this to you. I just no longer wish to hold it. Like I said, I'm an old man."

Lord Thorn screams, fully realizing his dire predicament. "This is your plan, Xavier? Let us both rot here until the end?"

"More or less." I raise my arms above my head, a glorious, languid stretch. "I'll wait and watch you fume, then inevitably panic, then beg, and then finally relent and do the thing that will benefit everyone I care to help."

"You'll watch me die."

"I'll take great pleasure in it, actually. And once I know you're gone, and Lyric is finally safe, then I'll join you. And the shadow will be left here until it disintegrates to dust. Because I won't willingly pass it along to anyone."

Lord Thorn scoffs. "You want to die?"

"What I want is peace. I don't expect you to understand. Truthfully, I don't care if you ever do." My lips tug into another smile—this is probably the most these muscles have ever moved. I suspect Cecilia is smiling somewhere as well. She may have minced the words, but she got the message across. A killdeer is a bird hell-bent on protecting its young. Perhaps I botched most of his upbringing, but I like to think I got this part right.

I pay no mind to Lord Thorn as he begins to shout and curse in futility.

Peace.

Finally.

May he judge me for this.

EPILOGUE
HENRY PRUDENCE

I smear my thumb across the jagged stone wall, leaving a line of blood. One mark of thousands. I'd lost count several hundred ago. I do it now more out of habit, a ritual to ground me.

A faint green light burns my eyes. I've adjusted to the eternal darkness, becoming a creature that knows only how to dwell in its depths. I haven't seen the sun in years, or maybe it's been centuries. My mind has lost all hold of the threads of time, along with most of my other faculties.

I'd almost given up. Surrendered completely. Let myself and my magic bleed into the prison that has been so eager to devour me.

Ice cracks along the line of my fresh blood, the remnants of my magic that remain. Winter in my bones, I'd known since that night in the meat locker: I'd known that the cold was no foe, but a friend.

And now I know why it has stayed with me for so long instead of being leeched out into this prison of nightmares I've been locked in. I understand now why death hasn't called upon me a second time.

A creature howls in the distance. Someone screams. It will only happen faster. You can't escape them once they smell your fear. You can't escape at all.

Unless . . . someone comes for you.

And she will come.

The winter in me calls to her.

For the longest time, I'd had no idea, for she was a secret well kept. And I was left to rot.

But someone left me a message, hidden in the belly of a beast I slayed.

The ice in your veins lives in your daughter.

Who was my mysterious benefactor? I had no idea. No messages ever reach a place like this.

But *she* will.

She will come for me.

Mullory Prudence will meet me in the labyrinth.

ACKNOWLEDGMENTS

Writing this sequel felt a bit like returning to school after a wonderful stretch of summer vacation. Reuniting with my familiar trio of friends—Mullory, Ellison, and Lyric—before the first bell rang. A reorientation with the strange sights and smells in a world where magic is every bit as wonderous as it is sinister. There's a sense of comfort, but also nerves, the knowing that it won't be the same as last year—friendships are different, classes are harder, and above all, now there are expectations. There were tears, and late nights, and what felt like failed exams, but in the end, I'd like to think this year was even better than the first. Now to thank all the people who made that possible.

I'd like to thank my agent, Brent Taylor-Hunt, and Laura Crockett at Triada US for getting the Mystery Royale books into the hands of readers across the globe.

To my editor, Brittany Rubiano, whose enthusiasm and love for this series helped keep my own spirits up and transform the story. Thank you for being such a spot of sunshine in a process that often feels forever cloudy. To Ashley Imanë Fields for stepping in at the final hour and helping me to get this book finished.

To the entire team at Disney Hyperion who championed this story. Sara Liebling, Iris Chen, Guy Cunningham, Monique Diman, Vicki Korlishin, Lebria Casher, Matt Schweitzer, Maddie Hughes, Crystal McCoy, and Daniela Escobar, thank you for all the hard work you've done behind the scenes.

To Neil Swaab, who illustrated, and Marci Senders, who led the design on a cover that is somehow even more magnificent and magical than the first.

To the Paper Garden Co, the most charming bookstore I've ever been to, thank you for spotlighting *Mystery Royale* and for hosting a lovely launch party.

Special thanks to the American Booksellers Association for picking *Mystery Royale* for Indies Introduce. To all the indie booksellers who loved and stocked *Mystery Royale*, thank you. Truly there is no greater feeling then seeing my book out in the world.

To all the friends and family I've gained along the way in Indiana, Pennsylvania. Until you've had the support of a small town, you can't possibly understand the power or the magic that dwells there.

To all students in the Heritage Conference who read *Mystery Royale* and reinstated the spark I needed to finish this sequel: Thank you for reminding me why I write books in the first place.

Bridget, my old gal, thanks for reading the very messy first draft of this book and for sending all those treats in the mail.

Billy, thanks for helping me realize how truly horrible I am with social media and for stepping in. For all your brilliant marketing ideas and support. Joey, thanks for all the encouraging texts and for driving five hours to stay with me (we all know I'm a baby).

Mom and Dad: A few sentences at the end of the book will never feel like enough. Because how can you adequately thank the people who gave you everything? Who sacrificed. And loved unconditionally. Who encouraged. And inspired. Thank you for giving me the world.

James: I'm not exaggerating in the least when I say this, I could've never done it without you. Not even close. It's more than you reading every word I've ever written, or for picking me up when I convinced myself I couldn't fix this book. It's all the times you watched Cameron so I could write, the sacrifices, the encouragement, the push you gave me. It's everything. You're everything. Thank you.

To Cameron. Thank you for putting everything into perspective. For the smiles, the snuggles, the endless hugs. I love you more than you'll ever know.

To Callum. You're in my belly, kicking at my rib cage as I write this, just three weeks away from being brought into the world. Know that I love you already.

To all those who read *Mystery Royale* and *Hunting the Strange*, who love this world and these characters as much as I do: Thank you for taking the journey with me.